DRAGON LORDS RISING

Lucinda Hare

Book Three of the Dragonsdome Chronicles

lucinda@dragonsdome.co.uk
http://www.dragonsdome.co.uk/
http://thedragonwhispererdiaries.blogspot.co.uk/

Published by Thistleburr Publishing

Dragon Lords Rising
Thistleburr Publishing, ISBN: 978-0-9574718-0-1

DEDICATION

To
Lucy and Phoenix Wilson
Jessica McConnell
Brogan and Bryony Varney
India Shackleford

MAIN CHARACTERS

People

Quenelda is the headstrong daughter of the Earl Rufus DeWinter. She has a gift for talking with dragons, but is hopeless at sorcery. Flying dragons and dressed like a boy, it is certain that she will *never* become a young lady! She does have hidden powers; although she cannot control or understand them, and her abilities only reveal themselves in times of dire need.

Root, son of SDS scout Bark Oakley, is the first gnome to be made up to esquire. He is determined to protect Quenelda, although his race does not take up arms. Scared of dragons and flying, he now loves his own gentle dragon, Chasing the Stars, with all his heart. He has been learning the rudiments of navigation and map making, and has sworn to the Earl that he will protect Quenelda.

Tangnost Bearhugger: legendary Bonecracker Commando and Dragon Master to the Earl Rufus DeWinter. Following the defeat of the SDS at the Battle of the Westering Isles, he fled with Quenelda to Dragon Isle. He has protected Quenelda since the moment of her birth, and with her new powers, his task is only beginning. Tangnost is about to lead her into the frozen north beyond the Old Wall to find her father.

The Earl Rufus DeWinter was Commander of the Stealth Dragon Services and Queen's Champion until he and all his regiments were betrayed by his childhood friend and mentor, the Lord Hugo Mandrake. No one returned alive from the Battle of the Westering Isles, and he is believed dead by everyone, except his daughter.

The Lord Hugo Mandrake, the Grand Master of the Sorcerers Guild. This powerful and dangerous man has been raised to the title of Lord Protector of the Seven Sea Kingdoms. Worse, he has been given leave to raise his own army, and to breed and fly Imperial Black battle-dragons, the greatest dragons on the One Earth. Unknown to the Court and Guild, he is a WarLock: a wielder of chaotic Maelstrom magic and the very person who betrayed the SDS. Allied with the hobgoblins, the true depths of his treachery have yet to be revealed.

Quester is the youngest son of a minor lord, and is esquire to Tangnost Bearhugger. Cheerful, gifted and ambitious, he befriended Root when no other esquires would, and they are fast friends. He hopes to earn a place in the SDS by feats of valour on this adventure.

Darcy is Quenelda's elder step-brother and is now Earl of Dragonsdome. Spoilt, arrogant and ambitious, he loathes his younger sister for upstaging him during the winter Jousts at the Cauldron. He takes his spiteful revenge by ordering the death of Quenelda's beloved battledragon, Two Gulps and You're Gone. He is everything his father is not, or is he?

Dragons

Two Gulps Too Many is a juvenile sabretooth with a serious weight problem. He eats just about anything, day or night. Chosen because of his quiet intelligence and similarity to his sire, Two Gulps and You're Gone, he is stubborn and lazy when it comes to flying. It doesn't look like he will ever get off the ground, let alone become a battledragon.

Stormcracker Thundercloud III is the Earl Rufus DeWinter's Imperial Black battledragon. Badly injured, he survived the Battle of the Westering Isles, bearing his Dragon Lord to safety before being captured by the Lord Protector and left to die in a brimstone mine. Following his return to Dragon Isle, he has become a symbol of hope.

Moonbeam Children's Book Awards 2013

Double Silver Medal Winner

for

Best young adult fiction: Fantasy/SciFi

Best book series: Fiction

Root's Drawing of the Smoking Fort

The Strangate Road

West Port

Spitting Alley Roosts

Sentry Fort

Runestone Tower

Dragon Port

Sabretooth Roosts

Vampire Roosts

Brimstone Pits

Ditch

Frost Dragon Roosts

Parade Ground

Cliff Edge

Moorland

The Old Wall

N

CHAPTER ONE

Betrayal

The battlegriff landed in a flurry of feathers, fighting the cruel bit that cut deeply into its delicate beak. As Darcy dismounted and carelessly threw the reins to a groom, the battlegriff bucked, lashing out at its tormentor. Grinning, Darcy struck back with his whip. Magic snapped, bringing the battlegriff to instant submission, singeing its feathers. Banned by his father from flying any hippogriff or dragon from the battleroosts, Darcy was now able to do as he pleased. Dragonsdome and all its dragons were his.

The young man glanced up to where a young Imperial was putting down on one of the higher landing pads anchored about Dragonsdome Keep. No such unruly behaviour marred the Lord Protector's flawless landing, but then dragon collars compelled obedience. Once outlawed by the Guild, the Lord Hugo Mandrake, Lord Protector of the Seven Sea Kingdoms had overturned that law and many others, reducing dragons, even mighty Imperial Blacks, to mere beasts of burden subject to the Kingdom's needs.

They had been planning the royal procession that would celebrate the Lord Protector's wedding to Queen

Caitlin in the new Year of the Lesser-Spotted Burrowing Cat, when a courier had arrived at the Sorcerers Guild requesting the young Earl's immediate return home. Alert and suspicious, the Lord Protector had returned to Dragonsdome with Darcy.

Striding to the Great Hall, Darcy threw off his heavy cloak and accepted the welcome of his steward and constable.

'So,' Darcy sprawled carelessly on his father's high chair. 'What important news could you possibly bear that you could not entrust to one of my men? That I am summoned from Court?'

Felix DeLancy, newly minted Dragon Master, hesitated, licking his lips nervously.

'My Lord, this news is for your ears only.'

'Clear the hall,' Darcy dismissed everyone. Unnervingly, the Lord Protector remained motionless in his richly adorned robes, eyes fixed upon the Dragon Master. Felix could not say why, but this powerful sorcerer, who ruled both the Guild and the Court, made him afraid in a way the arrogant young Earl did not.

'Well? Speak up!'

'A raven arrived at dawn, my Lord, from Bearhugger's esquire.'

Darcy glanced at the Lord Protector.

'I do not trust the SDS. Let the boy escape to Dragon Isle,' the Lord Protector had suggested to the young Earl. 'But first bring him to me.' Darcy had not asked why. His mentor did not welcome questions. If he wanted

Darcy to know, he would have told him why.

'And?' Darcy stifled a yawn. He had been out into the early hours of the morning with his friends, Darcy's Devils, and had a headache.

'They believe they have found the Earl's battledragon. I thought you would want to hear immediately.'

That brought Darcy out of his seat.

'They have found the Earl's battledragon?' The Lord Protector's voice was soft, flat with menace. 'Is it so? What makes you think that?'

Felix swallowed, mouth suddenly dry. Head down, he held up the small scroll with the broken wax seal.

'They returned it to Dragon Isle two moons ago,' Felix glanced up at Darcy. 'From your mine at Cairnmore, My Lord Earl...although it was badly injured. I don't know how they did it. The battledragon...' Felix paused, lest he sound soft in the head. 'The battledragon...' he took a deep breath and plunged on in a rush, words tumbling breathless from his tongue. 'They say that the Earl survived the battle also...'

'What?' Darcy rounded on the Lord Protector. 'But you said th-'

Silence!

The force of the Lord Protector's anger slammed Darcy back down onto the chair. *Be warned...not one word...*

'Tell me,' he commanded Felix.

Felix swallowed. Had he really seen the Lord Protector's eyes flare green? A trick of the light, surely?

'They say,' he licked his dry lips, aware of how ridiculous this sounded. 'They say the Lady Quenelda can talk to dragons. Her...esquire, that commoner...Root Oakley, says the dragon told her of the battle, that she can bond with the creature...'

So the rumours that the Earl's daughter had recovered from her mysterious condition were true, despite the SDS Commander's regretful denials. The Lord Protector's heart thumped. *Why do they conceal this news from me? Do the Queen and her Constable also know?*

Darcy snorted derisively. 'Talk to dragons? She has a talent with the brutes, that is all.' Not even he could deny that, after watching Quenelda fly to the aid of their father in the Cauldron at the Winter Jousts. But the Lord Protector did not laugh.

'Continue,' he commanded.

'They believe that the Earl was found badly injured, that he was taken in by one of the Clans who spirited him to safety. They – Bearhugger, the Lady Quenelda and her esquire – are going to search for him. Along with Bearhugger's esquire. They fly to the Howling Glen any day now. They-'

The Lord Protector's eyes narrowed, his handsome face suddenly stilled. Felix felt a sudden pressure in his head. *Which clans?* A cold voice demanded, making him shiver. *Which clans have hidden him?*

'My Lord Protector,' Felix swallowed, the command had not been spoken, he was sure of it. 'The message did not say.'

The Lord Protector's eyes narrowed. Felix squirmed, but then the cold interest diminished and was gone, leaving him shaking.

Darcy dismissed Felix with a careless wave of the hand, watching as his Dragon Master made his way unsteadily across the hall.

'Do,' the young Earl swallowed, face pale even in warm glow of candlelight. 'Do you think he could truly have survived?'

'If the Earl is alive, then why has he not returned? Nonetheless, it would be foolish to ignore them entirely.' *How could a child speak to dragons? They must wonder how the Earl's battledragon came to the mine.*

'Perhaps,' the Lord Protector mused, 'Bearhugger can find a trail that no one else has. If your father is alive, let them lead us to him, and we will kill them all; a chance to be rid of your troublesome sister.'

*Why did the girl fill him with disquiet? She was mocked at Court, hopeless at lessons...and yet...she was a threat...somehow...*he felt sure of it.

Darcy felt a momentary twinge of compassion, but it passed. If his father were alive that would mean he himself was no longer Earl, and he was enjoying his new found wealth and power too much to relinquish it. As for his step-sister, she had shamed him twice. There would not be a third time.

'What will you do?'

'Well,' the Lord Hugo Mandrake contemplated the young Earl. Soon he would reveal the boy's true parentage, and bind Darcy to him forever, but one step at a time. 'We must ensure that they get all the help that they deserve on their dangerous quest, must we not? I will set my dragon master Knuckle Quarnack and his men on their trail to see where it leads. Bearhugger's young esquire will betray them to us.' *And I will bring the hobgoblins inland to the Howling Glen and the Old Wall, ready to strike if needs be....*

He smiled wolfishly, his handsome face alive with anticipation. 'The north is *such* a very dangerous place after all; especially for an injured dragon, a young girl and her esquire. It will take more than even Tangnost Bearhugger to bring them home alive.'

CHAPTER TWO

Dragon Quest

Wooooooooooooooo. Woooooooo.

The sound of a deep dragon horn echoed round the flight cavern in the depths of Dragon Isle. Lights dimmed, so that the landing lights encircling the thirty dragon pads flared into sudden brightness, illuminating the Imperial Blacks rising from the hidden hanger decks and armour pits below. With a grinding of cogs and gears, and a vibrating metallic boom, the hangers docked with the dragon pad flight decks. Deck crew swarmed about the huge battledragons, as Bonecracker commandos and Sea Reaver marines from the III First Born Regiment prepared to board. Operation Knight Watch, to relieve the isolated garrison of the Howling Glen, was underway.

At the centre of this vast flight hanger cavern was the SDS Commander's dragonpad, but Commander Jakart DeBessart was not leading this battlegroup north. His task was to remain on Dragon Isle, commanding all his remaining regiments and protecting the Queen and Court. Nonetheless, on his dragonpad, wings still folded, knelt a fully-prepped Imperial Black.

This battledragon was huge; a young stallion that

should still be in his prime; instead, every bone in his emaciated body stood out, and slight differences in colouration betrayed a latticework of terrible wounds and puckered scars, some newly healed. The Imperial slowly stretched his great wings till the tips rested on the metal decking, revealing a right hind leg that had been badly broken and badly set, a weakness he would carry for the rest of its life. Unusually, this Imperial also wore dragon armour, a petrel and underbelly armour crafted with spells as well as hammers. Cast in mottled shades of black, the segmented armour was bound about with wards of *concealment* and *illusion*. The SDS Commander, a skilled Arch Battlemage, had cast them himself; because this Imperial was not able to cloak, was not able to conjure a cloak of invisibility that gave the name to the Stealth Dragon Services, the SDS.

Normally such dreadful injuries would invalide a battledragon out of service, but this was no ordinary battledragon. This was Stormcracker Thundercloud III, battledragon to the Earl Rufus DeWinter, one-time Commander of the SDS and Queen's Champion, now missing in action since the Battle of the Westering Isles. Rescued from a brimstone mine and healed with his daughter's help, he was leaving Dragon Isle to hunt for the missing Earl.

Unique though this SDS battledragon was, his flight crew were even stranger. No black armoured Dragon Lords with their fiercesome dragon helmets sat in the pilot and navigator's seats. Instead a skinny pale-faced girl sat in the pilot's seat, dwarfed by the spelled witchwood that towered above and about her. Her blond hair was cut ragged and tousled so that it radiated out like a dandelion, and her tawny eyes looked anxious.

Tentatively, Quenelda DeWinter stretched out her hand to the handprint inlaid in the right arm, but her touch did not awaken the runes and sigils of power that ran through the witchwood. Only her father's touch could achieve that. The witchwood felt cold and unyielding, even through the yellow scale on her left palm.

'It's nearly time.' Tangnost, SDS Dragon Master and veteran Bonecracker, was beside her, dark eye studying her far away expression. 'Ready?' His strong hand clasped her shoulder.

Quenelda nodded, unable to speak. He and Dragonsdome's esquires, Root and Quester, were risking their lives because of a dream, because they believed she was a Dragon Whisperer. What if she were wrong? What-

'Steady, lass,' it was as if the dwarf could read her mind. 'Everyone is afraid before a mission. It's no bad thing; it's what keeps you alive.' He turned and bellowed at the two youths down on the dragon pad flight deck sorting through equipment. 'Mount up, Root, and stow the equipment. Quester. Pre-flight check.'

'Sir! Yes, Sir!'

Root Oakley hefted the last storage pack on his back and

climbed up the dragon's tail and up to where waxed black canvas stretched between the giant dragon's spinal plates, to where nets of hay and thistles hung from hooks. Having stowed the last baggage next to the cauldrons of brimstone, he turned and called. 'Two G-'

There was a thundering on the overhead gantry and then a ball of golden red flew through the air bowling him over, slamming him to the deck.

'Two Gulps!' the young gnome protested as he lay winded, trying to wipe the copious slobber from his face. 'Whoa! Get-get off! You're squ-squashing me!' The juvenile sabretooth dragon's huge taloned toes had him firmly pinned to the ground.

'Stop stop!' He could hear the deck crew chuckling as he was neatly rolled over, trussed like a fly in a spider's web. There was a loud tear, and Two Gulps was happily chomping away at Root's cloak, his tongue searching out the pockets where the honey tablets were hidden. In moments cloak and tablets had gone. Burping contentedly, Two Gulps now allowed himself to be led into the roost, where Root firmly tied him up before seeking out his friends.

'Behave,' Root admonished, trying to sound like he was still in charge.

He was still amazed at the time it took him to walk from the tail to where Quenelda already sat on the pilot's seat astride the dragon's shoulders. Standing by his navigator's seat, he took one last look about him at the place that had been home in recent moons. It was barely dawn, but it seemed as if all of Dragon Isle had gathered on the gantries and ledges that ran about the cavern's walls to bid them farewell, the dark armour and garb of soldiers and Mages contrasting with the bright robes of the academics from the Battle Academy high on the cliffs of the island. But would they succeed? Would the Seven Kingdoms ever see the Dragon Lords rising again?

'Come on, lad,' Tangnost led Quester beneath the batteldragon. 'Final inspection. Pilot always checks the dragon is fit to fly before he mounts, but Quenelda has enough to deal with, so it's down to you and me.

'Right, let's see how much you've learnt.'

Quester took a deep breath. Taking hold of the neck girth rungs, he checked the great buckles that held pilot and navigator's seats; they were moulded to fit each individual dragon and were held by spells, but leather and brass still strapped them down. The young esquire made sure he did not touch the rune embedded in the wood that could eject the seat if the dragon crashed, a modification introduced after the Battle of the Westering Isles when dragon fought dragon for the first time since the ancient Mage Wars.

Scrambling down, he jumped lightly on to the battledragon's shoulder and gave him a signal by tapping a leg.

'I never imagined that an Imperial's muzzle was so soft,' Quester said, as Stormcracker turned his great head and bent it, so that gusts of warm air enveloped the pair in greeting. The youth examined the heavy silver bit and bridle to make sure they rested comfortably in that huge maw that dealt death to so many hobgoblins.

Climbing up from the flight deck, the esquire stepped out to examine Stormcracker's spread wings, while Tangnost checked their underside, calloused hands running over the raised scar tissue that had hardened like aged bark.

But who knew what hurts lay hidden within? The Dragon Master thought. Although they roosted in coombs, Imperials were creatures of the air. To be confined in the depths of a mine for so many moons, wounded, alone...who knew what damage that had done to the Earl's dragon? As it was, the Imperial's dragon magic was diminished by his severe injuries, and the Lord Protector's dark touch; and he was no longer able to cloak and hide them from prying eyes. That placed them in great danger should they ever be discovered. The Dragon Master glanced upwards to where Quenelda was. How much would the Earl's daughter be able to help them?

That Quenelda had power far beyond her twelve winters no one doubted. Not after the mayhem at the Cauldron; and Root had seen her sorcery unveiled when they had rescued Stormcracker from the mine, when she had prevented the exhausted dragon's headlong fall to certain death. But that power was erratic, dangerous to those around her: and no one, least of all the Earl's daughter, understood her true abilities.

But although she had tried and tried, always the Earl's daughter shook her head with frustration when Tangnost asked how lessons were going. On the verge of tears, she was becoming irritable, so that he no longer asked, and hid his anxiety. If she could even combine her power with that of Stormcracker to cloak, they could elude the Lord Protector's spies and minions, and their quest stood a chance. If not....

'Sir?' Quester was looking at him curiously. 'Sir, is everything alright?'

Tangnost cursed inwardly. He had to hide his worries.

'You've missed something lad...' he found a smile. To be fair, Stormcracker's harness and tack were modified for winter campaigning, and were yet to be standard issue. But they were heading far to the north of the Howling Glen as winter closed in, and Imperials suffered badly in the cold.

Standing on the dragon's claws Quester pursed his lips, mentally counting off his checks. He frowned as Tangnost pointed down.

'Oh!' Quester gritted his teeth. He was actually standing on the huge padded sheaths that protected the dragon's claws! 'I knew there was something I'd missed.'

Tangnost nodded. 'But well done, lad.' He frowned as Quester turned to examine the metal for corrosion or cracks. Although the boy had clearly been affected by his time at Dragonsdome with the young Earl Darcy, he was reluctant to talk about it. But the apothecary had quietly drawn Tangnost aside to tell him that Quester was suffering frequent headaches, although there was no sign of a head injury.

But Quester smiled as he bent to his task, the dragon master's approval calming him. For some reason he was anxious, as if he had an important task that he couldn't quite remember. He was tired, that was all. He had been training hard with bow and arrow as well as sword, at Tangnost's insistence: 'A sword won't help you in the air, lad, unless we're boarded.'

'T-5 and counting...'

They finished their inspection swiftly. Tangnost knew that the armourers, dragon smiths and roost hands had already done their job, but it was tradition that pilots checked their own mounts and armour before takeoff.

Alone of those venturing out in search for the missing Earl, Tangnost had experience of war and the wider world beyond the Sorcerers Glen. A Bonecracker veteran of sixty five years and over a hundred battles, he had also flown with the Earl on Stormcracker as the Earl's Shield, and knew the battledragon as well as Quenelda did. Success or failure of their quest would rest on his broad shoulders.

Tangnost had sent word to his blood kin amongst the clans of the north west; the White Raven, Red Squirrel, Capercaillie, the Narwhale and Ice Bear, and a dozen others. Following Quenelda and Root's successful mission to the Cairnmore brimstone mine, the Wild Cats at this very moment were guarding a precious caravan of brimstone wending its slow way overland to Dragon Isle.

If they were to find the Earl, they needed help from those still loyal to the Queen and the SDS, for rumours had reached Dragon Isle that the clans were divided, that the Dragon Lords had met with hostility when they put down for brimstone, supplies, and to recruit. There were as yet unconfirmed rumours that a small battlegroup from the IV Fire Storm regiment had disappeared somewhere in the Inner Isles.

The world had gone mad, and he was venturing out into the unknown with a wounded dragon, a girl, a boy, and an untested esquire. Tangnost shook his head. He must be mad too!

CHAPTER THREE

A Distant Dream

'T minus one...'

'Clear the pads. Clear the pads.'

Is it time, Dancing with Dragons? We fly to find Thunder Rolling over the Mountains?

It's time, Quenelda agreed with Stormcracker, hearts thumping against her ribs. She took a deep breath and lifted her head to show she was not afraid.

A deep bell tolled, its sonorous tone rolling around the cavern. It was now 2300 bells, or the hour of the sleeping hedgehog, as Quenelda would have said were she still at Dragonsdome, ancient home of the DeWinters in the Sorcerers Glen. But that life was now a world away, a distant dream that faded more and more each day; a dream, before battle and betrayal had taken everything Quenelda, Root and Tangnost had known, and destroyed it.

'Lift off...lift off!' the mission commander's voice sounded in Quenelda's helmet. 'Lift off.'

Quenelda could feel the battledragon's massive strength as his great hind leg muscles bunched and then, awkwardly, favouring his damaged leg, Stormcracker took off. Springing into the air, the battlegroup swept in perfect formation down to the dark cavern mouth and passed through a defensive ward. Rapidly gathering speed, they flew out into the rising dawn.

'Good hunting. This is Seadragon Tower out.'

Quenelda looked at the midnight battledragons about her. The SDS, ancient guardians of the Seven Sea Kingdoms, were now a shadow of their former selves. The best part of four regiments and their commander, Quenelda's father, had died at the Battle of the Westering Isles five moons ago, and two other regiments were badly mauled, bringing the hobgoblin's victorious advance to a halt near the Brimstone Mountains at the Old Wall.

Of all seven SDS regiments, only the IV Firestorms remained at full strength, and they were now stretched thinly across the Seven Kingdoms supporting operations from Dragon Isle to the Howling Glen.

And in their place the Lord Hugo Mandrake, then Grand Master of the Sorcerers Guild, had raised an army in the name of the Queen, had even been granted leave to breed and fly Imperial Blacks, the last of the noble dragons. With his new Army of the North, he retook the lost fortress of the Howling Glen from the hobgoblins and returned it to the SDS. Now the Guild and the common populace were under the thrall of their newly minted Lord Protector, and soon to be Prince Consort, and did not recognise their danger.

Quenelda shivered, and not from the icy cold of dawn. What was truly frightening was that it was the Lord Protector himself who had betrayed the SDS to the hobgoblin WarLord, Galtekerion, and his banners. Other than her companions and the new SDS Commander, Jakart DeBessart, only the Queen and her Constable knew this dangerous secret. And they could not prove it any more than they could prove that the Lord Protector was a WarLock, a practitioner of chaotic dark magic who had created the dark dragons that now bore their ancient enemy, the hobgoblins, deep into the heart of the Seven Sea Kingdoms.

The only reason they even knew was because they believed Quenelda was a Dragon Whisperer, gifted with talking to the dragons, a figure out of ancient myth and legend. Given her young age and nascent powers, it would be very dangerous to reveal the Earl's daughter as a Dragon Whisperer, and anyway, who would believe the word of a twelve year old girl grieving for her father, a commoner promoted to esquire, or a Dragon Master, no matter how famous, who had defied the wishes of the most powerful man in the kingdoms by stealing away the Earl's daughter to the safety of Dragon Isle?

When Quenelda's brother, Darcy, had her beloved battledragon, Two Gulps and You're Gone, killed, Quenelda had almost died too. Falling into what appeared to be a deadly sleep, she had finally emerged many moons later with new skills and knowledge that allowed her to heal SDS battledragons wounded by the Maelstrom's dark touch.

This burgeoning gift, and their lifelong bond, had led

Quenelda and Root north to discover Stormcracker, delivered to a life of servitude and death in a brimstone mine. Why the Lord Protector had not killed the Imperial Black who resisted his attempts to control it, no one knew, but as a result Quenelda had shared a memory with the battledragon of her badly wounded father surviving the battle, borne away by a dwarf clan on a longship.

And so they were setting off in secrecy, and alone, to find the missing Commander, taking with them Quenelda's juvenile sabretooth dragon, Two Gulps Too Many, for her to continue his training. No one knew when they would return. No one knew *if* they would return. Defying the powerful Warlock the Lord Protector, would be a dangerous, perhaps futile quest, and her father... No! Quenelda could not accept it. Her father may yet have died of his terrible wounds, in which case all was already lost.

CHAPTER FOUR

Broken

The mine? They had discovered the battledragon in the mine? How?

The Lord Protector's eyes blazed in pale fury as he flew north to inspect the Army of the North garrisoned near the Howling Glen at Castle Dubh, one of his northern strongholds. His men had sabotaged scores of mines to deny Dragon Isle any brimstone. And yet both the Cairnmore mine and the Earl Rufus's battledragon had somehow survived the explosion his men had engineered. The Wild Cats and Red Squirrel dwarf clans now guarded it night and day for the SDS, and he was not ready for open war on two fronts...yet. So the SDS still had their brimstone, but one single mine would not avail them. After all, he now had plenty of labour for his own mines in the north-west far beyond the Wall.

Someone, at least a BattleMage, must have broken the collar that bound the dragon's magic, but who? And how did they fly such a broken creature back to Dragon Isle? He had used a nexus, but no one else knew that ancient skill. Was that why they thought the Earl had survived? If the dragon had, then its master must have too? As for the rest... surely just a young girl's fantasy?

The clans, curse them. Was it possible they had found the Earl alive before his own men arrived? Well, given where the Earl's battledragon was found, there was only a handful of seafaring clans that could have sailed those winter storms. Swiftly he came to a decision. He would unleash both hobgoblins and his newly trained Imperials bearing the SDS banner of the triple-headed dragon to rain havoc on the sea clans, to sow distrust and fear of the SDS. He would teach the clans to fear their mighty stealth dragons, and the SDS would take the blame. In time they would all learn the price for opposing him. And if, indeed, the Earl had survived, he had plans to prevent them ever returning to Dragon Isle. He would summon Galtekerion, the hobgoblin WarLord, to Roarkinch, and between them they would seal the Earl's fate.

He should have killed the Imperial, but could not resist taking the Earl's battledragon as a trophy of war to lead his own forces; and to demonstrate his power, his triumph over the greatest soldier of their age. Anger still flared hot as he thought of the battle they had fought for supremacy.

First he had tried to command the Imperial, confident of easy success. It was weak and injured and should have obeyed him; he could use the pedigree bloodline to breed his own storm of dragons. But from the onset, Stormcracker Thundercloud had resisted his commands, had even tried to kill him. It had nearly succeeded before he bound it in cold iron and baleful spells; the bond between Dragon Lord and his mount was stronger than he had suspected.

Perhaps, the Lord Protector thought with disquiet, the ancient tales were true, that the Elder dragons had agreed to bear the greatest amongst men; a bond forged out of mutual respect and hatred for their mortal enemy, the hobgoblins. It was said that the bond was more powerful than any magic, that Imperials were both powerful and dangerous foes who had gifted the first Dragon Whisperer his powers, fireside tales he dismissed. If they were so powerful, why bend the knee to Dragon Lords? Dragons were beasts of burden, nothing more.

So he had tried to force the Imperial, used his Maelstrom magic to compel obedience. Unbelievably, the dragon had continued to defy him, although it had been further crippled in doing so. And so he had left it to die in the brimstone mine, delighting in the irony, and had turned to the Imperial juveniles the Guild had gifted him. Before long others, too, would labour in his mines, both dragons and men.

CHAPTER FIVE

Operation Knight Watch

'Three thousand strides', Squadron Leader Darkrogg commanded, as daylight flooded the world. 'Keep in tight formation.' he reminded them. He had received direct orders from Commander Jakart to conceal the Earl Rufus's dragon from all eyes, including those of the Lord Protector. He didn't understand why, but orders were orders, and the Lord Protector had Imperials of his own, and so could come upon them unawares. 'Skirmishers deploy to front and rear.'

Six Imperials peeled away, rippled and vanished into the pale sky. The remainder closed ranks.

'Arrow formation about Stormcracker.'

Quenelda held her breath as six Imperials took up station to port and starboard, above and below, in front of and behind Stormcracker. They were so close you could almost jump from wing to wing and the power of their wings drummed the air into a storm!

'Two thousand and climbing...'

To avoid detection, the battlegroup climbed, not as high or swift as Imperials in their prime, for these battledragons were mostly juveniles or old, and most carried injuries. But even without a cloak of invisibility

23

they would be hard to detect so high in Open Sky. There were no other dragons that could fly so high or so swiftly in the thin cold air, or who could drop like a stone to fall on their enemies unaware, striking them dead like thunderbolts from the sky.

For time immemorial, no dragon could challenge an Imperial, and ancient laws dictated that only the SDS could fly Imperials, for that meant the kingdoms would never fall. But that ancient covenant had been foolishly broken by the Sorcerers Guild; and now the Lord Protector, soon to be the Queen's consort, also had that right. And he was their enemy.

'Height means speed,' Tangnost had explained more than once as they prepared for their journey.

'Unless your target finds cover, he cannot escape you. Hold a v-formation and you slice through your enemies like a spear. Divided and alone, you are easier to kill. And what other advantage does height give you?' Tangnost asked, as they sat eating supper about the fire in his chambers above the roosts.

'The element of surprise,' Quester answered confidently, as he scooped more broth from the cauldron. He had been studying hard, joining tactical lessons with the SDS Commander's son, Guy, and the other young lords. Tactical lessons that now included dragon fighting dragon. That he was the youngest son of a minor lord, and an esquire, no longer excluded him from their discussions.

Tangnost nodded his approval. 'It is easy to scan open sky in front of you and below, but we don't have eyes in the back of our heads, and when the sun is bright you are utterly blind. We are only four, but Quester, with his sharp eyes, will guard our backs.'

Root grinned. Quester was also looking after the white winter ravens and ice eagles that would be their only link to the SDS in the frozen north, as well as being another sword to protect them all.

The battlegroup skimmed the soaring headlands of the Dragons Spine Mountains and headed north west, away from the rising dawn.

CHAPTER SIX

Beware of What You Wish For

'North vector two three seven...'

'Affirmative,' Root responded.

The quiet chatter between dragon crews faded to silence. For the first time in days Quenelda rolled her knotted shoulders and allowed herself to relax a little, although her stomach felt sick with nerves. How different this was from what she had imagined.

'Beware of what you wish for,' Tangnost had wisely warned the Earl's daughter one cold winter night when her father and his regiment had flown north. 'Look at what you have...do not wish it away...'

But with the carelessness of youth, she had. Now, as she sat in the pilot's seat on the greatest dragon in the Kingdoms, she would give everything to be back in Dragonsdome, for the reality of war was not how she had imagined it.

Barely a year ago, she had thought it would be a grand adventure to don the spiked black armour of a Dragon Lord and fight the hobgoblins, but too much had happened since then for her to believe in such childish daydreams. She had fought a dark dragon at the Winter Joust, a predator, and would have died but for the bravery of Root and Chasing the Stars.

As a reward for saving the Earl, they had been allowed to accompany her father to Dragon Isle, and the Queen had decided that all the young ladies at court would attend Quenelda at Dragonsdome to benefit from a better understanding of dragons.

Meanwhile, her father planned a bold strike at the heart of the hobgoblins' lands that would destroy their menace once and for all, and he would come home to watch his daughter grow to inherit the greatest Earldom in the Seven Sea Kingdoms.

But then, acting on false intelligence planted by the then Grand Master, the SDS had engaged with the hobgoblins on the drifting Westering Isles in midwinter, where, in an appalling blizzard conjured by him, they had been betrayed and annihilated. Not a single survivor, neither man nor beast, returned from the Battle of the Westering Isles to tell the tale.

As the weeks passed, fearful rumours of defeat and famine gripped the Seven Kingdoms, a brutal winter took hold and the north was cut off. Grimly the Queen's Constable, Sir Gharad Mowbray, had organised the Black Cortege in honour of the SDS and their fallen Commander. Returning grief-stricken to Dragonsdome, Quenelda had determined to flee with her battledragon, Two Gulps and You're Gone, to search for her father. But threatened by the young Earl, Darcy, Tangnost had been forced to kill Two Gulps to save Quenelda from a life of confinement in a young ladies' college and at

Court.

As the battledragon died in her arms, Quenelda fell into a deep coma from which she couldn't be roused. As the Earl's daughter apparently drifted towards death, the SDS suffered a second catastrophic defeat, and the Kingdoms north of the Old Wall fell to the hobgoblins. Spiriting the dying girl to Dragon Isle to prevent the Lord Protector from taking Quenelda as his ward, Tangnost abandoned Dragonsdome to Darcy.

Witnessed by all on Dragon Isle, Quenelda finally awoke and was drawn to the whispering HeartRock; home to the dragonbone throne, the seat of power of the Dragon Whisperers of old, where the first Dragon Whisperer had been nursed by an Imperial Black. Breaking deadly wards millennia old that bound unknown secrets, Quenelda claimed fealty from the six companion Imperials carved of stone, telling them the time was nearing for them to take wing again. With no memory of this, the Earl's daughter had woken to a world utterly changed.

But she too had changed. She now knew things as surely as if she had been taught them. Distant places and peoples...names...battles...sorcery and spells.

The Earl's daughter could now heal badly injured battledragons, and draw out the corrosive cancer of the Maelstrom. But she still only had twelve winters, and could not control her own power or summon it at will, and there were no scholars from the Battle Academy on Dragon Isle able to teach the young girl. They had an army to rebuild.

Food? Two Gulps Too Many nudged Quenelda. *Hungry...*he complained.

Oh, Two Gulps... Quenelda gritted her teeth and squeezed her eyes shut, as hot tears spilled down her cheeks. The death of Two Gulps and You're Gone, her beloved sabretooth battledragon; that was the bitterest blow of all. How could he? How *could* Darcy?

But her brother had indeed taken his spiteful revenge upon a dragon that had rescued him from his own foolishness, which had saved his life when his own battlegriff had bolted! She raised her left hand and flexed her palm where Two Gulps' golden scale had sunk into her skin, hard as dragon scales. Part of Two Gulps would always be with her; sometimes he whispered in her dreams, giving her comfort and strength.

But she had also woken to a haunting dragon cry that called out to her for help, tormenting her every waking hour, disturbing her sleep. Somehow, she knew, the answer lay in the north. Desperately short of brimstone, Tangost had allowed her and Root to fly north to a brimstone mine to warn his cousin Malachite of the Cat Clan to guard against sabotage by the Lord Protector. They arrived too late, and both Root and the battlegriff were injured by the huge explosion that collapsed the lower seams. Wanting to help, Quenelda had entered the stricken mine.

And there, chained and bound by cold dark magic, she had found her father's dying Imperial battledragon.

Using Stormcracker to help save miners trapped by the explosion, she had claimed him for her own. But the starved dragon had neither the strength nor will to return to Dragon Isle, seeking only death and oblivion. Fearing the pining battledragon would die, and that Quenelda could not bear yet another loss, Root had bravely flown through the night on their wounded battlegriff to raise help from Dragon Isle.

Carried home on a unique cradle by the SDS, Stormcracker was returned to Dragon Isle, the only survivor to return from Operation Crucible. The dragon's slow recovery had become a symbol of hope, a dream that the Dragon Lords would rise once again.

But the SDS and the wider kingdoms needed someone to rally behind, someone powerful to challenge the Lord Protector, the new Queen's Champion; someone who might be able to convince the peoples of the Seven Kingdoms to fight the deadly canker growing at the heart of the realm. And that person was her father, once Queen's Champion and Commander of the SDS, the Earl Rufus DeWinter, missing in action since the Battle of the Westering Isles.

CHAPTER SEVEN

Roast Goose

'Oow!'

The clack of wood on wood, and a cry of pain broke into her dark thoughts. Leaving the big dragon to maintain formation, Quenelda walked back along his spine to where her friends were. Watched by Root, Tangnost was training his esquire in the arts of war.

'Come on, Quester!' Root shouted encouragement to his friend.

Quester was dressed in a studded leather brigandine and a hauberk of chain mail that hung to his knees, almost doubling his weight. Having helped the esquire lace it on, Root knew how heavy the hauberk was. Quester might be of slight build, but he was strong and swift on his feet, and Root was heartfelt glad he was coming with them.

Eager to show what he had learnt, Quester suddenly thrust his wooden sword forwards, but Tangnost easily deflected it to one side, and brought his own sword round to smack the esquire on his sword arm.

'Ow!' Quester nursed his injury in pained surprise, earning a second smack on his other arm.

'Come on, lad,' Tangnost admonished the youth.

'You're on a battlefield, not in a ballroom! You don't dance about like that, or you'll be dead before you can blink. Guard up, like I taught you!'

Surprisingly light on his feet, Tangnost brought his blade down. Quester nimbly stepped to one side this time, deflecting the blow down his blade. Pivoting, he brought the wood around in an arc, letting his momentum do the work for him, only to find Tangnost's sword blocking him once again. The dwarf grinned.

'Better! Now, take up a shield.'

If it came to battle, Quenelda mused, their success would depend upon them both, Tangnost and Quester, and of course Stormcracker. No one could depend on her; the Earl's daughter allowed herself a moment of self pity. Nor her overweight juvenile dragon!

The harder she tried to master magic, the worse it seemed. She would never earn her wand, let alone the prized staff of a battlemage! Either nothing happened at all, or magic just seemed to explode from within her, causing harm to those around her. In the Cauldron she had unwittingly killed scores of people. Still the thought brought her shame.

She now had thoughts, skills and knowledge never gained in her short lifetime, power beyond imagining, and yet it remained a closed book to her, mere suggestions that floated just beyond her reach, like books stacked in a high shelved library. And maybe, given her lack of control, that was just as well.

'Oof!' Quenelda complained, as Quester stepped back

onto her foot. The pair collapsed in a pained heap.

'Oh!' Quester was mortified, red flushing his cheery freckled face as he helped her to her feet. 'Lady! I didn't see you there!'

Quenelda moved back to stand beside Root to see what she could learn.

'Keep your guard up!' Tangnost repeated as he adjusted the youth's grip, 'and use your shield as a weapon, too. Now, hold your sword up high....again, stay light on your feet.'

The wooden swords thudded together.

'Are you going to try?' As the sun climbed towards the hour of the inquisitive stoat, Quester wearily offered Root his sword and took a long drink from the offered water skin. 'I'm starving!' It was past time to think about the midday meal.

'No.' Root was not yet ready to take up arms, not ready to break with the traditions of his people, but it would do no harm to look and learn, he thought. He was Quenelda's sworn Shield after all. He had promised her father he would look after her until the Earl returned, and Root was determined to do just that, to justify the Earl's trust in him. But how could he if he did not know how to fight? Perhaps he could learn to use a shield as a defensive weapon?

Left to themselves, gnomes were a peaceful people, rarely fighting even to defend themselves. Cowards or fools some called them, those that did not know any better. The few that fought with the SDS as scouts, like his father, had been cast out by the Elders, but then their entire warren had died when a roving hobgoblin war band attacked. *Was it so bad to take up arms to defend those you loved?* Root wondered. *Would it not be better to become so strong you could not be attacked?*

Watching Tangnost and Quester, Quenelda reluctantly decided that she too had better practice magic. Her spell casting was woeful as her tutors had always claimed, although she could heal dragons without using a wand, which was both marvellous and baffling at one and the same time.

'Keep trying, lass,' Tangnost always encouraged her. 'Nothing of value comes easily. Only practice and more practice will teach you control!'

'But I feel just the same,' she protested. 'I don't have the power everyone thinks I do!'

'But it is not yesterday or today or tomorrow that you will feel a sudden change. It has been happening all your life, your power grows as you do. It would not be right for you to wield magic without first understanding sorcery, and we have no one to teach you. But look how you rescued Stormcracker. I can think of no man who could have done what you did.'

'But that's just it!' Quenelda complained. 'I don't know how I'm doing it! It just happens!'

'Then it will just happen again,' the dwarf said patiently, 'and each time you will learn more about yourself and what you can do. It is not in the nature of life that we are born knowing everything we need to succeed. We learn and we grow; each new place we visit, each new person we meet, challenging us, changing us, moulding us into who we are. Learn from me, and anyone you find willing to teach you.'

Walking back up to where their bedrolls and equipment were, she picked up a travelling stove and placed it carefully on one of Stormcracker's armoured plates, then stepped back. Sighing, Quenelda took her old battered wand from her boot and pursed her lips, unsure what to do next. Invisibility was a trick of the light and air. Carefully choosing runes in her mind for *concealment* and *illusion*, she raised the wand to fashion them into a spell, as she had been taught.

Closing her eyes she waited for the tingling that usually presaged her power. Nothing happened, not even the faintest tingle on the scale on her left hand. Concentrating fiercely, she held her breath. She could feel herself going red in the face. Still nothing happened.

'Oh, newt and toad!' she threw down her wand in disgust. As it struck the dragon's hide a red mote of energy ricocheted off one of Stormcracker's spinal plates, pinged off the cooking cauldron and shot upwards. There was a surprised squawk, and then something thudded onto Storm's back. A few scorched feathers drifted lazily down.

There was a short silence. Quenelda could feel everyone's eyes on her back. Another embarrassing failure... Her shoulders slumped. Then with a cry of delight, Quester leapt forwards, gathering the smoking object up.

'Anyone for roast goose?'

'Whoa!' Root said admiringly, as they crowded around Quenelda in congratulation. 'That's amazing! When did you learn to do that?'

CHAPTER EIGHT

You Fly!

Their journey to the Old Wall passed swiftly and safely. They flew above the same military road Root and Quenelda had followed when they visited the Cairnmore Mine in the Brimstones, but struck north where the road branched. This time, however, they put down at military forts and SDS castles along the way, and under Tangnost's watchful eye, Quenelda began training Two Gulps to while away their daylight rest hours.

Given that she could talk to dragons, and certain of easy success, things weren't going quite the way she had hoped. The dragon's wings were small for his age, unlike his girth which was the opposite, not that anyone was rude enough to say so.

Perched on Stormcracker's rump, the three friends were working very hard, unlike their pupil. Root and Quester were flapping their arms and running up and down to demonstrate the principle of flight.

Yes, Quenelda encouraged the young dragon. *Exercise your wings like Root and Quester...*

Ignoring the youths, the juvenile sabretooth nuzzled at her instead, trying to reach the honey tablets in her satchel.

Food? He demanded.

Wings, Quenelda said firmly, as the small dragon stepped forward, trapping her feet beneath his, tongue questing out. *Wings... and then food...*

'Here,' she flung the satchel at Root who deftly snatched it out of the air.

'Here, boy,' Root waved the bag enticingly, trying to coax the fledgling forward.

Grudgingly, Two Gulps spread his own wings for inspection.

'Mmn...a little on the small size,' Quester ventured, earning a glower from Quenelda.

'Stretch your wings,' she encouraged her dragon. *More. As far as you can.*

There was a short silence. 'He's never going to be able to fly with these,' Tangnost said flatly, as he stepped up behind them. 'Even if he was the right weight, which of course he isn't. The only thing growing is his stomach!'

They all looked accusingly at Quenelda.

'No, I haven't!' she protested weakly. She didn't mention the two geese that the fledgling had snatched when a skein had flown too close overhead. It was amazing how far he could jump on those huge feet. She stood on a telltale white feather.

'You know what he's like. If I don't feed him, he just eats something else.'

'Anything else,' Root muttered darkly, earning another glower. He had lost his left boot, and was convinced the hungry dragon had eaten it.

One flap and food? Two Gulps suggested, hopefully.

'One hundred flaps and then food.' It was as if the dwarf had read the dragon's mind. 'He has to strengthen his muscles and tendons and these wing membranes are still too soft from lack of use. From now on his diet must be strictly monitored. And no more honey tablets! Now, tell him to spread his wings and flap.'

Food?

No, Quenelda said firmly. *NO more snacks.*

The young sabretooth grudgingly nudged her in acknowledgement.

'Right. I think he's ready to try,' Quenelda optimistically offered. *Use the wind,* Quenelda encouraged her dragon.

Two Gulps pogo-ed up and down, only using the power of his huge feet as leverage, flapping ineffectually. Without the incentive of food, he barely got off the ground. Even Quenelda had to admit it was a feeble effort for a cave dragon.

Taking the satchel from Root, Quester held out an enticing handful of honey tablets. A long tongue snaked out, trying to snatch the treats from the esquire's hand. Quester was prepared. 'No! No food until you fly!'

He flapped like a deranged bat, keeping the honey tablets tantalisingly out of reach as the juvenile sabretooth waddled determinedly after him.

You fly!

Bad temperedly, Two Gulps kicked hard. There was barely time for a cry as Quester sailed overhead. A muted scream came from nearby gorse bushes.

CHAPTER NINE

The Razorback Queen

The Lord Protector stepped out of the vortex as it closed like a thunderclap behind him. The storm it had created died away to sudden stillness, but he noticed neither that, nor the bitter cold, as he crossed the Outer Bailey of Roarkinch.

A great fortress citadel was swiftly rising about him, unrivalled in all the Seven Sea Kingdoms; a citadel to rival those of the Elder Days. Gangs of enslaved peoples laboured under the whip, including tens of thousands of SDS prisoners-of-war, and gnomes and dwarfs captured by roving hobgoblin war bands or his own Imperials.

The Night Citadel was saturated with dark chaotic magic, sucking it up like a wick from the abyss deep below the stone bowels of the island it was built upon. Dark sorcery knitted the soaring ramparts and impossible arches and spires, and sorcery hid it from view behind a powerful defensive nexus.

'My Lord,' the overseer, a portly troll from the Silver Isles bowed low. 'We were not expecting you...'

'No...I dare say not...' the Lord Protector smiled coldly. *Nor shall I tell you....* 'How is the building progressing? My weapons of war?'

41

'My Lord,' the overseer swallowed nervously. 'We have them working night and day down in the lava pools, but - '

'But?'

The overseer flinched, the very air appeared to smoke about this man, and the ground froze and cracked beneath his feet. His very breath was winter.

'We need more slaves. The gnomes are soft and weak, they do not last long. We feed them to the razorbacks to train them.'

'And the dwarfs?'

'They are strong my Lord, but rebellious. We have to make...' he paused. 'Examples of many. They are a close knit people.'

'My Imperials bearing the standard of Dragon Isle are abroad, destroying holdfasts and settlements. They will bring you new slaves before the new moons rise.'

Taking only his personal guards, the WarLock stepped down into the razorback coombs below Roarkinch Castle. Here, bound by baleful spells, a creature of unmatched malice and cunning dwelt, a creature created by him. Avaricious for dragon flesh, for man flesh, she was a predator. The stench of chaotic magic lay heavy down here, slowly warping or killing those who guarded the castle; but they, too, could be replaced.

He had laid his plans carefully, thinking through the possible outcomes and how to deal with them. The Knucklebones had flown for the Howling Glen, and with luck would pick up Bearhugger's trail while it was still warm. A black Imperial that couldn't cloak shouldn't be too hard to find in the snow, especially since they did not know they had been discovered.

As winter closed in, Galtekerion's hobgoblin banners would move south to the Old Wall to harass the SDS without ever attacking in strength, luring them into a false sense of security. But if all else failed, he had his razorback queen. He moved over to study her, where she and lesser females protected the young.

The midnight creature that now rose up to watch him avariciously was a nightmare. Hatred of all living things stirred in her cold blood like poison. The Queen had been a sea creature of sorts once, an ancient predator, the last of her kind, or so her memory told her. But that was eons ago, before the Elders first swam the ocean deeps, and long before the hobgoblins had first spawned in the warm ocean shallows.

Last winter, as his mastery of dark power grew, the Lord Protector had drawn her up from where she slept in the ocean's deepest canyons, summoned her to give her boundless malice new shape and form. Fusing her with Maelstrom magic with his razorbacks, she was undeniably magnificent and deadly.

Dark sorcery played about the Queen like marsh fire. Compound eyes bulged out below the heavy brow. Razor-sharp barbs as cutting as flint stood up along the length of her body as he approached. A twisted creature, she had eight legs, double jointed and with huge taloned feet that could propel her over ground at breathtaking speed. The vestiges of wings were more like flippers, but she could fly over short distances. Bound to him by Maelstrom magic, within its dark aura she had grown beyond any living creature, filling the vast cavern beneath the cliffs. Then she had laid her eggs, releasing thousands of baby razorbacks into the sea, bound to the Queen as she was bound to him.

Her barbed tail lashed warningly from side to side as the creature watched the Lord Protector come closer. A bone-chilling hiss fogged the cold air, fatal to any other than those who served the Maelstrom, and the stink of carrion-breath hung heavy about her. Eyes avidly watched him, hungry, seeking a moment of weakness.

The Lord Protector smiled, driving her back with a thought, drawing a hiss from the creature.

'Oh no, my beauty,' he smiled. 'I have other meat for you...'

A dragon to surpass any Imperial in size and strength and power. If needs be, he would unleash her on Dragon Isle itself.

CHAPTER TEN

The Old Wall

The Old Wall, a name to conjure with: built in the First Age to keep the hobgoblins to the south as the ice retreated, now it was being rebuilt to contain them in the north-west, as the ice of a false winter drove them south, bringing death and famine in their wake.

The SDS battlegroup was making for the Smoking Fort close to the Brimstones. A strong wind had risen that slowed down their progress.

'ETA the hour of the creeping lynx,' Darkrogg's voice crackled in Root's helmet. 'Stormcracker, can you land in the dark, or do we need to transfer a pilot?'

Root didn't need to ask Quenelda, not after their midnight flight from the brimstone mine. 'Affirmative,' he answered, aware that his boyish voice was raising smiles. But they could laugh; nothing could take away the fact that he, Oak Barkley's son, was in the navigator's seat of an Imperial, the seat of a Dragon Lord!

With map and compass, and the light emanating from the runes embedded in the navigator's chair, Root felt confident he would get them there, even if they were separated from the battlegroup. Unlike dark-loving vampires, Imperials did not like to fly at night, but they could with help from their flight crew.

'It is still manned by Dragonsdome men,' Tangnost explained when Root asked why this particular fort. 'Your father's men, Quenelda. We'll attract attention and no mistake, but best in front of friendly eyes. With so many at war, it is not so unusual to find esquires flying dragons north to the front line, not Imperials, I grant, but unusual things happen these days. And remember Quenelda, your name is Quentin now, and you are a young esquire of Dragonsdome. Don't speak unless you are invited to. Keep your heads down, and don't get into trouble. Am I clear?'

'Sir! Yes, Sir!' they chorused. The adventure had begun!

When they put down to rest the dragons at a way fort, they found the North Road crowded with merchant wagons of timber and stone, hauled by dale dragons and shire horses, bearing weaponry and food, flints and heavy cloth, furs and boots, to supply the string of forts sprouting like mushrooms along the Old Wall. Some thirty thousand men now guarded the fortifications, and they all had to be fed and armed and kept warm, as did their mounts.

But as they swung north, the cobbled Military Way below was packed with troops marching to the Wall, or returning from the front line, many bearing wagons packed with the wounded and dying.

They flew over viaducts that spanned deep gorges and

bogs, and still the road ran straight as an arrow, northwards through forest and moor.

'Smoke! Bearing three four niner....'

Heads turned to the west, where a greasy plume of smoke was rising higher and higher.

'Brimstone convoy,' Darkrogg cursed. 'A hold's exploded... They must have fired it when boarded.'

Quenelda swallowed. *How brave is that?* Crews were firing brimstone convoys when boarded by hobgoblins and razorbacks, taking as many of the vile creatures to the bottom with them as they could.

'Stormcracker, Stormcracker, we are diverting to the convoy. Maintain height and keep your current course, and we will re-acquire you as soon as we can.'

'Acknowledged,' Quenelda said. No one knew about their mission, so surely they should be safe enough?

In fading light the following day, they were at three thousand strides when Quester on watch cried. 'Look! Look!'

Far below to the north and west, they could see the Old Wall long before they reached it, its undulating line picked out by hundreds of braziers in the growing darkness, fading away into the violet dusk. It was as if a line of stars had fallen to earth. Vampires were gliding above the fort set high on the cliff tops, looking tiny as bats against the rapidly setting sun.

'It's huge!' Root whispered. A wall that divided the

land from east to west, from sea to mountains! *What do my people make of it?* he wondered, *as they move south in the autumn to escape the winter.*

'Aye,' Tangnost agreed. 'Two hundred strides high and thirty wide, enough to allow three mounted dragons side by side to walk its ramparts.'

Root had been studying his maps. 'It runs all the way from the Brimstones in the west to the Grampian Mountains in the east!' Seeing it inked on a map, and stretching away into the darkness below, was as different as chalk from cheese. The sheer scale of it was breathtaking. SDS engineers from the mountain dwelling clans had been working on repairing and restoring the Wall since the Battle of the Line in spring. Now watch towers rose up every half league, and a string of forts was under construction, with a new fortress being planned.

The Smoking Fort, guarding strategic mines in the Brimstones, and one of the largest, was nearly complete. It was here they were to spend the last night.

Tomorrow...tomorrow... Root's heart skipped a beat; they would venture beyond the Wall into hostile territory, where the Lord Protector and his hobgoblins held sway.

But Quenelda felt her heart unexpectedly leap at the sight as they circled down, for she realised she had seen this wall before, countless eons ago when it was raised during the First Age. Forged of stone and molten sky iron by dragons and battlemages; it was redolent with Elder magic, shining like a lantern in the dark for those that

48

could see it.

Here, at the Smoking Fort, the wall was built on a high natural limestone ridge that plummeted down to the moorland beyond, guarding the fort's north and western flanks. The Old Wall had been all but forgotten – until the Battle of the Line in late spring. Now, Tangnost thought with pride, the dwarf masters and sorcerer battlemages were raising it up again.

'It's unbelievable...' Quester said, telescope ranging over the fortifications and the brightly lit dragon pads, as they began to lose height. 'Right out of legend. My ma used to tell me tales...' his tone dropped to the sing-song cadence of story tellers. 'When the Seven Kingdoms were being forged out of a frozen wilderness, the Old Wall was raised out of stone and ice, and bound about with wards to stop the hobgoblin banners...'

By the time Stormcracker had put down on the Stangate, the supply road that ran parallel and behind the wall, they had attracted a great deal of attention. An SDS officer accompanied by a half dozen troopers greeted them as they dismounted, introducing himself as Major Caldor, a battle Mage attached to the 4th Sappers Brigade, a young man with pale eyes and a hard face who had fought at the Battle of the Line.

'Bearhugger! Your reputation goes before you. We have no roosts here for an Imperial...' he looked keenly up at Stormcracker, then at the three boys who shuffled awkwardly under his gaze.

'Your...boys can take him down to the river...there is brimstone here, but he'll have to hunt for himself. There is a spare room in the barracks for your esquires; we just lost another patrol...Ceredic will show them,' he signalled a young trooper forwards. 'The mess hall is that way,' he pointed, 'near the south gate.'

'My thanks,' Tangnost gave Quester, Quentin and Root their orders, and then dismissed them without a backwards glance as he accompanied the Major to the tower chambers over the south port.

After a meal the boys were shown to a barracks room, small and sparsely furnished, lit by rush lights set into the wall. Despite the freezing temperatures outside, it was deliciously warm from the pipes that encircled the room.

'Battledragon roosts,' Root sighed with feeling, as he kicked off his boots and wiggled his frozen toes. 'To think I was scared of battledragons! Every warren should have one!'

'So,' Caldor said, as he and his guest stretched their boots to the fire, 'what brings you to the Wall in these troubled times with the Earl's battledragon and his daughter? Nay, man,' he put up a hand, as Tangnost started. 'I know who she is, but none will hear it from my lips, or those of my men.' He lit a pipe and drew on it deeply.

'You intend crossing the Wall.' It wasn't a question. 'Why? Why take an injured dragon and three...esquires into the hobgoblin heartlands? Only the Howling Glen holds out against them, and the Lord Protector.' He said the last with a grimace of distaste.

Tangnost studied the man. He had a reputation as a fearless fighter and unflinching loyalty to the Earl Rufus. Had that loyalty been changed to that of Darcy?

'I am the Earl Rufus's man,' Caldor continued as if he had read Tangnost's mind. 'Many rumours circulate the Wall....that the Earl's daughter has fallen into a deep sleep in Dragon Isle...that the Maelstrom is rising... wherever there are soldiers, there are bards and storytellers peddling their tales...'

Tangnost liked what he saw and decided to trust the man. He explained all that had happened, from the day of Quenelda's birth to the Battle of the Westering Isles, and the Lord Protector's treason. It had passed the witching hour before he finished.

'Legends coming to life,' Caldor said wonderingly, as he stood and stretched. He opened a shutter to watch the snow slowly falling, drawing in a deep breath of cold air. 'Great peril lies ahead for you, Bearhugger. I wish I could offer you an escort. At least as far as the Howling Glen, but I can spare no man from building the Wall. If they come again, it will be here that will bear the brunt of any attack. The lochs allow them to penetrate deep inland, like a spear to our heartlands.'

Tangnost shook his head. 'We did not expect one, and we will soon have to make our own way in the wilderness. Our escort to the Howling Glen should have arrived by now,' he bit his lip. 'I fear ill fortune has befallen them.'

'My task here is nearly done, Bearhugger.' Caldor stood and clasped the Dragon Master's hand, holding the dwarf's gaze for a moment. 'The fort and the Wall here should be complete by mid-winter. So should you need my help or my men's when you return, it's yours. We will hold the fort ready.'

Dawn broke clear and bright. Snow had fallen heavily during the night, and plummeting temperatures had frozen the crust solid as Tangnost, Quester and Quenelda carefully climbed up to the ramparts.

Quenelda frowned as they climbed the steps. The cold was making her skin tingle...no, that wasn't right. It wasn't the cold, it was the wall, but nobody else appeared to notice! These interlocking stones were forged with magic; the Wall was alive with it, tiny runes flowing through the battlements, old magic. She reached out, feeling the power of it thrum through her fingertips, and raised her eyes to find the major's watchful eyes on her. Dropping her hand she hurriedly followed Tangnost on his inspection.

They were using sabretooths to defrost the pads before raising them, but it was so cold that the water froze before it hit the ground. Icicles the length of spears now bearded every gantry.

Great catapults and smaller scorpion dart throwers lining the wall were mounted on emplacements that jutted out over the ditch. Quester climbed up to examine the thick wooden beams and cogs mounted on a swivel base of the seated catapult, looking at the strange design of its cup. Close by, a line of pots rimed in frost were stacked behind the parapet in small stone enclosures.

'Wildfire,' the Captain said following their quizzical glances. 'The hobgoblins call it dragonfire.'

'Dragonfire?' Quester made to move forward.

'Hold it lad,' the Major ordered, 'I wouldn't do that if I were you. It's highly volatile.'

'What is wildfire?' Quenelda asked, intrigued. She had no memory of her father mentioning it, but it tickled her imagination.

'Made by the Pyromancers and Illuminators Guild,' the Major explained. 'It's an ancient craft, none know their secret. The Commander – the Earl Rufus, that is,' he clarified, glancing at Quenelda, 'ordered their Mages to search their libraries and conjure it again. It wasn't ready for the Battle of the Westering Isles, but Commander DeBessart ordered the Guild to send its best craftsmen here. We've been field testing these last couple of moons, but it's still dangerously unstable.'

'May I?' Tangnost stepped forwards.

'Of course.'

Tangnost sniffed, testing the substance between his fingers. Despite the bitter cold it had a sweet sickly smell, and was as sticky as treacle. He tried to rub it off but it stuck like slug slime to his fingers.

'It burns like Imperial dragonfire, but with a blue flame; and like their fire it cannot be quenched, even under water. The hobgoblins fear it greatly. Could have done with it last year at the Battle of the Line,' he reflected. 'When they swarm, we lob these into their massed ranks. The clay breaks. It fills the moat under that crust of ice. If the fort is besieged we will fire it.'

'The Smoking Fort!' Quester realised. 'That's why it's called the Smoking Fort?'

'Yes,' Caldor nodded. 'And a barrage can stop a banner in their tracks – hate fire, the hobgoblins do, though their own dragons spew smoke that strips you to the bone.'

The esquires shuddered.

'We have one regiment of Sabretooths, two troops of Spitting Adders, a score of Vampires and not enough men. Those we do have are either too young or too old. All troops along the Wall are under strength and half trained. Casualties have been high. We've only a single troop in each league fort between here and the Brimstones. If the hobgoblins were to attack in strength, they would not be enough.'

'Have they attacked the fort since you began rebuilding it?'

'No,' the Captain shook his head. 'Not here at least. Strangely, no hobgoblin activity in over two moons, although the cliffs make it difficult for them. We can just pick them off from the air. They have nowhere to hide. But our patrols report frequent skirmishes barely ten leagues hence, and the moors and glens beyond are deserted and silent. Come, let me show you the gatehouse and outer ramparts.'

They were wending their way around the tower battlements when they heard cheering from those in the outer ditches. To their right, the frost-rimed cobbled Stangate ran as straight as an arrow eastwards. A patrol, tusked helmets and curving ivory swords catching the early morning sun, their argumentative mounts' hot breath clouding in the air, passed through the gatehouse tunnel and into the Outer Bailey, rapidly making for the ramp leading up to the North Gate.

'Raise the portcullis, drawbridge down!'

The esquires ran to lean over the ramparts as the drawbridge crashed down with a fearful thud, raising a flock of winter ravens up into the air with indignant squawks.

'The Boarhead Guards!' Quester's eyes were alight as he watched them dismount. No one could tame the wild boars save the clan that bore their name. 'I didn't know they were stationed here! They rival the Bonecrackers!'

'Root,' he turned automatically to his friend. 'Root look!'

But Root was in the Rune Tower. studying his maps, trying to keep calm. He had lost all his family to war, and now they were to cross the Wall, beyond which lay the hobgoblin banners and their dark dragons. And he was scared.

CHAPTER ELEVEN

The Man Who Would Be King

The Queen, hand laid upon the arm of the Lord Protector, arrived to a fanfare. The Court bowed down as she travelled the length of the Great Hall to where the throne stood, raised on a spreading dais of stone. Seating her, the Lord Protector stepped down.

Not for much longer!

The Queen raised serene eyes towards her Council as her Constable, Sir Gharad Mowbray, took his familiar place at her shoulder, knees and armour creaking in equal measure. The old man looked tired, and the Queen looked pale, her pallor heightened by the mourning robes of black she still wore, despite her betrothal to the Lord Protector.

Armelia, now one of the Queen's foremost Ladies-in-Waiting, was deeply concerned. Sleeping in the ante-chamber, she knew that the Queen suffered from endless nightmares; that she tossed and turned restlessly so that the weight was falling from her bones. Feigning disinterest, Darcy asked after the Queen's wellbeing often, but Armelia suspected that it was the Lord Protector who truly asked.

'How did she sleep?' Darcy asked. 'Who came to her

chambers? What did she and Sir Gharad talk about? What did she discuss with Commander Jackart DeBessart when the Dragon Lord attended Court from Dragon Isle?'

And Armelia was afraid of the handsome heroic Lord Protector. The man appeared from nowhere and vanished just as quickly. Whilst other ladies all but swooned at the feet of the hero of the Howling Glen, she resented the new Queen's Champion's influence over her fiancé, despite the extravagant gifts he brought her. But she was careful not to show her true feelings to either of them. Let them think her the empty-headed girl she was before she had met Quenelda.

The object of Armelia's concern considered the Queen's Constable with barely concealed contempt, as the old man banged his staff on the floor to signal the Council had begun. The old fool, the Lord Protector thought, creeping round the palace thinking none noticed. That he had a hand in the disappearance of the Earl's daughter from Dragonsdome was beyond doubt, though how he did it remained a mystery. Well, he had spies everywhere these days, and once he became the Queen's Consort, that interfering old fool would suffer a convenient accident; so easy for the elderly man to slip on the frost rimed steps...

And the Queen's reluctance to set a wedding date betrayed her hope that the Earl yet lived, so Caitlin, too, knew of Bearhugger's quest. She, too, put her faith in the

Earl's daughter, and her so called 'dreams'. Why, alone, did these few doubt him, when the Earl was all but forgotten, and the Seven Kingdoms hailed him as their saviour?

Caitlin lied sweetly, saying she needed more time, that she did not want to overshadow the wedding of the young Earl Darcy. But he had urged her Council persuasively; in times of famine and the defeat of the SDS, they agreed a strong man was needed at her side to lead the royal armies to battle. They supported his suit...well, most of them did. Even where there was doubt, gold had bought him friends. For those few who still opposed him, well, his Guild of Assassins had not lost their subtle touch, and a crown was within reach. And so a date for the royal wedding had finally been set, for when the new Year of the Lesser-Spotted Burrowing Cat dawned.

Soon there would be none able to oppose him, and the power of the Maelstrom would extend his rule to the seven corners of the kingdom, this world, and others. Other worlds, which the long lost Dragonsdome Chronicles were rumoured to foretell.

CHAPTER TWELVE

Battlefield

Taking off from the cliffs' edge and swooping east to where the cliffs gave way to rolling hills, Stormcracker followed the Kings Road north to the Howling Glen. Quenelda levelled him out at six hundred strides above the rolling moorland; a tapestry of peat bogs, bracken, heather and ice. Scattered everywhere were boulders and wind bent pines. Life was harsh north of the Wall. To the west, hidden in the dense morning mist, lay the hidden peaks of the Brimstones. Rannoch Moor in front of them would eventually give way to the ancient Caledonian Forest that covered great swathes of the Second and Fourth Kingdoms.

As the Wall faded behind them and was lost to view, they saw a horrible sight. Alongside the road below lay the discarded wreckage of tens of thousands of fleeing refugees rotting in the frozen bogs. Drunken wagons lay broken and abandoned, sunk in the frozen mire. And everywhere pale sun shone on the broken bones and shattered weapons of those who had never made it to safety in the spring. Here and there they could still make out the carcasses of dragons, the rearguard who had fought to the last man and dragon to save them.

As the day crept towards noon, the fog began to give way to low cloud, and Tangnost came up to stand at Quenelda's shoulder. Snow began to fall softly down. The Caledonian Forest now stretched as far as the eye could see; a dense canopy of birch, pine, aspen and rowan beneath a white blanket.

'Take him up, Quenelda,' Tangnost ordered, his voice tense. Major Caldor had forewarned him. Puzzled, Quenelda did as she was asked, rising to over two thousand strides before the Dragon Master was satisfied.

'What is it?' she asked. 'What's wrong?'

Root, too, was mystified. He studied his map again, scanning the distant horizon ahead where the forest began to rise towards the Dead End Glen. It gave no clue as to Tangnost's concern.

'Wait,' Tangnost said, searching the ground with his telescope. Then to starboard the soaring pinewood to the west gave way to a huge lake, silver against the snow. But it didn't look right, nor did the rippling yellow mist that hugged its surface.

Quenelda swallowed, suddenly queasy. She coughed. The stench of decaying spells still hung in the air, burning her throat. Only Tangnost had seen the aftermath of a battle, but she knew with certainly that they were looking at a battleground. Memories flashed through her mind, ancestral memories of other lives in other times. Other battlefields... the Mage Wars... There was battlemagic enough here to poison the One Earth for generations to come! Still potent, the saturated ground radiated a sickly heat, so that snow and ice evaporated long before it touched the battlefield.

Root cried out in dismay behind her as he saw the ground emerge through the yellow fug. 'But what's done this? What's happened?'

'This is where the SDS made their final stand,' Tangnost said flatly as the huge dragon glided silently overhead. 'This is where they held the line against a million hobgoblins, and turned them back.'

'Wild magic...' Quenelda said softly, suddenly certain, horrified. 'It's wild magic!'

'Wild magic?' Root was scared. 'What's that? I don't understand.'

Battle hardened, Tangnost drew a ragged breath. 'They-' his voice caught. 'They had no choice. They were desperate.' But he didn't answer Root's question.

It was a scene from the Abyss itself. The blackened and burnt hillsides rose up, scoured of all life, and the great gullies that sorcery had torn from the granite, lay in stark testament to the overwhelming odds facing the SDS, and their desperate rearguard action. Here and there, huge depressions pocked the hillside, now befouled pools of toxic rainwater. At the battlefield's edge, broken fingered skeletal trees rattled in the wind. Tendrils of lightning arced across the ash.

Below, frightened to foolishness by the huge dragon overhead, a herd of elk broke cover and galloped on to the hillside. Ash swirled and rose about them like the fingers of a fist then closed. Lightning flickered, and then the elk were gone. Bones clattered to the ground.

Root felt sick.

'Do...' Quester's voice was hoarse as he came to stand beside them. This did not look like heraldic tales of chivalry at all. 'Do...do battlefields always look like this?'

'No,' the dwarf shook his head as a hidden wind raised wreathes of smoke that spun like little tops raising a fine layer of dust.

'They rarely unleash battlemagic of this virulence,' Tangnost repeated as if in denial. 'And never near any settlements or towns. It will be scores of years before this land is habitable again.' 'Longer than that,' Quenelda said softly. 'Far longer than that...'

Silence lay like a shroud about them as they flew on, broken only by the whisper of Stormcracker's great wings rising and falling.

'Armelia's uncle,' Quenelda whispered, suddenly remembering.

Somewhere down there, Armelia's uncle lay in an unmarked grave, along with tens of thousands of his men, purchasing with their lives the chance that some refugees might make the safety of the Wall.

Fly swiftly, she urged the battledragon. They were all keen to leave the devastation behind. Ahead in the growing dusk, lay the Dead End Glen, and beyond, another day or two's flying, lay the fortress of the Howling Glen.

CHAPTER THIRTEEN

Foresight and Hindsight's Exclusive Emporium

Armelia's mother, Souflia, fanned herself frantically; the bridal suite at Foresight and Hindsight's Exclusive Emporium was no place for the fainthearted. One was quiet exhausted! With nothing as distasteful as a price tag anywhere in sight, it was clearly the kind of place where, if you needed to ask the cost, you would be escorted out – by the back door. If you had to ask, you were clearly not the right kind of customer.

Thank goodness Armelia's betrothed was paying for the wedding, and the Lord Protector – what a *wonderful* man, *so* handsome! – was paying for the festivities that would follow at Dragonsdome, and also in the city for the common folk. So wonderful that he had taken the young Earl under his wing, one couldn't wish for a more famous patron!

She and dearest Harold had spent their last groat on grooming Armelia at Grimalkins for just such an outcome. They had cast their net wide, hoping for a minor lord or baron, and had ensnared the greatest Dukedom in the land! Imagine! Finally, their once great house would be restored to its rightful place at Court, and all those wealthy merchants who had snubbed them because they could not pay their bills, would pay. Oh, yes, they would!

'Madam?'

Souflia started. A young lady was bending over with a silver tray on which a pale lemon drink bubbled in a crystal flute. 'Elderflower champagne, Madam?'

Madam allowed that a glass would be good for her health.

'Mama?'

Souflia turned to admire her daughter's entrance. The assistants fought for superlatives...

'My Lady looks so enchanting...'

'Enthralling...'

   'Beautiful

      'Dazzling...'

         'Exquisite...'

So, Armelia thought, were the dresses; frothy confections of brocade, lace and gold thread embroidery...each more extravagant than the last. Once the idea of unbridled luxury sank in, Armelia, unlike her mother, was really beginning to enjoy herself. It had taken six assistants to help her into this figure-hugging design by Esmerelda Witchwood, weighed down by rare dragon pears and moonshine beads, eighteen thousand to be exact, each sewn by hand!!

The necklace that Darcy had gifted his fiancée for the wedding was a glory of spun gold and emeralds that had cost a small fortune, and assured the loyalty of the

Goldsmith's Guild for evermore. Even the Queen had nothing finer around her slender neck. The engagement ring, equally exquisite, was the one the Earl Rufus had commissioned for his bride, Darcy's mother, Desdemona. Darcy had found it, along with unbelievable wealth, in Dragonsdome's deep vaults.

Armelia swirled. The layers of the dress fanned out, the momentum spinning her like a top. The huge crystal chandelier and mirrors that followed the curve of the dressing room, threw back the light tenfold. Dizzily she came to a stop. Her dress decided to join her soon after, almost making her knees buckle.

'Mama? May one have this one, Mama?'

Mama was moved to tears. Sniffing delicately into a lace kerchief, Souflia could only wipe away tears of gratitude that she was not paying for it.

The assistant nodded sympathetically. Indulgent parents were often afflicted in this manner once they saw the price tag.

Once the dress was chosen, an inexhaustible supply of slippers, stockings, tiaras, veils and designer wands were suggested and discarded. As she finally chose a veil of spun dragon gossamer all the way from the Third Kingdom of the Elves in the east, even Armelia began to feel exhausted. Flouncing down on a padded sofa, she accepted a flute of elderflower champagne; she may only be thirteen, but she was soon to be a Duchess, and a Duchess who commanded great lands and nobles.

Pausing for rest and a tray of canapés, they could hear

the muted background murmurs of delight and approval as those young ladies who had fought to catch Darcy's attention, were now fighting for the honour of being a bridesmaid at the wedding, hoping also to catch the Queen's eyes. Caitlin had yet to choose the royal bridesmaids.

'Slippers, my Lady?' An assistant knelt. 'The spun glass has been hand-blown, embedded with water dragon pears...an exclusive design, Madam,' the assistant trilled, imagining the sales bonus she would receive this month. In such difficult times, extra money was always welcome.

The slippers were exquisite, Armelia agreed. Exquisitely painful, cramping her toes. She would never go to the ball in these, they would give her blisters. Regretfully she laid them aside, pausing suddenly. Once she *would* have worn them because they looked so beautiful, but that was before she met Quenelda, who wore buckled boots because you could walk in them without breaking your ankle.

The entire bridal department and the exclusive bridal suite had been closed for two weeks while the future Duchess and her bridesmaids were fitted for their gowns. Cart loads of water pearls, moonlight beads and precious priceless spun gossamer had arrived at F&H's depository by the dragon load. F&H's seamstresses' and their assistants had been working day and night to finish the dresses in time. At Court the young ladies were all atwitter. Who would the designer be? Whoever it was would make a small fortune, as a host of young ladies were waiting in the wings, and a veritable army of seamstresses poised with needle and thread to copy 'the design.'

And then there had been the issue of one's coat of arms.

'Of course, my dear,' her mother had said. 'One must have a coat of arms to distinguish oneself from the common folk.'

For once, the reality was what Armelia had dreamt of, and more. She was to have her very own coat of arms!!...just like Quenelda. Once again that thought made her pause.

Armelia realised that she often thought of Quenelda. Her illness and mysterious disappearance remained a dark cloud on an otherwise bright horizon. Rumour said she had been spirited away to Dragon Isle by Bearhugger, even a few hinted that Darcy might have poisoned her. In the dockside taverns that crowded the harbours, pedlars sang that she slept in Dragon Isle, waiting to avenge her father's death in a time of great peril; whilst doom mongers foretold that such a time was already upon them. These ballads were being peddled in every tavern in the Sorcerers Glen, and even once at Court. Darcy had been furious when he heard.

But what Darcy had done to the dragon that had saved his life had shocked Armelia. Her parents had explained it away...the rashness and impetuosity of youth, they said. Darcy was a headstrong young man. And after all, Quenelda's claim to be heir to

Dragonsdome was arrant nonsense...and as for her dragon, well it was *only* a dragon after all, and it was not appropriate that a young lady should have a battledragon. Imagine the danger, Armelia's mother said, fanning herself, to the public if she lost control of it? Well, it was Darcy who could not fly, and everyone who had attended the Winter Joust knew that. So why did everyone refuse to believe what they had seen with their own eyes? And if one rumour was true, Armelia reasoned, might not the other one also be true?

CHAPTER FOURTEEN

The Howling Glen

Landing for the night at one of the way stations, Stormcracker joined a patrol of sabretooths from the IX, heading north the next morning, but, despite his injuries, they soon left the slower dragons behind. As dusk fell, along with more snow, on the eighth day out from Dragon Isle, they arrived at the Howling Glen, putting down on flood-lit dragon pads at the centre of the vast fortress built on the western shore of the sea loch.

Line after line of huge earth ramparts and thorn filled ditches encircled the fortress's high stone crenelated walls, with scores of small dragon pads encircling the high corner towers. Four massive double dragon gatehouses guarded by dragon pads faced east, west, north and south; but in these troubled times only the military road south lay open. The tumbled west gate and tower were still being rebuilt; huge chunks of masonry and rubble lay askew within the ditch. How the hobgoblins had dismantled them remained a mystery.

So, Root thought, as they dismounted and were escorted to sleeping quarters above the roosts. *This is where my father served and died, somewhere in this vast glen.* Tomorrow he would find his father's grave, and truly bid him farewell.

Restless and suddenly anxious, Root was up with the dawn, and promptly got lost in the maze of roads that criss-crossed the fortress with military precision. The wind was bitter with the promise of fresh snow, as he stood in confusion, utterly lost.

'Where are you going, lad?' The guard had just come off duty, his cheeks and streaming nose red. He was heading to barracks for hot food and sleep.

'The....' Root swallowed, emotion threatening to overwhelm him. 'The graveyard.'

'Outside the south wall.' The soldier's gaze suddenly narrowed. He hesitated. Not many gnomes lived within the fortress save the families of scouts, and this boy was dressed after the fashion of the Sorcerer Lords. The arrival of the Earl's battledragon, stabled in the roosts, had set the place on fire with rumours, as had his unusual crew.

'You're Bark's son?'

Root nodded.

'You need anything, boy, anything, and you can call on us. One of the best, your Da was. Saved many lives that night he died.'

Root nodded his thanks, and followed where the guard had pointed.

The military graveyard lay outside the southern fortress wall in the lee of the mountain overlooking the parade ground. Root couldn't help but notice that there were scores of recent graves, the mounds of raw dark earth not yet totally hidden beneath the snow. Threading through them, the young gnome searched for his father, and then he saw the small twin mounds side by side, covered with wild thistles, and he knew; they were the symbol of his home warren, long overrun by the hobgoblins. He knelt to scrape the hard hoar frost with his gloves, revealing the runes beneath the triple-headed dragon of the SDS, grateful to Tangnost and Quester that he could now read the inscription carved in the granite.

Bark Oakley
Chief Scout to the Earl Rufus and the III FirstBorn Regiment
And his faithful mount, Moonshine Memory

'Pa...' he whispered, tears stinging his eyes, blurring the runes as he rocked in distress. 'Pa. You would be proud of me now...You served the Earl. Now I serve his daughter...I'm following in your footsteps, Pa...'

Now Root could understand the bond between his father and Moonshine, remembering his childhood jealousy and resentment of the dragon that his father loved so, with shame.

'Chasing the Stars,' Root whispered, once again dreading what might have happened to his beloved companion, left at Dragonsdome when they fled to Dragon Isle with Quenelda, and now left behind again on Dragon Isle on this dangerous journey. If it weren't for

Quester, she might have been killed when a juvenile battledragon went on the rampage, driven to madness by the cruel collars Felix now used. Then as the sun turned the peaks of the Impassable Mountains to fire, he raised his head to search the glen.

'There,' a voice said.

Root turned to see an elderly gnome bent with age, skin gnarled and weathered as a walnut. His clothing marked him out as an Elder. Root bowed his head respectfully.

'That waterfall there,' the Elder raised his hazel stick. 'You're wondering where he discovered the coombs, aren't you? Where your Da died?'

Root nodded, searching the shadowed glen to where the Elder pointed.

'Hidden, behind that waterfall. The Commander sent the sappers to collapse the tunnels and all exits. Nothing gets past the dwarf masons. All caved in now. We think we've found them all.'

He turned his shrewd gaze on Root. 'He was a brave man. By what I 'ears you are too. We all heard about the Cauldron. You bring honour to your people and to your father's name, lad. He would have been proud.

'Times are changing, Root Barkley. Do not be shackled by tradition whilst all you love die in the coming winter. Follow your heart and not your head, or our people will be no more.'

Root blinked back tears. 'But what do you know of my thoughts? How d- ' He looked about, bewildered.

There was no one to be seen.

Wrapped in heavy cloaks, Quenelda and Quester were sitting on an icy boulder looking down on the fortress. It had taken them nearly two bells to reach the waterfall where Root's father had died. They sat idly, gathering their breath from the climb while Root explored the area. Several patrols had flown close overhead, one of them dipping their wings in salute.

It was only the hour of the blue spotted earwig, but already the sun was veering towards the west. The twin sickles of the Hunting Moons would rise above the mountain peaks in less than two bells. It would be their last night here. Tomorrow they would leave for the lands of the Inner Islands to begin their search for the Earl. With snow already blocking the Rannoch Pass to the north, Tangnost was afraid winter would turn them back before they had even properly started.

Root looked down at the fortress that his father had saved. It seemed impossible that a great fortification like this should be overrun by the hobgoblins, and yet the NightStalkers in the far north had fallen and were utterly lost, cast down, rumours said, as if they had never existed.

'How could the hobgoblins overrun a fortress this size?' Quester echoed Root's unspoken thoughts. A headache was coming on again, but the freezing temperature helped. 'There must be a garrison of what?

Eight thousand, and four hundred dragons?'

'Including forty Imperials,' Quenelda added. She was watching a small patrol of sabretooths as they made their way through the heavily guarded glen, taking huge bounds over scree and boulders. Their huge feet were stepping out almost at a run, their heads darting from side to side hunting for a scent of hobgoblins. In the air they were clumsy, inelegant, but on the ground they were surefooted and frighteningly fast and aggressive. Quenelda tried to imagine Two Gulps Too Many, last seen asleep in the sabretooth roosts after a large lunch, pounding in pursuit of hobgoblins, and failed. He had tried to come with them, but she had had to take him back because he had rolled back down the steep skirts of the mountain twice already, and was holding them up.

'I know!' Root came over to join them. 'It's the size of a city!' He was staggered, thinking of his warren of eighty souls. Only for the summer and winter fests did gnome warrens band together in temporary camps of hundreds. 'It's as large as the Black Isle!'

The great belfry, towering above the Strike Commander's dragon pads, rang half past the bell, its clear note carrying up the still glen.

'Come on,' Quenelda stood, stamping her feet and swinging her arms to get some life back in them. 'It's getting really cold, and anyway, Tangnost is expecting us by sixteen bells to get our kit.'

CHAPTER FIFTEEN

The Map Room

Tangnost was in the Map Room studying the huge map of the Seven Sea Kingdoms that once hung on a wall of the Earl's quarters, when he was summoned.

The Strike Commander, an old grizzled veteran left behind on Dragon Isle while the rest of the SDS gathered north of the Wall, entered, an esquire in his wake trying to remove his armour. He had just returned from patrol.

'Bearhugger, it is an honour,' Marcus Derango clasped the dwarf's arm. He had received the courier from Dragon Isle, and was intrigued. What could bring the legendary Bonecracker and his three esquires north in such haste and in secrecy with winter coming down? And on an Imperial of all dragons...and not just any Imperial! Derango still could barely believe that the Imperial bedded down in the battleroosts was the Earl's own mount, until he had seen him for his own eyes.

'Ah, Stormcracker,' he had greeted the dragon like an old friend as he examined the battledragon's many injuries. How had such a wounded dragon survived the battle and come to be here? These were strange times, the world had turned widdershins.

'You are avoiding our Lord Protector?' the Strike

Commander asked bluntly, dismissing his body servant. 'Why?'

Tangnost told him.

'Abyss below!' the old man swore as he poured himself a goblet of oat beer and offered one to Tangnost. 'I thought I had seen everything in my life - until this year.'

Tangnost nodded. 'I know.'

'So you want to know how far south the ice shelf reached, and the prevailing wind and sea currents? Back at the time of the battle?'

Tangnost nodded. 'Yes.'

'Follow me, we run ops from the Impenetrable Tower.'

They entered the round tower that straddled the East Gate, its wall thick and redolent with battle magic. Alone amongst the gates, this tower had suffered no damage when the fortress was overrun by the hobgoblins, nor had they been able to break the wards that guarded it, though many had died trying. It was also the oldest part of the fortress; the Impenetrable Tower with its spiralling turrets and dragon pads had stood since the time of the Mage Wars.

The tower hummed with soft conversations as air traffic control guided their patrols to attacks and incursions, from the Never Ending Glen to the south to the island of Minchie in the west.

They stepped off the porting stone and over to the operational map that hung suspended at the centre of the room, where tiny runes flickered and danced as patrols came and went. At a flick of a finger the map focused in on the rugged west of the Seven Sea Kingdoms.

'The Westering Isles lay about here,' Derango described an arc of light, moving the islands with a flick of his fingers. 'The ice shelf pushed them further south than usual, but since then...' he shook his head. 'This unnatural winter...the ice never retreated north of here this year, and they are landlocked in place. Now...' he frowned, brows knitting with recollection.

'The winds blow out of the north at that time of year...'

Another flowing light appeared. '...and the Dark Depths Current comes further south in winter, bringing the icebergs with it.' A pattern was emerging.

'That makes sense.' Tangnost nodded. 'The Earl put down on an iceberg.'

Marcus nodded thoughtfully, standing back to study his handiwork.

'I do not think Stormcracker could have borne the Earl beyond here. Not with the injuries he bears.' With a muttered word, the map he focused upon sprang into detail; a patchwork of high-cliffed islands, sea lochs and rugged inlets that studded the western seaboard.

Tangnost nodded. That, too, was the assessment of Dragon Isle, but after a lifetime serving in the Ice and Inner Isles, this man knew the winds and currents better than any. The Dragon Master studied the map thoughtfully.

'These are the clan lands of the Narwhale, The Sea Otter, The Seal and the Water Moose,' the dwarf gestured. 'If he was taken by a longboat, then that rules out the Sea Otter and the Seal. Their coracles stay close to shore. It is to the lands of the Narwhale we must fly, I think.'

'Bearhugger...' Grey eyes studied Tangnost and seemed to like what they saw. 'Even if the hobgoblins hibernate, and they seem to be able to withstand the cold better now, the Inner Isles are no longer safe. The Ptarmigan clan were attacked escorting a brimstone shipment here. This settlement to the east of the Howling Glen here was razed to the ground. Some of the dead were garbed and armed in the fashion of the Pine Martens...war is brewing amongst the clans. Old rivalries have been fanned. And...' he paused, frowning. 'Entire warrens have been disappearing.'

'Disappearing?' Tangnost looked baffled. 'Warrens?'

Derango nodded. 'Vanished. Even to the east far from the sea and the hobgoblins. They were just isolated reports to begin with, unsubstantiated rumours. But patrols are reporting there are now abandoned warrens everywhere, and few bodies are ever recovered. None know where they have gone, or why. The gnome scouts have brought their families here for safety, and I have patrols out escorting every warren we find, from here to the Old Wall.'

Tangnost frowned. 'Thank you for your warning. We'll take some of your snow eagles and ravens in addition to those from Dragon Isle. If I learn anything, I'll send a message.'

'Anything you need?'

'Winter supplies and equipment. Most of Dragon Isle's was lost in the two battles, and they had precious little to spare.'

'It's yours. I'll inform the quartermaster.' The Strike Commander paused. 'The Earl's daughter saw this?' The Strike Commander gestured at the map doubtfully. 'In a dream, you say?'

Tangnost nodded. 'Come, meet her. She's in your battledragon roosts right now, with your scalesmiths and healers.'

'But it is too dangerous! And she is still a child!' The Strike Commander was aghast.

'The black death?'

Derango nodded. 'We lost a dozen frost dragons and ten flight crew before word was sent from Dragon Isle to keep away from icebergs. We try, each time we try to save them, at great cost to our healers. But sooner or later we must kill them ourselves, to put them out of their pain. Men and dragons both.'

'My esquire can help you,' Tangnost repeated with quiet certainty.

Derango held his gaze, and then the old man nodded. 'Very well. We could use your esquire's help.'

The quartermaster, Tam Digworth, was a cheery man who was as wide as he was tall, and never seemed to stop talking.

'Right! Standard scouting winter issue the Strike Commander says...?' His curiosity was evident with every word, earning a warning glance from Tangnost. Tam shrugged. Gossip was his trade. 'May not look much, but this will save your lives. What your Da wore, young Root.'

'Ptarmigan feathers,' Tam answered Quenelda's unasked question as she held up the cloak doubtfully. It looked as if Two Gulps had had a go at it. Rips and tears, feathers and rags stitched here and there, mostly white but patches of soft brown and green and black.

'Breaks up your outline,' Root explained to his friends. 'Add in pine and bracken and no one can see you. Da taught me how; we used to play hide and seek. I could never find him!'

'That's right, lad!' Tam agreed. 'No one will spot you out on the ice,' he ventured speculatively, earning him a second warning look. 'You'll need heavy fur-lined winter breeches and jerkin, winter gauntlets and boots.'

Looking at the three esquires, he walked along racks of suits hanging on the wall with an expert eye, throwing kit at the struggling trio. Jerkin and breeches sailed through the air. Woollen under garments... 'Sealskin boots... White wolverine hooded jerkins... '

With a muffled cry Root sat down, buried beneath the sheer weight of equipment. 'These should do. Let's see the size of your hands, lad,' Tam bellowed.

Root stuck a hand out of the mound of clothes and

equipment and waved it around.

'Try these,' Tam rammed one on. 'Fit comfortably? Good,' he added without waiting for an answer. 'Boots, try these on. Boy,' he beckoned to Quenelda. 'Here's boots for you...Harness for equipment, and you'll need a belt with pouches and bandolier.' He paused for breath.

'How about weapons? Swords?' Tam looked at Tangnost quizzically, wondering where this strange group were headed. Veterans had recognised the Earl's battledragon, and the Dragon Master's reputation went before him. So if rumour was true, then this was the Earl's daughter and her esquire was Oakley's son. Where they were going and why was the object of much speculation.

The Dragon Master pursed his lips in thought, and then nodded. 'For the boys.'

'The boys? All two of them? Or all three of them?'

Tangnost cursed himself for carelessness. Tam was sharper than folk gave him credit for. 'All of them.'

After trying a number of swords and sheathes Root settled for a dirk, a short blade that fitted snugly into his right boot. Quenelda opted for a light sword crafted by the elves of the Second Kingdom. Only Quester could wield a standard issue SDS sword. He also chose an elven witchwood bow with three score arrows. Tam nodded approvingly. 'Aye, that's the best bow we have, boy, and very old. Well chosen. Put it to good use. Now-'

Tam handed a pair to Root who nearly buckled with the weight.

'Aye, they are heavier than you'll be used to, laddie. They need tae deal with snow, frost and high winds. Lighter ones would just come apart.'

Root gulped.

'Och, I know they look patched and faded. Take it from me, they're not. Just look that way to deter prying eyes. Get stolen else....now helmets. Orders say you're to get SDS helmets-'

Root's eyes lit up as he eagerly searched the racks.

'Nae, lad, not the dragon's head. Only Dragon Lords wear the dragon armour, magical it is, yours are made of much more ordinary stuff, but they will save you in a battle.' They were all shapes and sizes, and Tam and Tangnost left them to choose their own.

'Now. Equipment... You'll want camping stoves, dishes and mugs, eating knives. Resin torches, brass compass...waxed scrolls and ink ...mind you take some homing eagles from the courier post...'

The list went on and on.

CHAPTER SIXTEEN

Betrayal

Although the three esquires put on brave faces as they left the Howling Glen behind, they were all feeling nervous and tense. Two cloaked Imperials escorted them for the first twenty leagues, and then peeled off on patrol. Without their escort, the Open Sky seemed impossibly vast; their solitude frightening rather than reassuring. To begin with, they flew over a sprawl of crofts and farms that bordered the road north, and frequently saw the SDS patrols. Since then any dwellings were ruined and long abandoned. As they poked dispiritedly about yet another deserted warren, Root was baffled.

'But this is where they always camp,' he frowned in concentration. 'I remember because of those two peaks, the Large Shepherd and the Small Shepherd. And that warren yesterday down near the fork of The Black Adder. I remember that too. My Ma came from there. Where are they? Where have they all gone?'

But Tangnost had no reassuring answer for the gnome. Whatever had happened to the warrens, it did not bode well.

There was a loud robust boom. The tent flaps fluttered.

Quenelda groaned, and burrowed deeper into her sleeping bag like a grub into a chrysalis. She needed a good night's rest, they all did.

After five exhausting days flying into a westerly headwind they had finally crossed the sea to the island Knuckenmorrach, the second largest of sixty eight that made up the Inner Isles. There they had made camp at the foot of the Cuillins in a small dell between stands of rowan and silver birches. They flew by night or day, taking advantage of any break in the dreadful weather, resting frequently, but never for long, to make sure Stormcracker was not overly taxed.

The clouds bellying low over the mountains and high dark castles to the north held the promise of hidden threats. These were lawless lands now. Towards the second evening, they had caught sight of two SDS patrols, and during the night had seen the flash of sorcery lighting the sky as the SDS engaged with the hobgoblins in some inlet far to the south west.

In order to conserve brimstone stocks, they had released the battledragon to hunt. Unable to resist his favourite prey, Stormcracker had eaten one highland cow too many. The dragon had still not fully recovered from many moons of starvation, and too much rich food still made him ill. The noise from his digestive tracts and triple stomachs was indescribably vile, and that was before he started to break wind. After that began, the ground vibrated with explosive regularity, setting everyone's teeth on edge. But Stormcracker's internal plumbing wasn't their only concern. A storm was brewing, and Tangnost was concerned, although he had tried to hide it.

The temperature had been steadily dropping, too. As dark fell, sleet began a gentle tattoo on the dragon's outstretched wing and surrounding vegetation. Then, just as Quenelda finally started to doze, lightning flashed and thunderheads boomed. Heavy hail drummed off Stormcracker's armoured hide to pool where the dragon's great bulk had sunk deeply into the soft peaty turf. The wind began to rise. As water splattered onto his face, and began to seep into his sleeping blankets, Root heartily wished he could go into hibernation and wake up when this wretched adventure was all over.

In the middle of the night the tent decided it, too, had had enough, and took off into the storm, guy-ropes trailing like jellyfish tentacles. Tangnost strung up their hammocks military fashion, and Quenelda, Root and Quester spent the remainder of the night huddled beneath the doubtful shelter of Stormcracker's wing, emerging cold, wet and bad tempered.

Tangnost, having served sixty years in the SDS, was made of sterner stuff, slept soundly, and woke refreshed and unrelentingly cheerful. Turning out of his hammock in the dark, he set the kettle on a newly made fire and shook the youngsters, who had finally fallen into a miserable doze.

'But it's not dawn yet,' Root protested as he took the mug of steaming bramble tea. But it was – almost. It was in fact already a quarter past the hour of the yawning dormouse. Dark scudding clouds filled the sky and hung so low that it still felt like night.

The ground was so waterlogged that Stormcracker had sunk up to his spur claws, and the bogs squelched and sucked horribly. Off behind a boulder to answer the call of nature, Root got stuck, sinking up to his ankles and then up to his knees. Furiously embarrassed, he struggled and only made things worse as his boots filled up with peaty water. The mud was reluctant to relinquish its prize.

'Tangnost? Ummnn...Quester?' Face burning, he had to get pulled out by Tangnost, who told the embarrassed youth to mount up, to keep him from getting stuck again. Shivering, Root emptied his waterlogged boots with disgust.

The storm was getting wilder as they mounted up, and visibility poorer, but Tangnost was determined to press on.

It was a harsh unforgiving land of black basalt coastline relieved only by steep-sided craggy inlets and mountain-girdled sea-lochs, populated with heavily forested islands. Empty watchtowers stood a lonely vigil. They had been overrun when the hobgoblins swarmed during the previous spring, but some had now been garrisoned, whether by the Crown or the Protector's men they didn't know, and so avoided them when they could.

Day followed day, as Root, following the Strike

Commander's intelligence and Tangnost's instructions, set them a course that explored dozens of the westward islands using a grid of horizontal and vertical lines based on SDS search and rescue principles. Following the coast line, they surveyed beach after beach searching for a sign that Stormcracker might recognise.

Finding no trace of the Earl in the wilderness, they began to put down at the isolated fishing settlements that clustered around coves and river mouths, hoping to find food and shelter for the night, and hopefully some news, but the villagers were hostile, driving them away. Dragons, they said, attracted hobgoblins and the SDS were no longer there to protect them. Others threw stones and loosed arrows at them, cursing that SDS dragons had eaten their sheep and cattle, and the Dragon Lords had stolen their menfolk and young away on the back of an Imperial, forcing them to fight the hobgoblins.

The Queen's peace was clearly a thing of the past.

And when they did find a small community with a stout timber stockade and a warm welcome, it all went horribly wrong when Two Gulps raided their store of smoked herring and walrus meat, leaving the villagers with no food for the winter. Politely but firmly, they were asked to leave. Before they did, Tangnost sent Stormcracker and Quenelda to hunt inland, leaving a dozen giant elk to replace the food the juvenile sabretooth had stolen. Then he had taken the Earl's daughter aside to have some quiet words. When she returned to her pilot's chair, her cheeks were flushed, and she avoided Root's questioning glance.

'We're getting nowhere,' Quenelda was close to tears as they prepared to take off from yet another island three days later, where fisherfolk of the Seal Clan had refused to talk to them. She threw Root's torn and worn map down. 'How can we find him? They all refuse to speak to us, or say they don't know if there were any survivors. Papa could be on any one of them. And it is getting harder to fly.'

Tangnost nodded. 'We may have to over winter with my people to the east. But don't be too disheartened.' The dwarf laid a reassuring hand across her shoulders. 'The Clans have always been close-knit communities, and in these lawless evil days, rightly suspicious of any outsiders claiming friendship. But,' Tangnost admitted, 'I do not understand the hostility we have recently encountered, nor why we can find none of Root's people, but we must keep trying.'

As days turned into weeks and Root shivered in the unrelenting cold and even Tangnost grew tired, Quenelda felt guilty. *How can we find my father when the SDS have failed? What if he is dead and the dream was only a dream?* But it was too late for second thoughts.

CHAPTER SEVENTEEN

The Outer Isles – A Harvest of Dragons

Pink feathers of light tickled the horizon. Quenelda stretched and rubbed her eyes as it seeped into their cosy dark world.

'The snow has stopped!' She tried to push Two Gulps to one side, gave up, and crawled out of her sleeping roll fully dressed. The snow had indeed finally stopped, but she could see it piled eight hands thick on Stormcracker. For four days the blizzard had raged, burying them. The large dragon was curled about them with his wing outspread, creating a snug tent. Two Gulps had heated their little world in more ways than one...

Exhausted, dispirited, they had put down for the night as dark fell, on an ice island the size of the Black Isle, just a darker shadow on the ocean. Another weary day in the saddle beckoned. The remaining stars dwindled. Stiff and cold, they struck camp in silence. Even Tangnost seemed withdrawn. Failure, something the dwarf had refused to contemplate, now seemed a real possibility. Soon they would have to make a decision to over-winter with one of the clans as he had suggested, or turn back.

Moodily, Quenelda wandered down to the beach.

Emperor dragons, small, flightless dragons with a white chest and saffron crest, crowded in colonies of thousands, and filled the air with their high piping calls. Quenelda was captivated as they torpedoed out of the water at high speed to land on their bellies on the icy shoreline.

Root called her. With a sigh, Quenelda's started to stand. A pod of orcas broke the surface of the sea, catching her eye. Then her heart thumped, as beyond, she saw a lone small island rising up from the ocean on the horizon.

'Tangnost! Tangnost!' And she was running back to Stormcracker, her heart full of hope.

Rounding the headland they came across a small beach that rose rapidly into a narrow ravine, that in turn led steeply upwards towards thick woodland. And there, polished pale as bone at the foot of the cliffs, lay the skeletal ribs of longships, stuck way above the high tide mark. As Quenelda's heart missed a beat, Stormcracker's affirmation sang through her head.

I was here, Dancing with Dragons....

Tangnost didn't need to hear her words, Quenelda's eyes were enough.

'Put him down on that rocky outcrop,' he suggested. 'The beach is clogged with driftwood, and we don't want to crush any signs.' But even as the battledragon was dropping softly onto the rocks, the Earl's daughter sobbed and put her hand to her mouth in horror, and Root and Quester gasped in shock. Tangnost closed his eyes in sorrow.

What they had thought to be bleached driftwood was bones! The carcasses of countless dragons lay smashed and broken, thickly carpeting the beach, strewn haphazardly; the aftermath of a battle. The three youngsters had only seen dragon skeletons in Dragonsdome, and none that bore the trauma of battle and death.

*Brothers...sisters...*Stormcracker's sorrow swamped Quenelda with guilt and horror at returning him to this place; where the bond with her father was severed, and where the battledragon had been enslaved by the Lord Protector.

Am I doing the right thing...?

Taking a deep breath she climbed down and threaded her way through frozen rock pools to the beach. This, then, was the sanctuary her father had reached.

'Quester, lad, keep watch,' Tangnost ordered. 'Call if you see anything, see anyone at all. Quenelda, tell Storm to be prepared to take off at a moment's notice.'

'Sir!' Grabbing up his telescope, Quester took up station on Stormcracker's withers, his great shoulder blades. Raising the spyglass, he winced and closed his eyes. The bright light hurt his head, slammed into the back of his skull to explode in pain. Trying to ignore the agony of it, he began scanning the sky again. He wouldn't say a word, they needed him. They would never let him join the SDS if he was so ill.

Root was already on land, trying and failing to pick his way through the brittle bones that crunched beneath his boots, long since picked clean by hobgoblins and sea ravens.

Who were you? Tangnost asked softly, as he laid a calloused hand on the huge skull of an Imperial, finger tracing the marks of hobgoblin teeth. Melancholia suddenly gripped him. *Perhaps it would have been better that I had fought, and fell with you, than see the ruin of the Stealth Dragon Services...*

The wind moaned and whistled through the skeletons, adding its sad song to the deserted graveyard.

'Tangnost!' Root beckoned, excitedly. 'Over here!'

This time it was bleached wood that they gathered about; unmistakably, the broken splintered planks of a longboat. 'Here!' Root wrested a weathered shield from the driftwood, but the design on it was too faded to make out.

Tangnost suddenly leapt forwards with a cry. Looking at each other in confusion, Root and Quenelda followed. On Stormcracker, Quester had reached for his bow.

'Look!' The Dragon Master looked up, eye bright with triumph. The broken figurehead of a longboat rose out of the wreckage, unmistakably that of the Narwhale Clan despite the battering it had taken. The twisted horn had been snapped off.

'Right!' Tangnost said, suddenly full of hope and energy. This was the clue they had been hunting for. 'Root, take Quester with you and scout the island. See if there are any more clues as to what happened here, then after a rest, we fly to the Narwhales.'

He considered the Earl's daughter, who had returned to stand motionless beside Stormcracker. *Give them time to grieve...*

Gently Stormcracker's neck stretched out to nuzzle some bones. Blowing softly he breathed on the smashed ruins of Imperials, and then raised his head high.

KKKKKKKkkkkkrrrrrrrrrrrrrrrrrrqqqqqqqqqqqqqqk!

He roared his grief to the sky, purple plasma jetting outwards. The bones crumbled to dust, and were caught by the wind, and vanished. Quenelda wept.

Stormcracker was warming his wings up and down. The wind had veered round and freshened, and Tangnost wanted to leave to take advantage of it. One mistake in the dark, and they might miss landfall. None of them would last more than heartbeats in the freezing sea.

'Sooo...' Root examined his map, carefully adding more detail to it with a quill and ink. 'We plot a course for...Innerskinch?'

'No...' Tangnost pursed his lips in thought. 'Not their heartland. I think your father would have been taken to the Isle of Thornsea. That is their true holdfast. It is hidden, and few know of its existence outwith the clan. It is very old. If they were hiding him that-'

'But,' Quenelda cut in, asking the question everyone was avoiding. 'Why,' she bit her lip and took a deep breath. 'Why have we heard no word from them? If they have Papa?'

'I do not understand,' Tangnost conceded. *There must be a reason...maybe he has died?* 'But I am sure they will talk to us!'

CHAPTER EIGHTEEN

The Island of Thornsea

The overcast sky was the colour of pewter, draining colour from the day. Quester's sharp eyes were the first to see the heavy plumes of smoke over the horizon that defied even the rising wind.

'What is it?' Quenelda asked Tangnost, who was seated astride the battledragon's neck in front of her.

The dwarf shook his head. 'I don't know, lass, but I fear it doesn't bode well. Smoke like that means battle.' He handed the spyglass to Root, who checked his calculations and instruments.

'That heading is exactly where we are aiming for,' the young gnome confirmed.

'Take us up as high as he can manage,' Tangnost said. 'I don't want to be caught unawares if there are hostile dragons about.'

As they drew closer, Quenelda could see why they might have brought her father here. The island far below was the largest of three, cliffs rising sheer out of the sea and guarded by a necklace of smaller rocky outcrops and islands that jutted raggedly from the sea. It was heavily wooded, and riddled with deep ravines, save for the crown which was cleared.

Small powder flakes of ash were floating in the air as they closed in. Several mounds about the rocky shore were burning. As the tide washed over them, they fizzed and fumed and sent spume high into the air. The greasy black smoke lingered as if the wind were not strong enough to shift it. Broken hulls and shattered timbers from longboats floated belly up about the island.

But there were no other dragons in sight. Although there was a risk that it was a trap and other Imperials might be cloaked, Tangnost told Quenelda to take them closer.

As they dropped slowly down, a feeling of danger grew in Quenelda's mind. Darkness was close at hand. The taint of the abyss hung faintly here.

'What?' Tangnost had noticed her sudden stillness.

'Wait.' *Storm, go closer, down to those rocks...*

With a sense of foreboding, they descended. The closer they got, the more the smoke clogged their throats as they circled the base of the island, making them cough.

Away, Storm! Quenelda had made out the shapes. She had only seen them through Stormcracker's dream, but she knew them, enemies of old risen in new form.

'Razorbacks!' she said flatly.

'Razorbacks?' Root's heart missed a beat as he swung his telescope down. They looked like burning rocks to him. He handed the telescope to Quester.

Tangnost stood. 'Take us up,' he said grimly. 'And keep out of range!'

Keeping the battledragon upwind, Quenelda slowly

brought Stormcracker up level with the crown of the cliffs, to where a great hall and longhouses and had once stood. Circling round the cliff tops they could see the ruins of devastation. Stone walls tumbled; bodies scattered like broken dolls. Great swathes of wood and grass had been scorched. Finally they were noticed, as dwarfs ran out of their smouldering longhouses and streamed up out of their cliff defences. A shower of arrows arced up, but they were well out of range.

'They're firing at us!' Quester was shocked. 'Why?'

'Perhaps,' Tangnost said thoughtfully, 'like the villages and warrens on the mainland, this is not the first Imperial they have seen...let's convince them of our good intentions. Break out the colours, Quester. Quenelda, take him in low, but stay within the protection of your seats.'

But as Quester unfurled the triple-headed dragon of the SDS, another hail of arrows arced up with faint cries and curses.

'What can we do?' Quester asked.

'Give them a token they believe in.'

This time, as they passed just out of arrow range, Tangnost cast his torque, a heavy necklace of gold, its ends shaped like bear paws, to the ground where it was scooped up by a child who ran to a group of Elders. The dwarfs then lowered their weapons and stood watchfully whilst Quenelda brought the dragon down beside the smoke blackened fortress, whipping ashes into a storm.

'Wait,' Tangnost warned, 'till I beckon you forwards.

If I don't return, prepare for immediate take off...we no longer know who is friend or foe. Quester? Cover me.'

The youth nodded. An arrow had already been notched; he had a second to hand.

Tangnost descended Stormcracker's wing, arms stretched wide, palms upwards in the universal sign of friendship. A grizzled dwarf came forward, guarded by his house Carls, who held their weapons loosely. The Chieftain had bloodstained bandages about his head, and his cloak was soot stained and torn. The veterans who guarded him bore wounds too. Watchful eyes brightened as Tangnost reached them and removed his helmet.

'Bearhugger!'

'Tamrock!'

They clasped each other warmly. 'Old friend!' The Chieftain stepped back to consider his visitor, as his men lowered their weapons. 'Uglier than ever! You come too late! You missed the battle!'

'You have been attacked by an Imperial.' It wasn't a question; there were few dragons who could melt rock. 'An Imperial flying the SDS flag?' he guessed. 'They took prisoners?'

The Chieftain nodded, glancing at the great battledragon who had taken a thunderous step forwards, and the three boys who were dismounting. *An esquire... piloting an Imperial? Bearhugger has brought a crew of boys? This will make a good tale!*

'Ouch*!*' Quenelda turned to tell off Two Gulps who was hurrying after them. He had been curled up since they took off, digesting a seal he had caught. Quenelda had hoped to leave him snoring in the care of Stormcracker. *Ouch,* she complained to him more forcibly as he tripped her, and she fell. *Stop treading on my heels!* she snapped, embarrassed. The fledgling had already wrecked a pair of boots with his talons, and Quenelda's legs were covered in bruises.

Trying to stop, but still clumsy, Two Gulps tripped and went head over heels. Bowling down Stormcracker's wing, he rolled over Root who tumbled after him, to land in an untidy heap on the charred grass. A number of young children shrieked with delight.

*What? A sabretooth fledgling. Stranger yet...*Tamrock turned back to Tangnost.

'You seek the same thing as they did, do you not?' Keen hazel eyes searched Tangnost's face. The Dragon Master nodded.

'It is no coincidence then that you arrive within days of each other. Come, we have forgotten our hospitality for friends in our grief. Come into our halls and break bread and salt with us, and then we will talk of your purpose.'

He led them through the ruins of the upper fasthold and through a smashed and blackened oak gate. At the threshold, bodies were being laid gently on the charred ground.

'But he's my age!' Root blurted in disbelief, as he knelt beside a pale faced boy who still gripped a broken sword in his stiff fingers. Suddenly the danger seemed all too real.

'That he is, lad,' Tamrock agreed gently. 'The war has not only taken our warriors, but it has taken our children also.'

'Root lost all his family to the hobgoblins,' Tangnost explained, as the shocked boy was helped to his feet by Quester. 'It was his father who saved the Howling Glen last year.'

Tamrock reached out to squeeze the young gnome's shoulder. 'You are amongst friends here, boy. No shame in tears.'

Winding through the burnt wreckage of a battle, Tamrock led his guests down a steep stair cut into the island's bedrock. To begin with, the corridors were littered with bodies and weapons, and shattered stone that crunched beneath their feet. Oily soot clung to everything, and made them cough. Several heavily armoured bodies lay heaped carelessly about a great arched door.

'Mercenary scum,' Tamrock spat in contempt.

On either side now sheer walls rose up, punctuated with arrow slits. Root glanced up to where holes gaped in the ceiling above them.

'Murder holes,' Quester had followed his friend's gaze. 'They pour boiling oil onto attackers and fire it!'

Root shivered, and once again wondered whether it was best to take up arms and die fighting like this clan, rather than to be slaughtered. Is that what the Elder had meant?

The corridor curved and then curved back again, sinuous as a snake, the stonecraft so subtle, that the cracks were barely a head hair in width. They passed through three more doors, the last one made of stone, two hand widths thick. Then they found themselves on the threshold of a vast cavern, and in it was a city.

CHAPTER NINETEEN

Bones of Stone

It was the first time Root, Quenelda and Quester had been in a dwarf fortress, and it was remarkable, as different to Dragon Isle as night was to day.

'Newt and toad,' Root whispered, only to find his words echoed beneath the vast stone dome. Quenelda and Quester were no less impressed.

'It looked just like an island from the air!' Quester shook his head in amazement.

'The lost Stone Citadel was said to be carved out of an entire mountain.' History was one of the few lessons that Quenelda had paid any attention to, especially military history.

Dragon coombs and limestone caves had been crafted into something beautiful and spacious, lit by a thousand streamers of daylight that entered through narrow flumes to the outside world. *How did they carve those windows?* Quenelda wondered.

Towers, halls and homes were carved out of columns of stone. The rock beneath their boots was polished, the houses and halls brightly tiled. They were led along a winding street and into a hall. It had no roof; only the cavern ceiling high above!

The hall was lined with elaborately carved stone pillars that corkscrewed upward to flower overhead like budding trees. Quenelda had always imagined dwarf cities to be strong and sturdy, powerful, like the Wall. Yet this had an unexpected elegance wholly lacking in Dragon Isle, built with beautiful flowing lines and airy arches that spanned great chasms between towers and spires.

The Narwhale Bone Caster they were introduced to was surprisingly young; pale hair short and clean shaven after the manner of the SDS. Logarth nodded in acknowledgement as he was introduced to the travellers.

'I was studying at the Battle Academy when my master and mentor was killed at the Battle of the Westering Isles. I returned here as soon as I was able. Ooki chose to protect our sons and daughters in battle, but none returned, so I try to continue his work here as best I can. Though,' he added longingly, 'I would love to return to Dragon Isle one day, and take up my quill and scrolls again.'

After they had been made comfortable about one of the fire pits, spiced dwarf cider was brought, and freshly baked bannocks off the griddle, sweetened with honey. The cider was golden, tasted like apples and smelt like cinnamon. As the warmth spread throughout their cold and aching bodies, the travellers relaxed. Finally, they were back amongst friends.

'I shall begin,' Tamrock offered. 'You seek news of the

Earl?' the old man had been openly studying Quenelda with keen eyes, making her flush. 'He has long since gone from our keeping.'

'Gone?' Quenelda blurted, earning a warning glance from Tangnost. He would have to caution her again against revealing who she was.

But Quenelda's hope of being reunited with her father had turned to cold ashes, and she didn't care who saw it. 'Gone' she whispered. Her father was gone! She couldn't keep the despair from her face.

'Nay, not dead,' Logarth said, as he saw Quenelda's despair, 'At least not when he left our keeping.'

'But wh-'

'Let me start at the beginning of the story.' Tamrock rebuked her gently. Heads nodded around the fire. Stories were not to be rushed, and no one yet understood its meaning, or how it would end.

'We were hunting whale to see us through the end of winter. The ice was creeping ever southwards, and soon we would no longer be able to put to sea, and our children would starve. Then we saw lights on the horizon. Some thought it the northern lights, but those of us who had fought for the dragons knew it to be sorcery.

'Several of our boats were still out to sea; others were on shore harvesting our catch. We had pulled our boats high above the winter tides and were rendering oil for lamps, smoking whale meat on the racks.

'Then just before dawn, the tide withdrew suddenly, sucking those boats that were beached out to sea, tumbling men onto the rocks. Then we heard a great roaring and a huge swell that grew as it approached the shore. Our oarsmen could not fight it, and a piercing wind rode it. Many ships were dashed on the rocks. Only those of us already on shore survived by climbing the cliffs, but even so our ships were badly damaged by the wave and the debris it brought.

'When the sky cleared we could see dark clouds gathering in the west, and so we set out to fell trees and make repairs. Then we saw an Imperial half a furlong out from shore, heading towards us. Our veterans knew it was badly wounded, for it barely cleared the waves, and it made a difficult landing, destroying anther of our ships, and killing a half dozen of our sailors.

'The moment we approached it we knew there was something wrong, something uncanny about it; for both dragon and men bore wounds such as we have never seen before, and many were dead. They burned, and green tendrils grew under the skin of dragon and men both, and their flesh grew black.'

All round the hall, hands reached for charms to ward off evil.

'It was as if they were being devoured from inside, and rotted before our very eyes. Those few that still lived, spoke of dark dragons and darker sorcery.

'We feared the Earl himself was close to death; delirious, crying of treason: we think only his own power had saved him; Dragon Lords are not so easily killed. We took the Earl and some of the wounded into our care.

Then we –'

But Quenelda did not hear the rest of his words, could only hear the thunder of her own heart as the accusation rose hotly.

'But why-why,' the words choked in her throat. 'Why did you leave men for the hobgoblins to kill, leave the Imperial alive? How could you? Would it not have been a mercy to kill them?'

'Peace, lad,' the Chieftain held up his hand. 'To do so would have betrayed our presence to any who followed, who would in turn follow us. And they chose to stay behind...they were dying anyway, and feared to kill us also; for even those not wounded in the battle were dying. And if there was pursuit, they would say the Earl had long since died of his wounds. One was my sister's son,' he added.

'But the dragon. H-'

'The dragon was dying also, and we had no power to save or kill it. Imperial's magic is beyond our ken.'

Tamrock's eyes calmly met those of Quenelda till she lowered her gaze, ashamed. *I am too quick to anger...she* thought. *Too quick to blame. What kind of courage does it take to wait for the hobgoblins and certain death? What could they have done?* What could she have done if she were in their shoes? *How do you kill an Imperial?* She realised that the dwarf was still silent and looked up, to see sympathetic brown eyes fixed on her. He nodded before continuing.

'Before we could finish our repairs, the storms closed

in again. We waited five days and nights, then put to sea and returned here to our holdfast.

'It was a perilous journey, aye, but so, too, no dragon could fly to see us, and so we were hidden from prying eyes behind winter's cloak of snow.

'Then, as the spring moons turned, men on frost dragons came with news of the battle, wearing the badge of the Grand Master and the Guild. They said they were seeking survivors throughout the Inner and Ice Isles: that none had returned, and the SDS had fallen.

'They pressed us hard for news; offered much gold for word, left birds of prey to send a message. But we do not betray our friends, and sent no word. Instead we sent messages north to our cousins the Ice Bears, for their lands are vast and hostile to strangers. And our narwhale travel more swiftly through the ocean deeps than any hobgoblin. We-'

Root's eyes were wide as twin moons as his curiosity overcame his caution.

'You...you command narwhales?' he asked in awe.

Tamrock turned to the boy, a faint smile on his lips. 'We do not command them, boy, no. But they are our animal guides, our spirits, and they choose to help us. Long have they fought the hobgoblins, and their numbers are greatly diminished. We protect them as best we can, for our lives are bound to theirs.

'The Ice Bears heard our call, and launched all their ships; their ships are heavy and metal shod at the bow to break the ice, and they are the greatest sailors amongst the coastal clans. They came despite the storms, at much risk to themselves. By the time they anchored in our harbour, they had lost three ships. They took the Earl and left with the next tide.'

'Since then,' Tamrock continued, 'Dragons have twice put down to ask after survivors. The last time they bore the badge of a black adder on red, crossed with the royal unicorn, for the Lord Protector is now betrothed to the Queen. Each time they were turned away empty handed. A-'

'Where will they have taken him?' Quenelda interrupted a third time.

Tamrock glanced at the esquire. 'In truth we do not know, boy. We agreed it was better that way.'

'So we fly north?' Quenelda asked excitedly.

'Wait,' Tangnost cautioned her to be still. 'The story is not yet finished.'

'We heard nothing more for many moons,' Tamrock continued, 'and thought we were safe. Then last night the hobgoblins and dragons came, in the coldest darkest hours before dawn. We had relaxed our watch, and they took us by surprise. Dark dragons rose up from the sea, bearing hobgoblins that swarmed over our fleet and entered the lower sea caverns. Dragons swooped down on our long houses and our cliff top defences.

'We could not see the Imperial,' Tamrock shook his head, beard bristling in fury. 'But we could see its purple fire as it lit the night, and burned us from our upper stronghold; then it put down and scores of soldiers who wore no badge, attacked us. We fought hard, and then fled below. We held the stair and the upper holdfast against them. Then, just before dawn, they melted away into the darkness. Leaving this behind.'

He passed the muddy torn fabric to Root who shook it out. Shock rippled about the hall. Quenelda's jaw dropped. Her eyes were wide with horror.

'B-but, that's – that's-'

'The triple-headed dragon flag of the SDS!' Tangnost completed for her. 'I thought as much.'

Tamrock took a deep breath. 'There is more! They-'

His voice cracked with emotion, and he paused to cough to hide his grief. Tears pricked his eyes as he completed his story. 'It was not until dawn and we had searched through the wreckage and the island, that we finally realised many of our people were missing, carried away on the Imperial, for what fell purpose we dread to think.'

'But that is like my people!' Root leapt to his feet as everyone turned to look at him. 'My people, their warrens, they are all deserted and no one knows where they have gone!'

Tangnost nodded grimly, placing a comforting hand on the gnome's shoulder.

'It is as I feared,' he admitted. 'Reports had reached the Howling Glen that entire warrens were vanishing! And many villages and settlements we came across on our travels were hostile to us, accusing the SDS of stealing their folk away, destroying their crops. Now we know how they did it.'

'But not why,' Tamrock added heavily.

Chapter Twenty

The Dragonsdome Ring

'But,' the Chieftain turned quizzically to Tangnost. 'You now know our story. But you have one to tell. How did you come to be here? How could you, or those others, how could anyone know we found the Earl? The clan swore a blood oath on pain of death, never to betray his existence. And why now, after so many moons, has a pursuit begun?'

'I do not know how they came to be here, and that worries me,' Tangnost admitted. *How can the Lord Protector know?* 'But I will tell you why *we* are here.' He took a drink, and lit his pipe. It was going to be a long evening.

'The Imperial above who guards us. It is he who led us here. He is the Earl's battledragon, the very same one that you left behind.'

Excited conversation broke out. Listening, Quenelda was amazed to find that suddenly she understood some of it, although she had not been taught the language of the dwarfs, save for a few words she learnt from Tangnost. Almost every day, something strange became familiar.

'But,' the Chieftain protested. 'How can that be? That

111

dragon was dying, like all those of our people we left behind. It could barely move, let alone fly, and was alone and far from home. The cold would have killed it. And who knows what a creature, no matter how mighty, may witness? I do not understand.'

Tangnost beckoned Quenelda forwards. She stood reluctantly; suddenly shy of telling her story. The dwarf frowned at the scruffy esquire. Her appearance gave no hint of who she was.

'Your ring.' Tangnost commanded.

Quenelda held her hand out. Examining it, Logarth instantly understood, for he had cared for the Earl. 'The Dragonsdome ring...passed from father to son,' the Bone Caster affirmed. 'It is the twin of the Earl's'

'But you are too young,' Tamrock protested. 'You are still a youth. All know the Earl's son to be a man grown.'

Tangnost took a deep breath, about to reveal Quenelda's true identity, when the red gold ring uncoiled about her thumb, causing those closest to her step back hastily, including Tangnost himself. Root stifled an unmanly squeak as the dwarf's iron shod boots trod on his toes.

Spreading its wings, as the girl lifted her hand in wonder, the tiny dragon flamed blue and purple, and in the flames' flickering depths, another world took shape around them; a world embroiled in war.

At its heart were two armies coming together, hobgoblins and the peoples of the Seven Sea Kingdoms. More hobgoblins than Quenelda had ever dreamt of.

Battlemagic struck, throwing them back, but they kept on coming. Suddenly waves of virulent dark sorcery lashed across a moor and the hobgoblins turned to ash.

'Wild magic, chaotic magic,' Tangnost muttered.

The image wavered and then dissolved as a vast citadel rose up before them. It was floating amongst the clouds! There were murmurs of awe and amazement. A floating city!

'The Sky Citadel...' Quenelda whispered so softly only Root could hear her. 'I knew it well...' But all about its battlements and in the air, Sorcerer Lords fought...each other! And dragons flamed and fell smoking through the air, plunging down through the clouds.

Horror and fear rippled outwards.

'What is this?' Root was frightened.

'The Mage Wars...' Tangnost spoke as if in a trance. 'It's our story. It's Quenelda's story.'

Huge swathes of land were devoured by magic, leaving barren landscapes behind. A great stone city crumbled to dust. Then suddenly the image changed to a castle high on a cliff.

Tangnost's eyes narrowed. It was the Battle Academy... similar, but not the same. There were strange towers and spires, great curtain walls and drawbridges, no longer at the Academy they knew.

Smoke curled. Books and scrolls piled on a cobbled quadrangle burned, feeding the flames... crumbling to ash.

The end of the Mage Wars... Quenelda knew. *They burnt all records of Maelstrom magic.....so that the knowledge would be lost forever...*

Suddenly it grew cold and dark in the great hall. Quenelda shivered as they saw a cloaked and cowled figure materialised out of the smoke. Bearing a shuttered lantern the figure hurriedly stole through catacombs and tunnels to place a book deep in stone archives...buried, forgotten...sealed with wards of *concealment* and *sleep.*

The seasons came and went..Stars wheeled across the sky...Eons passed...

Now daylight entered the world. Two young men stood talking, laughing, friends; both handsome, one tawny haired and one dark, and behind them the towers and dragonpads of Dragonsdome.

Night fell. A pinprick of light grew. The dark haired youth in novice clothes moved silently through the dim depths of a library searching, wand held aloft casting a cold light. He was scattering ancient scrolls and manuscripts carelessly to the ground...trampling them underfoot in his haste. The scene faded...

A huge hobgoblin covered in tattoos and kill fetishes stood...in a cavern beneath a castle....and a figure in black, face hidden by a mask...talking!

Another battle but far smaller: Royal and SDS standards whipping in the wind on the battlements of a half built fortress. Cut off from their dragons three men stood there wielding their staffs. The tallest wore the crown of the Seven Sea Kingdoms, a second younger man fought at his side, a thin circlet of gold about his helmet, the third in SDS black armour beneath the wolf's paw standard of the DeWinters. The standards fell one by one...

'The Isle of Midges,' someone whispered. 'When the king and the Black Prince died...'

Where my grandfather died, Quenelda thought. *Where they were overwhelmed by a banner of hobgoblins...everyone said it was a chance encounter... but it wasn't! He betrayed them!*

The flame now revealed a young woman, richly dressed, on a dark balcony looking out across the Sorcerers Loch, waiting. The same woman dressed royally, a crown being set on her young head. At her shoulder, the young Earl, Rufus DeWinter, younger than Quenelda could ever remember, and on her left a young Lord Protector in his Guild robes with a smile on his face and fury in his eyes.

Snow was falling softy as a young man in spiked dragon armour raised a golden-eyed baby wrapped up in furs to an Imperial which bent its mighty head as the tiny child raised a fist to touch the dragon's huge muzzle. A broad shouldered dwarf in a bearskin cloak stood protectively at his shoulder, a double headed battleaxe strapped across his back.

'It's you, Quenelda,' Root said, squeezing her hand. 'It's you and Storm and Tangnost!'

Then, for the first time, Quenelda recognised an awkward child in breeches and boots playing with girls in lacy dresses, being tormented and mocked, running, hiding, weeping...

The same lonely child standing forlornly on the battlements of Dragonsdome, watching her father fly away, wishing with all her heart she could fly with him.

Quenelda cried out in rage and pain as an image of chained and dying dragons in a dank cavern formed. The bodies of countless hobgoblins also lay rotting in that dark place, and there in strange robes stood the Lord Protector conjuring twisted creatures in their stead... razorbacks...

Suddenly they were on the snowy slopes of a dark island dominated by a smoking volcano and hot sulphurous pools. A fleet of battle-galleons lay at anchor as troops poured onto the beaches.

'It's the Battle of the Westering Isles...' Quenelda said. 'This is what I saw in my dream.'

Dark dragons erupted from beneath the ice. Everything was milk and moonshade ...A wounded Imperial rose above a howling storm bearing the dead and dying...green veins creeping along its flanks...

The vision changed to a battledragon roost and a dying sabretooth, cradled in the arms of a stricken girl, and a young boy trying to comfort her. The vision swirled and tumbled...The same girl but pale and thin, her outline touched with white fire, reaching for an injured battledragon, drawing out poison like ink in water...

A gasp went round the watching group.

'The black death,' Tangnost cursed.

Then once again they were in Open Sky, seeing the curve of the One Earth far below; and above, a legendary sky citadel floating in a clear sky, beneath stars where a storm of Imperials flew between its spires and towers. A young woman in black-scaled armour that fitted like a second skin stood, her outline shimmering, changing aspect....into a young Imperial, with a flash of gold scales on its left claw...the dragon took off and swooped down into the night...

Quenelda lifted her hand to see Two Gulps' golden scale pulsed brightly in the dark, and as she did, the Dragonsdome ring coiled about her left thumb, and became a simple ring once again. The vision died away into stunned silence.

No one moved. Light returned to normal. The call of voices outside seemed loud. Quenelda blinked, as if waking from sleep.

'Remove your helmet,' Tangnost ordered. She did as he asked, her dirty hair matted and dishevelled.

The chieftain stared at her in confusion. 'A girl?' Frowning, he turned to Tangnost who nodded. 'That was you..? Then you must be-'

'May I introduce the Lady Quenelda, daughter of the Earl Rufus DeWinter, Dragon Whisperer, and true heir to Dragonsdome.'

The Chieftain knelt, followed by all those in the hall. Quenelda turned to Tangnost in confusion.

'They acknowledge you as the Earl's true heir,' Tangnost said softly. 'You bear the ring of Dragonsdome, as does your father. You are one and the same.'

'Lady,' the chieftain stood, helped by one of his Carls. 'You are most welcome in these troubled times...the Narwhale remain loyal to the noble house of DeWinter, though it has cost us dear as you have seen. You only need to call and the Narwhale will rally to your standard. We are yours to command.'

Root watched as Quenelda lifted her head proudly and accepted the fealty of the Narwhale as one by one they kissed the Dragonsdome ring, certain that no one else noticed her bite her lip, or her fingers anxiously tapping on the hand behind her back.

*She is growing...*he thought proudly. *Already she has achieved more than Darcy...she deserves to join the SDS no matter what they say about girls...that's just stupid!*

'That you are heir, Lady, I understand,' Tamrock turned back to Tangnost as he took his seat and accepted a drink of water. 'But I do not understand much of what I saw, nor how you come to be here. How did you know where to look for your father?'

And so once again Tangnost explained part of the vision, telling them about the night of the battle when Quenelda bonded with Stormcracker; how she had then found the broken and injured dragon in the mine, and how she had shared the battledragon's memories so that they knew that the Earl had survived, and where to begin their search.

Logarth nodded. 'The sagas foretold a Dark Age when the triple-headed dragon would fall, and so it has happened in our time.'

Murmurs of fear ran round the hall.

'But,' the Bone Caster lifted his voice. 'The lost Dragonsdome Chronicles are said to foretell the birth of one born to both dragonkind and mankind who will rekindle the ancient glory of the dragons. It is ages beyond count since a dragon whisperer trod the One Earth. Such legends became myth long ago, and few believe the ancient prophesy. And yet, here we have living proof that the heir to Son of the Morning Star walks amongst us.'

'But...' Quenelda protested. This was happening too fast. 'But I'm not. I have a gift with dragons, that's all. I may be my father's heir, but I can't even wave a wand without an accident happening. I'm not – I don't... Tangnost tell them,' she appealed.

But to the astonishment of Root and Quester, the Dragon Master knelt and took her hands in his.

'I swore on the night of your birth, on my oath, to be your Shield; to guide and teach you, to keep you safe from harm. I swore to your parents that I would never leave your side. Nor will I ever do so until death takes me.'

CHAPTER TWENTY-ONE

The Hunters Become the Hunted

Supper platters were cleared away. Whale oil lamps had been lit about the halls, and the fire pit stacked with dried seaweed and fresh wood by the time the travellers and Elders gathered to debate what to do, and to ask how the Lord Protector had come to search for the Earl days before Tangnost had arrived. Treachery was the unspoken word on every lip.

Above, Stormcracker lay curled about the ruined longhouses on the crown of the island. After telling the battledragon the tidings that they were on her father's trail, that these were indeed the same wingless ones who had rescued his Dragon Lord, Quenelda had warned Stormcracker to stand guard in case the Lord Protector's Imperial returned, for it surely had been him. None other had writ to fly Imperials.

You *may have to fight your own kindred... an Imperial attacked this clan two days ago...*

No, they will heed my words. Lesser dragons may be compelled, but my kindred do not fight our own brothers and sisters... We bear Dragon Lords because we chose this alliance long ago. We will not serve the hobgoblins...

But they may be compelled by the same collars with

which you were bound in the brimstone mine... Those same that bound you in the Mage Wars...

Then they will wish for death as I did. We are creatures of the sky and cannot live shackled to the ground, or to another's will. It will be a kindness to kill them... unless you can free all dragonkind from their bondage, as you did me?

Quenelda paused. *No,* she protested. *I do not know what I did to free you. Maelstrom magic is forbidden, none now know how to fight it...*

But you did. You freed me...

It just happened! Thinking back, she remembered anger hot in her blood like dragonfire, and then Storm's shackles had fallen away. *What did I do?* She sighed. *When I try to conjure, I can never remember what I've have been taught, and I never paid much attention to my tutors. And yet...and yet when I needed to help Storm fly from the mine, to free him, then I managed...*

Only, she still had no idea what she had done.

You are not fully fledged yet.., Stormcracker cautioned her. *You cannot even fly... Power will grow within you as you grow. It is no gift to have too much too young...*

I don't want power... I just want to help my father, my friends. I want things to be the way they were...

But that is foolish... Now you talk like a fledgling... You must harden your scales and your heart...We will find Thunder Rolling over the Mountains...he will teach you much of what you need to know... I too will instruct you... Now, go and rest...

Quenelda hesitated.

I will watch, Dancing with Dragons, the huge dragon reassured her. *They will not come upon us unawares. Rest well...*

The witching hour passed into another day and the three esquires had long since fallen asleep on low benches wrapped in blankets, and the fire had been stoked and fed twice with bones and wood. Tangnost and the Elders of the Narwhale clan had still not puzzled out how the Lord Protector came to learn of their quest, nor how he had moved a badly injured battledragon such a great distance. Puzzled, they turned their attention to the future.

'You fly north to the Ice Isles now? A storm is closing in,' Logarth warned Tangnost. 'I have seen it in the fall of the bones. Evil stirs; this is no natural winter that is coming.'

The Earl's Dragon Master nodded. 'Then we must make haste, before it is too late.'

Logarth slipped an amulet bag from around his neck and opened it.

'We told the Ice Bears that any who followed would bear a token to tell friend from foe.' He turned to Quenelda who was sitting up, yawning and knuckling her sleep eyes. 'Lady, take this.' It was a narwhale horn amulet, the length of a thumb, spiralling to a taper attached to a light leather thong.

'It's beautiful,' Quenelda showed Root and Quester,

before slipping it over her head and tucking it safely beneath her doublet. Other than the Dragonsdome ring, and the Wildcat torque given to her by Malachite of the Wildcat Clan, she had never worn jewellery, but the carved horn nestled warmly against her skin. And it took her one step closer to finding her father.

'But beware, Tangnost,' Tamrock warned again. 'Things have changed since the battle. Strange rumours are carried by the wind and the waves. Not all the clans will welcome you. There may be peace in the Sorcerers Glen, but here in the Fourth Kingdom we fight for survival. Many clans lost all their sons and daughters on the Westering Isles, and their grief has been turned to bitterness against the SDS. There are some who spread fear and ill will amongst us. Others are simply afraid and try to hide from the rising darkness.

'Strangers are not welcome amongst them,' Logarth agreed. 'And a few have openly turned their backs on the Old Alliance, and the Seven Kingdoms, and seek to rule themselves once again as they did in the days of old. Beware the false face of friendship on your travels.'

Tangnost closed his eye in sorrow. He took a deep breath.

'There was rumour of this at the Howling Glen fort. A patrol disappeared in the west. Quester? Send one of Strike Commander's ravens with this news. Clans are changing allegiance. War is brewing.'

'Sir!' Quester nodded and left.

'Root, your map? The one you have been creating.'

Root went to fetch his satchel from his bedroll. Returning, he set the vellum out on a stone table, stretching and weighing it before carefully bringing a shuttered lantern to illuminate his neat handwork.

Tangnost was impressed. Root had marked clan lands with their symbol, a narwhale, otter or ice bear; and red ink marked out their boundaries. Quenelda's esquire had added to it as they journeyed; small islands, places to camp, flying times, where the winds were strong, particular mountains and streams.

Few amongst the clans save their Bone Casters could read maps; nonetheless Logarth had never seen the thin horizontal and vertical lines that crossed it. Root quietly explained to the fascinated dwarf, while Tamrock spoke quietly to Tangnost.

'The Orcas have new ships and much gold,' Tamrock informed him, as Logarth studied the map. 'The Ptarmigans have turned our traders away, saying they do not need our petty goods. Their guards have new weapons of forged steel, and armour inlaid with enamel and silver.'

'The hobgoblins do not attack them,' Logarth listening, looking up. 'You would be best to avoid them.'

'And... they all border the Lord Protector's lands,' Root pointed out.

Tangnost nodded. 'Yes, lad, you're right. It will be too risky. We'll have to fly seaward.

'Root, prepare a flight plan, and then to bed. We shall leave at first light.' Tangnost started to rise.

There was the sound of running feet, and raised voices. A young woman arrived; she had just come up from the harbour.

'Pardon,' she spoke between breaths. 'Elder Father, forgive the interruption.

'A messenger has just arrived from the Red Squirrels. She came with one of our longboats. I thought your guests might wish to hear.'

'What?' Tangnost was instantly alert. 'What did she say?

'She says - that - all chieftains and Bone Casters from loyal clans are commanded to attend the Yule Festivities in the Sorcerers Glen. The wedding of the Queen to the Lord Protector is to take place on the first day of the Year of the Lesser-Spotted Burrowing Cat.'

Tangnost's heart thumped against his ribcages. *He must know! He must! He brings the date forward to secure his hold on power. But how can he know?*

'The Queen?' Quenelda was aghast. She had always believed they would have returned with her father long before the wedding took place.

'But she can't marry him! Why would she marry him? She knows what he's done!' her voice rose in denial. 'He betrayed the SDS! He betrayed Papa! How ca-'

'Hush, child,' Tamrock softly interrupted her. 'She will have no choice. If he is so truly powerful as you say, if he is the Queen's Champion in times of such dire need, the people would rejoice in their union.'

Tangnost pursed his lips thoughtfully. 'Such will have

been sent to all corners of the Seven Sea kingdoms. The elves from the Third Kingdom may come; the trolls from the Fifth Kingdom; the giants from the Sixth, and the gremlins.'

'The giants? And the gremlins?' Root was wide eyed. 'But they haven't been seen for centuries!'

'No, Root. It will be the greatest gathering of the Third Age!'

'To attend Court over the winter festival? But,' Quenelda thought out loud. 'But they will not be able to return home before winter breaks in the late spring.'

'I think,' Tangnost speculated, 'that that is exactly the point. The Lord Hugo would then have hostages of high rank to buy the co-operation of those who resisted him! He will truly rule the Seven Sea Kingdoms, and all its peoples!'

CHAPTER TWENTY-TWO

Sleepwalker

It was still dark when Quester softly rose from his bed roll. Pleading a blinding headache that left him sick and dizzy, he had slept outside where the cold night had helped with the pain. Silently, he pulled aside the heavy hide and stepped softly into the night. Stormcracker barely stirred as the boy padded to where the winter ravens were caged. The birds knew him well, and allowed him to come close. Reaching inside his doublet for a scrap of waxed paper, Quester stowed it in a tiny brass cylinder. Throwing the winter raven aloft, he went back to bed.

CHAPTER TWENTY-THREE

WarLord and WarLock

The huge razorback cut effortlessly through the waves, rising and falling with the dips and swells, plunging deep beneath the towering icebergs in their path that drifted southwards. Galtekerion revelled in the razorback's power as it responded to his slightest command. To think that they now rode dragons, their ancient foes! So swift! So fierce! Twisted dragons, to be sure, bonded to the thirteen tribes by blood and bone; but surely now they would defeat the hated Dragon Lords?

Behind him, his Chosen surged forwards, five thousand strong. They were all battle hardened warriors chosen from the thirteen tribes who rode in the vanguard of his army. Borne on the backs of razorbacks in their hundreds of thousands, his banners were heading for the Brimstones, and the deep sea loch that snaked inland about its northern flanks, to await his orders.

Despite the late season, the hobgoblin WarLord had been summoned by the rebel Dragon Lord to war. A brew, poured into the spawning pools of the Westering Isle, promised that his warriors could fight over winter instead of falling into hibernation. What he had not been told was that the price would be death in late spring;

death, once the battles had been fought and won. But even had he known, Galtekerion would not have cared, for the tribes were millions strong.

Ahead, the volcanic island of Roarkinch loomed out of the perpetual fog that hugged its sheer flanks. Galtekerion shivered. Something hidden lay here, other than a crumbling castle clinging to the cliffs. Lava poured down its eastern flank into the sea from a smoking mountain, raising spume and fog into the frigid air. And everywhere the ocean was alive with juvenile razorbacks, filling the sea with their savage song.

A vast, broken, arched cave loomed up ahead, the slap of the tide echoing about the dark emptiness beyond. But then, as Galtekerion passed beneath the island's portal, there was a strange sensation, as if the world about him shivered and shifted. He felt dizzy and sick, almost falling from his razorback.

A ward! Galtekerion's skin crawled. Gripping his dragonbone weapons in fear, he hissed his displeasure, hearing the muttered curses of his warriors. Like all his kindred he loathed sorcerer magic; and secretly he was mortally afraid of this rogue Dragon Lord whose malice and power seemed boundless. But he was the first WarLord ever to rule all thirteen tribes, and for now he must bend his knee until his people were so strong they would need no alliance.

And so Galtekerion bit down his dread and spurred his mount on, just as a different world shuddered into focus about him. A world like the Killing Caves of the Westering Isles.

A great harbour lay concealed within the cavern, alive with activity. Battered merchant galleons bearing the tattered flag of the Guild crowded the docks, and beyond, jostling for space, lay swift war galleys with reefed sails and three rows of shipped oars, dark as night, the badge of the striking adder on their prows.

Great cradles hanging from clanking chains held the bare skeletons of new galleys in the air above, swarming with figures on scaffolding hammering and sawing and planing wood. Others caulked the clinkered timbers with steaming cauldrons of pitch raised up on pulleys and yard arms. Leagues of rope were being crafted into rigging, and all black as night.

As the hobgoblins moved further into the cavern, Galtekerion saw uncountable thousands of prisoners chained and shackled in gangs, unloading pirated brimstone galleons of their precious cargo for the WarLock's battledragons. Vast cauldrons were being winched up through flutes in the roof of the cavern, up to where the battleroosts lay. Galtekerion sniffed the air, tasting the scents carried on it: gnomes, trolls, dwarfs, men, they were all toiling here under the lash.

'Aahh,' a gnome cried as a cauldron of ore slipped from his grip to spill over the ramp into the sea. He cowered, but not swiftly enough. The overseer's whip lashed out, ripping away rags to reveal sharp bones and moon pale skin scarred with weals and unhealed wounds. The gnome fell and curled up as the blows rained down. With a cry, a second captive tried to help his fallen friend by covering him. The heavily armoured guards laughed.

'Ain't no use to 'is Lordship anymore. In with them!'

Cries of horror rose as a careless kick tumbled the inert prisoner into the sea, and those chained to him followed. Galtekerion's huge razorback lunged forwards, snapping at lesser rivals. The sea fountained red as they fought over the pickings. Chain gangs all about the cavern froze in horror.

'Move, you scum,' a guard shouted, flicking his barbed lash, 'or it will be you next time. If you're too weak to work, then you can serve as food for the Master's pets.'

Slowly the captives shuffled forwards, weighed down by chains and captivity.

Black steps rose out of the sea where a second archway beckoned. Diving from his razorback, followed by his bodyguard, Galtekerion rose out and climbed up to where black armoured soldiers stood guard.

'This way!' A guard gestured gruffly, gripping his spear tightly. He was sweating. Towering over him, Galtekerion could smell his fear. He bared three rows of serrated teeth, satisfied as all those near him tripped over each other in their haste to get out of his way.

He followed them upwards, suckers gripping the

flawless black steps, pausing in consternation where heat and light leaked out of an adjoining cavern, making him shrink back. A stream of lava flowed down to be diverted along dozens of flues and troughs, to furnaces where sweating dwarfs worked molten iron with great tongs and hammers, using the volcano's heat to forge weapons and armour for both dragons and men.

'Go there.' The soldiers stopped as the tunnel opened up into a vast chamber, a hollow cavern at the island's heart, empty and yet not empty. The hobgoblin's skin crawled with fear as he stepped forwards onto the smooth ice-glazed floor, hearing the slap and echo of his webbed feet and the clack of his bone armour echo hollowly about him.

The very air here vibrated with power, and the WarLord could sense a darkness, where no light ever penetrated, that pulsed about him; a darkness that oozed and shifted as if it were a sentient creature whispered about him. Flickers and sparks of pale green threaded the darkness, emanating a hideous cold that froze him to the bone. Fear trickled and dripped.

'So,' a deep voice said everywhere and nowhere, 'welcome to my Night Fortress. Come; take a ride to the cliff tops.'

He stepped reluctantly forwards towards a vast porting stone that flared into life, followed by his bodyguard.

'Only you,' a black armoured guard said, spiked spear

thrust aggressively forwards barring their path. 'Stand there. The rest wait down here.'

Galtekerion licked his lips.

His knees buckled and his senses blurred, and then the wind struck him full in his face with its ferocity, but it was not that that make the WarLord hiss. Instead of finding himself on the windswept cliffs in the ruins of a castle, a vast fortress towered about him. Black as night, covered in a tracery of frost, it reached up into the clouds, and about it Imperials rode the wind. Fear coursed through him, what sorcery was this?

Given shape and form by malice, it was stitched together with chaotic magic that howled about the spires and towers, pulsing like a heartbeat.

'Are you afraid?' a voice mocked. 'Or is it the cold that makes you shake so?'

He turned to find the familiar dark cowled figure right behind him. He had not heard the WarLock's approach. He no longer hid his face but he had no need. The WarLock's flesh was almost black and was threaded with veins of green.

'I have a task for you that will be to your liking.'

Galtekerion kept silent, waiting.

'The Dragon Lord Commander we thought was dead,' eyes flared green making Galtekerion step backwards. 'He has survived.' The WarLock's tone indicated that he would not be for much longer. 'As has his dragon.'

'Hissss dragon?' Galtekerion licked his lips anxiously. 'Ssssurvived?'

'Come...'

They stepped through the seamless black polished stone into a room where scrolls and books lay in alcoves, looted treasure from the archives of the Guild library.

'This dragon has flown north to the Ice Islands with the Earl's Dragon Master and daughter, pursued by my men. The Imperial Black is wounded, a shadow of its former self, and it cannot cloak.

'Move six of your tribal warriors into the great sea loch that strikes inland around the Brimstones to await my orders to move on the Howling Glen. This will be no stealth attack but an open assault. Move the remaining tribes secretly and with great care into the great Caledonian forest by night. Send your young warriors to attack the Wall, but never the Smoking Fort. And only attack in light numbers; hold the greater part of your warriors far to the north in reserve. The woodands are full of boar and deer and rivers of salmon, so your warriors may feast there.' *Though so many will soon strip it bare and be starving...and in a frenzy to kill..*

'Watch for a lone dragon's return...there are no roosts for an Imperial, it will put down close to the south gate near the brimstone pits. I have a man amongst the soldiers. He will slip out of the fort bearing a token none can mistake. Give me a token of your over-lordship, one that none will confuse.'

Galtekerion laid down his weapons and removed a green amulet carved after the fashion of a dragon skull from around his neck.

'From the bonesss of a ssseadragon...they are long dead...'

The Lord Protector nodded. 'It will be returned to you by one of my men. Now, this is how you are going to attack the fort.'

Galtekerion looked at the map and saw only lines and colours.

The WarLock cast his hand, and the Smoking Fort shimmered into view and rotated. A huge wall and there, a fort built on the crest of a ridge....

'The brimstone pits are here,' the illusion shifted. 'You will attack along the length of the wall...' And so the Lord Protector carefully lay out his plans.

'And then?' Galtekerion asked. 'When we have killed the Dragon Lord asss you command? Will another not rissse in hisss ssstead?'

'And then,' the WarLock smiled. 'We will attack Dragon Isle and cast the Dragon Lords down for ever.'

'But, my Lord,' Galtekerion licked his sharp serrated teeth. 'It is set about with fearful ancient magic...even with our dragonsss we cannot beat them and their Imperialsss.'

'I have a dragon greater than any Imperial, a creature of water and air, that their magic cannot stop. She will attack Dragon Isle and the Dragon Lords will fall.'

CHAPTER TWENTY-FOUR

The White Fox

Stormcracker took off as the sky lightened. Tangnost was anxious for them to be gone. It was clear the Lord Protector not only knew of their purpose but that pursuit was close behind, or laying in wait for them. And staying would only draw danger to the Narwhale. There was no point in hiding his concern any longer; they would need all their wits about them.

'We must assume they are searching for us; how close the hunters are I don't know, but I fear our path is far more dangerous than we had hoped. They are unlikely to attack before we find the Earl, for they will fear to leave him undiscovered and alive. But we must fly like the wind now.'

He looked round at the anxious faces. Quester's eyes were slightly unfocused and he was white as a sheet. *I must talk to Root,* Tangnost thought with concern. *The youth is clearly ill, despite his denials.*

He found a smile for them all. 'But we have one advantage; they do not know they have been discovered.' He turned to Quenelda.

'Take us up, lass, as high as he can go without getting lost in the cloud. From now we must be on our guard.

Quester, take point and keep your eyes peeled.'

'Sir! Yes, Sir!' Quester lifted the brass and leather spyglass. His head was thumping. He felt sick from the pain. *What has happened to me?*

But fearsome headwinds meant that four days later they had barely made thirty leagues. Hopping from island to island between storms, they had been repeatedly grounded, and the bitter cold was taking its toll on Stormcracker. Unlike other Imperials who never liked the cold at best, he no longer had his magic to shield him, and was as vulnerable as a juvenile with soft scales. He had a half dozen cracked talons, and patches of scaly blue sores were forming all over him. Two Gulps, plump and glossy, nestling in the shelter of flight roosts, seemed full of life. But he was the only one.

Exhausted, running low on food and brimstone, Tangnost decided to stop to rest everyone in the clan lands of the Snow Lynx, whose land they would have to cross or take a long route inland.

Dark was swiftly coming down before they sighted the low lying isthmus of Inversnekkie. It was a wilderness of round topped hills, frozen black bogs and thick woods, broken only by crude hill forts set about with earth defences and wood stockades.

'It is a hard land,' Tangnost told his esquires. 'There is little here to hunt or trade. The land is too boggy, the coastline craggy, with no natural harbours for fishing. They only have coracles and canoes: alone of the Ice

Clans they do not venture far from shore. Next to their main settlement, they used to have a way fort, where travellers could take on brimstone, fodder and food, in return for goods. We will have to risk it.'

Blazing braziers lined the stockade encircling the highest hill, as they circled to land. In a clearing nearby they could see a brimstone pit and fodder under a crude shelter of turf, but it was crowded in by trees and bog, not meant for Imperials. In the end Quenelda told Storm to fold his wings and drop down – an SDS tactic for Imperials landing in confined spaces.

Crack! Pop!

With loud sharp creaks and bangs and splinters, popping like fireworks, crushing a huge area of woodland, Stormcracker landed. It would provide the clan with a lot of felled winter firewood.

The Chief and a deputation of clan Elders stood quietly waiting, along with, Tangnost alone noticed, several score fully armed warriors. Not unexpected given hobgoblin incursions. But still, something did not feel right to the Dragon Master as he dismounted. It was as if they had been expected. But the Snow Lynx stood silently, and made no hostile moves, their faces were hidden in shadow.

'Wait here with Storm,' Tangnost bid them, as the snow swirled more thickly.

Tangnost strode down Storm's lowered wing, as the dwarfs backed away fearfully. Holding his hands palm up, the dwarf dismounted and moved forwards. Quenelda peered in the flickering light of flaming brands.

'Bearhugger, you are known to us,' the Clan chief greeted Tangnost when he declared himself. 'And this is our Bone Caster.' A dark hooded dwarf with many beads and feathers nodded curtly. 'Few fly in such bad weather. We have not entertained visitors in over two moons.' But her eager eyes roved as she spoke to the three youths as they dismounted, bringing with them Two Gulps. A frown creased her face.

'Leave your dragons here,' she suggested. 'I fear we have little brimstone and they will need to hunt...'

Tangnost kept his expression neutral, inclined his head in gratitude, and beckoned his esquires over. The Bone Caster nodded as Quenelda hesitated to leave Two Gulps. 'They will be safe here, boy, and our people are not used to dragons in the compound. It will cause fear and alarm, and we are a peaceful people.' But Tangnost's experienced eye had caught the glimmer of weapons in the woods.

'Bade Storm be ready to fly...' Tangnost said softly, as he bent to lace his boot.

Storm, do not allow Two Gulps to forage....we may have to fly...

Leaving Two Gulps under the watchful eye of Stormcracker, the travellers followed their hosts through the boggy woodland on a network of crude raised wood slatted walkways and up through the outer ditches of the stockade. As they climbed through a second steep ditch, the high gates were softly closed behind them. Then, as they passed through the inner ditches and ramparts, the Chieftain seemed to slip right next to Quenelda. The Earl's daughter instinctively put out a hand to help her, the Chieftain slipped again, tearing the glove from the girl's hand and hanging on to it.

'Forgive an old woman, boy. Old bones grow stiff in this cold. Here, lend me your strong arm.' *So....it's true... the dragon ring as they said...* She patted the girl's hand with a satisfied smile.

As the Chieftain shuffled forwards, Tangnost relaxed his grip on the dirk at his belt. He was becoming suspicious of everything.

'Come, Dragon Master,' the Chieftain welcomed them to the settlement. 'Break bread and salt with us.'

They were led along dirt paths to the largest hall, where Tangnost was seated beside the fire, his three esquires further back near the door. It was poorly built, and the icy air crept through a dozen gaps between the upright tree trunks and badly cured hides. Bowls of fish broth and platters of jellied eel, smoked eels and bannocks were brought.

Tired though she was, Quenelda could not help but notice that the White Foxes, like the Narwhale, were either mostly young, or very old. Just like the SDS, she thought. *They have lost all their young warriors...*

'Aye,' the Chieftain caught her glance. 'Many of our young men and woman were lost at the Westering Isles. Many children have no parents, many grandmothers no sons or daughters; but this clan is close knit. We take care of our own as we always have, for we are far from the Sorcerers Glen.'

Although his face was hidden by his hood, the Bone Caster's eyes gleamed in the dark, sending a shiver of disquiet up Quenelda's back. *They hate us,* she thought with new found insight, *but it is the hobgoblins who are to blame for their kinsmen's deaths, not us...*

Moments later, saying he had a sickly child to attend to, the Bone Caster departed. A fiddle struck up a refrain accompanied by a drum. The lament was soft, sad, relaxing. The Clan Mage did not reappear.

At the crown of a nearby hill a watch beacon was fired.

Root started to fall asleep.

'The hour grows late,' the Chieftain suggested, 'and you must be weary. We will speak on the morrow. Meanwhile rest in the hut we have prepared for you.

'Dargon,' she beckoned a grizzled dwarf forwards. 'Show our guests to the beds that have been readied for them.'

Limping, Dargon led them out into the night. Dipping a resin torch into a brazier that burnt just outside, he lit their way as they threaded through a maze of dwellings, past the forge and midden heap, to far within the high stockade of felled trees.

The damp turf-roofed longhouse they were shown to was barely warmed by the miserly peat fire burning in the hearth, or the mildewed hides that hung on the walls. The floor was packed dirt, and the ceiling dark and low slung. It stank of sheep fat being burned in the few wall sconces. Their eyes stung with the bitter acrid smoke, and it tasted foul on the tongue.

'Warmed milk,' a toothless old woman mumbled to Tangnost. 'For the lads.'

A child following her brought a small cauldron and hung it over the fire. 'Sweetened with honey,' she filled three horn mugs.

'Thank you,' Quenelda drank deeply, feeling the warmth steal through her. Root hugged the leather mug to his chest, letting the warmth seep through into his hands, sipping, but Quester just fell into a pallet, and was softly snoring within minutes.

'Dragon Master,' a small cask was brought just inside the door. 'Oat beer...' a pewter flagon was left on a small wood stool. 'And some pipe leaf for you,' a pouch was left for him too. 'Sleep well,' the old lady reassured them. 'You are safe here.'

Are we? Tangnost wondered as he stuffed his pipe with the tobacco. They had broken bread and salt together, and so were protected under guest laws that stretched back into antiquity, and pipe leaf was a kingly gift in this part of the world. Yet a sense of wariness had hold of him... He rolled his shoulders, trying to relax. He was seeing dangers in every shadow.

Tangnost stretched out his legs and rubbed his thigh. The bitter cold and damp were making the old wound ache. He shook his head. He was too old to be flying in mid-winter. He tried the oat beer which was surprisingly good; drinking his fill, he set the tankard aside and lit the tobacco with a twig from the fire embers. Drawing deeply on his pipe, pulling his cloak about him, he let his head rest against the high-backed chair.

Sweet scented smoke curled. His head felt heavy. His fingers relaxed and he fell asleep.

Crack!

His clay pipe broke on the fire pit stones, jerking him awake.

Sleep weed! The dwarf cursed. Kicking the broken clay into the hearth, he lurched unsteadily to his feet. The fire had totally died down, so at least one bell had passed.. It was quiet outside; too quiet. N*othing that might disturb our sleep...*

Tangnost softly tried the wooden door. It was barred and shuttered from the outside! He tried the low windows. They too were barred. He looked round, running hands over the rough stone walls, pressing and pulling, looking for a weakness. It would take him too long, and rouse the guards who were no doubt out there.

He checked his esquires. Root lay slumped at the hearth. Tangnost thought swiftly. *Fool! 1 should not have been so trusting.*

He shook the boy. Root mumbled and stirred groggily. 'On your feet, boy', he said softly, shaking him again. 'Boots on, quiet now.' He moved on.

Quester sat up. 'Wh-?' A hand covered his mouth.

'Hush,' Tangnost warned. 'Get your cloak and boots, and weapons. We must flee. Protect us, while we escape.'

He turned to the Earl's daughter, but she didn't stir. He shook her again roughly, urgency now growing on him. This stank of a trap. How close were the Lord Protector's men?

'Quenelda,' he hissed, 'Tell Stormcracker...it's a trap, we're in danger!'

'Trap?' Quenelda's head swam. She felt like falling to the ground, slumped in his arms. 'Leave me,' she complained, trying to shrug off the dwarf's grip. She just wanted to sleep. She was so tired...

'Trap,' he repeated, as he dragged her to her feet. 'Tell Storm, he *must* come. Now! We are in danger!' His voice was urgent, demanding, breaking through the veil that fogged her brain. 'Storm must collapse the wall; tell him he must protect us. I know it's dark, and we do not know this place; but we will have a fight on our hands if we are to flee.'

'He may - may be too far...' Quenelda was breathing hard, her words slurred. 'He may not hear me...'

'Then shout,' the dwarf said simply, shaking her shoulders roughly. 'You have reached all the dragons on Dragon Isle. Project your voice. We need him, or we are all betrayed. Like your father!'

Betrayed! Like Papa! Storm, she said, her thoughts exploding outwards...*Storm to me. We are betrayed!*

Betrayed!?

Raw anger surged through the dragon, and his third

stomach churned and boiled as flame rose to his throat. Thunder Rolling over the Mountains was betrayed. Dancing with Dragons is betrayed...! He would not lose her too. Out in the darkness he sprang forwards with a roar of rage that lit the night like day. The ground vibrated. Stormcracker was on his way.

The sound of the battledragon coming was immense in the night. Uprooted trees splintered as the dragon half flew, half charged towards the hill fort, talons gouging furrows, tail thrashing from side to side in his haste. Rudely awakened, Two Gulps bounced off one spinal plate into another trying to find his feet. Stormcracker's claw tore through the outer earth works dragging the gate and its guards into a shattered ruin. There were screams of confusion and fear.

Within moments Stormcracker's great mouth tore away the feeble roof. The battledragon was gently lifting Quenelda up to the safety of her pilot's chair as the first torches were seen converging on their devastated hut. A horn sounded the alarm, but it was too late.

'Go! Go! Go! Stoner Manoeuvre!' Tangnost urged Quester out into the darkness onto the dragon's wing, grateful that he had made them train like troopers for just such an emergency. 'Up the wing, Root,' he instructed the half drugged boy. 'And get strapped in!'

Then a figure was on them, and a blade outlined in flame arced out of the dark. It shattered on Tangnost's axe haft.

'Quester, with me, lad!' Already the dwarf was pivoting round, his blade taking the warrior in the side. A torch was thrust in the Dragon Master's face, blistering his chin... Four more were coming at him when the nearest fell to an arrow. Quester was already nooking a second, when Stormcracker flamed. Like a tidal wave, dragonfire rolled across the timber fort, torching thatched round houses. The perimeter fence blazed to charcoal.

Arrows thudded about him as Tangnost slipped on an icy patch on Stormcracker's icy wing and landed heavily. A sword whickered by his ear, before he heard a grunt, and the man fell with an arrow through his chest.

'Use the nets!' a voice cursed. 'We want the girl alive!'

Weighted fishing nets were hurled through the air.

Tangnost was already retreating up the wing when a weight whispered past him and caught Quester on the back of the head; the youth folded like a hinge. Tangnost lunged as the boy started to slide downwards towards the attacking clansmen.

Stormcracker's head turned to snap as axes thudded into a claw sheath. A half dozen of his attackers died, but the battledragon had a nasty gash on one of his claws.

'Stormcracker! UP! UP!' Tangnost threw everything into the command, hoping the big dragon would hear him over the din.

Hearing a familiar command, the dragon lifted his wing, staying Quester's descent, and tumbling the youth back towards Tangnost. Grasping the boy's brigandine,

Tangnost hauled the dazed youth to his feet, and almost carried him between the spinal plates. Stormcracker tensed to spring up, great wings sweeping down, wreaking havoc below.

Root, saw a sudden movement in the shadows, then a figure was racing towards the Dragon Master who was kneeling next to Quester. Root turned to call, but who would come? In that split second he made a decision. Tangnost was a second father to him. Armed only with love, Root charged, screaming.

AAAaaaaaaaaaaaargghhhhhhhhhhh!!!

He had a fleeting impression of the Dragon Master's startled face turning towards him, and then he and the attacker were tumbling down the wing together. Hands were closing around his throat when Root's assailant screamed. Ripped away by sabre teeth, there was a resounding 'thunk' doled out by a huge taloned foot, and a dazed Root watching the body cartwheel over the wing as Stormcracker leapt skywards.

'Oh, Two Gulps,' Root said huskily, rubbing his aching throat as the sabretooth nudged and helped him to his feet. 'Let me find you a honey tablet.'

They rose above the trees. Fading sparks flew in the air as another round house collapsed. Stormcracker's weak trailing leg caught briefly in branches, and then they were up and away!

'Fly!' Tangnost urged Stormcracker, as he carried his unconscious esquire to the roosts. 'Fly!' he bellowed, not caring for the damage his great speed would do. They disappeared into the night, the downdraft tumbling trees in their wake.

Tangnost's heart finally slowed as the night shrouded them. The blazing compound was a dying speck lost in the swirling dark. He turned to Root.

'Are you alright? That was brave but foolish!'

Root nodded.

'Then tend Quester for me!' Tangnost ran to the pilot's chair, hoping to find Quenelda at the reins. He did, but she was slumped in her seat, head rolling from side to side, and so he lifted her gently to the roosts as well. Leaving all three guarded by Two Gulps, he took the pilot's chair.

It was almost impossible even to see Stormcracker's head, and their headlong flight at night into unknown hostile country was fraught with danger, so he took the battledragon as high as he dared to avoid collision. Worse, they had taken off into a strong headwind that stung his face. He wasn't sure which direction they had taken, let alone where they were. Wasting a precious flare he checked the compass. They were heading north. That is all Tangnost knew.

CHAPTER TWENTY-FIVE

Iceberg

To Tangnost's dismay, a grey dawn revealed that they were over open ocean, heavily populated with icebergs. The wind had changed, now pushing them westwards out to sea. If his esquires had felt miserable flying blind in the dark, that was nothing compared to how they felt now.

Tired, wretched, and still suffering the effects of the sleeping potion, Quenelda was repeatedly sick. Slumped in his navigator's chair, Root was not much better. Quester had a large bump where the weighted net had struck him, and was white with pain.

'I'm alright,' he lied. Taking the spyglass he stood watch while Tangnost retook the pilot's seat. But without sight of land or a sun to navigate by, Tangnost had no way of knowing how far north they had come.

Hiding his worry that they might not make landfall before the battledragon tired, Tangnost searched for a place, any place, for the dragon to put down to rest. As morning wore on they came upon an island, little more than a spray soaked rocky outcrop in the ocean. Tangnost put the dragon down to rest, and to assess their situation. Walking the circumference of the small craggy rock, Tangnost thought he recognised where they were.

'Here,' he pointed to a waxed map of the islands. 'I think we're here.' They were all sheltering from the weather under one of Storm's wings. 'We're on the Minchkin Rocks.'

'But we've hardly made any headway.' Still queasy, Quenelda was not feeling charitable. 'And we're too far west!'

'I know!' Root snapped back, fear making him angry. The land had been their only guide, and without the sun and with a grey horizon stretching in every direction, he was lost. Totally lost. The runes set in the navigator's chair were beyond his understanding. 'It's the wind! It's still blowing offshore.'

'Well,' Tangnost said calmly, hiding his dismay. 'We had better make landfall before dark.' *It must be forty leagues to land against the wind!*

They struck out again, this time landwards, but the howling wind scooped them up and drove them ever westward. Massive swollen waves beneath them rose and fell in frothy peaks, soaking them in endless icy spray.

'Rope up!' The Dragon Master instructed them all. 'Don't want you being washed overboard. In this sea you'd be dead of cold before we could rescue you!' He didn't say *if* we could rescue you...

Storm, Quenelda pulled on the reins, as if her strength would make any difference. *Can we not turn landward? Into this wind...?*

His answer chilled her. *I can do no more...* the large

dragon hated to admit defeat, hated the weakness injury and cruelty had cast on him. His once mighty strength was failing. So was daylight. The deep ocean swell dipped so deeply and then rose up, that danger then came upon them unawares.

'Hard to port!' Tangnost suddenly shouted.

The beautifully sculpted icebergs were becoming larger and larger, many towering threateningly above the dragon. Root forgot about being airsick, and found time to be seasick instead. Then as time passed and no land materialised out of the storm, he began to fret about the vast size of the ocean and how very, very small, Stormcracker suddenly seemed.

Tangnost sent the boy back to the roosts for a change of clothes and some sleep while Quenelda and Quester stood watch together. For once, even Two Gulps had no interest in food. Cradling each other miserably, boy and dragon retched into the sodden hay.

Searching the gloom for icebergs, Quester's eyes were raw and red, and he longed for the SDS helmets with their close fitting clear visors, instead of the half helm he had chosen because it looked like a warrior's helm. Salt and ice crusted his lips, and burned his cheeks raw. The wind was screaming like a banshee, pushing them first one way and then another, tossing the huge dragon around as if he were a mere sparrow. Boot spikes or not, he struggled to keep his feet, rescued more than once by the rope attached to his flying harness.

Stormcracker, too, was approaching exhaustion,

although the dragon said nothing. Sensing things her companions could not, Quenelda could feel the tremor in his tendons, the beginnings of a fiery ache in some of his muscles where ice was forming on his wings. Sometimes, when she was tired, it was hard to tell where his feelings left off and hers began. She told Tangnost.

'Quester, ice on the wings!' Tangnost warned. 'Out you go, lad, but take care!'

The wind shoved and tugged as Quester stepped out onto the wing, grateful for Tangnost's training at Dragonsdome which had prepared him for moments like this. He touched his amulets for luck, as he played out the two ropes that were attached to a cleat in one of Storm's spinal plates, and lifted his wand cast to an easy rune. Light spread with a glowing orb at its heart; the ice sizzled and turned to steam.

The casting was easy; it was his strength and skill that would be tested; Stormcracker's wings were huge. Half a bell later Quester was exhausted, trembling from the effort of staying on his feet in the headwind, of endlessly casting the spell. If he had more practice, had a more powerful wand, he could cast his power more widely, but he hadn't, and his blinding headache made it hard to concentrate. Now, no sooner had he de-iced part of one wing, he had to begin on the other, and the melted snow was freezing almost instantly, so that both wings were bearded with icicles.

The temperature dropped along with the dark. Things were now desperate, and Tangnost began to question his reasoning. *Is it all to end here in the freezing ocean? What end have I brought us to in my folly?*

Powdery snow floated down, kissing noses and lips and catching like burrs on cloaks. Frost rimed and cracked their clothes. By now both Root and Quester were clutched together with Two Gulps in the roosts, who wrapped his wings around them and flamed to warm the air.

A wave of panic washed over Quenelda as they failed to spy the mainland before darkness fell; freezing her to the marrow more than any sea wave could do. What had she been thinking of, hauling her friends and Storm out over the freezing ocean? What made her think that she could do the impossible? Find her father when the SDS had failed to... because of a dragon's dream?

Doubt gnawed at her. Exhaustion claimed her and her eyes drooped.

On his own again, bracing himself against the gale, Tangnost stood in his stirrups searching, searching...

An iceberg materialised scant strides off the dragon's port wing. Too small to land on, but still dangerous!

. 'Up!' he commanded Stormcracker, deftly pulling on the left lower and then both middle reins softly. Responding immediately, Stormcracker stalled, allowing the wind to fill his wings and scoop him up smoothly like a kite. Not a moment too soon. A huge milky-white iceberg reared up beneath them, tall as a cliff, blue-hued and deadly.

'Iceberg!' Tangnost bellowed. 'Iceberg to port! Climb! Climb! Climb!' He roared encouragement, throwing up a gauntleted fist as the milky hued giant filled his eyes. But he needn't have worried. The huge dragon was already climbing steeply while banking sharply to the left despite the treacherous battering of the wind.

They were so close to the berg that Stormcracker's talons gouged great grooves in the iceberg as he struggled for height, weighed down by ice and exhaustion. But the scrabbling dragon made it over the lip with the help of a gust of wind.

As the iceberg dipped once again into the saddle of the swell, Stormcracker folded his wings and dropped. Muscles bunched to cushion the fall, the battledragon screamed as yet again his bad leg buckled in a burst of hot pain that failed to wake Quenelda. The battledragon slid forwards like a seal on the smooth scales of his belly, slewing round and round.

'Anchor! Anchor!'

Tangnost's shout was almost buried beneath the ear splitting screech of talons and scales scraping along ice. Tendons tightened and tensed. Sixteen talons and four dew claws scored and gripped. The great tail whipped around, the sharp point driving into the ice, anchoring them. Wing spurs struck ice wherever they found it. As the iceberg dipped dangerously, they ground to a halt.

It was not a moment too soon. The battledragon was utterly exhausted. Each heavy tread vibrating through the ice, Stormcracker circled around, until seemingly satisfied that the bulk of his body blocked the wind, the dragon collapsed, curled his long tail wide around Tangnost and his own body, and then stretched out one wing across his coils like a tent. The howl of the battering wind immediately lessened, and stillness settled on the protected crown of the iceberg. Nobody moved.

Pumped up by adrenaline, Tangnost quickly stirred himself into action. Now was a dangerous time for them all; cold could kill them quickly.

Breaking a flare he held it up. With a veteran's practised eye, Tangnost assessed their situation. It was a huge iceberg, more like an island that towered above them, sweeping down to a near level plateau larger than a dragonpad – it would serve their needs well. Quenelda, Root and Quester needed heat and food and sleep, in that order, and the battledragon rest. After his recent excesses, Stormcracker wouldn't need to eat for days, which was just as well, and Two Gulps needed to lose some weight.

As Tangnost reached the roost, the juvenile sabretooth in question was anxiously nuzzling Quenelda, trying to wake her up.

Food? Food? He demanded. He had not been feeling too well, but was rapidly recovering. His persistence was beginning to tickle the edge of Quenelda's awareness, but she didn't want to stir.

Food? Hungry... he complained.

He gave her a gentle kick, followed by a slightly harder one when she didn't respond. Frustrated, the little dragon lifted back his head in agitation and flamed. As yellow fire curled about her, singeing her sodden clothes, Quenelda stirred and stretched. The scale on her left palm glowed with sudden energy, and tiny scales raced up her arm and appeared on her brow, faint beneath her skin. Suddenly she felt warm and alive.

The hay she lay on went on fire, but was doused by the wind. Unfurling like a fern in springtime, Quenelda soaked up the heat, drinking in the flame till she shimmered and her outline blazed. Then just as quickly the flame about her died.

'Two Gulps?' She seemed startled to find herself sitting in the middle of a burnt bale of hay, more startled as she lifted her eyes and saw the faint glow of their iceberg.

'You put down on an iceberg?' she said to Tangnost. 'Just like Papa!'

She laughed and kissed her dragon's nose. *Two Gulps, what have you done to the hay?*

Tangnost watched with amazement. *I would not have believed it if I had not seen it with my own eyes! She is becoming more like a dragon, although you cannot see it yet!*

Relinquishing the tattered remnants of her cloak to Two Gulps, who ate it with relish, Quenelda stood, noticing for the first time her two friends shivering and semi-conscious at her feet. Root was coughing in the damp smoke. Quester was still unconscious. Neither responded to Tangnost's anxious questions.

Her eyes widened with concern. 'What's wrong with

them? They are so pale! It looks like they are sleeping!'

'They are, and so were you till Two Gulps flamed. It's snow sickness,' Tangnost judged. 'I've seen too many die on winter campaigns, especially the injured. They go to sleep and never wake up.'

'But what can we do? Two Gulps would kill them if he flamed on them.'

'Old SDS trick....' The dwarf told her what they were going to do.

Instructing Two Gulps, Quenelda dismounted to prepare. Two Gulps, too eager, half jumped, half flapped, slipped, then tumbled down, smacking into Storm-cracker's coils where he bounced and rebounded. He immediately jumped to his feet and plodded over to Quenelda, to see if he could get some honey tablets sooner rather than later. Tangnost shook his head; nothing seemed to slow Two Gulps down.

Tying a rope to Quester's flying harness, the dwarf lowered the esquire down to where Quenelda gathered him up and repeated it with Root.

Next she chose a spot just beneath the protection of Storm's wings and commanded Two Gulps to flame. Careful of Tangnost now stringing up a makeshift tent, Two Gulps breathed in, and then released a narrow stream of fire. Within moments the outer crust of the iceberg melted and in the blue depths of the ice, a bowl of toasting hot water steamed. Clouds of vapour billowed and sparkled.

'Good!' Tangnost nodded. 'Now, you string the

hammocks, and get some hot food and drinks prepared, and yes, give him some tablets,' he added as Two Gulps bumped his arm encouragingly.

Inside the tent Quenelda set a fire of heather and resin logs and a kettle of water to boil on a portable tripod, whilst preparing porridge. Meanwhile, Tangnost turned to find Quester conscious and recovering a little. 'Help me with Root,' he asked. 'He hates the cold so.'

Taking off Root's sodden cloak and helmet, Tangnost removed the boy's flying leathers, leaving the thick wool survival suit. Then he hauled his esquire into the steaming hot water, rubbing his hands and feet.

Root squealed. It felt like unbearably sharp pins and needles as blood began to circulate. Rummaging around in the boy's saddlebags Tangnost found towels and dry underclothes.

'Strip, towel down and get dressed, inside the tent for hot food and then into your hammock,' he told the youth handing him clothes.

Once the pink-faced boy was warmly dressed, Quenelda gave him a mug of spiced tea, a bowl of porridge and their last wild boar sausages. Within moments of tucking himself into his hammock, Root was sound asleep.

Fully dressed and comfortably warm, Quenelda, too, curled up in her hammock slung under Stormcracker's outstretched wing, and fell deeply asleep. Quester and Tangnost soaked some of the knots from their stiff muscles in the hot pool, before joining them.

Snow piled up on the outside of their dragon-wing lean-to, sealing the four travellers and two dragons in a muted black world that drifted north east on the deep sea currents.

CHAPTER TWENTY-SIX

Dragon Down

Dawn brought a clear day, with land only a few leagues to the east. The deep ocean swell had calmed. Two Gulps had kept them warm as toast, and Root and Quester felt much better. Making good time, they put down to rest where forested hills gave way to a rugged mountain range that stretched away to the east. They had reached the Snow Fell Mountains. Beyond, the land became a rugged wilderness of hot pools, rivers and forest where the giant elk, ice wolves, moose and grizzly bear ranged, and beyond that lay the arctic wastes.

Tangnost released Stormcracker and Two Gulps to hunt; the juvenile sabretooth was perfecting his technique of taking a huge leap and squashing his prey under his huge feet, squashing two capercaillie intent on a squabble with one bound. Quenelda asked him to catch some geese for them, but when they looked at the squashed offering he brought back, they decided to eat what Root and Quester could forage instead.

The good weather held, and in the following days they rested and recovered, eating well and enjoying the journey. Food was abundant, and Tangnost and Quester hunted, gralloched and smoked meat, against the time when the forested hills and ice-bound lakes would gave way to a rugged blue mountain landscape rising up steadily about them. Deep ravines scored the snowy flanks of the Smoky Mountains, and glaciers ground slowly down towards the sea. Steaming hot pools belched mud, and towering, smoking volcanoes dwarfed the lone dark dragon flying ever northwards to where the lands of the Ice Bear clan lay, and where, they all hoped in an agony of suspense, they would finally find the Earl.

The Frost moons waned as they crossed the Wilderness Straits to the Ice Isles. The passage beyond the cliffs of Cape Wrath was only open to ships for a few months at midsummer. Now, thick pack ice was broken only here and there by seal holes and cracks where beluga whales came up to breathe. Ahead lay the vast expanse of the Ice Isles, and the land of the Ice Bears rolling out white to the horizon.

Its sheer brilliance almost blinded them. 'Put on the masks that Tam gave you,' Tangnost ordered. 'Otherwise you risk becoming snow blind.'

The dry cold was breathtaking, exhilarating and frightening all at once; Stormcracker, a mere speck of night against the white immensity.

The first days passed without incident and no sign of pursuit. Every now and then they saw small flights of frost dragons on the wing, and a huge pack of white direwolves. As dark fell, a large snowy owl swept silently above the dragon. There was a series of soft hoots answered by another.

Two Gulps sprang upwards. He was feeling decidedly hungry, but the large owls remained infuriatingly out of reach, as if taunting him. Then it was silent, only the breath of the wind as they passed over the flat ice, silver in the moonlight. They changed watch.

Root was dreaming of Chasing the Stars, that they were skimming along beside Stormcracker all harnessed in white, when his sleep was disturbed.

'Root! Root!' Quester called the youth's attention away. 'Root, come and see!'

As he ducked out from beneath the dark canvass, Root saw dappled colour playing over the huge dragon's back. Puzzled he stared at it.

'Silly!' Quester punched his arm, and pointed a finger skywards. The sky blazed with wild colour that spun and trembled.

'The Dancing Lights!' Root looked in wonder at the incandescent colours dancing across the heavens, their soft hues of rose and green and violet reflecting on the snowy world beneath. 'Some of the Elders spoke of them, but I've never seen them before!'

'They're beautiful!' Quenelda, too, was gazing upwards at the wash of colours competing with the stars.

'Most of it is ice,' Tangnost explained to Quenelda as they skimmed above the white brilliance for a fourth day. 'Only a small part is truly earth, the rest is ice, countless fathoms deep, that grows or shrinks with the seasons.'

It was hard to know what time of night or day it was, as the sun barely rose before it began to set. They changed watch again. By mid-afternoon they stopped to rest and eat. They had flown over endless icy wastes, only broken here and there by jagged cracks that looked like black lightning against the snow. The only living creatures besides themselves were the great white bears that gave the clan their name, seals, and pods of black and white whales with large dorsal fins who came to blow holes then disappeared under the ice. Soft wind formed peaks, and hummocks now dotted the landscape.

Then white clouds appeared on the horizon, racing towards them at impossible speed. Within moments the world around them had disappeared, to be replaced by a blizzard.

'Root! Root,' Tangnost shouted. 'How high are we above ground?'

Root rubbed the snow from his visor and looked at the instruments and dials. He had no idea how most of them worked. The wind dial was rising rapidly, the compass needle spinning crazily as the dragon was battered one way then another.

'I can only tell you that we are still on heading vector nine five zero one, although the compass is going a bit wild.'

'Stall!" Tangnost shouted in Quenelda's ear. 'We need to lose some spe-'

They never saw the hummock until they slammed into it. The impact wrenched Stormcracker fully around

163

before ploughing through the snow, until the weight of it finally brought him to a halt. Tangnost was thrown; he had a fleeting sensation of Stormcracker flaming in anguish, and then nothing.

CHAPTER TWENTY-SEVEN

White Out

Quenelda unbuckled her flying harness with shaking hands and stood on wobbly legs shedding chunks of snow. Her shoulders ached with the wrenching impact.

'Tangnost? Root?!' Nothing! 'Quester?' There was an edge of panic to her calls. 'Anyone?'

'Quenelda?' A snowman stood up. A hand poked out, followed by a helmet. Root shook his head, spitting out a mouthful of crystals, and wiping the blood from his lips. Quenelda sagged with relief. Root was alright! But they were not all so lucky.

Storm? Storm, you're hurt!

The battledragon was flat out for his full length, half buried. In reply he raised his head, and turned it to nuzzle her, warm breath turning ice crystals to water.

I have pain... He awkwardly fought to free a crumpled wing, heavy with snow; he had more trouble with the other. But it was his hind leg, already injured in battle that had been twisted. Half scrambling, half stumbling through the deep snow, Quenelda dismounted to inspect it, whilst Root went in search of Quester and Tangnost.

Two Gulps! Quenelda realised with a start. Where

was he? *Two Gulps?* Where was the sabretooth? 'Two Gulps?' she shouted. The faintest of replies reached her, but she could not hear it well enough. 'Two Gulps? Where are you?'

Root was not having any better luck. The driving snow was reducing visibility to scant strides. 'I can't find either of them!' he told Quenelda, having skirted round the prone dragon several times. 'Wait!' he put his hand up for silence. 'There! Do you hear it?'

'Tangnost? Tangnost?' The muffled voice was urgent, distant. 'Tangnost?' This time the call was edged with fear. It was Quester!

'You go! Find them, and I'll see what I can do for Storm to ease his pain.'

Root nodded and was gone into the white out.

'Tooth and claw!' As he stumbled over ruts and the snow ploughed up by their landing, Root was staggered by how far their crash had taken them. With a navigator's eye he paced it out: over five hundred strides!

The Imperial had gouged out a deep trough littered with debris; helmets, fodder, camping gear and pots and pans....and an irate Sabretooth, whose back end was stuck out of an icy mound. Steam was rising from his efforts to free himself, and his strong tail whipped from side to side, showering Root in stinging crystals.

'Oh, Two Gulps!'

Despite his worry, Root smothered a laugh as a hind leg broke free, but desperately anxious, he left the sabretooth, and ran on ahead to the lip of a huge impact crater.

'Quester? Quester!' he cried, as he searched for his friend.

'Root? Over here!' The esquire stood to wave his arms. 'Over here!'

Root ran down into the deep crater. 'What's wrong? What's happened?'

'I don't know! He's not moved! I think he's dead...' Quester's voice cracked. 'He-he's so cold. He hit his head on the ice,' he pointed at the dwarf's dented helmet.

Root knelt. 'Give me a knife, a sword, anything metal. Quick!'

Puzzled, Quester handed his friend his small flying knife. Bending over the dwarf, Root held it to Tangnost's lips.

'No...' he blew out his cheeks in relief. 'No, he's not dead.'

Quester's hammering heart slowed down a fraction. His legs felt wobbly with relief. He sat down.

'How do you know? He's so white!'

'So are you,' Root replied with a smile. 'You should see yourself. But look,' Root sat back on his heels. 'His breath, see...? It's clouding the blade. He is breathing!'

'How bad is he?'

'I don't know,' Root admitted. 'I'm not a skilled Healer. I know how to forage, and what certain herbs look like and their uses. I can make poultices and clean wounds, maybe even splint a break. But if he is hurt inside....' He pulled his glove off and examined the head injury with numb fingers. 'His head wound is shallow, looks worse than it is. Can we find anything to bandage it?'

'Maybe he's just been knocked out?' Quester said hopefully, as he offered Root his flying scarf.

Root nodded fervently as he knotted the scarf as best he could. It was a clumsy attempt. He hoped so, too. He then examined the dwarf, gently lifting arms and legs. 'Quester, give me a hand. Lift, no gently, lift and push then back again. I can't feel any breaks....'

Tangnost groaned, making the pair of them jump.

'Tangnost?' Root bent over the inert Dragon Master. 'Tangnost? Can you speak? Are you alright?'

Root swam into focus, and then the Dragon Master passed out again. The next time he managed to hold on to his senses. It was full dark by then, but the rising half moons cast the ice in a pale glow.

'Root?' He blinked, putting his hand up to his bandaged head, it came away sticky with blood.

'Tangnost? Are you alright?'

'Wait...' the dwarf lay there a moment longer, until he had time to think. His head thundered and he felt dizzy. He was also freezing...his limbs felt like lead. Even if his legs were broken he wouldn't feel them.

'I've cleaned the wound with snow and bandaged your head roughly,' Root informed him. 'But head wounds bleed a lot and I think you had better rest. You took a bad knock against the ice. We were afraid you weren't going to wake up!' They had been petrified. If Tangnost died, they would be utterly lost.

The dwarf tried to sit up, and grunted. Every breath was painful. 'I think-' he put his hand to his chest. 'I've cracked some ribs. Help me up,' he took a deep breath against the pain to come. 'Gently.'

'Who else is injured?' Tangnost cried out as he got to his feet with Root and Quester's help and looked about. He frowned, wincing. 'Where's Quenelda? Is she alright? Where's Storm?'

Root nodded. 'She was strapped in. But Storm isn't. He's injured! Quenelda said his broken leg is bad. She is healing him.' Root was anxious to get back to her and the big dragon before the snow buried the trail.

With one arm about each boy's shoulders, they still struggled to get Tangnost out of the huge crater. Despite the cold, the Dragon Master was running with sweat from the pain. Painfully slowly, the trio hobbled slowly forwards in search of Stormcracker and Quenelda.

Two Gulps had managed to dig himself out, and was now poking around looking for anything edible amongst the debris, which, Root noted, in fact was about anything within reach. He had found a couple of cooking pans, and had devoured most of the esquire's dragonwings.

They almost tripped over Storm's half buried talon sheath that had been ripped off. Trying not to bend too much, Tangnost examined it. It lay buckled and twisted, and the snow about it stained with blood. 'Must be a bad fracture...'

Within moments they came upon the dragon's tail. Tangnost frowned as he searched for Quenelda. 'Which way?'

'Quenelda?' Root bawled, squinting into the driving snow.

'Here,' came back the reply.

'Over there, there!' Quester pointed to a dim dark shape in the whiteness.

She was underneath a wing. Leaning against the big dragon, as if drawing strength from him, Quenelda had removed her heavy mittens. Flexing her left palm she pressed the golden scale against Storm's ice crusted hide, and closed her eyes and her mind against the bitter cold. She felt her fingers tingle, and then tiny motes of light sparked and danced. A golden nimbus of power formed about her hands creating a cave of light beneath the dark wing that then flowed into the battledragon. It was like watching a pouring jug, Tangnost thought. *And one that is not bottomless, no matter how we might wish it.* He reached out a hand as if he could lend her his own strength.

'Tangnost!' Quenelda opened her eyes with a start. 'Oh! You're hurt!' she looked frightened.

'I'm fine,' he lied, trying to take shallow breaths. 'Just a knock. How is Storm?'

'His muscles were torn. I have healed them, but they will still give him pain. And his talon is cracked, but I,' she put her hand to her head. '– I haven't managed to fully heal that yet. I keep having to rest. It will be days before he can fly, perhaps a week.' She was shaking, from cold or exhaustion – or both. 'What do we do?'

She's too thin, Tangnost agonised. Her eyes looked huge in her moon pale face, and beneath those furs and sealskin her skin was hanging from her bones.

'He needs to rest,' Quenelda added.

And so do you, Tangnost thought but didn't say. Instead, 'We had better make camp; it is far too dangerous to continue. We were lucky!'

It was a long night. Curled within Stormcracker's coils in her sleeping roll, Quenelda closed her eyes. Slowly she stopped shaking. She was feeling thin...as *if the dragon fire in my veins was burning out...* Although she had healed Storm's torn muscle and sinew, nonetheless his flesh needed time to recover, and the bruise was a constant ache at the edge of awareness. Two Gulps attempted to wrap her in his wings, bestowing fiery kisses, so that eventually she fell deeply asleep.

The snow had stopped.

'What do we do?' Root repeated the following morning as he tried to gulp down his porridge before it froze. He glanced at his friend who was still sleeping. 'Quenelda says Storm can't possibly fly for days. How can we find the Ice Bears now?'

'We won't have to, they'll find us.'

'Where are they...?' Quester was baffled, as he scanned the hummocks and snow drifts. 'I can't see anyone!'

'Ah, but they're out there.' Tangnost said

mysteriously, a smile twitching the corners of his mouth, although he looked grey with pain.

'Where?' Followed by Quenelda, Root clambered up a snowy mound. 'But there's nothing here!' he repeated, just as the ice beneath him shifted and rose.

'Argh!' The gnome youth stepped backwards as fearsome shaggy figures rose up out of the snow and surrounded the pair, plumes of icy breath fogging the air. The icy blue eyes of snow bears looked down at them, great claws poised to rip them apart.

'Ice bears!'

They were gigantic! Fearless when facing dragons, when faced with these huge shaggy creatures, Quenelda stood stunned, unable to move. Summoning his courage, Root fumbled for his flying knife and the small shield slung across his back.

He couldn't get the knife out; it was frozen to the scabbard! Those claws would surely rip them apart in moments.

'It's stuck!' Shoving Quenelda behind him, the youth frantically tried to free it. 'It's stuck!' The blade suddenly came free whickering in a circle, making Quenelda duck.

'Aahhh!' She fell back headfirst into soft snow

The great shaggy head lowered till the blue eyes were level with his, hot breath clouding the air between them.

'Put that away, boy,' the bear advised gravely, as it considered Quenelda's waving boots and Two Gulps' concerned snuffling. 'You might do yourself a mischief.'

CHAPTER TWENTY-EIGHT

The Ice Bears

The bear towered above Root as Quenelda scrambled to her feet. A paw went up to its huge black snout, the fearsome ivory teeth...and pushed back the fur hood to reveal a white mask almost hidden beneath shaggy white hair. Blue eyes glittered through two slits. It was then that Root noticed the ivory spear it carried in its other paw. He was wobbling so much he fell to his knees with relief.

The dwarf was tall, taller than Tangnost, but as broad shouldered; so large he looked like a bear himself, Quenelda thought.

Eyes on Stormcracker, looming hugely black against the snow, the figure spoke. 'Who are you that have come amongst us in these perilous times? Who dares cross tracks with the Ice Bear?'

'I – I do,' Quenelda said unhelpfully.

'Your amulet,' Root hissed, giving her a poke. 'Show them the amulet!'

'Yes! Here! Here, let me show you,' Quenelda fumbled to open the toggle on her jerkin, and lifted out the amulet.

The nearest dwarf lifted it, eyes glinting keenly. There

was a brief conversation as the other bears crowded forwards.

'Norgarth of the Narwhale gave it to me,' she answered their question in dwarfish. 'We – we crashed...' she pointed. 'Our dragon, we hit a snow bank.'

There was a moment of shocked silence while everyone looked at her in disbelief. Root realised his jaw was hanging open and closed it; like magic, for Quenelda had always been hopeless at languages until now.

'*Your* dragon, boy?' The eyes flicked to the Imperial.

'Storm... But one of our party....he's hurt, we need help. We don't know how bad he is...over there. Tangnost. He's..'

'Tangnost?' The bears moved closer. 'Bearhugger?'

'Yes!'

'Tangnost?' The dwarf scrutinised the blood crusted face.

'Barlad!' Tangnost grinned, despite his pain.

'We thought you had died on the Westering Isles. Can you walk?'

'My ribs are broken, and a leg.'

'Falfir, Goodrin; spears and a cloak!'

He turned to scrutinise Quenelda, Quester and Root, all stamping their feet to keep warm.

'Take the youngsters down, Dimlock, before they freeze.'

'But...' Quenelda hesitated. 'But my dragons?' she gestured towards Two Gulps at her shoulder.

Barlad shook his head. 'Your sabretooth will get taken

to the Ice Caves; apart from the bears...The Imperial must stay here.' He looked expectantly upwards at the Imperial. Frowning, he turned to Tangnost.

'How many men are with you?'

'None. These three only.'

'Only three ch-? You travel north in winter on an Imperial with just three boys?'

Tangnost nodded. 'We seek the Earl as you now know; we thought one dragon might pass unnoticed.'

Barlad nodded. 'We have waited a long time for someone to come. Well, your tale can wait. Go, boy, and rest. Your dragons will be fed. Go!'

Reassured, Quenelda murmured her thanks and bade the dragons wait and rest as the three esquires followed the dwarfs to one of the dark holes in the ice.

'A seal breathing hole?' Root was confused.

Dimlock smiled. 'No, boy.'

On closer inspection, Root could see lots of tracks about it, bear tracks. It looked for all the world like a large burrow in the ice. Next second, one of the Ice Bears gripped the outer rim, held his weaponry against his chest, swung his legs and disappeared from sight.

It was the esquires' turn. 'Cross your arms and lie flat,' Dimlock advised.

Quenelda and Quester hesitated. Root stepped boldly forwards. 'This is like our burrows, only our warren entrances are larger and cut with steps. I'll go first,' so saying, he gripped the edge and swung himself forward in one smooth motion and disappeared. Moments later a shout echoed up the funnel. 'Come on, it's easy! And it's warm down here!'

Watching them as he was being lifted to the stretcher, Tangnost nodded approvingly. Bark Oakley's son was growing in confidence with every day. He knew Quenelda hated small spaces. Seeing the ease with which her esquire disappeared, and setting aside her qualms, Quenelda followed.

'Aaaaaaaaaaaaaaaaaaaaaaahhhhhhhhhhhhhhh!!!!!!!!'

Quenelda's scream followed her down the icy flume as she was thrown high up the side, first one way then the next at unbelievable speed. Then the ice flume rose to slow her descent before it spat her out into the waiting arms of Root and a heaped pile of furs. She had barely stood up, when Quester arrived, followed by Dimlock.

'They're not bringing Tangnost down one of these flumes are they?' Root asked doubtfully.

'Nay, boy,' Dimlock smiled. 'There are other hidden entrances, this is a swift one, and easy to defend.'

They found themselves in a small underground dome, crafted of curved ribs that rose together to a point above. The walls were of packed snow, smoothed till they shone. A deep pit of burning bones gave out a steady heat, the smoke curling through a tiny vent in the ceiling. Small sconces were carved into the ice, holding lamps with wicks set in whale oil. They shone dimly, and the highest bone rafters were blackened with soot.

A number of dwarfs were going about their tasks, but Dimlock introduced them to a young woman, tall and slim by dwarf standards, not much older than Quenelda. Already she had a warrior's bear tooth hung about her neck. She had killed a hobgoblin!

'Come,' Chinka invited them. 'Take off your outer garments, be warm and rested.' She led them deeper underground, down steps cut in the ice to a second much larger chamber. Root had never seen such large tusks.

'Mammoth,' Chinka caught Root's look of wonder as they all shrugged out of their heavy outer garments.

'B-but...' Root stuttered. 'Mammoth are just fireside tales!'

'No! They were hunted to extinction,' Quenelda said sadly. 'Their tusks were carved into necklaces and chess pieces...'

'No, young friends,' Dimlock shook his head. 'You are both wrong. The white haired woolly mammoth have survived here in their northern fastness, as few predators can survive in their frozen world. Even we do not go there willingly.'

They settled around the long firepit, where a haunch of caribou was roasting, a young girl turning the spit. Various steaming cauldrons were hooked above the burning embers. Other children were bringing elk horn platters and carved ivory knives and forks, and bowls from an adjoining alcove for their guests.

'Eat!' Chinka invited them.

As Quester tore into the roast meat, Root tried the soup, gratefully feeling its warmth spread through his body.

'It's good! What is it?'

'Seaweed and white cap mushroom broth, thickened with reindeer moss,' Chinka told him. Root also chose a pale green tuber, it had a strange earthy taste, slightly waxy but filling. He sighed contentedly, but Quenelda had picked at her food, pushing it about her platter without eating anything. Closing her eyes, she fell asleep where she sat. Not long after, Root and Quester bedded down on low pallets beneath furs. An elderly woman, who had sat quietly dozing in a corner, lifted a wool blanket and tucked it in around the sleeping girl. She stood there a moment lost in quiet contemplation. So, this was the girl the bones had foretold. The time had finally come, and the task had fallen to her.

CHAPTER TWENTY-NINE

Drumondir

Quenelda woke late. Soft light, a deep bottomless blue, filtered through the thick ice. She could sense Stormcracker sleeping above, his great bulk curled about the caves, and Two Gulps somewhere closer, eating. She lay there a while, warm and comfortable but still exhausted, but sleep didn't come. She started to rise, searching for Tangnost as she pulled her boots on. For once they were warm. An unfamiliar voice made her turn.

'Your Dragon Master is well,' a grey haired woman said softly, as she sat at her spinning wheel, teasing out a card of mammoth wool. 'As are your dragons; do not fret on their account. I have tended Bearhugger, and bound his wounds. He is built as strong as your sabretooth, although not blessed with the same appetite.'

'Who...Who are you?' Quenelda shivered into the sealskin jerkin laid out for her and closed the bone toggles. It was lined with dense felted fleece of a kind, and wrapped her in warmth.

'Drumondir,' the old lady bobbed her head, making the carved ivory necklaces and bracelets at her bony wrists clack. 'Bone Caster, and Elder Grandmother.'

Quenelda in turn nodded her head in respect, before

studying Drumondir. She was stocky, and still powerfully built despite her evident age, her wrinkled face dark and seamed as a walnut. Tattoos were painted on her cheeks and forehead, and decorated her bare arms with intricate patterns in soft blue, with a glint of gold. Her voice was deep, almost like a man's. But it was the eyes that instantly caught Quenelda's attention; for like her own, or like an animal's, they seemed to glow in the dim light.

'Here, drink this,' Drumondir went to the fire where a blackened kettle hung. She held out a steaming bone mug. 'Drink, child, it will help you. You must look after yourself, as well as others.'

Quenelda rubbed her eyes, and had a sniff.

'It will not taste nice,' Drumondir said, as the Earl's daughter wrinkled her nose. 'But it will do you good...girl,' she added softly, as Quenelda started. 'Yes,' she nodded. 'Bearhugger told me your story.'

Quenelda nodded and drank, trying hard not to pull a face. It tasted like the bottom of a pond!

'Now,' Drumondir moved to the griddle over the stove where pancakes were stacked and a bowl of red berries and a pot of honey waited. 'Eat, child, and break your fast.'

'No – no, thank you, I feel...I'm not hungry.'

Drumondir accepted the lie, hiding her concern.

'They say you have a gift with dragons,' she said instead, raising wise eyes to consider the Earl's daughter. *And great power, though you do not yet know it...* 'That you saved your father from a rogue dragon, and then brought his injured battledragon home when it could not fly?'

Quenelda shook her head. 'No, they're wrong. They're exaggerating. It was me and Root together, and the SDS. I couldn't have done anything without Root and his dragon, Chasing the Stars. They saved Papa's life, and mine. More than once.'

'Is it so?' Drumondir bobbed her head, bird like. 'Yet Bearhugger says you lend strength to this great dragon above? You can heal wounds? You are too young to have served any apprenticeship, yet you draw on the *elements*.'

Quenelda shrugged her shoulders. 'No. Yes! I-since I woke on Dragon Isle, after' – she took a deep breath to steady herself, yet her voice cracked – 'After my brother killed my dragon – I have been able to heal dragons. But I feel hollow...empty afterwards. Cold,' she hugged herself. 'I'm always cold.'

The Bone Caster cast alarmed eyes at her before veiling them. 'That is not good, Lady. But...you must let the power flow *through* you, not *into* you; that is why your people use wands and staffs to conjure with. Few can act as vessels for magic without swiftly dying. You need to be trained how to use your gift.'

'I can speak with dragons,' Quenelda acknowledged. 'And I can help heal them...but,' she took a deep breath. 'I'm hopeless with a wand!' she indulged in a bout of self pity. 'I'm hopeless at sorcery! Everyone says so.'

'Do they now?' The Bone Caster looked at her quizzically. 'Those who can draw on the *elements* without having to study for many long years will always be the object of envy and fear. And,' she added, 'jealousy. Many are frightened of strange things, or those who are different.'

'They're right to be afraid! I can't control it,' Quenelda blurted. 'I can't summon it when I want, except to heal, and so, when I do, I – I hurt people. Kill people.'

'I do not know how much I can teach you,' Drumondir conceded, 'but if you will accept me, I will come with you, and teach-'

'Come with us?' Quenelda didn't know why, she hardly knew this woman, and yet she liked her, felt reassured by her quiet certainty. 'Yes!'

'Then, child,' a gap-toothed smile broke Drumondir's face. 'I shall come.'

'Where is Tangnost?' Quenelda asked, feeling better. Maybe she was hungry after all. She picked up a bannock.

'Talking with the clan Elders. They will come in their own time. Let your friends sleep. The fair haired boy,' she glanced at Quester. 'He is unwell?'

'Yes – how do you know that?'

'I examined his head injury, but it is what is hidden within that hurts him. Well, we shall leave that for now. Come, child, introduce me to your dragons. I have never flown before!'

'Yes, and I can introduce you to Two Gulps, my juvenile sabretooth!'

Whilst waiting for the Council of the clan Elders to

break, and finding Stormcracker still sleeping, Quenelda decided to continue with Two Gulps' training. It was a chance to show off her dragon skills to Drumondir.

The baby sabretooth's wings had grown larger, and now that she thought about it, the 'juvenile' dragon was not so small anymore. In fact his shoulders topped hers by several hand spans, and his wings now reached down to the ground. He was big enough for her to fly....he was probably eating or sleeping.

But as they emerged from a hidden entrance beneath a hillock, Quenelda found her sabretooth already the centre of attention.

*I cannot fly right now....*the dragon was lying on his back, huge feet wiggling, surrounded by young children who were throwing morsels of food in the air, screaming with delight as the young sabretooth flamed them before gulping them down.

Two Gulps, she said, aware Drumondir was watching with an amused smile. *It is time for lessons. You must learn to fly.*

Why should I fly? I do not need to fly! Another charcoaled morsel was devoured.

Two Gulps. Of course you must fly! Quenelda huffed in exasperation, aware that an interested crowd was gathering. *You have wings. You should have fledged long before now...*

But, Two Gulps protested with flawless logic. *You cannot fly either! You also are carried by Stormcracker...I have not seen you spread your wings. Why should I?*

Well I don't know h- Quenelda stopped herself just in time. *Men cannot fly,* she blustered.

But, Two Gulps protested indignantly in clouds of smoke that made their audience draw back, *you are of Onekind...you are a dragon inside, even if others cannot see it, I can...Why don't you show me how to fly?*

He's right, she thought. *I haven't flown yet...I haven't shed my skin....I'm afraid...*

It was true. She was bossing the young dragon, berating him for failing to fly, and yet she, too, was resisting the changes that were stealing up on her... And how many esquires had she humiliated just because they couldn't fly? She had not been very nice towards them.

She flew in her dragon dreams. In that world her other self was scaled, strong: were those dreams truly who she was inside? She looked at the golden scale on her hand, and then peered more closely. Were those tiny black scales creeping up from her wrist to her elbow? They were almost translucent, barely visible beneath her skin.

'Hello!' Root arrived, shyly smiling at the children who had gathered. 'What are you doing?'

'Trying to get Two Gulps to train!'

'Mmmn,' Root looked at the plump dragon and frowned. 'Is it my eyes or does he not look...well...even fa...rather full?' he hastily amended, knowing how tetchy Quenelda could be when it came to her charge.

Two Gulps burped. Root ducked, but he was too slow, and it caught him full in the face.

'Oh yuk!!' he tried to wipe the saliva off as the

children shrieked with delight. 'Newt and toad, this stinks!' He held up his hand dripping with goo in disgust. Bits of what looked like fine bones and scales dropped to the ground. 'What's he been eating?'

'Nothing,' Quenelda was baffled. 'There isn't anything for him to steal here.' The enforced diet was good for him. The small dragon might not be happy, but Tangnost surely was.

She turned as they heard raised voices, and moments later Chinka came towards them looking worried.

'What is it? What's wrong,' Quenelda asked...

'Wild ice bears must have broken into our storage caves during the night and eaten a quarter moon's food supplies...'

'What, err, what sort of food is stored down there?' Root asked casually, standing on a scrap of scales.

'Walrus and seal meat and fish, for us and our bears.'

'Why, yes,' Quenelda hastily added, feeling a guilty flush rise. 'That's dreadful! Umm...' she hovered on the edge of admitting who the suspected culprit might be. 'Where are the storage caves?'

'They are in the Crystal Caves beneath the ice, next to our polar bear stables.'

'Oh!' Root said brightly. 'Can we visit your polar bears?'

'An excellent idea,' a voice said as they all turned to find Barlad and Tangnost, hobbling on crutches, behind them. 'I was just going to suggest that myself!'

CHAPTER THIRTY

The Crystal Caves

The crystal cave they descended into threw back the reflections of daylight above in half a hundred hues of blue and green. The air was surprisingly warm and slightly musty, with a tang of fish overlaying the smell of wet fur and waxed harness. Two massive upright sabretooth ice bears carved out of the ice guarded the entrance, drawing a gasp of admiration from Root.

He reached out a hand to caress the sculpture, lovingly carved and perfect in every detail. It was both beautiful and terrifying. And huge!

'That's not,' he began, looking doubtfully at the huge canines. 'I mean', he swallowed. 'Are they really this big?'

'Only a few grow so large now,' Barlad answered sadly. 'But in past ages they were even larger and roamed in huge growls. They are ever hunted for their pure white fur, and for their sabreteeth, which many use for weapons or ornaments.'

'A growl?' Quester asked, wide eyed. 'What's a growl?'

'A group, a pack,' Chinka explained. 'Come and see!'

Eying the ice sculptures warily as if they might spring to

life, the trio passed through and into the vaulted stables. The ice sparkled like starlight, and the sound of water passing along channels and troughs was background music. Stalls of ice stretched away from them.

Barlad led them forwards to a stall where a golden eyed bear grunted a welcome, and bounded forwards to growl softly as he rubbed noses with the clan chieftain.

'How are you today, White Spirit?' Barlad ran his fingers through the bear's shaggy fur. 'They can kill an adult frost dragon with one blow. They are raised and trained from cubs by their riders, and we form a lifelong bond. They can live thirty years.'

They walked down the lines. Many bears were curled up sleeping, others feeding. 'What are they eating?' Root wrinkled his nose, it smelt horrible. 'Do they go hunting?'

'Walrus meat. And yes, they are free to roam where they will, and when we are on patrol, we hunt together. We freeze half of what we hunt in the summer down here in a store,' he led them to a dark cavern that reeked of the sea. 'Our stores of frozen walrus, fish, and seal. And we have a smoking room also.'

'All this for the ice bears?' Quester was fascinated.

'Not just the bears. For us also. We have elk and caribou too,' he gestured to great sides of frozen meat hanging on hooks.

'Let us return. Talking of food has made me hungry. The midday meal is being prepared and will be growing cold. We sh-'
The jingle of harnesses sounded up the lines, and a noise

like drumming thunder vibrated through the ice. There were faint calls and answers, and then a bear entered the stables at the far end and was loping towards them, the thunder of its huge strides eating up the distance at unbelievable speed. The ice bear came to a halt in a shower of ice chips...as its rider shed her stirrups and dismounted in a flurry of snow. Billows of steam rose from them both as she struggled for breath.

'Frost dragons... have crossed our borders...three days ago. They carry no banner. They killed Falfir and our entire troop, save me. They are all dead!'

There was a stunned silence, and then cries of anger broke out. Ice Bears ran for their weapons.

'Where?' Barlad's calm voice commanded silence. 'How many?'

'Dozens. We could not clearly see. They camped since they made landfall at Sailor's Wrath. Yesterday when the weather cleared a little, they moved inland to Snowspike Fell, where we challenged them. They have a Mage!'

But only Root, the navigator, realised what that meant. 'But...' he frowned. 'That is *exactly* where we made landfall, and our first camp!'

Tangnost considered him gravely. 'You have the nub of it, young Root. This land is vast. It is no coincidence. Somehow they are tracking you.'

The group exchanged horrified glances. How could anyone know where they were?

CHAPTER THIRTY-ONE

The Moot

'But what do we do?' Quenelda had just dismounted as Tangnost and Quester examined the lame leg and fractured talon. 'He is struggling to get airborne! He needs at least another day's rest. If the weather clears...' she shrugged. 'Perhaps he might manage.'

'We must wait for better weather....' Tangnost reluctantly agreed. *But better weather will bring our enemies upon us!*

Bruised and battered, Stormcracker had struggled to take off, and flying was clearly painful. Once the blizzard died it would be easier, but they would never be able to fight off so many enemies if they were caught on the ground.

'But how can we evade them if they are coming here? Storm stands out against the snow!'

Tangnost shook his head. How could they hide a black Imperial if they were bring hunted?

Barlad joined them beneath the dragon's wing with a grizzled old dwarf swathed in white seal skin fur, and introduced him as Sigurd.

'Tis the boy what gave me the idea,' Sigurd nodded to indicate Root who was jumping up and down beside him.

'He was talking about his Da, Bark, who served as a scout...'

'Yes!' Root interrupted, too excited to wait for the old man to finish. 'Camouflage!'

'Aye!' The old man pursed his lips in disapproval, 'camouflage,' he repeated. It was his idea after all. 'Build a hillock for t' dragon.'

'Yes...' Barlad nodded thoughtfully. 'Yes, it might just work. Call everyone out, man, woman and child; we have a lot of work to do! And summon all the other caves to a Moot. Send out our swiftest bears!'

'Camouflage?' Tangnost was instantly intrigued. 'Where? How?'

Barlad indicated the hummocks that littered the landscape. 'Just as some of these guard the entrance to our stables, could they not also hide a dragon? Even one as big as this?'

Tangnost considered the suggestion and nodded, smiling at Quenelda's anxious face. 'How can we help?'

And so the Ice Bear Chieftain explained the plan to Tangnost and his esquires.

Throughout the day Ice Bears arrived in dozens and scores on their huge white mounts and began helping those already digging a deep hole in the ice. Great saws were used to cut blocks, and simple tackles and weights on a tripod used to lift and swing the blocks into place. What was difficult, back-breaking work became a lot simpler after Quenelda explained to Storm what they were trying to do.

A roost? In this white world where I am dark as night?

Yes! A roost of ice. It will keep you warm and will hide you from our enemies...it will make you invisible just as if you could cloak..so you can rest a little longer.

Carefully directing him according to shouted instructions, Storm's long tail effortlessly lifted huge blocks of ice, setting them about the excavated hole, so that three walls went up swiftly. By then the Ice Bears were coming up to touch the fearsome dragon, to offer him morsels of frozen walrus and seal.

If a dragon could be said to be pulling a face, Stormcracker was.

It tastes like rotten meat, the battledragon observed sourly.

That is all there is here...

*But there are bears...*Stormcracker looked around at the hundreds of ice bears tethered or resting or being led down to the Crystal Caves.

'What? Be-' *No! You must not touch the bears.....* Quenelda looked guiltily about her, but no one had noticed her outburst. *No! Not bears!* She said severely. *They love their bears as we love you, a life bond...*

The battledragon blew a disgusted plume of smoke across the ice, raising cries of alarm and causing several blocks of ice to melt, but their silent conversation was interrupted by Tangnost.

'Ask him to come and stand in the crater,' he directed Quenelda. As the battledragon stepped forward, the broken snow beneath him was crushed, and creaked and sank even deeper. Soon the walls grew ever closer about him, and the cubes of snow grew smaller and smaller till they arched above him, leaving only a small breathing hole. Within a bell the driving snow had layered it thickly so that the cubes of ice were totally hidden.

'What happens when we're ready to fly?' Root asked. 'If we have to leave hurriedly?'

'Why then,' Tangnost replied, a twinkle in his eye. 'All he need do is flame and he is free.'

But for the scores of footprints, also fading, it looked like an ordinary hummock. Elated but exhausted, the Ice Bears and their guests returned to the caves for a hot meal, and afterwards a moot.

'Yes,' Barlad raised his voice so all could hear, as they sat gathered in the great Moot cave, the greatest of the Crystal Caves save for the stables. 'Your father was here in our care that is true. But we decided it would be safer to t-'

'Where has he gone?' Quenelda impatiently butted in, earning an exasperated glare from Tangnost.

'He's on Inversnekkie.'

'What?' Quenelda and Quester spoke in unison.

Root scrutinised his map, straining to read in the low light. 'I can't find it...' he said, puzzled.

'That's because you are looking too far north,' Tangnost suggested.

'What? Where?' Root looked again at his map. 'I

don't understand.'

Neither did Quenelda. She angrily shook her head in frustration.

'Sit, lady,' Barlad invited her. 'Have patience! We knew if any came looking for him, they would expect him to be hidden in the far north, where none dare go; so we reasoned. So...although he was here, and we cared for him for two moons, he has long since gone south, passing from our care into the lands of the Inner Isles.

They are many clans, many islands, many warriors, and many ships. And they are close knit, for they bear the brunt of the hobgoblin incursions. They said they would pass him from clan to clan so that only a few ever knew where he was. They intended to call a coven of Clan Bone Casters in an effort to heal and protect him.'

'How can we ever find him?' Quenelda burst out, fists balled in frustration. She was too tired and dispirited. 'How can we possibly find him?' A treacherous hot tear trickled hotly down her cold cheeks.

'Every time we arrive he's already gone! And,' she swallowed, 'midwinter is almost on us, Storm is weak, and we may not be able to fly for much longer!'

'But we are on his trail,' Root tried to cheer her as she sat down. 'And he is alive. Don't give up hope.'

But we are not the only ones on his trail, Tangnost kept his thoughts to himself. *It can be no coincidence they have put down exactly where we did! And who knows what damage chaotic sorcery had done to him? WarLocks went mad; forgetting who they were,*

193

forgetting friend from foe in their desire for power...and the Earl has been injured...weakened...he may already have changed. We may not know him even if we find him. What then? Something must be wrong or else he would have sent word...

Quietly he considered Quenelda.

Will she be able to help her father? Can Drumondir teach her to understand her gift? It is draining the life from her... He looked up to find Drumondir's uncanny eyes upon him. She nodded reassuringly, as if she had read his thoughts.

'Ten of our young warriors, and our Bone Caster took him,' Barlad was saying. 'They knew they may never return home, for they would fight to the death to save a DragonLord; but they wanted vengeance for their fallen brothers and fathers, their sisters and mothers, and so they took him south by sledge to the sea at Carcass Island. I believe he is still alive, or they would have returned to us.'

'We have told you all we know,' Barlad accepted a horn mug of tea. 'But your tale is just as strange; now tell all my folk your news,' he gestured to his people crowded into the Moot cave. Younger children were already dozing by the fire but everyone else was wide awake eagerly anticipating a new story. 'And what truly happened to our folk at the Battle of the Westering Isles, and in the heart of the kingdom in the Sorcerers Glen?'

And so Tangnost, ably assisted by his three esquires, told their story once again. There were cries of dismay as the Lord Protector was unmasked, and of amazement as Quenelda was revealed as the Earl's daughter and heir.

'Reckon you'll need all your courage and craft Bearhugger,' Barlad said, 'if the Lord Protector is a WarLock, and evil truly wears the guise of friendship and walks amongst us.' He stood.

'What say you, people of the Ice Bears? The Earl's daughter needs us. Our brother, Bearhugger needs us. Do we prepare for war?'

There was a heartbeat of silence, and then a one-armed old warrior stood and brandished his walrus spear.

'Aye,' he said. 'My three sons and sister-son died at the Westering Isles.'

'And I,' another veteran stood, then another.

'And I,' a young woman stood, until it seemed to Root that the whole clan had pledged themselves, and the Crystal Caves boomed and echoed.

Barlad nodded, baring his teeth in a wolfish smile. 'The Ice Bears are yours to command, lady. Elder Grandmother?'

Drumondir came forwards. She was dressed in ceremonial robes of white, stitched with white crystals that sparkled, and an ice bearskin hung from her head like a cloak. Gold earrings and a necklace in the shape of bear paws hung from ears and throat. She carried a small wooden bowl of dove-blue paste, and a fine bone needle.

'Sit, girl, and bare your right arm.'

Wide eyed, Quenelda did as she was instructed. She

had to bite back tears as the Bone Caster pricked a pattern about her right wrist. It felt like it had taken forever by the time Drumondir dabbed away the blood and stood back to admire her handiwork.

The Earl's daughter raised her arm to admire the intricate pattern of a dragon intertwined with bear paws that was painted on her wrist like a bracelet.

'It's beautiful,' Root said admiringly.

Drumondir nodded, one artist to another. She had seen the esquire's charcoal sketches of Barlad's mount White Spirit.

'Behold!' Barlad took Quenelda's arm and raised it. 'The mark of the Ice Bear! The Ice Bears and the dragon will fight side by side. Offer your allegiance to the Dragon Lords!'

As Tangnost, Root and Quester flanked her, Quenelda felt a fierce sense of hope grow. Finally now, they had a chance of success with so many of the clans behind them. They were no longer alone. Despite the dangers, there were many still loyal to the three-headed dragon. The Dragon Lords *would* rise again!

It was nearing the witching hour and the fire pit had died to ashes and many in the hall had fallen asleep when Quester offered to stand watch with the dragons in the ice roost. Tangnost frowned. 'No, you're not well, lad.' He had seen Drumondir preparing an infusion of butterbur and ice thistle to help numb the pain. 'No need. We're no longer on our own.'

'But I can't sleep, and the cold helps.' Quester felt awful. Sometimes it seemed as if he had had no sleep, and once or twice he had woken to find himself outside in the snow with no cloak or boots on.

Holding the youth by his shoulders at arms length, Tangnost examined his esquire. Quester was pale as snow, and his brows knitted with pain. His eyes were sunk in bruised shadows, and his skin had a greenish tinge to it. 'Right, lad,' he nodded. 'You take first watch. The caves are well guarded, but you can stand watch with Storm.'

'I think he's sleepwalking,' the Bone Caster said in answer to Tangnost's anxious questions. 'I spoke to him and Root earlier in the day. He is clearly ill. He gets violent headaches that have no logical pattern. Has he suffered a blow to his head recently?'

'My head hurts,' the pale faced youth had acknowledged, when Drumondir asked how he felt. The esquire looked dreadful. 'I can't think straight...' How could he reveal the alarming loss of memory? They might leave him behind, if he said he were ill.

'Drink this,' Drumondir gave him a bone mug that steamed. 'This should dull the pain, and help you sleep.'

CHAPTER THIRTY-TWO

They Are Coming!

It was still dark when warning came. A scouting party had returned.

'They are coming,' the young woman warned. 'They split into four groups under cover of darkness. Some one hundred frost dragons. They are now converging on us.'

'They are coming *here*?' Barlad was astounded as he rubbed the sleep from his eyes, while the fire was rekindled and the lamps lit. 'How can this be?'

'W-what do we do?' Quenelda was horrified. 'We can't take off in this, we'd need a dragonpad.'

'Be calm,' Barlad comforted her. 'Rest safe and sound tonight, and prepare to fly at a moment's notice. We shall decide what is best. Do not fear, no one can defeat the Ice Bears in their own land.' The chieftain motioned to Tangnost, and the pair of them moved away.

'This blizzard is beyond even our craft,' Barlad warned. 'So I do not understand how they come to be making directly for us. Our ice caves are hidden...our tracks are the bears, and none save us would know the difference. I fear you are betrayed.'

'It is as if they know everything we do,' Tangnost agreed. 'But The Earl's battledragon is weak. I fear if we

198

take him any deeper into the north he will succumb to his wounds, and the cold. And,' he hesitated to give voice to his innermost fears, 'I fear for Quenelda's health. She is not yet strong and the dragon drains her strength.'

'The snow will stop soon, and then they come. We must lay a false trail for them to follow, lead them where they expect to go, and they will be blind. We have the advantage of our own land. They are the strangers here. Many will never leave this place; they will die of the cold, men and dragons both. That will reduce their numbers further.'

'They will not know they have been discovered,' Tangnost agreed. 'They think that they can bide their time, and come upon us unawares. That will make them confident...and careless.'

'None will suspect that the Earl is so close to home, and it is to the lands of the Inner Isles you must fly with all haste. We will lead them deep into the Frost Marches first and ambush them there, and you must slip away once they have passed.'

No one could sleep. Drawing the cave together, Barlad explained their plan.

'W-' Quester blushed as he interrupted.

'Lad?' Barlad said kindly.

'But won't the frost dragons kill you? There are so many of them.'

'This is our land, boy, and they have to find us first. They cannot survive without food, and I doubt those southerners have the skill to find any on the icy wastes. They are also not equipped for the cold as we are. And see, the adult ice bear stands eleven strides tall, and can bring down a frost dragon. We are not easily killed.

'Now! We will leave a trail that even a babe could follow...to tempt them to folly.

'Hai!' He called his warriors to him. 'Saddle and armour the bears!'

CHAPTER THIRTY-THREE

Camouflage

The Ice Bears had long gone; some eighty bears had left towards noon, leaving six trails to confound their hunters. Six trails to force them to split into smaller groups.

Only the young and very old remained in the Crystal Caves. The last light was vanishing into the sky and the twin moons rising; thin slithers on the horizon that cast little light. Inside the ice roost, tension was rising. Tangnost had discovered about the spoiled stores.

'I'm sorry!' Quenelda said defensively, cheeks burning. 'He was just hungry. How many times do you want me to say that I'm sorry?'

Tangnost grimly pursed his lips, clamping down the pain. 'Sorry isn't good enough anymore! This is no game, Quenelda. No story book adventure.' The dwarf shook his head in disgust. 'Two Gulps is undisciplined and greedy, and he has destroyed a large part of their winter stores. Some of what he didn't eat, he toasted. It cannot continue. Unless you take his training more seriously, I am going to have to take Two Gulps' training away from you.'

'Take aw-?' Quenelda flushed to her hairline at the

reprimand, knowing Root, Quester and Drumondir must have heard in the silence. Her hearts thumped with shock. *Take him away from me? Is he that bad?*

'And he should be flying by now. At the very least, be able to get off the ground!'

'But I do tell him he must fly before he gets food, just as you instructed.'

'But then you give in,' Tangnost said flatly. 'Every time.' He took a deep breath, trying to contain his frustration and fight down the pain that fuelled his anger. 'If you don't force him to fly, he will never be able to forage for himself, he will never become a battledragon. His battle training should have started so that he can protect you. Look at him, Quenelda,' Tangnost forced her. 'Look at him! He is fat. He waddles. Those wings of his are pathetic!

'You must be cruel to be kind. Let him go hungry! That is not a request. It is an order!'

Tangnost asked Quester to fetch his whetstone from the baggage, and began sharpening the edges of his axe. He shook his head. The juvenile was totally out of control, and even if Quenelda did not see it, Two Gulps was getting bigger by the day; and not just his stomachs. Four shields had disappeared overnight, and it wasn't hard to guess where they were! The Ice Bears could not afford such losses in a harsh winter. And neither could they; not if they were going to have to fight their way home!

Daylight vanished into the dark. A patchwork of stars

appeared overhead through the smoke holes. The temperature dropped like a stone.

'But his breath,' Quester said softly, pointing to where Stormcracker's smoke now curled thickly through a hole into the freezing night air. 'It will be visible for leagues!'

'Hot pools and smoking mountains lie everywhere in this land,' Drumondir softly reassured the young esquire. 'Many hillocks smoke...no one will notice.'

Bored with nothing to do and nothing to eat, Two Gulps began to nibble Root's prized mammoth wool cloak, sucking it in like a worm.

CHAPTER THIRTY-FOUR

Friend or Foe?

Despite the bitter cold outside, it was stiflingly close, and tension was a palpable thing inside Stormcracker's ice roost. Quenelda had fallen asleep in her pilot's chair, wrapped in warmth by Two Gulps' embrace.

In her dreams she flew. Her powerful black wings were spread to catch the rising thermals as the sun peeked over the mountain ranges. Below, in the still dark glens, great herds of elk and deer scattered in fear as she passed over them, but she had already fed, and drunk her fill from the ice cold streams that tumbled down from the mountains. Higher and higher she spiralled effortlessly, as the mountain ranges and great rivers shrank to silver ribbons and the great ocean merged with the blue sky. Up and up to where her kindred flew in storms so dense they blotted out the sun, and frost turned her wings to sparkling starlight. Up to where a great citadel of spun glass hung in the vast immensity of space.

In these dreams, Quenelda fled the unrelenting cold, leaving her fears and doubts behind, taking refuge in another place, another time, long ago; the first Age of the Elders, before the age of men.

They are coming... Stormcracker hissed a warning in

204

her mind.

A hand was on her shoulder, another held gently but firmly over her mouth.

'Ta-'

'Hush...' a voice whispered in her ear. *'Not a sound.'* Tangnost held his finger to his lips in warning. 'They are coming...the idiots are using torches to track!'

Quenelda cocked her head, and hearing nothing, listened with her inner dragon senses. *There!* At the edge of her hearing...the jingle of harness, the careless clash of chain mail and weapons. Her heart started racing. These soldiers were coming to kill or capture them...her and Storm.

Food? The smaller dragon complained. The slab of walrus meat he had found at the very edge of the camp had filled a little space and no one appeared to have noticed. But that was several bells ago. *Hungry!*

No! Stay still and be silent...! Quenelda rocked the little dragon on his feet with the force of her thoughts. *Give their dragons no cause for alarm. Two Gulps!* She added severely. *Don't move...not a talon!*

Everyone could hear them now. The crunch of claws...the murmur of conversation and complaints, muffled by the ice walls.

Tangnost stood, head against a listening hole punched through the ice.

'I tell you,' a voice insisted. 'There is nothing here, the boy lied. I have circled the area twice.'

Tangnost stiffened with shock. *What? The boy lied?*

'Wait,' the first voice insisted. 'He said he would leave a token. Fan out.'

'What are we looking for?'

'Abyss below! How do I know?' It was Knuckle Quarnack, the Lord Protector's Dragon Master! 'Something that shows they're hiding around here.'

Tangnost cursed silently. Who else would be on their trail? They had crossed paths before. Next time, next time, Tangnost swore, there would be a reckoning.

'Or we are lost in this forsaken land!' a voice complained. 'One hillock looks much like another beneath the pole star. We could have gone in a circle and be right back where we started! We'll not know until their Imperial flames us to toast, like ours did for Wentlock. They don't seem to know friend from foe.'

'Damn fool to get so close,' Knuckle laughed. 'It's a killer through and through; those collars control them, dragon magic or not. Wentlock knew that, he just got careless. The Lord trains his Imperials to kill; makes the common folk afraid of the SDS.'

'T'aint no Imperial we should be worrying about here, Flint! It can't cloak, this wounded one, we'll see it a league away in the snow,' A new voice worried, as Tangnost listened, horrified.

They knew that Stormcracker couldn't cloak? *How do they know?*

'But those damn ice bears are on you before you know it!' the soldier continued. 'We've lost a half dozen more men and dragons already. And it's so cold! Can't feel my feet or hands no more! And don't want to eat seal meat ever aga-'

There was a thud as a dragon stumbled into Stormcracker's ice roost, raining down snow inside, almost drawing a cry from Drumondir as chunks fell on her. Outside a soldier cursed. There were shouts.

'Dead!' A voice whined. 'My Adder's just died. Now I'm done for!'

'Take Storlock's,' Knuckle told him, kicking the cooling carcass. 'He's not going to last much longer, anyhow. And let's get out of here; this scent of death will attract those ice bears!'

There was a cry and a curse and the sound of drawn steel. A grunt and then nothing but the crunch of dragons' feet moving off.

Two Gulps burped. The ice bear talon amulet he had found lying next to the dried seal carcass was giving his third stomach a bit of a problem. He could feel it tickling his innards.

As the voices and lights faded, Tangnost let out a sigh of relief, but raised a finger to his lips to maintain silence.

'How long?' Quenelda whispered, shivering. 'How long should we wait?'

'If we flame now, they'll see it a hundred leagues away. We must wait for first light.'

But dawn had not arrived when they heard the thunder

of approaching bears. A young man hurled himself off his battle bear's back, with a crash of harness. The bear reared up, growling in protest, its flanks heaving.

'Bearhugger!?' There was no effort to hide the exhaustion and anguish in the voice.

'Stay!' Tangnost barked, as he kicked through the thin wall of snow.

'There has been a fight at Black Sound.' The man was breathing heavily and blood stained his left leg and his bear. 'On the slopes of the Smoking Mountain. They have a Mage. We are fighting a rearguard action. Barlad is wounded. Go! Make it worth the deaths of our people. Go, with the blessings and friendship of the Ice Bears.'

The men clasped in farewell, and then the Ice Bears were gone, heading back into the ice fields and the fight.

'Mount up!' Tangnost ran back inside. 'We must fly,' he commanded Quenelda. 'The time for stealth is gone. Take off as soon as his wings are warmed up.'

'But it's still dark and cloudy,' she protested. 'What if we crash again?'

'I know, lass! Do you think he could manage a vertical takeoff? And then take him up to three thousand strides or as high as he can manage. That should keep us safe from harm and pursuit. Let me talk to Root about which way to go.'

Storm... Quenelda commanded as she scrambled up the girth rungs. *We must get airborne before they find us... wait, on my command...*

Root was already in his navigator's chair as

Drumondir strode up the dragon's tail as if she had been doing it all her life, followed by Quester who took up position on the dragon's tail to watch for pursuit.

Tangnost had been drilling them for this. 'Heads down! Shields up! Fire in the hole...! Fire in the hole!'

Purple flame licked out as Stormcracker swept his head left and right. The hummock about them was instantly vaporised, creating billowing clouds of steam that froze and showered them with ice crystals. The battledragon lashed out with his tail and stamped his legs, slowly stretching out his stiff neck. He shook himself from his snout to his tail, shivered the frost off his wings, and began to warm up.

Chapter Thirty-Five

Lift Off! Lift Off!

Stiff with cold, the battledragon's first attempt to get airborne failed. Although Quenelda had healed his damaged leg, it was still weak and ached so that he stumbled, sending them all tumbling save Quenelda and Root who were already strapped in. Like a broken winged black swan, he glided and hopped over the ice, great wings thrashing up and down. Tangnost hid his anxiety; neither on the ground nor in the air, they were very vulnerable to attack if any of the Knucklebones should be nearby.

'Up! Up, Storm!' Quenelda urged the battledragon, imagining their enemies falling upon them. It was only heartbeats, but it seemed to take forever before they finally sprang into the air. Circling slowly, the big dragon gradually gained height until Quenelda levelled them out at one thousand strides, well clear of the hummocks that had so nearly ended their search.

'Lady?'

Quenelda's eyes flew open. The sun was high above in a clear sky. She must have fallen asleep in the pilot's chair. Tangnost sat astride the battledragon's neck a dozen paces in front, reins loosely in hand. He didn't look round.

The Ice Bears Bone Caster was looking at her with shrewd eyes. Drumondir sensed power, and yet the girl had no aura about her. Why? 'Child, walk with me,' the Bone Caster invited.

'I know little of sorcery; but I know magic, and I believe you do, too. Wild magic, what is now called Elder Magic, exists in every living thing, but men have long since forgotten; those times now live only in their legends. Those who wield it today have to learn the art. It takes many years, even for those who are gifted.

'Come, show me what you can do. Try and move that cooking cauldron.'

Quenelda wilted. *More pointless lessons! More embarrassment!*

'But I've told you! I'm *hopeless* at sorcery! I haven't even earned my first wand.'

'Nonetheless,' Drumondir encouraged her.

Huffing with exasperation Quenelda pulled out her warped old wand from down her boot. Curious, Tangnost joined Drumondir.

Nothing's happening! Quenelda balled her fists and bit her lip, trying not to cry. Two Gulps couldn't fly, and despite all her practice, she couldn't cast the most basic of spells! Only in her dreams was she the person everyone said she was. Gritting her teeth she tried again.

Drumondir bobbed her head, deep in thought. 'I think she is spellbound,' she said softly to Tangnost.

'Spellbound?' Tangnost shook his head, confused, as Two Gulps trundled up to the Earl's daughter to give her a clumsy embrace, treading on her toes. *I have never seen such a clumsy yearling!* he thought distractedly.

'I have seen her lend strength to your Imperial, the mightiest of dragons. Even wounded and his magic diminished, this dragon has power, it ripples about him. And yet Quenelda herself has no aura. Only when she unveils her eyes, does she reveal her inner dragon.'

She paused to draw deeply on her pipe.

'Those who are skilled in the art of sorcery may hide their aura, shield themselves from their enemies as the Dragon Lords do; but she is far too young for such knowledge. And the first time I saw her, just for a heartbeat, threads of many colours wove her in white, but then were gone in the blink of an eye.'

'But,' Tangnost frowned, shrugging his shoulders and immediately gasping with pain. 'What does that mean?'

'I do not know. I have no certain answers, but I think it is well meant. I think, somehow, someone is protecting her. She is spellbound, so that she can hardly cast magic at all. So that she will always remain unnoticed.'

'Except for her unusual passion for dragons!' Tangnost said dryly, 'that has always marked her as different to other young ladies at Court. And at the Cauldron all the Seven Kingdoms saw her skill, saw her fly a battledragon to save her father!'

'Yet none saw her cast her power did they? They saw a girl who could fly! No one, not even the Lord

Protector, truly saw her...so perhaps it is true? None can see who she truly is...least of all she herself.'

'But!' Tangnost objected. 'The Cauldron, her dream of the battle, the brimstone mines...I witnessed wild dragons singing on the night of her birth...'

Drumondir nodded. 'Do not misunderstand me. It seems to me that when the need is dire, she can unleash her power; but she does not yet have the training or the wisdom to control it. And so it remains hidden, dormant, until she is ready.'

Tangnost nodded, stroking his chin. 'That makes sense. She strikes erratically like lightning. Now she fears to hurt others. Two score died at the Cauldron, and she blames herself, not the dark dragon and its master.'

'She cares,' the Elder Bone Caster agreed. 'And that is a good beginning. If she truly is a Dragon Whisperer, Bearhugger, her road will not be an easy one. She is at a crossroads; belonging to both mankind and dragonkind and yet to neither; she bridges elder magic and chaos. She will draw many to her standard, but others will envy and fear her.' She paused. 'Whoever is watching over her has shown great wisdom.'

'Can you train her?'

Drumondir nodded. 'Yes, she has the light to fight the shadow. But we must tread carefully, teach her enough so that she can protect herself, and that may be hard enough if she is spellbound. But she needs you also...I think you alone have been a constant anchor in her life, always there for her, whilst others have always left her behind.

Do not die, Bearhugger for your paths crossed before she was even born.'

Tangnost looked at her sharply, seeing the wisdom in those strange almost amber eyes. How old was Drumondir?

'She always wanted to follow her father, to fight at his side. She wanted to be a son to him, to fight, to fly in the SDS. A foolish dream most people told her. She was mocked for being different, children can be cruel. And yet...'

'And yet', Drumondir smiled. 'Here she is piloting the greatest battledragon on the One Earth. Dreams do come true, but they are not always as you imagined.'

'I am sworn to her, from the moment of her birth to be her Shield.'

'That is why you departed the Bone Crackers? Why you became Dragon Master? Her father always absent. Her mother....'

'Yes,' Tangnost's hazel eye held her gaze levelly. 'My injuries were real, and we agreed they would mask my true role; to teach and guide her.'

'But your people are-'

'Are ruled by my brother.....I made my choice long ago.'

'I can't!'

Quenelda gave up with a curse and threw her wand at the cooking cauldron where it landed in the embers and went on fire. The girl gave a gasp of dismay, and tried to kick it out; ashes and the cauldron went flying. Deftly intercepting it with a single bound, Two Gulps barely crunched it before swallowing. He gave a metallic burp of satisfaction.

'But...' Root's shoulders dropped. 'But that was our lunch!'

'I told you!' Quenelda was angry. She had known all along she would fail. 'I am hopeless!'

'Tut,' Drumondir admonished her. 'You were not listening, child.'

'What do you mean?'

'Think, child. When your power flows, are you using a wand? Think carefully.'

'N-no...!'

'Then throw away your wand, and forget your lessons.'

'Throw it..?'

'It serves no purpose. You do not need it. Stop trying to do what others tell you. Be yourself.' Drumondir held out her hand.

Quenelda bit her lips doubtfully. Embarrassed, she reluctantly handed the charred wand over. It was still smoking. 'Now child,' Drumondir said briskly, letting go and watching the wand disappear. 'Believe in yourself, and follow your own instinct. Look inwardly for answers. Come, try! Move your dragon.'

'Two Gulps?' Quenelda was horrified. 'But he weighs a ton!'

There was a short silence. Quenelda was aware that everyone had stopped whatever they had been doing. She had always hotly denied her juvenile sabretooth had a weight problem.

She looked up to find Tangnost's amused gaze on her. He tilted his head towards Two Gulps and nodded.

'Relax, child,' Drumondir said softly.

'But I can't just do it! It never works.' Quenelda felt like stamping her foot like a child. She was just too tired for this. Tired of everyone expecting her to be someone she wasn't!

'That is because you are still thinking how to cast a spell, rather than upon what you wish to happen. And you are paying too much attention to those watching. Cast them from your mind.' Drumondir rebuked her mildly. 'And nothing of value is easily earned; I served a full score years at my master's side.

'So! Draw threads from the elements around you and weave them to your will.'

Quenelda drew a deep breath and tried to ignore the fact that Tangnost was behind her, the familiar warm scent of his tobacco filling the cold air.

Relax! They are risking so much for me, for us...let me succeed!!

She tried to calm herself and concentrated on Two Gulps Too Many.

Boom...boom... her hearts slowed. Her fingertips tingled.

Boom...boom...

Abruptly the living Earth came into sudden brilliant focus: threads swirled, dozens of colours, the elements of earth, wind, fire and water, stone, metal and wood, alive and vibrant.

The ice beneath them, a thousand hues of blue and green, the accumulation of millennia, layer upon layer of snow falling, reaching back into history, each layer a story reaching down and down towards the freezing water below. The vast blazing cauldron that was the core of the volcano that rose up to their right, where they were going to make camp. The cold whispers of the silver white stars glinting above in the darkness. An ice bear and her cubs hidden in a den, meshed threads of amber and russet bound in white. People alive, threads of softest rose almost aglow, hearts beating strongly...an aura about Drumondir; soft, muted like autumn gold. Tangnost, comforting earthy colours of iron, and stone.... Stormcracker's magic shining but fractured like broken ice and...and Quester, pale as the moon and bound about with threads of black!!

She jerked around, eyes wide, as Drumondir came swiftly to her, placing a finger on Quenelda's lips, knowing eyes acknowledging what the girl had seen.

'So, child, you see it too?'

Quenelda nodded, wide eyed.

'I will speak of it to Bearhugger.'

Quenelda's eyes flicked to Quester; the boy was setting up another cauldron, preparing for the meal.

CHAPTER THIRTY-SIX

The Enemy Within

'That was excellent elk stew with dumplings,' Tangnost said, patting his full stomach. 'It is marvellous to have someone who can cook! I shall sleep well tonight.'

'I'll take first watch, I can't sleep,' Quester offered.

Tangnost nodded. 'Thank you. Wake me at three bells... the hour of the dozy hedgehog,' he explained to Drumondir.

Root yawned gratefully and curled up in his sleeping roll. The Bone Caster lay back and nurtured her mug of ice berry tea. Two Gulps breathed fresh heat into the fire stones, and Quenelda curled up with the dragon beside her. Ash drifted down. The twin moons began to rise. Quester sat silently.

The witching hour had passed before the esquire suddenly rose from the Imperial's back. Eyes unfocussed, he moved to study his friends. Tangnost, Drumondir and Quenelda lay silently; Root was dreaming of Chasing the Stars, shifting and turning.

Quester moved softly to where the ravens slept in their cages. Lifting a raven out in its white winter plumage, he twisted a little canister concealed about its leg, and threw the bird up into the night. Turning he sat down again.

'Take her,' Tangnost whispered as the raven made for the ice shelf.

There was a blur, just a sense of movement white against white, and then feathers falling lazily down like the snow. Tangnost was already striding out, his spiked boots crunching as he crossed to where the snow eagle sat, tearing at its prey.

'Here girl,' Tangnost offered up some dried beef. With a lazy hop the eagle accepted its reward.

Drumondir raised a shuttered lamp as Tangnost returned with the bloodied rook and removed the paper from the canister. Swiftly reading it, he called loudly to Root. 'Fetch Quester.'

'Now?' Root sat up in his bed roll. 'Why?'

'Now, lad,' Tangnost looked grave.

Quester was tired, his face pale. 'What? What's wrong?' He appealed to his friend. 'W-why are you all looking at me?'

Tangnost handed the message over, watching his esquire keenly for any sign of guilt, and seeing only bewilderment. 'It has been you who has betrayed us every step of the way.'

The boy frowned as he read it, rubbing his head. It ached so, and he was having trouble focusing on the three words scrawled hastily.

The Inner Isles

He looked up at the ring of silent watchers.

'I don't understand....'

'I heard them, Quester; the Knucklebones, the soldiers

hunting us. They spoke of a boy who sent them messages. Who was going to leave a token to betray where we hid. It had to be you, but Drumondir confirmed it earlier today.'

'What? How? What do you mean?'

Root reached forward to look. 'It's your writing, Quester!' Root was stunned. 'You wrote this,' he pointed to the scrawl.

'No!' The youth looked horrified. 'I would never betray you! Never! Why would I write this? Who would I send it to?' He was on the verge of tears.

'No, lad,' Tangnost said thoughtfully, reaching out to put a reassuring hand on his shoulders. 'We believe you.' he sighed. 'Come here!' He clasped the shaking boy to him, as Quester let out all the pain and confusion that had dogged him since he left Dragonsdome.

Quenelda gently reached out her hand to the youth, resting Two Gulps' scale against his clammy head. There was a thread of darkness coiling through his thoughts, muddling him.

'He's been *touched*,' she confirmed, suddenly remembering, suddenly afraid.

'Touched?' Now Quester was really scared. 'What does that mean?'

'He tried to do it to me,' Quenelda said. 'After the Winter Jousts...the Lord Protector, he touched me....he was digging in my mind, trying to find something.' She shivered. 'But Sir Gharad and Root came...'

'I remember!' Root agreed. 'But we thought you had

fainted. You were on the ground.'

'Do you ever remember being alone with him?' Quenelda asked the frightened esquire.

'I...' Quester frowned; trying to remember. 'Yes! No! I...I think so. Felix, he told me the Earl wanted to see me. The Lord Protector was there...I don't remember anything after that.'

'It's not your fault, Quester,' Root reassured his friend. 'He's a WarLock. He-'

'But I'm a danger to you all! How will I know I won't betray you again? I might do something worse, and never know! You could never trust me!' Quester was desperately afraid. He was trembling when Quenelda placed her hand on him again.

'Wh-?' Quester felt her hand vibrating, growing warm.

'Hush,' she said. 'Trust me.'

Drumondir's eyes watched like a hawk's as a soft glow suffused Quenelda, as threads of white and gold spun around the injured youth, spinning faster and faster. Brighter and brighter it became and then a tiny thread of black leaked out and was caught up by the cocoon, pulled out like an unravelling garment. And then it was gone.

Quester collapsed into Tangnost's arms.

CHAPTER THIRTY-SEVEN

Roarkinch

It was barely the hour of the yawning dormouse when they broke camp.

'We must fly with all speed,' Tangnost warned them as they prepared to take off. 'Quester has no memory of when he last sent a message. They may already know the Earl is not in the Frost Marches, but on the Inner Isles. They may be close behind. Stormcracker must fly like the very wind!'

'We are now facing a flight of a hundred and fifty leagues over the sea, without making landfall, because these lands,' Tangnost indicated on the map the coastline of Moray. 'These lands are owned by the Lord Protector. Quenelda, the weather is fine and the wind with us. Take him up as high as Storm can go, and keep well out to sea. In a few hours I'll take the reins, and you get some sleep.'

But by the hour of the osprey the sky to the south was as leaden as the sea. Dark storm clouds tinged with green were gathering about a distant island, and a dense fog hugged the coastline. A strange westerly wind sucked them towards it.

'It must be this volcanic island here,' Root pointed

222

towards a large island in the Forgotten Straits, surrounded by a necklace of lesser islands. 'Maybe all those clouds are coming from the volcano?'

'Mnn,' Tangnost said doubtfully, casting a glance at Drumondir. 'Well, with this wind we can hardly avoid it, but we had better not get too close.'

Quenelda was dreaming when something woke her. Heart stopping terror gripped her. Crawling out of her bed roll, she looked around. A sticky mist coiled about them. Shaking with dread, legs weak with fear, she ran up to where Tangnost was seated in the pilot's chair, Drumondir was seated on the battledragon's withers to one side.

A large volcanic island loomed to port. Wild and thick with tangled forest and rugged broken cliffs; it was crowned to the north by an ancient castle that had tumbled slowly into the sea. Quenelda frowned, blinking. The island shimmered as if through a heat haze on a summer's day. A dark aura hung about it, drawing in energy from all around.

A nexus....concealment....what power to hide an island! A voice, a memory, not hers, whispered in her head. She blinked. Her head was suddenly pounding.

'W-what island is that?' she gripped the side of Root's navigator's chair.

Root consulted his map. 'Ermmm...it's...Roarkinch.'

'Roarkinch?' Quenelda searched her ancestral memories for the ancient meaning of the name. 'That means Heart of Darkness...it's a dangerous place!'

'What? What is it?' At her side, Tangnost tried to keep the anxiety from his voice. 'You've gone white.'

'I...' Quenelda felt quite ill. The island emanated a sickness, a crawling stench of fear and suffering. She looked again, seeing through the nexus to where dark, green-tinged clouds knotted the sky above it; lightning branched down, and at its centre, a hole, the Abyss.

'The island!' Drumondir answered for her. 'It is not what it seems, Bearhugger. Something evil is hidden there, something I cannot see. But I can sense it.'

'We must get out of here...' Quenelda felt suffocated. 'Tangnost,' she gasped for air as if she were being crushed by a great weight.

Then her voice changed, became deeper, older. Smoke whispered from her mouth. 'We must go,' the voice commanded, '– now.'

Her inner eyes flared smoking sulphur. 'I-I am not yet ready for this.' Her breathing was ragged as the dwarf caught and clasped her flailing hand in his just as she collapsed into Drumondir's arms.

'The Abyss is rising...'

Tangnost cried out in surprise when Quenelda gripped his hand so hard he thought the bones would break, and then he saw why. Her left hand and wrist, save for the gold scale on her palm, were sheathed in small black scales, hard as diamonds! A living skin of scales!

Drumondir's calm eyes were intent as she pointed Tangnost to where black scales had also appeared on

Quenelda's brow and cheek bones, where the dragon tattoo coiled.

Struggling in Drumondir's arms, Quenelda turned once more towards the mist wreathed island, the same island; yet now the castle rose skyward and its vast jagged battlements and towers were lit by a thousand braziers flickering green light. Tiers of ramparts encircled the island, wall after wall, gate after gate, bastions and spires, catapults and ballista and dragon pads, patrolled by ranks of black armoured soldiers, drilling and training with weapons of war.

This was a fortress island.....a dark citadel to rival Dragon Isle was rising; it grew, filling her vision.

And then suddenly she was there, soaring around the barbed spires and towers, spiralling and weaving about them wings outspread; and all around her, Imperial Blacks rode the winds.

You do not see us; she commanded them as she swept closer and closer. *You do not see your brother...*

As the detail came to her, her hearts slammed in her chest. This was where they were, Root's vanished people, and those taken by the Lord Protector's dragons, and here too were SDS prisoners. Shackled and chained on gantries and scaffolds, building this dark fortress. Pulling great blocks of stone, raising up battlements. A whip lashed out and another exhausted prisoner fell dead, like so many before him; a young boy, Root's age! With a cry of horror she fell backwards as if punched, and found herself back in Drumondir's arms on Stormcracker once again.

'It's...it's not what you see, Tangnost,' she struggled to explain. 'This is an illusion. There is a black citadel here, built with chaotic sorcery!'

Dumfounded, Tangnost searched the ruined castle and the black cliffs down to the base where the rough sea broke on the rocks. Only those weren't rocks...those dark craggy shapes...they were moving in the sea beyond the reach of the nexus. Razorbacks! Thousands...tens and tens of thousands...

'Abyss below!' His voice cracked. 'Fly!' He commanded Stormcracker, seizing the reins as Drumondir tended the shaken girl. 'Fly, Storm! Fly!'

CHAPTER THIRTY-EIGHT

Odin's Eye

It was not until nightfall, when they put down on the lower slopes of a wooded dell, that Tangnost finally relaxed. Somehow they had passed unnoticed; there were no signs of pursuit! After the next five days of easy travel, resting Stormcracker frequently, they were flying around the rugged west coast of Fintry, heading for the Inner Isles, when Quester called out.

'There's a....a longship over there,' he lowered his spyglass. 'It's ...' The youth was baffled. 'It's going round in circles...it doesn't make sense.'

'Where?' Tangnost asked.

Quester started at the dwarf's urgent tone. 'There,' he pointed past a rugged stack of weathered stone. 'Where the sea's deep green, and it's foaming.'

'Odin's Eye!' Tangnost said wonderingly, shading his eyes from the glare. 'You've found Odin's Eye!'

'Odin's Eye?' Quester was baffled.

'I've heard Pa mention it!' Root offered. 'It's a whirlpool isn't it?'

Tangnost nodded. 'One that opens a portal into the Netherworld! It's deadly because it is always shifting position. It disappears and reappears somewhere else, and it's sunk countless boats, and taken many lives.'

'Fly, Stormcracker, fly like the wind.' Quenelda urged the dragon.

Soon the wind was rushing in their ears as Stormcracker sped for the stricken ship. As they drew closer, the terrible struggle of the crew became clear. The sixty-oared longship was made of dark caulked timber with a magnificent high-carved dragon prow painted red and gold, declaring the clan's allegiance to Dragon Isle. Colourful round shields lined the sides above rows of hobgoblin spikes, each matched by a long oar. The single bright red sail had a white bird on it.

'The White Raven,' Tangnost called, as they circled the ship. 'That's Chief Thorfinn's longship!'

By now they had been spotted, and several of the dwarfs were waving to them. The rest were still futilely fighting the deadly suck of the whirlpool. The roaring vortex and spume flecked the air about them.

There was a sudden commotion at the raised stern, a crack they could hear above the roar, and a dwarf was thrown forward onto the deck. The longboat tilted. Several pieces of wood were snatched from the surface of the sea and disappeared down the throat of the whirlpool.

'The rudder's snapped,' Tangnost shouted. 'The rudder's snapped! They've no chance now!'

Without its rudder, the ship was yawing violently. The boom swung round, sweeping several crew into the sea. They disappeared in moments, drowned by the weight of their armour.

Deftly moving between the battledragon's huge spinal plates to rummage amongst their equipment and packs stored in netting, Tangnost seized heavy coils of rope. 'Hold him steady,' he bellowed to Quenelda. 'Knot these ropes,' he instructed Root and Quester, 'and attach them to the spine plate cleats.'

'Quenelda! Take us as close as you can!'

Quenelda took the dragon down as low as she dared. Stormcracker's beating wings creating swirls and curls of spume. Cold spray hung like a feathered plume in the air, the moisture clinging to visors and hands, making everything slippery.

The milky green vortex below was huge. Quenelda could feel its cold breath sucking greedily at them. Only Stormcracker's great strength kept them safely out of reach.

'Right, lads,' Tangnost instructed his esquires. 'Hurry now, and anchor the ropes from there and make sure your flying harnesses are roped up, too.'

The Sea Raven clan heaved at their oars.

Tangnost rappelled down the dragon's great flank with surprising speed, followed by a more cautious Quester. Securing himself in turn to the harness webbing, he threw the long rope down. The dwarfs had guessed what they were doing and several were frantically trying to catch the lifelines as they dangled above them. Peering anxiously over the Imperial's shoulder where it met the wing, Root could see that the rowers were visibly tiring.

Above them, Quenelda could feel that Stormcracker was also was having trouble maintaining a steady hover in the roiling air above the stricken boat. Light-boned Harrier dragons were made for hovering; heavy boned Imperials were made for speed and brute strength. Their journey and his injuries had taken their toll.

It is trying to suck me down, Dancing with Dragons... Can you hold position?

As you command... came the proud reply, but she could feel the edge of doubt in his mind. Tangnost would have to hurry.

'A little forward,' the dwarf was shouting to Root, who relayed his instructions to Quenelda from a sling he had roped up. 'A bit more.'

Hanging almost horizontally from the side of Stormcracker's dragon-harness, Tangnost never took his eyes off the floundering boat. 'Stop! Too much... Back a little...' the dwarf gestured with his free hand. 'They've got it!' he cried triumphantly as the rope was caught and secured.

Quenelda felt as if the first dwarf was taking forever to climb the knotted rope and onto the webbing that covered the dragon's flanks. She could hear Tangnost shouting encouragement, but it seemed like bells before she saw the top of a bronze-tipped helmet emerge around the dragon's belly, as the dwarf climbed up the webbing. A double-headed axe and heavy studded shield were strapped to his back. A bearded face soon followed, followed by a heavily armoured torso. Two ice blue eyes looked up, saw the young esquire in the pilot's seat, and widened in surprise. The Norseman's face was flushed, despite the bitter easterly wind. He skinned back his lips in a white-toothed smile. 'My thanks,' he saluted, then turned away to help Tangnost.

Hooking his legs into the webbing, the dwarf began to help Tangnost pull the rope in, hand flying over hand. Trying not to stare, Root could see why. The dwarf was as wide as he was tall, and corded muscles stood out on his neck and arms. His battle-hardened body was criss-crossed with scars. *But...but he is hardly older than I am! Everyone has warriors except my people...*

A second then a third and a fourth dwarf swiftly arrived. But the big dragon was tired with the strain of maintaining a hover, longing to let the wind catch his wings and take him up high. Quenelda could almost feel Stormcracker adjusting to the added weight as each dwarf climbed up from the boat.

Below them, the whirlpool began to make a ghastly sucking noise like water spilling out a drain, as the power of the swirling vortex grew more powerful.

It was still too slow! A fifth rope then a sixth and seventh rope were sent down as the dwarfs desperately hauled their comrades up.

Two score...forty one...forty two...

But the faster they rescued their comrades and kin, the fewer dwarfs were left to fight against the frothing whirlpool which was growing ever larger and stronger.

'Climb!' Tangnost shouted his encouragement. 'It's

going!'

The longship was tilting further and further over. There were only a dozen left now, still fighting Odin's Eye, still trying to turn the longship from its fatal grasp.

'Fifty three...fifty four...' Quenelda could barely hear Root's shout above the thunder of water. 'fifty eight...'

The remaining dwarfs were no longer rowing. Instead they were fighting to keep their balance as the boat keeled further over. Shields and oars were falling away into the sea. Stormcracker was getting weaker by the heartbeat. Quenelda could sense the ache in his injured wings through their bond. What was she thinking of? Leaving her saddle she clambered back to help.

'How many more?' Quenelda shouted. 'We're going down!'

Tangnost held up three fingers. He was panting hard.

'Tell them just to grab hold of the ropes. Tell them to grab the ropes,' Quenelda shouted at Root, running back to her pilot's chair. 'And we'll move away and then haul them up.'

Root relayed Quenelda's words to Tangnost, who nodded, gesturing to the dwarfs below to hang on for their lives. Suddenly Stormcracker veered violently to one side, the tip of his wing dipping in the sea. The suction from the vortex had caught him. There were screams and shouts of alarm as the rescued dwarfs tumbled across Stormcracker's back and the ropes went slack. With a cry, one of the exhausted sailors fell into the sea.

Grabbing an empty water bladder, Drumondir

wrenched off its stopper. Blowing into it, she then jammed the cork back in. "Flying harness off!" she barked at Root, as she perched on the shoulder of one of Stormcracker's wings and threw the wine skin down to the drowning dwarf who clutched desperately at it.

Realising what Drumondir intended, Root shrugged out of his harness. Swiftly knotting it to a rope the gnome passed it to Tangnost who threw it down whilst the other dwarfs desperately pulled the last two survivors up. The flailing dwarf hooked an arm and leg into the harness, and hung on for grim death as one and all pulled the rope.

There was still an agonising wait. Finally Tangnost and Root gave Quenelda the thumbs up. Fighting hard, Stormcracker rose up, letting the wind fill his wings. Beneath them the ship's timbers cracked like eggshell and were crushed. The red sail, with its proud raven, crumpled and was gone.

'Head for Inversnekkie Island, Root.' Tangnost was being thanked by the White Ravens. Checking his map, Root passed on their destination to Quenelda.

The large island to port, Stormcracker. Food and rest! The dragon peeled away into clear air.

A hand fell on Quenelda's shoulder. She looked round and into the wind-burnt face of the last dwarf to be rescued. He had taken his battle battered helmet off, leaving his grey-flecked fox-red hair and beard to whip around his head. Holding unsteadily onto the pilot's chair, the old dwarf nodded at her.

Tangnost leaned forward to speak in her ear. 'This is Thorfinn Andmusson, Chieftain of the Sea Raven clan.'

'My daughter,' the Chieftain pointed to the young dwarf rescued from the sea, who was still hacking and coughing up water while being tended by Drumondir. 'My daughter, Helgard' he repeated in the common tongue. 'My thanks. My clan are indebted to you, boy.'

'We are brothers in arms,' she replied in Dwarfish custom, making him start. Smiling with delight, the chieftain thrust forward a calloused hand and gripped Quenelda's free hand in a vice-like grip. Then the dwarf's eyes suddenly widened. He turned her hand to look at the Dragonsdome signet ring on her thumb. It coiled beneath his grip.

He barked a guttural question at Tangnost. A rapid conversation followed before Tangnost turned to Quenelda, his eye afire.

'Quenelda,' his trembling voice was cautious. He blinked away a tear. 'We may have found your father. He is on Inversnekkie, in the care of the Elder Council!'

'I know!' her face was lit by a radiant smile. 'I know!'

CHAPTER THIRTY-NINE

Gathering of the Clans

'Elder Grandmother, Bone Caster?' the young woman marked with blue tattoos and robes stitched with runes, bowed respectfully to Drumondir as she descended Stormcracker's wing. 'My master, Loki, First Bone Caster and Mage to the Elder Council, asks if you will speak with him?'

'Of course,' Drumondir did not seem surprised that her arrival was already known, before she even set foot on Inversnekkie. Smiling reassuringly at the Earl's daughter, she followed the young woman towards a strange wooden dwelling near the cliff edge. Quenelda had never seen anything like it.

The circular stone wall was some thirty strides tall, adorned with the bones and skulls of many creatures. Steps that corkscrewed about its outer wall, led up and up about a spiralling roof that rose high into the sky. It was all set about with braziers on the top of poles.

The Bone Caster's four companions were shown to a small roundhouse near the centre of the settlement, undistinguished from a score of others. Pulling back the weighted leather apron, they found themselves immersed in rank smoky warmth. Their guide beckoned them towards low benches that surrounded the crackling fire. Dim light streamed in the smoke hole above. He gestured towards low pallets covered with blankets and furs, set against the walls.

'We have arrived in time for a special gathering of the clans,' Tangnost explained as the man left. 'The Sea Ravens were heading here when they got caught by Odin's Eye. Clan chieftains of the Inner and Northern Isles have all been summoned here to take counsel.

'They will bring us food and drink,' Tangnost continued. 'And there are pallets here where we may rest. At dusk they will come for us. There is much to decide other than our errand, no matter how urgent that may seem to us. Many of these people live far from the safety of the Sorcerers Glen and the SDS, and war gathers about their shores. We must be patient. Your father-'

'But Papa,' Quenelda protested, starting for the door. 'I want to see Papa now!'

Tangnost caught Quenelda. 'Be patient.' he said gently but firmly. 'They will not disturb him while he sleeps. We must wait until he wakes, and then they will see if he is himself.' He felt her sag in his arms in defeat. Had he prepared her for this moment? Would she cope if the Earl did not know her?

'Quenelda,' Tangnost cautioned her. 'He was badly injured. Sometimes he is wild, and they cannot restrain him; this may not be the father you knew. His mind comes and goes. He is still gravely ill. The dark of Maelstrom has touched his heart and mind. You saw what it did to Stormcracker. He may not even recognise you. So please,' he appealed to her. 'Don't expect too much.'

Defeated, Quenelda sat heavily on a fur-covered bench. She *was* feeling light headed with exhaustion, and the smoke was making her dizzy. Then the food arrived; smoked fish and freshly baked bread and honey for Root, walnuts and almonds and sweet apples, and suddenly she realised how hungry she was. A diet of frozen fish and seal-meat had left them all hungry. They fell on it ravenously, and ate till full and contented.

Afterwards, Quenelda allowed Tangnost to lead her to a pallet, and within moments she fell deeply asleep, Root curled protectively at her feet. Two Gulps barrelled through the door and curled up beside them. Smiling, Tangnost slipped out quietly. There was much to discuss before tonight's moot. A little later, Quester came by and quietly led Two Gulps down to the shore.

At dusk, children came for the esquires, bringing gifts of warm cloaks and soft boots before guiding them to the Moot Hall. Quenelda and Root first went to check that their dragons were being well looked after. They found them down on the shore, already being tended to by Quester, resting amidst beached longboats. Light snow drifted down. Two Gulps looked fit to burst as he waddled sleepily up to Quenelda. Stormcracker raised a dripping muzzle.

Greetings, Are you hungry? Will you share food with me? The hunting is good here...

Quenelda looked at the hindquarters of a cow that fell out of the dragon's mouth to slap wetly in the sand, and swallowed.

Many thanks, Stormcracker, she replied formally, *for offering to share your kill with me, but the Elders are holding a feast in our honour. It would not be proper to go to their table already full...*

Thankfully, the dragon accepted her refusal and turned back to his dinner. A rib cage cracked with a crunch of breaking bone.

'I am happy to care for them,' Quester said, oiling and rubbing down some of Stormcracker's cracked scales. He was looking much better to Root's eye, but was still ashamed that he had betrayed his friends, and refused to go with them.

Trembling with nerves, Quenelda paused for breath outside the Moot Hall where Root and Tangnost awaited her. Shouts and yells and crashes and bangs rattled the door frame. Someone was playing the pipes and fiddle at a furious pace. After a hard year, this was a time to renew friendships and rivalries, and for clans to compete in friendly games. It sounded as if they had already started.

Tangnost put out a hand to steady her. She smiled weakly.

'It's just...' she swallowed. 'I've been hoping for this

moment for so long. And now it's arrived...I'm really afraid.'

'I know, lass. So am I,' Tangnost admitted.

Quenelda and Root looked at the dwarf in surprise. Somehow it made Quenelda much feel better to know the tough Dragon Master was as nervous as she was. There was no sign of it on his stern face.

'Ready?' Tangnost asked.

Quenelda took a deep breath and nodded. 'I'm ready.'

Without warning, the doors flew open and a dwarf hurtled out at shoulder height. Curled like an armoured hedgehog, he spun through the air before bouncing three times and coming to a gentle stop against a midden heap, where he unravelled with a sigh, and an empty goblet rolled from his hand. His helmet clanged and bounced along the path after him.

Eyes wide with shock, Quenelda and Root turned back from the inert body to the hall, almost staggering backwards as they were engulfed by the wall of noise and heat, and the eye-watering smells that rolled out over them.

Root coughed, his eyes watering. Smoke billowed out in pungent clouds, followed by the sweeter tang of heather ale, oat beer and roasting meats that almost, but not quite, disguised the bitter tangs of sweat and damp fur and wild boar.

The rowdy noise was incredible, new and almost overwhelming to the esquires who had never even set foot in a tavern before. Stepping tentatively forward, they peered into the fug, trying not to cough.

The Moot Hall was held up by a dozen huge carved wooden pillars that soared up to the sooty wooden hammerbeam roof. As Quenelda looked around, and her eyes adjusted to the low light, she saw that the walls of the hall were covered in bright round shields and hung with animal skins and thick tapestries of longships and battle.

The hall itself was thronged with dwarfs, dressed according to the traditions of their many Clans. Quenelda recognised the weaponry and furs and feathers of the Sea Eagle, the White Fox, the Ptarmigan, the Arctic Wolf, the Blue Stoat and the Orca before she lost count.

There were dwarfs drinking tankards and horns of oat ale and slicing roasting meat at long trestle tables with their dirks, with hounds and boar rooting around underfoot for scraps. Others were playing chess with exquisitely carved ivory pieces, or dicing. A raucous wrestling match was taking place over on the far side of the hall between clan champions, and betting on the outcome was fierce.

Whatever they were doing, Quenelda noticed that they all had one thing in common; they were heavily armoured and armed. The war might be over in the Sorcerers Glen but out here on the borders of the realm it was still being fought.

Tangnost was greeted warmly with raised drinking horns and respectful bows. Accepting both, he led the two dazed youngsters up the hall past the fire pits to the raised dais at the far end, where the Council of Elders were seated around a huge table, and on lesser chairs and tables, clan chieftains and the clan mages. That was where Drumondir had got to! The Elder Bone Caster caught Quenelda's eye and nodded. There were two empty seats between the Elders and Tangnost took one, indicating his esquires to stand behind.

Then Quenelda noticed a great bone horn curled about one of the pillars. Intricately carved, she recognised it as a mammoth tusk, a giant mammoth tusk! A young woman was standing silently by it. At a signal from an Elder, she bent forwards. The sound slowly grew so that its persistent call vibrated through the floor, making Quenelda's teeth tingle. As it grew deeper the whole hall seemed to shake. When it ended there was utter silence.

Quenelda found many curious eyes intent on Tangnost, but few paid attention to his esquires. An Elder stood up, wearing a cloak of many colours interwoven after the fashion of the clans.

'We welcome our brother, Tangnost Bearhugger, to our halls, and...' he paused for dramatic effect, knowing the impact his words would have. 'The Lady Quenelda, daughter of the Earl Rufus DeWinter, and her esquires, Root, son of Bark Oakley, and Quester, who is tending their dragons. Today, they saved the lives of Thorfinn Andmusson and those of his daughter and fifty seven of his men. The Sea Ravens are forever in their debt, as is this Council.'

Whispers ran around the hall like a rising wind. Feet

were stamped in approval or mugs rattled on table boards. The Elder bowed towards Tangnost and his two esquires, who flushed red with pleasure and embarrassment.

'These travellers have come south from great danger, seeking someone dear to them; someone whom the Clans are sworn to protect; someone whom we, the Council, are sworn to protect. Their purpose and ours coincide, for we are gathered here to discuss the fate of the Seven Sea Kingdoms, and within that, the destiny of our own Kingdom.

'The Abyss is rising. The SDS have fallen, and some say into ruin and despair. Some ninety thousand of our kin fell on the Westering Isles. More have died since, defending our holdfasts and longships against the hobgoblin swarms. The Lord Protector says that our people fell through the folly and arrogance of the SDS, who led them to their deaths. His messengers secretly say that the Sorcerer Lords care naught for those who serve them, and old oaths should be sundered.

'He soothes us with honeyed words and gold. He promises us that his armies will keep the hobgoblins from our shores, and that this fight is not for us. That our kingdom should be free again as it was in the days of the Old Kingdoms in the south. The Ptarmigan and the Midnight Owl have heeded his words, as have others whose lands lie to the north on his borders. They sent no one to speak for them at this Gathering of the Clans.

'The White Fox betrayed Bearhugger and the Earl's

daughter to the Lord Protector's men, and they were forced to flee into great danger. Y-'

Outrage and disbelief eddied about the hall.

'Yet,' the Elder repeated as the sound died down. 'War gathers about our borders, and many die. Our ships disappear.' He paused to look out over the silent gathering. 'Over the last moon we have heard many arguments for and against. But now perhaps,' the Elder looked at Tangnost. 'Now, perhaps for the first time we will learn the truth of it. The Lord of the Isles has a tale to tell that leaves little doubt as to who our true enemy is.'

He nodded to Tangnost, who stood. As he did, the dwarfs all went down on bended knee. Confused, Quenelda and Root looked at each other.

'What! Do you not yet know who your companion truly is?' A mocking voice softly said behind them. They turned to see Chieftain Thorfinn's daughter, Helgard, whom they had rescued.

'This is Tangnost Bearhugger of the Bear Clan, Lord of the Inner Isles. Thirty six clans owe him their allegiance.'

And so, as Quenelda and Root stood, eyes wide in amazement, Tangnost told the hushed hall the story of the Winter Jousts and the Earl's brush with death. Their belief that the rogue dragon was the result of tampering with forbidden Maelstrom magic by the greatest sorcerer of his generation: the Grand Master himself, now the proclaimed Lord Protector of the Seven Sea Kingdoms.

'And on the night of the Battle of the Westering Isles...' Tangnost continued, to describe how Quenelda had become one with Stormcracker, and had seen the betrayal that brought down the SDS, and had seen the face of the Sorcerer Lord who had ordered the battledragon into captivity.

Quenelda and Root were stunned as Tangnost then answered questions, telling for the first time the full story of how wild dragons had witnessed the Earl's daughter's birth. How she had then 'died' with her battledragon, Two Gulps and You're Gone, only to emerge with healing powers and knowledge far beyond her years.

'Here, bear witness that the Earl's daughter carries the mark of her battledragons.' So saying, Tangnost took Quenelda's left arm and held her hand high, so that those nearest could come forward and see for themselves the golden scale that was now part of her, and the tiny black scales that were now spreading to her wrist and creeping up her arm.

By now there was great excitement as Tangnost explained how she had used that Elder power to heal the battledragons on Dragon Isle touched by the dark of the Maelstrom, and went on to rescue Stormcracker from the Brimstone mines. And following that dragon's broken memories that the Earl had survived, how they had set out on a quest to find him, and return him to Dragon Isle, so that the Dragon Lords could rise up from defeat.

As he ended his tale, a storm of noise broke out

throughout the great hall.

The Elders let it flow for some time before they called for silence. A second Elder stood. He was old and stooped, and was missing an arm. 'It is as we feared,' his thin reedy voice quavered. 'The Lord Protector has sought to deceive us. A storm is coming. Do we stay out of this war, or do we raise our battle standards? The ancient Ice Sagas are said to have foretold the rising of a new Dark Age, and it has come upon us. The Earl's heir is here, yet she is young, and cannot lead us into battle. She is ours to protect until she comes into her own.

'We would now hear the counsel from one who once commanded the armies of the Seven Sea Kingdoms. If he is well and rested, fetch our guest. We would hear the counsel from the Earl Rufus.'

CHAPTER FORTY

Eternal Night

And then Quenelda felt her father's approach. *Power attracts power*, a voice whispered in her head, and she recognised him because his aura was shadowed and fractured, brittle, like Stormcracker's. Her father was badly injured. It should have prepared her, but it didn't.

Behind the Elders, in the shadows, a flickering light briefly flooded the hall then died down again. A number of the Elders' Carls parted ranks and formed a corridor. A hunched figure stood there in the shadows, head attentively cocked to one side as if listening; behind him stood another, an elderly dwarf. Clan tattoos and dress showed him to be Loki, the Bone Caster Mage, the most powerful amongst the clans, who kept her father in his care.

Quenelda's heart began to beat wildly. Her legs suddenly felt weak. Tangnost put a restraining hand on her shoulder, his strength holding her upright. Leaning heavily on a wooden staff, the figure hobbled forwards into the light with the shuffling gait of a very old man, back bent like a bow. The rasp of his breath was harsh in the silence, his face hidden by a large hood as he passed her by without a glance. She caught a glimpse of a tangled mane of golden hair streaked with silver, that hung in long warrior's braids from his shadowed face, before the Bone Caster helped him gently to the lowest chair on the dais. Although the figure was swathed inside a dark patched cloak and leant heavily on a staff, there was something familiar in the way he stood, in the way he moved.

For a heartbeat the world seemed to hold its breath as the figure turned. All about the hall, fists were held on heart and heads bowed in salute to a Dragon Lord. Then the figure put up a shaking hand to turn down his hood, punching a gasp from Quenelda. Behind her, she heard Tangnost swear in Dwarfish.

The Dragon Lord had been handsome once, but now half his face was burnt black, and the mane of tawny hair was streaked through with silver. Both eyes were milky blue, and stared sightlessly ahead from sunken bruised eye sockets. The face behind the unkempt beard had caved in against the skull, giving the face a cavernous look. Yet the figure threw back his cloak, and proudly raised his face towards a light he could not see.

The weight and strength had fallen from the Earl, so that to Tangnost he seemed like a bag of bones knitted together by sinew and parchment-thin skin; all sharp angles and twisted, desiccated flesh. They had carved him another staff to replace the warped twisted thing they had found fused to his hands, but it lay dead and lifeless in his hand, as if his power had gone with his eyesight.

It was as if time itself had stopped, as if this moment

was being drawn out into eternity. The fire popped and cracked. A dog barked. A dwarf belched. Quenelda took one tremulous step forwards, hand outstretched as if in appeal. Uncertain of what she saw before her, that this desperate creature was once her father.

'Papa?'

The man's blind eyes turned towards the sound of her voice, and then she was weeping in his arms. The man only said one word.

'Goose...'

CHAPTER FORTY-ONE

Two Hearts Beat as One

'Betrayed?' The fire flickered red on the pacing Earl's burnt face, turning it to the colour of rust. 'Yes! They knew when we would come, and what our plan was, what our tactics would be. It was a trap.' The Earl fell silent, lost in memories.

'Papa?' Quenelda reached to take the trembling hand, anxious lest her father slip away from her into a world of his own, forever.

The Earl shook his head. 'The hobgoblins – they rode dragons, dark dragons twisted to madness by the Maelstrom – they have come to be called razorbacks. We were beset on all sides; the reserve wings were destroyed before they could come to our aid. The fleet was destroyed by...' he shook his head helplessly. 'A great wave... Nearly four regiments swallowed up by the Maelstrom. We lost one hundred and fifty thousand souls!' The Earl raised weeping, milky eyes, and cursed.

'The touch of the Maelstrom robbed me of my sight and my reason. I have no memory of the aftermath of the battle beyond our flight over the Ice Fortress, where I saw the wounded being slaughtered by those who feigned to be friends. They told me that Stormcracker took me to the Outer Isles, seeking sanctuary. He found the Narwhale, who stole me away on their longboats, along with five of my men who still lived. They put to sea immediately, leaving Storm and the dead and dying. Ah, Stormcracker,' the Earl's voice broke, and he put his head in his hands. 'Ah, Gods! He was badly wounded, or they never would have been able to take him...'

'But – ' Root started eagerly forwards, desperate to give good news to the broken man.

Stop, Tangnost signalled with the palm of his hand before putting a finger to his lips for silence. Confused, the gnome obeyed.

The Earl suddenly staggered.

'My Lord!' Tangnost leapt forward from his seat as Quenelda grasped her father's elbow. 'My Lord,' he repeated with such tenderness and love that it made Quenelda weep. 'Take my seat.'

'Tangnost?' the broken voice husked. 'Is it truly you, old friend? After all this time?' Leaning on Tangnost's strong arm, Quenelda's father allowed himself to be seated. The dwarf then called forward a cup bearer to bring the Earl a drink to refresh his voice. After a moment to gather himself, the Earl continued.

'As I lay delirious, I was moved from clan stronghold to holdfast. Despite the winter storms, word of the battle had spread on the wings of winter ravens. None knew what had happened, only that the SDS had been defeated by the hobgoblins or the winter blizzards, so utterly defeated that no survivors returned.

But by then the Elder Council of the Inner Isles sent word to the Ice Isles, to the northernmost lands of the Ice Bears, and bade them come for me. Locked in by ice, they carried a ship over the White Wastes before they could put to sea!

Over the ice! The visitors exchanged awestruck looks! The seafaring clans murmured their wonder and admiration. This would make a saga!

'They carried a longship over the ice?' Root repeated softly... 'How can you do that?'

'Our bard has composed a saga: *The Dragon Lord and the Sea of Ice....*he will sing it for you,' the Chieftain's daughter said softly.

'Over one hundred leagues,' the Earl was saying, 'losing a half dozen men on the way to injury and frostbite.'

The Ice Bears amongst his audience nodded grimly. The Earl paused as the noise died down, lifting a hand to rub his ruined face.

'Rumours abounded. A search and rescue mission found the Ice Fortress had fallen with no survivors, only half eaten bodies. The starving hobgoblins feasted for many moons on the leavings of the battle. Reports said some survivors were found, but that they were quite mad. None understood what ailed them, and they all died. They call it the Black Death.

'Then the whispers began. Softly, insidiously they spread like cancer, sowing doubt and anger. Many took them up saying that Operation Crucible should never have been attempted; that we had destroyed the SDS in our folly. As the weeks wore on and no survivors were found, fear grew.

'The ice shelf crept south, bridging the Westering Isles to the Seven Kingdoms. Law and order began to break down on the margins of the kingdom. The Grand Master sent his army in and declared martial law, garrisoning all the Royal castles north of the Old Wall. Then, when Spring finally came, so did the hobgoblins; swarming in their millions as the ice bound rivers melted. The NightStalkers fell, and the Howling Glen was besieged.' The Earl paused to take a drink offered by Tangnost.

'Outlying strongholds in the west fell to them one by one, first in the north, and moving ever southwards. And so finally, the clans brought me here to safety, so close to home that none came to look.'

Tangnost nodded as the Elder Grandfather stood again.

'These islands are heavily fortified and defended, within range of Dragon Isle and the fortress being rebuilt on the Isle of Midges. The Hobgoblin Tribes would not dare come against us openly, at least not yet.'

There were murmurs of agreement and feet drummed on the floor.

'Then, gradually as the Bone Casters cared for me,' the Earl continued. 'About midsummer, my memories returned little by little, fragments, like pieces of a jigsaw puzzle. I remembered who I was, but little else. News came of the Army of the North and that all the lands north of the Old Wall, save the Howling Glen, are now held by the so called 'Lord Protector'.'

The Elder nodded. 'By then, the Lord Protector had secretly sent emissaries to us, offering us our sovereignty; to free us from the ancient dominion of the Sorcerer Lords.'

'We have yet more news, Elders, my Lord Earl,' Tangnost added urgently, standing so that all could hear him. 'That none other knows,' he glanced at Quenelda. 'The Lord Protector is building another a fortress to rival Dragon Isle, with an army of hobgoblins and other twisted creatures, men and dwarfs and those disaffected with Dragon Isle who seek power of their own as his minions. Your daughter saw through his illusion... On the Isle of Roarkinch, far to the north, hidden behind a nexus, he has built a black citadel that reaches to the sky, whose bowels are sunk deep in the pit of the Abyss.'

Tangnost hesitated, glancing warningly at Quenelda. They had not told Root this. Understanding, Quenelda laid a hand protectively on her esquire's shoulder and nodded.

'He has enslaved the weak, and those taken captive who had opposed him, for the citadel and brimstone mines.' He heard Root cry out. 'The gnomes, their warrens are wrecked and abandoned north of the Old Wall; an entire people have vanished. He has taken them.'

'Ah, Gods,' the Earl hung his head. 'This is bitter news!'

'He holds the Sorcerers Guild in the palm of his hand,' Tangnost added. 'The populace are in thrall to him, and now...now,' Tangnost hesitated, reluctant to cause the Earl more grief. 'He plans to marry the Queen at the turn of the year.'

The Earl gasped as if dealt a mortal blow, and hid his head in his hands. The Elders had not shared that with him, mindful of his fragile state. Now his greatest fears were coming true.

'But, Papa', Quenelda's eyes were bright, her voice eager. 'We are here now,' she gestured towards the hall. 'We've come to take you home. Home to...' she faltered. *Where is home?* She thought of Two Gulps and You're Gone... Home was a time now, no longer a place.

'Home to Dragon Isle,' she cradled his scarred hand to her chest. 'Where you can be treated by the scholars and battle surgeons who understand your injuries, who can find the ancient lore needed to heal you. We can stop the marriage! You are the Queen's Champion! We ca-'

'No,' the Earl shook his head. 'I cannot come with you.'

'No?' That single final word stunned Quenelda. She had never truly believed, even in her wildest dreams, that if she found him, her father would refuse to come home with them.

'No?' Her face crumpled as she searched his ravished face for a clue. 'But why? Why not, Papa?'

As I feared, Tangnost stepped forward to comfort her, but the Earl held out a clawed, burnt hand blindly, to find his daughter's. 'Goose, look at me.' His grip was so fierce it hurt. He pulled her close.

'What do you see? Truthfully?'

She stared at him, reluctant to speak, reluctant to put the changes she saw into words. It was true. He was like a once magnificent raptor, broken winged and shackled to the ground. She hung her head before lifting anguished eyes to Tangnost. She opened her mouth but could not find the words. 'But...' she said in a small voice. 'But who else can take back Dragonsdome, Papa, if not you? Resurrect the SDS?'

'I'm crippled and blind.' The Earl said it for her, his voice flat and strangely empty. 'It cannot be me.'

'But, Papa-'

'Hush, Goose, hush. I am wounded, and would be a danger to everyone near me. I cannot fight or wield my staff in anger. I could never fly a dragon again. I would be a burden, a danger to all around me. I could not live like that. Here I have a measure of peace. Quenelda,' he continued gently, 'I love you. You are precious to me,' his voice cracked, 'and...the Queen...but I cannot return home with you, crippled, burnt, an object of pity. Those who love me would eventually turn away from me. Tell me you understand?'

But Quenelda didn't want to. 'But, Papa!' she argued. 'Darcy is destroying Dragonsdome. He squanders gold on racing and banquets, and your stud is scattered and destroyed. The Lord Protector controls the Court and the Guild. The SDS stand alone against the Hobgoblins!

They need you. The Queen needs you,' her voice finally broke. 'I need you!' she wept.

'Ah, Goose!' The expression on her father's face changed as swiftly as clouds across the hillside on a windy day. Doubt, anger and indecision warred on his scarred face, but he shook his head again.

'You can!' she shouted at him. 'You can! Why don't you want to!?'

'Quenelda!?' he called out, as she hurtled past him out of the hall, but she was gone.

CHAPTER FORTY-TWO

Bonding

Searching in the dark, Tangnost found Quenelda and Root down on the rocky cliff overlooking the cove below. She was weeping silently and Root was at a loss how to comfort her. He looked helplessly at the dwarf as Tangnost laid his burning brand down on the damp ground.

'Quenelda,' Tangnost, too, was troubled as he sat down beside her on a moss-covered rock. 'I did try to warn you,' he took her cold hands in his, rubbing them. 'He is injured, both in body and mind. His old life has gone beyond his reach. Imagine a life without dragons, without flying. Your father was Commander of the SDS and Queen's champion. He was a great soldier. You cannot expect him to be the father you once knew.'

'And...' he thought about the Queen and the court. 'He was handsome, admired. Now he is a ruin of a man.'

'No! No!' Quenelda denied it angrily, shaking off his hands. 'It doesn't matter what he looks like!'

'It will! Men will pity him. Women will turn from him.'

But Quenelda shook her head furiously. 'No! No, they won't! I won't let them!'

'Think about it,' Tangnost spoke softly to calm her. 'It was for these very same reasons that you fled Dragonsdome. Would you have survived at Court?

Tangnost ventured hesitantly into unknown waters. 'Can you imagine yourself in bows and satin, in a world of ...ummn...' he floundered helplessly trying to think of ladylike pursuits.

'Fashion and accessorising...' Quenelda helped him out.

'And...'

'Dating etiquette and organising dinner parties...'

Tangnost tried to smother a grimace. *Who would be a nobleman's daughter?* Root, too, looked horrified, but that was Tangnost's point. 'Can you imagine yourself happy in a world like that? No dragons. No flying. No terrifying the living daylights out of hapless esquires?'

That produced a wry smile.

'I didn't think you could. Well, neither can your Lord father. His, too, is a world of dragons and flying, a creature of the air. He is a warrior, he can live no other way, just as you are not a -'

'Young lady...' Quenelda finished for him and nodded reluctantly, wiping her nose on the back of her hand. She was hearing the truth and she knew it. But how could she leave her father behind?

'Perhaps...perhaps we could stay here, too?' She offered tentatively '...forget about Dragonsdome...forget about the SDS...what is there to go back to? My family, you, Root, Papa, Two Gulps,' she sniffed.

'Perhaps,' she hesitantly explored the new idea in her mind. 'We could all stay here?'

'Perhaps,' Tangnost acknowledged, nodding. 'Go to bed, lass. Let's us all sleep on it. It's late, and everyone is highly emotional. No one can think clearly. Go to bed, and we'll discuss it in the morning.'

But Quenelda could not sleep. Aching and queasy, she slipped out of the roundhouse as the sky began to lighten. A shadow swept overhead, more felt than seen. The cliff shook as Stormcracker put down and crossed the crescent bay below. The battledragon had been out hunting.

You are in pain, Dancing with Dragons? His great head lifted up and snuffled around Quenelda caringly, nudging and blowing gently. He was puzzled.

But we have found Thunder Rolling over the Mountains....?

As she explained, she started weeping helplessly again.

Thunder Rolling over the Mountains will not return to our home roost with us? Stormcracker's distress mirrored her own. Steam erupted from his nostrils, making a dozen seagulls who had settled on the remains of his kill shy away with raucous shrieks of anger.

He is crippled. He is blind. And so he cannot fly. He cannot fight...

Is that the only reason?

Storm! Quenelda was astounded at the dragon's hard heartedness.

I was crippled. I could barely fly. I could not flame.

You cared for me and now I am myself again...

No one can cure blindness...

No, the dragon conceded. *We can do many things together, but not that. But you, Dancing with Dragons, you are of One Kind. You have the magic of all Dragon Kind and the Dragon Lords running in your veins. You and I, together we can give him his sight...*

Quenelda looked baffled. 'But he is blind!' she protested out loud as Tangnost arrived. He raised his brows questioningly at her.

'He is saying I can give Papa his sight back.'

You have the power to help him see. When we bond we become one, do we not? When you dream you can see through my eyes, feel the beat of my hearts. He is of your blood, and bound to me by love and loyalty as I am to him. He raised me from the day I was first fledged. You can bind him to me as you are bound, if it is my wish....

Quenelda's hearts were galloping, her mind racing. Was it true? Could she help her father bond with Stormcracker? If she could, the possibilities were endless.

'What?' Tangnost saw the hope kindle in Quenelda's eyes.

'Storm thinks that somehow we - I, can help Papa see...' she bit her lip. 'Do - do you think...do you think he would come home if he could see again?'

'Let's find out, lass.' Tangnost was already on his feet and striding towards the Moot Hall.

But I don't know how...

You do, Dancing with Dragons. Look within yourself and ignore the counsel of others. The memories are there. The knowledge of Dragon Kind lies there. The power lies there. Bring him to me...

But it was a long agonising wait for Quenelda. It was the hour of the irritated bumblebee before her father rose, and by then she was waiting impatiently at the door of his chamber.

'Quenelda?' He sensed her before he saw her, not needing to see the aura that flickered about her, to hear her impatient tread. 'Sweetheart, I-' He did not know what he was going to say, but whatever it was, he was never given the chance.

'Papa,' Quenelda interrupted, hope and fear in her voice. 'I have something to show you. Please, Papa.'

'Now?' he almost smiled.

'Yes! Now!' She took her father's twisted hand and, biting down his pride, the Earl allowed his daughter, who had crossed half the Kingdom to find him, to lead him down the path that curled around the cove and down to the shore.

The tide was out. With his acute sense of hearing, born on the back of blindness, the Earl could hear the soft roll of the waves and the call of the sandpipers as they fed. Barnacle- and limpet-encrusted rocks crunched beneath their feet and fat seaweed popped. They stopped. The sun was beating down. To the west, gannet dragons were headed out to sea to hunt, the whisper of their flight faintly audible on the wind.

On the shoreline Quester and Root watched with bated breath. As word sped round the gathering, they were soon joined by Drumondir, and then dozens and scores and hundreds, so it seemed like the entire gathering had turned up to watch the Earl's reunion with his battledragon.

Something shifted in front of the Earl, its vast bulk moving the air. Sand squelched and sucked, reluctant to part with its heavy load. Quenelda's father felt the whisper of warm breath on his cheek, soft as a kiss; smelt the heady breath of brimstone, the tang of scale oil and wax. The Earl suddenly tensed. For a heartbeat the world held its breath about him. Then he held out a withered hand as tears ran down his ruined face.

'Stormcracker, old friend,' the Dragon Lord said simply, as the great spurred tail curled tenderly around him, and raised the weeping man up onto the battledragon's back.

'But how?' he shook his head, bewildered. 'How can this be?'

The Earl sat on his battledragon, where he never thought to sit again. Emotions overwhelmed him as he reached out to touch the fearsome snout that now nudged him gently, the tip of his dragon's forked tongue tasting the salt of his tears.

For a full minute after Stormcracker lifted her up

beside her father, all Quenelda could hear was the desperate sound of her own body panicking, until the big dragon turned his reptilian head and regarded her with his grave eyes.

Be still, Dancing with Dragons, he gently counselled her. *Just reach within yourself for what you want. Seek to make Thunder Rolling over the Mountains one with us and it will be so... Reach out to him......you have the power...we have the power...I will lend mine to yours...and maybe in time...bonded with me, he will find his own again....as the Dragon Lords of old did...*

Obeying, Quenelda reached out for her father's left hand so that the scales on her palm lay against his skin. 'Papa,' she swallowed, glancing nervously at Tangnost as he climbed up beside her father to stand at his shoulder. 'Storm and I are going to try something.' She took a deep breath. 'We are going to try to bond you and Storm, so that you can see again.'

Her father gasped then went rigid. His hand tightened in hers, but he said nothing. Her other hand rested on Stormcracker's pebbled, armoured hide. She closed her eyes and emptied her mind, let her fear and worries drain from her. She let the frantic galloping of her hearts slow to the dragon's deeper beat. Let the knowledge of dragonkind flow from her inner dragon self into her conscious mind.

Suddenly, she became the dragon of her dreams.... sheathed in midnight scales...power flowed through her from tail to talon...

Boom...boom...boom, boom......boom, boom......

She heard the indrawn hiss of Tangnost's breath...

Memories came to her as the sun beat down, spells and words of power surged through her mind like a rip tide, and down tingling into her fingertips, into her talons. Elder magic, the most ancient of all... She whispered a word that only Stormcracker understood. A word of *making*, a word of *mending*...a word of *bonding*...

The sea wind from the east was cool on the Earl's red-raw face and hands. He tasted the bitterness of kelp on his tongue. The scales on his daughter's hand were cool and hard to the touch, yet flexed and trembled. The Earl puzzled over what it might be. They pulsed against his skin with a deep, slow rhythm that tingled through his arm. The Earl held himself still and tried not to hope, to dare to hope, to believe that his daughter held such a gift within her power. She *was* changed. *Power attracts power...* she had the aura of a Mage... and something else....

The Earl had spent his life amongst dragons, and he could sense a quality of *otherness* about her, a presence that radiated from her, that he could sense without his sight but with the sixth sense of a Dragon Lord. His fingers tingled with the tension. Then, barely, with his shattered senses, he became aware of a disturbance, a ripple in the magical field that surrounded her.

Quenelda slipped effortlessly into her inner dragon skin.

Tangnost drew in a ragged breath. What was happening? Briefly, her outline shimmered, grew larger, the outline of a dragon. Her sulphurous eyes glowed bright, reflecting another world. There was the faintest touch of black above her brows as if tiny scales again became visible beneath her skin. Scales swept up her left arm, sheathing it entirely in black. Her fingernails grew and hardened into talons, and then the outline faded leaving only the gold of her eyes.

'Reach for him, Papa,' she encouraged her father with wonder, knowing for the first time that she was the teacher and he the pupil. 'Reach for Storm's thoughts and then you will be able to share them.'

And so the Earl obeyed, reaching blindly beyond his dark world with his mind; leaning forward to touch the battledragon's pebbled armour, feeling its warmth rise beneath his twisted hand. The tingling grew stronger. The beating of the dragon's two hearts grew louder and louder, overlaying the rhythm of his own. He could hear the great puffs of breath as the dragon filled the huge bellows of his lungs with air. In...out. In...out. Without realising it his own chest began to rise and fall to the same rhythm.

Then the strange tingling spread and began to wash over him like a hot bath and a faint whisper sang to him. He listened to the strange melody, tilting his head to one side. He felt a voice in his head rather than heard it.

And then he understood!

Welcome, Thunder Rolling over the Mountains, the

dragon's thoughts sang through his mind. *Open your mind to me... ...*

He understood!

Now he knew the true wonder of Dragon Whispering. But how could this be? How could his daughter make him understand too? Then power poured through him, surging like a rip-tide, bringing warmth and a sense of security. The ache of his wounds faded, and he felt his muscles relax as the dragon's strength filled him. Stormcracker gently broke into his thoughts.

Thunder Rolling over the Mountains...?

Thunder Rolling over the Mountains...? He echoed...

*So we have named you...*the dragon affirmed. *Now bond with me...*

With a sudden jolt, the Earl felt a massive punch of adrenaline flow through his veins, as the dragon's mind and his began to merge together, infusing his crippled body with hot energy and new life. His sense of self faded away... Then new sensations and strange reptilian thoughts tumbled wildly through his mind and body, dulling his pain, clearing his mind, and washing away the lonely bitterness of exile.

With sudden wonder, the Earl felt the sun on the dragon's scales as if they were his scales, the slap of the tide against his taloned claws, the vast power and strength that were his to command. But more than that, he could see through his dragon's eyes; see the blue sea stretching to the horizon; see the cloudless arc of the sky; see his daughter turned in her saddle, watching him with the sulphurous eyes of her birth day, and a slight iridescent sheen on her brow, anxiety evident in every tense bone in her body; and behind her Tangnost, watching intently, a broad rare smile breaking his weathered face. He raised his fist against the chest in salute to his Commander.

The Earl held out a trembling hand to take his daughter's and a second to Tangnost, and smiled at the tears that poured down their faces as the three linked. His daughter was moon pale and thin, her cheekbones and brow more prominent in her pinched face, but it was not that that drew a gasp from him. As an ArchMage he could see on the magical plane, and clear as daylight a light hung about her, and it had the aspect of a dragon.

He felt his mind soaring, up and up...He raised a fist to the watchers below who cheered, a soft sound that grew into a groundswell that swept about the beach as swords were rattled on shields.

Then it was all too much. His heart started to race, his breath sawing in his chest as if he had fought a battle. Black spots danced in front of his eyes and exhaustion overwhelmed him. His heart hiccupped. He cried out as he saw his own body fall.

*I am breaking the bond...*Stormcracker whispered in his mind, in Quenelda's mind, and then the dragon was gone. With a violent jolt the Earl was back in his own racked body, and then he lost consciousness. Quenelda watched as her father's gleaming copper eyes dulled to a milky blue hue. He groaned as he slumped forward in his saddle.

'Papa!'

Tangnost was already at his Earl's side, easily holding the fragile man in his arms. 'He's weak, Quenelda, that's all. His body and mind are badly damaged. He'll need rest.'

His body and mind are injured, Dancing with Dragons, the great dragon confirmed. *He is not damaged by the bond…trust me in this…it requires great strength and Thunder Rolling over the Mountains is weak. We will not, we must not attempt this again until he is strong again…*

And Quenelda knew the truth of it, for she had dipped into raw magic. If they were not careful, the power of such sorcery would tear his frail body apart. Her father had to gain his strength so that he could control the bond, or the raw power could consume him.

CHAPTER FORTY-THREE

Wings of Vengeance!

The fire in the great Moot Hall flickered red on the circle of dwarfish faces, painting dancing shadows on the carved timber walls. It was a War Council. The Elders and Chieftains of the Ptarmigan, White Fox, Narwhale, the Sea Otter, Ice Bear, Fat Seal and dozens of others were gathered together to decide the future of their clans. Their votes were cast.

Tangnost stood, Lord of the Isles, along with the Elder Council; his strong face as intent as his voice, carrying to the far reaches.

'The Fourth Kingdom *will* go to war. We will not forsake the old alliances made by our forefathers. The Fourth Kingdom will answer the SDS call to arms!'

Quenelda's face shone as she stood by her father.

She has done it! Root thought with pride. *She is at her father's side!* Then with a pang he closed his eyes. *Oh, Pa! How I wish you were here to guide me, and the Earl! To take us home...*

'Choose runners from amongst your young,' Tangnost was saying. 'Your best hunters, who can move unseen through the forests and glens. Send secret word to the Clans, we will give you tokens of good faith. New longboats must be built, new weapons forged and tempered in battle. The very old must teach the very young.'

Late into the night, they laid their plans.

'Soon we fly to Dragon Isle,' the Earl leant forward in his eagerness. 'It is not yet time to fight. I must regain my strength first. I must learn to fly with Stormcracker, to become one with my battledragon as the Dragon Lords of old did. Then I will have my revenge!' He clasped fist to chest in the salute of the SDS.

'Wings of Vengeance!'

'Wings of Vengeance!' The SDS battle cry was raised.

The dwarfs thumped axes on shields, eager for the fight that was to come. Horns of ale and grog were thrown down throats.

'Go on, lads,' Magnus said. 'Get it down you....you cannot fight if you do not know how to drink grog!'

'Tastes like the bottom of a swamp,' Root pulled a face.

'I'll stick to cider,' Quenelda decided.

'I like it,' Quester declared. He was beginning to look and sound like his old self, Root thought, though his friend still had the odd headache.

'And we will be at your side, my Lord Earl,' the Elder Council stood and raised their drinking horns as the Earl raised his daughter's right hand, just as he had at the Cauldron.

'DeWinter! DeWinter!' Taking and raising Quenelda's left hand in his, Tangnost raised the Earl's battle cry to the rafters.

The Earl raised a hand to greet his daughter standing on the rocks watching, fierce delight on his injured face. Both man and dragon, wounded, crippled, their joy at their reunion was a palpable thing that brought delight to everyone who saw it. Bonding with Stormcracker had both rejuvenated and exhausted him; yet the growing power evident in his voice and bearing gave them all hope that his power may return, too.

CHAPTER FORTY-FOUR

Dragon's Bane

'What's wrong with him?' Tangnost asked, as the Bone Caster Mage felt the Earl's cold clammy forehead with the back of his hand.

'I had feared this,' Loki sighed, glancing at Drumondir who was examining the inert Earl. 'But I could not be sure.' Turning, Loki lifted the small cauldron that hung beside the fireplace in the Earl's chamber, and held it out. Tangnost leaned forwards curiously as Drumondir dipped a finger in and tasted it. She shook her head.

'A dried herb?' Tangnost guessed.

'Yes,' Drumondir nodded. 'But not one I am familiar with.'

'Then, come,' Falfir motioned them. 'I will show you. We have been treating him with a herb, and were not certain how much it helped; but I fear now it was more than we guessed. And the more he bonded with his battledragon, the more he has consumed.'

The Mage's dwelling was empty, but inlaid in the floor were steps spiralling down into the rock of the island. A scented brazier smoked nearby. Picking up a resin torch, Loki dipped it in. Holding the burning brand aloft, the trio descended down.

'When the Earl came into our care,' Loki explained. 'I searched our scrolls for any wisdom they might hold. The collective wisdom of my forbears lies here.'

The cave they came to was reached through a long tunnel. Braziers burnt in alcoves to either side. Skins hung across the entrance, tied back with thongs. Runes were burnt into them and chiselled about the entrance into the stone. They glowed faintly, flaring as the Bone Casters approached.

Loki lit a shuttered lamp, and placed it on the single stone table in the centre. Tangnost let his eyes adjust to the gloom.

The vast cave was shaped and honeycombed like a dovecote, only no birds nestled here in the nooks, but scrolls, books, and, Tangnost saw when he turned, seeds, ground powder, oils, inks and paints...

'The First Cave,' Drumondir nodded. 'A privilege I have long waited for.'

Loki nodded. 'My ancestors and those of other clan Bone Casters carved this out of the living rock,' he explained to Tangnost. 'Normally only I set foot in here, but now is not the time to be shackled by tradition or secrecy. Now...' He lifted a scroll and carefully weighted it down on the table.

'It took me many moons to find this.' The waxed hide was stained dark with use, and dotted with oily spots. Cracked around its edges, the scroll was faded in patches. Tangnost peered at the complex runes and glyphs written there and frowned. Its meaning was beyond him.

'This is the record of my people from the time of the Mage Wars,' the Bone Caster explained, finger tracing his translation. 'When my family served with the Sorcerer Lords in the Air Citadel, long since lost.'

'It says, back then, that the Sorcerer Lords fled from the hobgoblin banners who filled the seas and overran the land, so that they had to retreat to the Air Citadel, the city in the sky. There they first wielded Maelstrom magic so that they may cleanse the land of all hobgoblins. Their healers also studied chaotic magic, and learnt how to weave wards and spells to protect their men and dragons.'

'I have also heard such a tale,' Drumondir added. 'But all such lore was destroyed by the Dragon Lords, lest it destroyed them first. Now there are none who know how to wield it who still live.'

'Save one,' Tangnost said darkly. '*He* has unlocked the secrets of chaotic magic...now we must do the same, or we are lost.'

Loki drew his finger adorned with carved bone rings down, passing over a stained portion.

'It is hard to read, the runes are faint, and their meaning unclear, but it refers to a 'weed that helps those afflicted' by what we now call the Black Death.'

'There is no such lore in the land of the Ice Bear,' Drumondir admitted. 'Few herbs survive the cold.'

'A weed?' Tangnost was astounded. 'I've never heard of such a thing!'

'Nor I, but I searched our store of herbs, and tried all that we had.' He mounted the steps that coiled up and up. 'And here,' he indicated an empty nook, 'We found one that helped. We steeped the leaf to make an infusion like tea. We gave it to him as he lay delirious...and it calmed him, and killed the fever....but as he gained strength, so our store dwindled. This,' he lifted a pouch, 'is all that remains. Seven days ago I began to make the infusion weaker, hoping that he was healed now, that his bond with his battledragon would mean he would no longer need it...'

The meaning of his words finally sank in. Tangnost's eye widened in horror. 'You are saying you have no more of this herb?'

Loki shook his head. 'Yes. But I think I have identified it. I found this volume. Its cover had been cut away, and the bindings are worn and brittle. Here,' he turned the crumbling pages to show Tangnost and Drumondir a faded drawing of a bush, with detailed renditions of the leaves and flower, and a withered stem pressed between its leaves. 'It is described as a sea plant only found on the shoreline. It is said to grow like a weed on the sandy dunes....but there is none to be found on our islands. We have searched.'

'But there is more,' the Bone Caster Mage turned several pages. 'It was 'used with caution' it reads,' Loki ran his finger lightly over the complex runes... 'Then this part is lost, and here it reads 'sends dragons mad,' then again the words are not clear.'

He looked up at Tangnost's intent face and shook his head. 'I do not know what that means, but it is clearly a warning. We have had no dragons here save yours, so it has not mattered.'

'So if we do not find it, the Earl may die?'

Drumondir shook her head. 'We do not know that, Bearhugger. His power is returning. The bond with his dragon grows stronger by the day.'

Tangnost looked doubtful. 'Yet his body is growing weaker. But if we *do* find the weed, it might endanger our dragons, may endanger Stormcracker. And without his battledragon-'

'He is blind once more,' Loki finished for him. 'And I think his spirit would break.'

Tangnost sighed. 'Then we must use it with caution till we understand the meaning of the warning. Perhaps the scholars of the Academy will make sense of it. Root is skilled at foraging; his people may know the plant. We must find it, else the Earl may die before we reach the sanctuary of the Sorcerers Glen, and all this will be for nothing.'

Loki nodded. He covered the book in a soft hide and then gave it to Drumondir who bowed gravely. 'I will treasure it, First Bone Caster, and return it into your keeping in better times.'

'Root!'

'Sir?' Quenelda's esquire ran over from packing equipment for their departure. 'This plant,' the Dragon

Master explained as Drumondir showed the esquire the page. 'Do you recognise it?' They watched anxiously as the youth studied the drawings intently.

'Here is the dried leaf,' the Bone Caster gave him the delicate stem with its pressed leaves to examine.

But Root shook his head. 'N-no, there is nothing like it in our lands to the south. Is it important?'

'We think so, boy,' Drumondir answered. 'We believe it helps those touched by the Maelstrom.'

'Memorise it, Root, and keep the dried plant to help you.' Tangnost turned to where his other esquire was loading the last of their food supplies.

'Quester, prepare three eagles immediately for the Howling Glen, the Smoking Fort and Dragon Isle. And three winter ravens.'

'Sir?'

'One eagle and one raven for each. Just in case one doesn't make it through, the other surely will. Our enemies will be watching for couriers and carrier birds. I would if I were them. Tell them we have the Earl and are making for the Howling Glen with all haste. We need an SDS escort.'

'Sir, yes, Sir!' Two coded glyphs that would mean nothing to anyone but the SDS.

CHAPTER FORTY-FIVE

The Dark Citadel

High in his Dark Citadel, the Lord Protector, renegade Dragon Lord and WarLock, watched as his Dragon Master, Knuckle Quarnack, and his followers, the Knucklebones, put down on a dragon pad. His mood was as dark as the thunderheads above. He was overdue at the Howling Glen, although the treacherous weather could be blamed. The Guild were becoming ever more fractious at the taxes levied, and the deployment of troops around the Kingdom. They still had to deal with the hordes of refugees and the starving, clogging the streets and harbours of the Black Isle.

And, he held out his shaking hand, he was burning up inside. The elixir was no longer enough. He would need to take more drastic action. Or perhaps not yet. Perhaps this might be the good news he had been waiting for.

The Knucklebones had been in a fight; that much was evident from the wounded being helped onto the gantries, and the injured dragons on the sinking dragon pads. They would be killed, he had dragons and plenty to spare. There were no seriously injured men of course, they would have been killed, too, the price for failure.

None would live to betray him, were they captured by the SDS.

Dragon spurs and armoured boots sounded on the stone steps.

'My Lord,' Knuckle went down on one knee, not without a hiss of pain. His head was crudely bandaged, and he had a new scar across a face already cross hatched. The Dragon Master's armour was rusty and cracked, and his heavy cloak dripped onto the black flagstones. He had hoped for the warmth of a fire, but the chamber was so cold that tendrils of ice painted a delicate tracery across the black stone.

He said nothing, waiting, heart hammering. How much did his master already know? Finally he felt forced to speak.

'My Lord, if the Earl lives, we are closing in on him.'

Eyes flared green then died back. *So...he is alive...* 'And Bearhugger and the daughter?' His voice was cold. 'Do they yet live?'

'We nearly captured them in the lands of the White Foxes, my Lord, heading for the Ice Isles. The clan betrayed Bearhugger for gold and food, but failed to stop them escaping before we arrived. They paid for that carelessness and will not fail you again.

They fled into a storm on their Imperial and we thought they may have died for they did not make landfall. But then a raven came, bearing a message that the Earl was in the lands of the Ice Bear; that Bearhugger knew where to find them. So we set out in pursuit once again.

A second message came, saying where to find them in the wilderness. We could find no token, but we followed their trail into the White Wastes where their armoured bears ambushed us. We managed to break free, but we lost track of the Imperial. It was not there. We fought free, but I lost nigh on fifty men, torn apart by those bears of theirs. A blizzard came and we could not fly, and their bears came at us time and time again.'

Knuckle hesitated to spell out the depth of his failure.

'There have been no more messages, my Lord. They vanished into thin air.'

'So...' the Lord Protector mused. 'Either the boy is dead... or they have unmasked him, and know we are hunting them.' He shook his head. 'They would not have the skill to discover him. So, then, they are alive and you have lost them?'

'No! My Lord, no! Bring her in!'

His men dragged in a struggling figure swathed in bloodied white furs and threw it on the floor. Weighted about with chains, she still struggled as the Lord Protector dragged her by her hair into the light....

A young girl, bloodied and beaten, spat in his face. He lifted the milky tooth worn on a thong of leather and pulled her close. 'So...you know where they are? You will tell me before the day is done. Take her!' He tore the amulet from her neck.

CHAPTER FORTY-SIX

The Earl's Esquire

The moment the weather cleared they had flown, a strong south-easterly wind chasing them all the way. They made a hundred leagues in two days. Their plan was to put down after dusk for a short rest, before flying throughout the night due south-east over the Mull of Chriachdubh, making landfall early the next morning on the tiny Athol of Rumtollin, hopefully avoiding the chain of watchtowers that ringed the rugged coastline. From there they would fly over the sea until they came to Loch Etive, leading inland to the Octarine Pass over the Shard Mountains. That would lead them further inland to the Howling Glen fortress, and beyond that to the Old Wall and safety.

Early dawn on the third day revealed a steady stream of dragons that had been trapped like Stormcracker by the weather. They were rising up and heading for the mainland, migrating south for the winter. Some would over-winter in the Sorcerers Glen. Dozens of galleons and longships were also heading south east, bearing the last precious cargoes of seal fur, whale oil, wool and wood before the sea lanes closed for good for the winter, trapping any remaining boats for four or five moons in the inhospitable north.

Passing into the Earl's tented quarters stretched between Stormcracker's spinal plates, Quester, followed by Tangnost, crossed to the pallet and the figure that sat there. The night before, Drumondir had given the Earl the last precious preparation of Dragon's Leaf. Some of the Dragon Lord's strength had returned, and he was preparing to rise, although it seemed to Tangnost that the familiar motion of flight and the keen air had also revived him.

'My Lord Earl?' Quester knelt beside the bed, though the blind man could not see.

'Quester de Northwood, my Lord Earl,' Tangnost said.

'Quester? You are Gortrod's youngest?'

'Yes, my Lord. I ...my Lord, I wish to offer you my fealty. My Lord, let me be your esquire. Tangnost has taught me well.'

The Earl reached out a hand to touch the youth's face, running his hand over it as if to remember the contours. 'I am not an easy master. I-'

'My Lord,' Quester swallowed, his hand rubbing his brow. 'The...the Maelstrom has touched me also. I, too, am tainted...'

Tangnost had told him, and the Earl could sense the same anger and pain, the same determination that burned in his own heart.

'Swear then, boy.'

And so Quester knelt and offered his sword, witnessed by Tangnost and Drumondir. 'I swear to be your right hand, Lord, by night and day, in winter and summer, in war and in peace, I will shield you from all enemies...' he faltered, not remembering the right words. 'With my life...' He glanced up at Tangnost who nodded.

'That was well done, boy. Well done!' The Dragon Master squeezed the youth's shoulder as he stood. 'Your first task is to dress him after the fashion of the clans.' Tangnost indicated the equipment that lay in an open chest.

'Now,' the dwarf sorted through the pile, choosing dark and worn clothes, and a light chain mail. 'Make sure he is well protected, but hard to identify from those around him.' *Lest we are attacked*, he did not say.

'My Lord?'

Quester carefully lifted a soft under-tunic over the Earl's raised arms, trying to ignore the burnt skin, rough as bark beneath his fingers. Next the esquire pulled on and laced a pair of soft breeches, padded at knee and thigh, followed by a quilted eiderdown under-tunic, settling it comfortably on the Earl's broad shoulders. A light hauberk of ring mail followed, split at both hips.

'Here, lad,' Tangnost unfolded a cloth to reveal a thick belt clasped with the wolf's head sigil of the deWinters; and a sword. *And what a sword!* Quester thought, as he unsheathed a hand-span of its length.

It was forged of folded steel, rippling like the blue scales of a fish, redolent with a magic of its own. Long but light, its black handle was carved from an Imperial's jaw bone. Tangnost held it out to Quester, letting the esquire present it, hilt first, to the Earl.

'Your father's sword, my Lord Earl,' Tangnost revealed. 'From your quarters in Dragonsdome. I took it when we fled to Dragon Isle.'

The gnarled and twisted hands settled around the hilt and slowly drew the sword from the scabbard. A weapon, Tangnost thought with sorrow, for a Battlemage who had lost his power. For still, although he laid his hand on his witchwood pilot's chair, the Earl could not yet bring the runes to life.

'Here boy,' the Earl held his reversed blade out. 'If you are to be my esquire, if you are to be my Sword, then you need a weapon to defend me with. This is *jaw breaker,* ancient blade of my ancestors. Unsheath it only in anger, and earn honour with it.'

'My-my Lord Earl,' Quester was stunned. 'I-I don't deserve such an honour, I have not earned it...'

'You have. You have been touched as I have and have fought bravely. It should have gone to my son, but...' the Earl's face creased with pain. 'I have no son. You *will* earn my trust, boy. Take it!'

Smiling, Tangnost nodded. And so Quester took the beautiful blade and buckled it about his brigandine. His eyes were shining and there was a bounce to his step.

He is healing... Tangnost thought, slapping the boy on

the back in congratulation. *The Earl has given him his life back.*

And so Quester armoured and dressed the Earl after the fashion of dwarfs, so that if they were in a battle, he would be hard to spy. Boots of seal-skin bound with thongs, and a seal-fur lined, hooded cloak completed his disguise. A small shield, the clans called a targe, was slung on his back. A dirk was strapped to his right leg and another scabbarded at his hip. A half-visored helm, with nose and cheek-guards, completed his disguise

CHAPTER FORTY-SEVEN

Wedding Cake

Hammers rang throughout the Great Hall. Dragonsdome was being decked out for Darcy's wedding which was to open the festive season, and his bride to be, Armelia, was in a fluster. The Queen's own wedding was now to take place at the beginning of the Year of the Lesser-Spotted Burrowing Cat, in barely three weeks' time, and not in the spring. Two weddings, and Armelia was to be the bride in one and the bridesmaid in the second!

In all the excitement, they had somehow overlooked a second dress: to look splendid but not, of course, as splendid as the Queen's dress! And so Dragonsdome had been invaded by an army of Foresight and Hindsight's best seamstresses, By Royal Appointment, to remedy the oversight.

Below stairs, carts of fir and holly and scented candles arrived from the Guild, barrels of honey mead and oat beer, smoked meats and cheeses from the mongers and butchers and brewers had been arriving for weeks to be stored in the great slate-lined larders and cellars. Gifts, too, were being laid beneath the huge fir tree in the Dragon Hall, ready for the festivities. Other gifts were brought in a steady stream to Armelia's chambers;

wedding gifts from the Earldom's bannermen and lords.

The harbours were forests of galleons and clippers, disembarking dragons and men-at-arms. A steel serpent of shining plate and mail coloured by surcoats, with shields and silk flags, wound its way up from the docks to the castle, and to the city palaces of the realm's greatest lords. Others made their way across the two great causeways that joined the Black Isle to the Sorcerers Glen and Crannock Castle.

Darcy's lords and bannermen had claimed most of Dragonsdome's huge palace, and the roosts and paddocks were packed with every breed of dragon imaginable. But an even rarer sight were the highborn lords and nobles from all Seven Kingdoms

Highborn Sorcerers and their vast retinues had claimed every room in the royal palace on Black Isle and Crannock Castle; the Elves had struck their city of coloured tents amongst the woods on the lower slopes of the Five Wizards. The trolls, coming from the south, chose to stay in their yurts further to the south where it was not so cold. Few dwarfs from the north had made it; the passes were already blocked by snow and the seas treacherous. Of the gnomes, no one knew what had happened to them, they had vanished. The giants and gremlins of the Sixth and Seventh Kingdoms had not been seen in centuries, and many believed they had never existed, save in stories.

Darcy was being fitted for the ceremonial armour he

would wear for both weddings. He had refused to wear the beautifully crafted armour passed from generation to generation of DeWinters that now lay unused in the armoury. He wanted something more dazzling and glamorous. And anyway, as he told his fiancée, it was far too heavy and old fashioned.

'Careful, damn you!' Darcy swore as his new gold-chased breastplate and back plates were buckled by nervous body servants, whilst their Master goldsmith and silversmith made appropriate noises of appreciation at their own work.

'My Lord Earl, I am lost for words,' Guild Master Woodfellow admitted, truthfully for once, wringing his hands, brows knitted like a badger's. 'One of the most exquisite pieces ever tooled by our craftsmen, if I may say so. Only Her Royal Highness has such plate.' *And one of the most expensive*, he thought gleefully.

'Helmet!' Darcy snapped as his valet trod on his unbooted toe. 'It's rather heavy...' He was not used to bearing the weight of battlefield armour.

'My Lord Earl!' Woodfellow protested. 'It is has been beaten feather light by our silversmiths. But the gold inlay you wanted is as heavy as it is-'

'Expensive...' Darcy finished for him, allowing his servants to place the magnificent helmet on his head, with its stunning golden unicorn tail that hung to his shoulders.

'Precious, your grace, I was going to say precious. The hobgoblins...' Woodfellow wrung his hands in anguish. 'Many of our gold mines lie beyond the Wall...'

'Hmmnnn,' Darcy regarded himself critically in the huge mirror that nearly took up one wall of his bedchamber and nodded. He turned to the huge mirror in his ante-chamber to admire the soft doeskin breeches that were so tight he had had to lie down to get them on, and the thigh-high polished black boots stitched with juvenile scales.

Woodfellow quietly let out a sigh of relief. It was almost impossible to please this brash, ill mannered young Earl whose only redeeming quality was that he had a seemingly bottomless supply of gold.

Armelia was now down in the kitchens supervising the baking of the wedding cake, currently wrestling with an enormous bowl of flour, eggs and candied fruit that was to be the centre point of the feast. Thankfully, thought the Upper Cook, Agnes Dimpleweed, the girl's wretched mother, recently made a Dame by the Queen, was 'quite exhausted,' and had taken to her bed with a migraine. Souflia's repeated interference was causing mayhem below stairs, so that everyone heartily wished she would take herself above stairs where, thankfully, she belonged.

'Thirteen layers,' Darcy had told his betrothed. 'One for each year of your sweet life, sugar plum!'

Behind her, Armelia hadn't seen Rupert's eyes cross, or Simon pretending to throw up. She only had eyes for Darcy, soon to be Master of the Unicorn, an ancient title to be bestowed upon him on his wedding day by the

Queen. Why, he would be the youngest in living memory! What some of the battle-hardened veterans from the 7th and 9th Armoured Brigades who made up its ranks thought, no one had dared to ask.

Dragonsdome's bells rang out the hour of the howling wolf. Agnes was exhausted, her nerves utterly wrung dry, as she commanded an army of under-cooks, maids and servants and scullions still at work in the labyrinth of kitchens, pantries, sculleries and cellars below stairs. The Queen and the Lord Protector himself were to attend the wedding feast, and the young Earl had spared no expense. A thirty-five course dinner to rival that of the Royal Wedding had been ordered, along with some particular dishes favoured by the Lady Armelia, soon to be Duchess of Dragonsdome!

She clapped her hands. 'Time for bed!'

After all, the scullery maids had to be up in barely four hours to set and light Dragonsdome's two hundred fires, and she herself had to rise at the hour of the yawning dormouse to prepare breakfast for one hundred and thirty two lords and ladies, never mind the army of servants below stairs who attended them!

'Come on, Darcy!' Rupert drawled as he pushed away his trencher and threw a bone to the hounds. 'Only a few nights of freedom left! Time to sample the taverns. The night is young...' The groom to be, stood and stretched and nodded. Not that he intended to change his ways once he was married!

There was great excitement out on the cobbled streets of the Black Isle. Already packed to bursting with refugees, the populace of the city had grown fourfold as those from near and far flocked to see the two weddings. Only three days remained until the first of them.

CHAPTER FORTY-EIGHT

Come Maelstrom Black

The Lord Protector's eyes glittered dangerously as he left the dungeons deep below his Night Citadel, and the chained wreckage that had once been an Ice Bear warrior. The young woman had shown surprising courage, but it had not helped her in the end. So... the Earl was hidden somewhere in the Inner Isles and Bearhugger had flown to find them. He had been so close all this time!

Well if he were there, where then would they hide him? In one of their strongholds? No...Confident their secret would not be betrayed, they would hide him in plain view. It must be Inversnekkie, where the Elders dwelt. And their Bone Caster Mage! Yes!

Royal couriers, his men now, had been there only a week ago, bearing the Royal Standard and summons to the Queen's wedding. They had reported a Clan Gathering, some sixty strong. Warmly welcomed by the Council, the Elders had promised their Chiefs and nobles would set sail to attend with all haste. Yet none had arrived... the Earl must be with them!

Stepping from a porting stone, he moved swiftly to the Impenetrable Tower high above Roarkinch to consider the great map of the Seven Kingdoms that he had stolen from the Guild's Library. The fools had not known what a treasure lay discarded in its depths. This map was old, *very* old, and marked places of power...like this island. It had taken him some time to discover its secrets, but it was worth the effort, for now he had the power of the Maelstrom at his command.

The Earl's Imperial was indeed crippled, injured further by an accident in the lands of the Ice Bears that had also injured Bearhugger himself. That meant, even had they already flown, that they must be somewhere in the Inner Straits heading for the Octarine Pass through the Shard Mountains and then the safety of the Howling Glen.

Time to destroy the Earl and his companions once and for all! They were no match for his power; and he would break them, and destroy those stubborn dwarf clans of the north who had been a thorn in his side for too long. A Maelstrom would destroy them, he thought with grim satisfaction; else smash them against the Shards. He stepped back to the porting stone.

In a heartbeat, the Lord Protector was back down in the frozen black bowels of Roarkinch, that monstrous freezing hollow where no other living creature could survive. Crossing an ice glazed span hanging above the unguessable depths of the Abyss, he stretched out his arms, palm up. Green spirals formed in the depths of the pit below, slowly swirling and braiding about him like a cocoon, drawing up chaotic magic from below to sheath him in green spun darkness.

Threads leaked outwards like black ink in water. This was dangerous magic, he must be careful to contain it. The Lord Protector raised his arms higher. Spinning, the Maelstrom grew in size spiralling upwards, with the WarLock at its centre. Higher and higher it reached into the sky, a vast spinning nexus of power. Vast it became; the wind shrieking about the Night Citadel. Green lightning flashed and struck. Around him, the island shuddered to its stony bones.

The Protector's voice cracked with the corrosive magic of the spell.

Come Maelstrom black
And let them all take flight
Make them ride the gale
Beneath your endless night
Come ice and hail
Earth and stones
Fire boil their blood
Stone break their bones
Crush wing and talon
Tail and snout
Teach them fear
And bring them doubt

Come Maelstrom black
And Maelstrom dire
Weave Earth and Wind

Sea and Fire
Come thunder, lightning
Wind and rain
Burn them up
Watch them flame
Sweep them up
Bring them down
Into the ocean
And watch them drown

Like a monstrous spinning top the Maelstrom rose and twisted westwards, out over the sea. Sucking up sea water, it grew with every heartbeat, gathering clouds about it as it reached to the heavens.

The wind slowly died and calm returned beneath Roarkinch. The WarLock shuddered with the effort of it. No matter where they hid, this would find them. And if they had already flown, it would drive them eastwards in haste towards the Howling Glen where he would command his banners to attack in force.

And so, they would seek the security of the Old Wall and the Smoking Fort, where Galtekerion and his hobgoblins were gathering beneath the dense canopy of the Caledonian forest.

As soon as he was strong enough, he must return home, from the battlefront of course, with yet more tales of triumph over the hobgoblins. Darcy's wedding took place before the week was out, and he had his own wedding plans to finalise with a full Council of the

Court.

Perhaps it would be a double celebration? Soon, he would be Prince Regent, with the Queen and highborn nobles of all the Seven Kingdoms in the palm of his hand, hostages to ensure obedience. Then he could begin his search for the fabled Dragonsdome Chronicles, and the secrets contained within them; lost since the Mage Wars of the Second Age.

CHAPTER FORTY-NINE

Weave Earth and Wind, Sea and Fire

The sun crawled lazily towards noon. Quenelda was asleep. The Earl held the reins loosely in his hands, his joy at seeing familiar islands and the distant cliffs of the mainland evident to Tangnost who stood at his side, the Earl's Shield once more. Almost, for a heartbeat, the dwarf imagined nothing had changed, and they were returning home after a mission. Almost you could believe it, almost, until you saw the terrible injuries they all bore.

They were flying over the tiny outer islands of the Muckle archipelago when they felt the first hint of danger. Greenstone dragons from the outer ocean were rising up to form long skeins, flying east towards the mainland. The air filled with their raucous cries as they clustered about Stormcracker.

There was a strange brooding quality to the air. A cold wind began to blow from the south. Drumondir raised her eyes from studying the ancient book of the Bone Caster Mages and frowned. The wild dragons about them were increasingly unsettled. She sniffed the air. A storm was coming.

Tangnost arrived. 'You feel it too?'

Drumondir nodded. 'I don't know what it is. Just a sense of...menace...'

Stormcracker....? Wounded and powerless as he was, something pricked the Earl's senses, as if dormant magic had just been awoken.

I feel it also, Thunder Rolling over the Mountains... the dark is rising...

Search the skies, old friend....he is looking for us...

The Imperial swung his head around so that the Earl could see through his eyes...searching...searching...

Danger... some other self whispered in Quenelda's head as she lay dreaming. *Danger...* She snapped awake! The feeling of dread flooded through her. Just like Roarkinch! On shaking legs, she moved backwards to find Quester.

'What? What is it?' Quenelda's fear was palpable.

'Give me your spyscope,' she asked urgently. Worried, the Earl's esquire handed it over.

Baffled, she looked about her at the bright sky. No sign of pursuit... she relaxed. *No sign of danger...*

'Wait!'

Far to the north, welling up like black ink on blotting paper, was a storm. A distant rumble reached them as thunderheads stalked the darkening horizon on crooked legs of lightning.

'Just a winter storm,' Quester shrugged. 'It's too far away for us to worry about. We're in no danger.'

Quenelda nodded. *And yet...?* 'It's coming from the

north! From Roarkinch! Against the wind!'

This time she knew this was no ordinary storm, just as a warning wave of darkness hit her like a physical blow and she staggered, caught only by Quester's quick reactions. 'This storm is dangerous; it reeks of chaotic magic and madness!'

'Tangnost?' Quenelda shouted urgently, running towards the Dragon Master and waving her arms. 'Drumondir!'

'Behind us!' She pointed. 'It's behind us!'

'What?' Tangnost scanned the sky. 'I can't see any danger!'

'No! No!' she tugged his jerkin. 'Look! Look!'

Running up to the highest point of the dragon's back, Tangnost and Drumondir looked to where she pointed.

Stretching open armed across the ocean, the storm was racing southwards towards them, hungrily gobbling up the daylight. A huge wave was forming, running ahead of the storm. The sky convulsed. There was a distant flash of purple followed by a deep rumble, and the calm winter's day around them evaporated.

'Odin's Hammer!' Tangnost swore, just as Stormcracker's great head swung round to look behind. Next second, the Earl's hoarse cry cut through the air, confirming Tangnost's worst fears.

'Maelstrom! Maelstrom!' The Earl was trying to get to his feet, casting around for a staff that wasn't there, for power that would not answer him!

'What's happening? Look at the wind gauge,' Root

started to rise out of the navigator's chair. 'What's happen-'

A gust of wind picked up the huge dragon and effortlessly rolled him almost twenty degrees to port. There were cries of alarm from Quester and Drumondir who were standing just behind them. Legs akimbo, strong hand clasping the back of Root's saddle, Tangnost held on with practiced ease, but Root tumbled forwards, cracked his head off the pilot's chair, and fell. The safety harness played out, and Root jerked like a broken puppet before being grazed by a rising wing talon.

'Root! Root?' Tangnost shouted, trying to peer around the dragon's belly. There was no response as the dwarf swiftly hauled up the unconscious boy with powerful arms.

With the dwarf's and Drumondir's help, a dazed Root struggled back into his seat, where he slumped like a boned fish. White as a sheet, his eyes were unfocused. 'I will tend to him,' the Bone Caster told Tangnost. 'Do what you must to save us.'

'Boy?'

Gently shaking the gnome's shoulders, Drumondir held up a hand. 'Watch my finger.' But Root's eyes remained unfocused. She examined the swelling bump on his head. 'A bad knock...but no worse injury,' she assured him. 'I will stay with you. Here, sit on my knee and I will strap us both into this witchwood chair of yours!'

Stormcracker's cry of warning rang painfully in

Quenelda's head at the same moment as her father's raw cry, freezing her marrow.

'Wind and Water!' she whispered to herself, as she raced back to Stormcracker's great shoulders. No one got caught in Open Sky by a Maelstrom and lived to tell the tale.

'What do we do?' Quenelda, still a child of only twelve years, was panicking as the first gusts of the Maelstrom's brittle energising breath reached them with frosted finger tips. 'Where do we go?' she asked her father and Tangnost.

'We have to have to find land and shelter. If we stay in Open Sky,' the Earl said grimly, 'then we're dead. We must find sanctuary. I will keep us ahead of the storm until you find an island or inlet that can shelter us!'

'Bring us down then, my Lord,' Tangnost agreed. 'As low as you dare, whilst we three search for sanctuary! Quester, Quenelda, rope up and look for cave or cavern large enough to hide Storm! Go now! Quickly!'

Like the advent of night, darkness continued to swallow all that lay in its path.

As they lost more height, great flocks of blue gilled seagulls now cried and squabbled loudly around them. The bickering raucous birds normally kept clear of carnivorous dragons. Now they seemed to be congregating where the storm of dragons was thickest, as if seeking sanctuary from a greater danger. Dozens were colliding with Stormcracker. Two Gulps was so full he

301

could barely move.

There was a sudden ear-splitting crack, and a finger of lightning lanced down, striking Stormcracker's back, splitting into coruscating tendrils that crawled all over the dragon's back as if searching. Several struck the back of the pilot's seat, just as Quester's scream cut through the smoke-filled air.

Slicing his tether rope, Tangnost raced down between the dragon's spinal plates, to where the Earl's tent was on fire. Further down, wreathed in green flame, Quester frantically beat at his cloak. Smoke skirled about them.

'Roll!' Tangnost forced the esquire to the ground, throwing himself on top to smother the flames, ignoring the explosion of pain from his cracked ribs.

'Drumondir!' He bellowed. ' I-ugh!'

He looked up to see Drumondir calmly throwing the cooking cauldron away, an ironic twitch on her lips. 'Water never fails, Bearhugger.'

Smoking, sooty, wet, he got sheepishly to his feet, hauling the esquire with him. 'Alright, lad? Good, come with me!' With an embarrassed nod at Drumondir, Tangnost raced back to the Earl.

'My Lord! The storm seeks you out! It struck both your chair and your tent. Let the witchwood protect you!' he turned to the Earl's esquire who was still smoking.

'Quester, care for my Lord Earl. Defend him with your life!' He held the boy's eyes for a moment to be sure his meaning was understood. Wide eyed and pale, Quester nodded.

Then Tangnost was back again at Quenelda's side, straddling the dragon's neck. It was not the time to tell her of her father's danger. She needed to concentrate.

'We have to find shelter.' He urgently scanned the approaching storm. We won't survive many more strikes like that.'

The cold air running before the storm finally brought Root fully around. The youth's eyelids trembled and flickered into awareness. The world wobbled uncertainly into focus, bucking and yawing. Blinking groggily, Root saw that the streams of birds and dragons all around were merging into a moving storm of wings, teeth, feathers and claws. Sitting forwards, he craned round to see what pursued them.

'Tooth and Claw!' the youth's voice was shrill with fear.

'Have no fear, boy,' Drumondir gave Root another fright, making him jump as the gnome realised he was sharing the witchwood seat with her. 'We are as safe as we can be here. Trust to your companions. There is nothing we can do to help. They will save us!'

The air grew colder still as the storm sucked in energy from everything around it, feeding and growing stronger by the heartbeat. Jagged spikes of green and purple lashed out. Warring gusts now clutched at the huge dragon, who was struggling to make headway in the swirling wind.

'Ten leagues, and rapidly closing!' Tangnost judged calmly. 'We aren't going to make the safety of the mainland, and we won't to be able to outrun it. We have to put down on an island and take our chances.'

'Ooooff!' As the dragon suddenly rose upwards the air was punched from his lungs, bringing Tangnost to his knees with an oath, sending a spike of agony through his chest.

At the edge of her awareness, Quenelda could feel the strike of chaotic magic that sought her father out. *Power attracts power...he is hunting us...will he find me?*

Already, the first tendrils of the storm were probing ahead, and hungrily grasping at them with frozen gusts of turbulent air. A tendril struck a greenstone dragon which shattered into pieces. And the vortex at the centre of the Maelstrom grew darker and darker in the greater brightness, spiralling greedily inwards, swallowing the whole sky, merging seamlessly with the towering wave. At the heart of the firestorm, baleful green eyes watched. A cold voice laughed, and then faded into darkness.

Injured or not, Stormcracker was using every ounce of his and Quenelda's strength to draw ahead of the thousands of birds and lesser dragons disappearing into the ominous dark hole growing at its centre. Static energy crackled, making their hair stand on end. They were flying low now, racing twenty strides above the whitecaps. The rolling waves rose higher and higher until, like the fingers of a hand, they almost curled above them, a wall of darkness. The noise of the waves' advance was deafening.

A flare shaped like a hand curled forwards, fingers outstretched. Another greenstone dragon overhead disappeared. Ash and cinders floated down. Quester's eyes were streaming as he frantically searched for somewhere to hide. Close by, now back in the navigator's chair, Root tried to breathe in the searing cold air and choked, as his throat seized as the air was sucked from his lungs. It was like being in the battleroosts without ceramic armour on, Root thought wildly; as if he would be sucked dry of all moisture and left like a desiccated autumn leaf to crumble in the wind.

Only Stormcracker and Two Gulps, creatures of fire from the molten heart of the One Earth, were untouched by its searing, grasping, greedy touch; and Quenelda, a fledgling dragon whisperer who barely noticed.

Breathing shallowly, flexing numb fingers, Tangnost ignored the fierce cold and grimly calculated their odds for survival. They weren't good. There were high-cliffed islands up ahead, but none offered even the dubious shelter of woods; trees could not survive on these small windswept rocks.

But then the wind turned on itself, raising a huge waterspout that reeled drunkenly across the surface of the sea, striking northwards away from them. An island was enveloped in the whirling spinning Maelstrom. Chunks of rock were ripped up. By the time the island appeared out the other side it was stripped down to a dark chewed up rock face. Smaller water spouts began to form around them.

A ragged finger of raw energy flicked out so close to the Earl it rebounded from his pilot's seat, glanced across Quester's shield and singed the skin on the esquire's face. Almost at their wingtips, a dragon touched by a tendril exploded in a mess of blue blood and scales.

'The Mainland, my Lord, we must reach the caves in the cliffs!' Tangnost shouted to the Earl. It was becoming hard to speak in the oily vacuum.

Panicking, Quenelda searched through the darkness. Where could they find sanctuary? The lay of the islands below suddenly seemed familiar. Yes, that low group of islands coming up swiftly to port...guarded by three stacks. She recognised them – how? When? It was hard to concentrate on ancient memories through a haze of raw fear. She searched the gloom ahead, eyes flickering bright gold.

Then a sense of calm descended on her and her fingers tingled. Her hearts slowed and her mind cleared as power settled about her like a cloak.

'No...'

*Papa? Let me guide Storm...*she said to her father. *Give Storm to me!*

Quenelda banked Stormcracker hard to port and into the teeth of the oncoming storm.

'My Lord? Quenelda?' Tangnost was instantly again at her side as Stormcracker struggled to turn. Ice flaked off his wings. They were gasping for breath with the force of the wind coming straight at them. 'What- what are you doing?'

'There are dragon coombs over there,' she shouted. 'Down on that island, where the stacks are!'

Tangnost's brows knitted as he swung the spyglass round. 'How do you know? You've never been here before.'

'I know,' she acknowledged, as her eyes flared. 'But there are caves down there, by the stacks. Seadragon coombs from the days of the Elders,' she pointed to where three shadowy pinnacles of rock punched up from the churning grey sea. 'I know they are! I...I've been here before...'

Tangnost came to a swift decision and nodded. He would take her words on faith; she had never let them down.

He nodded his assent. 'Take us there.' If she were wrong, well then, they were all dead anyway; the maw of the Maelstrom was almost upon them.

Storm, Quenelda's thoughts were urgent. *Fly for those stone stacks... can you feel the Elder power?*

The big dragon rolled steeply to port and struck out with all his mighty strength. *Coombs...*Quenelda whispered to herself. *Seadragon coombs...the SeaDragon Citadel...*

The turbulence was getting worse as they levelled out scant strides above the waves, their spray soaking them. As the stacks reared up to port, the treacherous winds slammed smaller dragons and sea birds into the rock; wings crumpling like paper they tumbled lifelessly down with flakes of stone into the sucking sea. The wind was becoming unmanageable.

'AAahhh!!'

Quenelda fought down her rising panic as they, too, were tossed sideways towards the cliffs. She raised a hand and a wave of air rebounded and pushed them to safety.

The wind snapped and popped. The cold air hissed and steamed. The dragons bucked and lurched. Flashes of electric green and purple lit the seascape in eerie detail, then sank back into darkness. In the fading light, small fish dragons were struggling to land safely on cliffs and beaches around them.

'There! There!' Quenelda twisted around, shouting over her left shoulder, and pointed through the seething, swirling air down to where a dark chasm snaked inland like a serpent's tail. To where sea gave way to shale and sand, to where the sea smashed on the headlands and led to a vertical opening that loomed in the growing dark. The wind pulled at her words, shaking them apart, then snatched at her, almost lifting her from the dragon's shoulders. Then Tangnost's strong hand was on her shoulder, steadying her, anchoring her.

He squeezed. 'Stay calm.'

Then the world disappeared and the storm's savage roar rattled their skulls. Stormcracker was pitched and tossed as if some giant predator shook them in its mouth.

Strange words, harsh runes swirled about Quenelda's

head; ...ancient words from another lifetime. She sensed someone, some living thing at the heart of the storm; a looming threat of ancient darkness casting its net over the north to see what it may gather in. The violent music of the Maelstrom rose up around her, trapping her in its twisted melody, dragging her down into its dark soul. *Such power* ...she thought dreamily...

'Quenelda!' Tangnost cried as an alien power swept through her and about her like smoke, and the light in her eyes faded. 'Quenelda!'

But her eyes were now black as pits, and the mocking laughter that rode the wind was not hers.

CHAPTER FIFTY

I Do

'I do,' Darcy said, slipping a beautifully wrought ring of dragon gold from the Third Kingdom onto his fiancée's slim finger.

'You may kiss your bride,' the Lord Protector said, his eyes almost aglow with a fierce light as Darcy bent to kiss Armelia.

My husband... Armelia surrendered to the kiss. She could hardly take it all in, the Queen's apartments, the sumptuous gold-embossed carriage of spun glass drawn by and escorted by a troop of the Household Cavalry and the royal band, the great shire horses with their kettle drums, the extravagant gifts from Darcy's lords and bannermen that had been presented over the course of the week. Except...strangely, no gift from the Lord Protector. But Darcy hadn't seemed to notice.

My fiancé...no! My husband! Armelia thought proudly. Darcy was clearly as overcome by the day as she was, and moved as if he were in a dream.

'Lord Protector? Uncle?' Darcy had prompted the day before. He was tense with anticipation. What had the Lord Protector to say, that would bring him wealth and power?

The Lord Protector turned from the fire, and considered the young man standing before him. The dark hair worn fashionably long, the striking eyes; Darcy had inherited his good looks from both his mother and father. His own square jaw and height, his mother's eyes. But it was not what was outside that interested the Lord Hugo Mandrake; it was the young man's behaviour. Reckless, ambitious, he lacked the subtlety for Court politics and the courage of a soldier, but he would teach his son that, and more.

'You are not like your father, are you?'

Darcy's eyes narrowed at the implied criticism. Still one year on, the fact he had not defended his father at the winter jousts in the Cauldron was a bitter memory.

'I-' he began angrily.

Hugo Mandrake held his hand palm up to forestall the defensive reply.

'Shall I tell you why? Why you are more kindred to me than to him? Because you are not his son, but mine.'

Darcy's eyes widened with shock. 'Not...what? I'm *your* son?'

The Lord Protector stayed silent, letting his son work it out for himself.

'My mother...' Darcy queried, remembering his childhood. 'It was *you*?' Of course, his father was away on campaign half the year, and his best friend was a frequent visitor to Dragonsdome. Who...always listened to him as a boy. Made time for him, brought him extravagant gifts, encouraged him.

The Lord Protector nodded. 'Why did you think I took such an interest in your upbringing?'

'I – I' Darcy was reeling.

'I promised you wealth and power beyond your imagination, did I not?'

'But I am Earl, you, you promised me that. How? How did you know before anyone else?'

'All in good time, my son. You will marry your young lady. In less than a moon's time, I marry the Queen, and her Council will make me Prince Consort.

'Then together, my son, you and I shall rule all the kingdoms of the One Earth...and beyond.'

CHAPTER FIFTY-ONE

The Seadragon Caves

'Give me my daughter! Quester!' the Earl cried, feeling the Maelstrom's touch blot out her aura. 'Bring her to me!'

Battling the elements, held only by his tether line, Quester yanked Quenelda off her feet with strength born of desperation.

As he struggled forwards, the blind Earl pulled his daughter down onto his witchwood seat and wrapped his arms about her. Cursing he tried to awake the chair, placing his palm on the cold wood. 'Nothing!' He cursed. 'Nothing! No power!'

With a hiccup, Two Gulps barrelled his way forward through all the debris to the Earl's side and spread his wings, protecting them both from the bones and branches and stones that were whipped up by the wind.

Cradled by Drumondir on the navigator's seat, Root hung on to for grim death. His copper skin was clammy and pale; he felt violently sick and had retched till he was empty. His eyes were swollen and sore from the battering rain, his throat raw from screaming. How could Tangnost still stand in his stirrups and defy the storm?

Roarkinch's great citadel rose in Quenelda's mind, its obsidian surface smooth as glass, up and up it rose, its spiralling towers reaching up into the cold dark of space between the stars. It was beautiful! Dark dragons, their twisted carapaces gleaming coldly, their green eyes burning fiercely, swooped beneath arches and under the pathways that spiralled up behind its spiked walls. *So* beautiful...

At its foot, broken mountains and jagged chasms scored the smoking landscape, where pools of lava belched and bubbled, their noxious gasses glittering in the frigid air. The only familiar things in this world were the stars, twinkling coldly overhead.

Stormcracker banked his wings through the churning darkness as the chasm rushed up to meet them. But the heart of the vortex also changed direction, hunting them down. It spun closer. Stormcracker was distracted, his mind half on his mistress as a huge boulder cannoned into his right wing, skimmed and bounced between two spinal plates, deflecting the dragon from his true course. Desperately, he stalled his bruised wings to gather air, knowing the danger that the *dark* might take them at any heartbeat from behind.

'We're carrying too much speed!' Tangnost shouted as he finally fell to his knees. 'We're carrying too much speed! Up, Stormcracker, up!' He hauled desperately on the reins, but it was too late! They were going to hurtle into the base of the cliff!

'We're going down! We're going down!' The terrifying words sounded in Root's helmet com. 'We're going down.'

Unaware, Two Gulps, talons curled about Quenelda in the pilot's chair, bugled his anxiety as he felt her slip further away into darkness where he could not follow, her voice falling silent in his head. She was leaving him alone in the dark...

Dancing with Dragons...? He flamed, his desperate dragonfire wrapping her, and the dormant pilot's chair in golden flames. The chair shuddered...then runes came alive in the witchwood; runes in brilliant colours forming and reforming in the grain. Beneath Quenelda's hand, her father's palm print sprang to life. The chair tingled as it wrapped Quenelda in a defensive nexus, shielding her and her father from the Maelstrom.

With the song silenced, Quenelda's mind struggled to free itself, to break free of the last dark threads of confusion that coiled in her mind. Where was she? It was still dark, but there were no stars, only stabs of lighting and the rushing of the wind.

'Quenelda! Quenelda!' At that very moment, Root's terrified cry broke into her trance as an uprooted tree tumbled towards them. In that instant, her golden eyes snapped open, and she lifted her hand and deflected it with a flick of her fingers, at the same moment as she saw beyond it, the cliff face looming, and knew with certainty that it was too late for Stormcracker to pull up.

'We're going down!' Tangnost was not yet aware of Quenelda as she stepped free of her father's arms.

Up, Stormcracker! Up!

Threads of gold, russet, red, green and blue, half a hundred colours spun towards her hands, braiding together. White light blossomed in the darkness as she raised them up in a blinding bright cocoon of spun magic that was still sheltered from the Maelstrom; and the battledragon rose within it, up, up... but not swiftly enough!

Tangnost was flung into the air as the weaker of the Imperial's claws was slammed backwards with the impact, the battledragon's talons scoring deep grooves across the cliff face. Tangnost struggled to his feet by Quenelda's side to retake the reins. Rocks gouged out by the dragon's claws crumbled into the hungry foaming sea below. White hot pain lanced through the battledragon as he smashed his injured talon and then...

And then they were rising, ploughing vast furrows of turf and stone as Stormcracker scrabbled for height over the craggy island, and his tail swept to gain momentum. Side by side, Tangnost and Quenelda roared with the effort, their screams competing with the wind as the battledragon almost tripped and somersaulted, then his hindquarters swung down and the Imperial's claws swung forwards and sprung, and they were up, free of the earth's grip, only to be grasped by the Maelstrom.

Light pulsed from Quenelda as she lent her strength to

Stormcracker's and then she felt her father, his sorcery powerful yet weakly cast, anchoring their efforts with his knowledge. Flickering lightning coruscated hungrily about them, seeking for weaknesses, but did not pierce their cocoon. Wheeling around into the teeth of the wind, they turned for a slower approach, struggling to find the caves again in the near dark.

'Brace for impact!' Tangnost warned. This was going to be a rough landing, for the vortex was now almost upon them. 'Brace!' he screamed at Drumondir, face moon pale as she hung on to Root in the navigator's chair. 'Brace for impact!'

Quester ached with the effort of hanging on to the pilot's chair with one arm and keeping his shield raised with the other. Debris was battering his unprotected body but he stood fast.

This time, compensating for the rising wind by stalling and spilling air from his wings, and using his long tail as an anchor, Stormcracker swooped down into the chasm at an ungainly run, his great claws slipping and sliding on the wet rock, pitching them all violently from side to side.

Thrown forwards from his chair, the Earl was reaching Quester's hand when a finger of lightning found the pilot's chair and a tendril struck him. He spun about like a broken doll, and was taken by the wind before Quester could react.

The gap's too small!

So much of the cliff had fallen into the sea since

Quenelda last knew this place countless centuries ago. *Countless... millennia ago?* Quenelda lifted a fist, and a pulse surged forwards to strike the fissure at its apex. Tons of stone were vaporised to dust, drowning Quester's cry of anguish.

Then outriders of the huge wave swept in, carrying them swiftly forwards toward sanctuary. Foam surged around the dragon's legs then fell away, sucking him backwards on a moving bed of shale, back and out to sea. But nothing could stop the big dragon and Quenelda now, not even the Maelstrom.

'Down, everybody down!' Tangnost screamed as Stormcracker folded his wings. Slithering on his belly, the battledragon squirmed sinuously forwards, dipped his head and shoulders and disappeared through the dark rocky arch. His rising spinal plates thumped into the cliff. Fractured rock fell where Quenelda had weakened the arch, and then they were through, and into storm-strobed darkness and safety.

CHAPTER FIFTY-TWO

Dragon Isle

The winter raven was spent, its lifeblood drained. Half starved, injured and with one wing broken; how it ever made it home the Keeper would never know.

Within half a bell of its arrival, Commander DeBessart was in the briefing room, where tiers of seats rose up in a horseshoe shape about him.

'The Earl is alive and with Tangnost Bearhugger and his daughter on Stormcracker heading south with enemies hunting them. The message came from the Ice Isles, so who knows what flight path they have chosen. But I think it is safe to guess they will head for the Howling Glen or, following Major Calder's report, the Smoking Fort. I want every dragon we have out there, fully armed, night and day and every scout, every dragon we have airborne. If they are pursued, then they could be taking any route home. We must find them first!'

CHAPTER FIFTY-THREE

Seadragon Caverns

Climb, Storm, climb! Quenelda urged, not knowing how she knew it. *The sea will rise and flood these lower caves! Climb to the upper chambers...*

Shale rattled as Stormcracker limped awkwardly forwards up the rising slope of the cavern, while trying to protect his shattered talon. The wind outside howled like a living creature robbed of its prey. Lightning lit the caverns in flashes of sickly green, and tendrils groped about the entrance but came no further.

Deeper and deeper into the dark caves the battledragon moved, mindful of his precious burden, as rough hewn rock gave way to carved pillars, and the rocky floor to smooth flagstones. Runes sprang to light guiding their path, then faded back to darkness behind them. Then the wave was on them, bursting into the caves below in a frothy explosion of water that roared through the lower levels, drumming through the rock.

'There, Storm,' Quenelda's dragon eyes had picked out a huge carved archway, knowing it would be big enough for an Imperial because adult Seadragons were larger yet, and that there was a plaza high above sea level. As swiftly as they climbed, the water rose with them, up and up, frothing in its fury. Then, as Stormcracker's pain became unendurable, the sea began to drain away, and the shriek of the wind slowly receded to a mere whisper. The huge Imperial lay down with his flanks heaving and froth flecking his muzzle.

Shaking so hard he could barely grip the girth steps, Root unbuckled his flying harness and half clambered then fell to the ground, his legs collapsing beneath him, only his padded hauberk saving him from further injury. Barely managing to pull his helmet off in time, the gnome was wretchedly sick. Drumondir sat quietly, slowing her breathing. Her first flight had been...interesting!

'How are you, lass?'

Quenelda turned, fending off Two Gulps' joyful embrace, revealing normal eyes. Tangnost visibly sagged with relief, a smile twitching his lips. Time to discuss what happened later. Shaking, she was flushed with adrenaline.

'What is this place?' Tangnost asked, wonderingly. He could see little clearly, save the soft glow of her and Two Gulps' eyes, and the faintest glow from the stone.

'I have been here...' she replied, lost in memory. 'This was an Elder city once, the Sea Citadel; the realm of the long dead seadragons and Dragon Lords of old; but the stone still remembers them, their language...their laws... their lives...

As she spoke, runes, all the colours of the rainbow, sprang to life on the smooth walls, bathing the city in soft warm light. The scale of it was breathtaking. They were standing on a plaza, the floor of which was an intricate mosaic of pink coral and white, greenstone set with concentric runes and glyphs. The cavern was immense, the buildings on many levels, and beautiful!

'Seadragons...' Root said, still on all fours, amazed by the beauty of the fluted dragons of the undersea world that came to life beneath his hands. Already forgetting his fear and exhaustion he looked around eagerly. An undersea city!

'The Maelstrom cannot touch us here,' the Earl's daughter finished, hearing fading whispers about them. 'There is power enough here to guard us from him...'

She's changing, Tangnost thought, *although she doesn't see it. The child I raised has already become so much more in the last year. Whose memories are these she draws on? Whose voice does she speak with? Or is she simply growing towards the young woman she will become?*

He glanced at her, marvelling that she had saved them from crashing. The Maelstrom had almost won, but with the help of her father and Two Gulps, she had overcome it. That thought made him hopeful.

'And Papa, Tangost! I felt his power join mine! His power is returning, isn't it? We did it! You and me, Papa and Storm! Together! We-'

The pilot's chair was empty and smoking. And then they heard Quester's cry!

Following Quenelda, Tangnost charged down the

Imperial's back searching for the Earl, finding him lying in the wreckage of his tent, Quester on his knees beside him. He looked up, tears running down his face.

'Thor's hammer!' The Earl's burnt face was dark with fine green veins creeping beneath the skin.

'He isn't moving,' Quester sobbed.

'Papa!' Quenelda screamed. 'Nooo!'

'Oh, no! No!' Tangnost grasped for the Dragon Lord's clawed hand, and lifted his eyelids. Instead of milky blue, the Earl's eyes were black with green threads! The dwarf put the back of his hand to the Earl's throat, feeling for a pulse. The injured man groaned, his eyes flickered then closed again.

'Alive!' Weak at the knees, Tangnost could hardly breathe for the pain in his chest.

Drumondir arrived, albeit a little wobbly and pale. 'I will tend him,' she said calmly. 'I will do what I can for him.'

'Come, lads, eat some broth and bannocks if you can, and then sleep. Feed Two Gulps and keep him with you. Who knows when this storm will end? There is nothing we can do to help,' he glanced back to where Drumondir and Quenelda had disappeared into the city. The Bone Caster had had no trouble lifting the Earl's wasted body in her strong arms, and the pair had long since vanished.

'The Earl's injuries are beyond our power. We need to be rested if we are to help them, and ready to fly at a moment's notice if we have to.

'But first, Root, the moment the Maelstrom dies down, you must search for dragon leaf, dragon's bane.' He carefully lifted the precious book from the few baggage rolls that had survived from the wreckage of the Earl's tent. 'Study this carefully, and take the dried plant with you. Quester, go with him and make sure he doesn't get into trouble. We can only delay a short while; we must get the Earl to the Howling Glen and safety as soon as we can.

'Now, get some sleep!'

'Sir! Yes, Sir!'

These streets and steps were impossibly wide and saddle backed, worn down by countless Elders and those who lived and fought with them; five-score paces wide, Drumondir counted, before they dropped another level and moved into a new cavern where delicate bridges spanned great waterways.

Light glowed in soft orbs that drifted overhead in some unseen breeze, as Quenelda led the Bone Caster to a deep pool, its depths fading to black as the lights sent ripples of gold and coral across its surface.

'Here was where the dragons came to eat,' Quenelda gestured to the surrounding shallow basin of smoothed stone, 'pulling their catch up through the crystal clear sea, up into the shallows of the pool...' Her voice was soft, her gaze distant as she tried to remember.

And it was there they found it, carved of green hued rock, the head and shoulders of a seadragon emerging from the pool, and on its neck, near the shoulders, unmistakably a Dragon Lord; but armoured in scales of glittering green, and with a helmet that mimicked the fronds of the seadragon he rode. But there was one other difference: this Dragon Lord's hands were webbed, and on his neck was a delicate tracery of gills.

'They bonded as we do, but it changed them. They became more like the dragons they rode.'

'Just as you are changing also, child.'

'Am I?' Quenelda turned her palm to where Two Gulps' scale now lay nested within others, smaller, black. 'I suppose I am, but I don't feel any different,' she shrugged. 'The dragons taught us their magic, and together we grew stronger than any other race on the One Earth.'

'Until the hobgoblins came,' Drumondir observed softly.

'Yes, until the hobgoblins came,' Quenelda agreed sadly. 'And then, in desperation, we turned to chaotic magic... and it nearly destroyed us.'

'Is it much further? This place of healing you seek?'

But Quenelda could only shake her head. 'I don't think so. I can't be certain. It was so, so long ago...'

They walked silently on, each wrapped in their thoughts.

'Here! This is the place!'

Great columns carved with glyphs rose up in front of them, rows passing into darkness beyond. And between the columns were stone dragon lords on their seadragons, each the same and yet different. Down the centre of the aisle lay empty stone slabs.

'What happens now, child?' Drumondir asked. 'This is a place of great power, I can sense it. I have seen nothing like it before. Is it a tomb? Have we brought your father here to die?'

'No!' Quenelda shook her head as if banishing sleep. 'Yes, they came here to die, the last of the Seadragon Lords and their mounts, bonded together for eternity, changing back to stone, slowly returning to the One Earth. But it was also a place of healing. Lay Papa down here,' she gestured. 'Before they died, they tried to fill the stone with their ancient lore and healing for those in need that followed. Only Dragon Lords may wake the wisdom within. I-' For the first time, she seemed uncertain. 'I don't know how much remains,' she bit her lip, fighting back tears. 'No one has set foot in this city since the Second Age, since the last of the seadragons died!'

'Look, child!' Drumondir seized her arm as a soft light blossomed about them. 'Look! The stone is coming alive!'

Night fell, but nobody noticed. Then, as the hour of the strutting cockerel was breaking, the wind died just as suddenly as it had begun, and the sea calmed.

Tangnost was the first to notice the silence that had fallen, or so he thought. As he bent to rouse Root and Quester, he noticed that Quenelda and Drumondir had not yet returned. Two Gulps, forbidden to go with Quenelda, had finally settled at the esquire's feet and was snoring.

'Right, lads, break your fasts, get some hot food into you. We mount up in two bells. Then out you go, see if you can find this weed. If not, we have to hope Dragon Isle knows where to find some.'

'Um,' Root looked embarrassed. Quester looked anxious. The pair of them were staring at their boots.

'What?' Tangnost had no time for this. 'What have you done? Out with it!'

'I – I – left it out, with my paper and inks and....He ate it,' Root's voice was a whisper.

'He **what**?' Tangnost growled, The Dragon Master didn't need to ask who 'he' was. 'He ate the book!' Tangnost's eye flashed in rare anger. 'Hav-'

'No, Sir, no!' Root hastily shook his head... 'N-no, not the book! Only the plant!'

Tangnost subsided, only slightly mollified. 'Did you memorise its characteristics? Could you draw it?' he asked Root, who nodded. 'Just as well! I'll deal with you later.' *And Two Gulps and his mistress!* 'Now go, and make amends by finding this plant. And take Two Gulps with you,' he added as an afterthought. 'If he likes it so much, perhaps he can help you find some more.'

Taking the guilty dragon with them, the pair fled, glad to escape the dwarf's wrath, and determined to find dragon leaf to redeem themselves in his eyes.

The young esquires clambered over fallen rocks and

debris that clogged the cave's entrance, out into a silent ravished world. An oily sea haar hung thickly about the water, drifting slowly over the sea's smooth surface, and the corrosive stench of a decaying spell hung in the air. The sun was rising, pale as a poached egg through the white mist.

'Oh, Tooth and Claw!' Root choked as he emerged ahead of his friend.

'Abyss below!' Quester had taken to swearing like a soldier. The friends stood side-by-side gaping in horror. The outer cliff which had weathered the worst of the storm was unrecognisable, and two of the ancient stacks that marked this island had crumbled into the sea, leaving a single battered stump.

Great sections of broken cliffs were burnt black and smoking where fingers of lightning had struck, and here and there the smouldering remains of wild dale and smaller greenstone dragons lay like fallen boulders, limbs and bodies broken, bones pale in the weak sun.

'Look, Root! Look!'

The shattered hulk of a merchant galleon lay beached on top of the cliffs, its bared ribs smashed open to the sky, the silk guild flag tattered. And everywhere, the hoar frost glittered, sprouting like coral, the cold kiss of the Maelstrom.

Through the fog's drifting coils, they noticed bodies moving sluggishly in the shallows, trapped by the kelp beds. Birds, bodies, dragons, broken ships and shredded sails wallowed thick as stew, now being washed up by the tide.

Horribly afraid, fingers nervously on the short swords Tangnost insisted they both take, the pair set out along the dunes, searching through the debris and high grass looking for the spiked leaves of dragon's leaf. Two Gulps followed them, half waddling, half hopping, loudly flapping his wings, sniffing hungrily at everything, grumbling to himself. The youths ignored him, angry that he had got them into trouble.

They were kicking bad temperedly at clumps of grass when there was a loud squeal and Two Gulps took off... more of a flying hop from dune to dune on his huge feet with his wings whirring, followed by a huge pounce.

Quarrkkkkkkkkkkkkkkk!

Baffled, Root and Quester looked at each other. Surely there was nothing left to eat after the storm? Running after the dragon they crested a dune, breathing hard, bent over with their hands on their knees.

'Two Gulps!?'

The dragon was in the middle of a clump of large bushes with bright yellow flowers, wolfing it down. Sniffing and snorting, he sneezed. A couple of branches caught fire and smouldered, raising a thin plume of smoke. The sabretooth sucked it in with seeming pleasure, and then he fell over on his back, with his legs wiggling in the air.

'Two Gulps!'

'Two Gulps!' Root ran up to the dragon... 'oh, newt and toad,' he moaned, head in hands. 'Quenelda will kill us. He must have eaten the bush...He's foaming at the mouth and rolling on his back. He's poisoned!'

Tangnost had roused the sleeping Imperial with unexpected ease. The big dragon had turned to nuzzle softly at him as if to reassure the Dragon Master that he was ready to fly.

It must be this place! Tangnost mused, rubbing his leg. *I hardly feel any pain, and I feel rested. It must be the same for Storm! But where are they? What if he has died?*

'Bearhugger!' the call echoed across the plaza.

'My Lord Earl!' Tangnost's joy lit his face as he looked up to see the Dragon Lord crossing the plaza beside his daughter and Drumondir. 'But how? How c-'

'I do not fully understand either, old friend,' the Earl took the arm offered, although it did not look like he needed it. For the first time since they had found him, the Earl stood upright and tall again.

'But I feel better than I have since – since the battle. As if the darkness has lifted from me. Ironic is it not,' he said with a trace of his old irony. 'He sought to destroy me and instead...we took refuge here in this forgotten city and I have survived, stronger than I was!'

'I-'

'Where are Root and Quester?' Quenelda looked exhausted. Even Drumondir looked weary. Whatever had happened in the seadragon city, they had not had any sleep. 'And where is Two Gulps?'

'Out looking for dragon leaf. The island has, or had,

beaches before the storm. I thought perhaps...perhaps here we might find some.'

Cautiously leading Stormcracker, Quenelda moved outside just as Tangnost sounded the bugle a second time; Root and Quester still hadn't returned from their foraging. Apart from her father up in the pilot's seat, she alone knew what she would see in the aftermath of a Maelstrom; for the dragonsong had long since fallen silent. It was just as she had feared, but the reality was even more frightening than the memory. The storm had scoured all the life from the islands.

Brothers, brothers and sisters. Stormcracker's thoughts and those of Quenelda overlapped in silent horror. The battledragon lifted his reptilian head and roared a keening cry of lament that echoed unanswered in the vast empty silence.

The cry tore the heart out of the Earl as he looked down on the devastation.

'This was no rogue storm. No accident of nature. This storm was *summoned*,' he growled to Tangnost. 'You can still feel the threads of *Air*, *Water*, *Fire* and *Wind* warped together as they should not be ...this is the ruin of Maelstrom he unleashed upon us in the Westering Isles.' His broken hand instinctively went to his ruined face

'He will pay,' he swore. 'One day he will pay for this and all his betrayals.'

*Where **have** the pair of them got to?* Tangnost was

anxiously scanning the bay and the headlands for Root and Quester. Were there any hobgoblins? They could be out feasting on the wealth of death caused by the Maelstrom. *Thor's Hammer, please protect them!*

There was so much debris, it was hard to make anything out in the broken landscape. Behind him, the Earl bonded with Stormcracker, anxious to see through his dragon's eyes. The Elder magic of the ancient city seemed to have both healed him and given him strength. He was preparing to take to the air to search for the missing pair when Quenelda pointed.

'There!'

Just disappearing out of sight amongst the dunes, Root was shouting and waving. But something was wrong. He was stumbling and falling.

'But where are Two Gulps and Quester?' Quenelda cried.

Running forward, ignoring the grind and crack of his ribs, Tangnost reached the boy. 'What's happened?'

Root was exhausted, cut and bleeding. Tangnost held the youth up by his shoulders.

'What's wrong, lad?'

'I I-I think we've found Dragon Leaf,' Root was in tears, 'but – oh Tangnost! H-he's poisoned. Oh, Tangnost! I think he's dying! That's why they call it dragon's bane!'

CHAPTER FIFTY-FOUR

The Dawn of Days

'Two Gulps? Oh, Two Gulps!' Quenelda was beside herself, as she tried to calm the thrashing dragon while Tangnost, Root and Quester attempted to tie him down for his and their own safety.

'Arggh!' The dragon's tail whipped the legs out from under Root, knocking him out.

Eyes heavenward, Tangnost sighed. The esquire was going to have a fine pair of black eyes.

Two Gulps was drooling, and his normally golden eyes were black as midnight. Boulders, trees, and general wreckage made it difficult to move him, even without the juvenile dragon's excessive weight. The fact that he was rolling around and kicking huge feet in the air didn't make it any easier.

'Two G-ooof!' Quenelda got caught by the rising powerful jaw, tumbling her head over heels into a jagged bush. So upset, she barely noticed the thorns that snagged her jerkin and tore her hands as she tried to get up.

'Come away, lass, you'll only get injured,' Tangnost lifted her to her feet. 'Call Storm, or someone is going to end up with a serious injury.'

Summoning the Imperial to her, a distraught Quenelda

bade him put down beside the stricken sabretooth. Nuzzling him curiously, the battledragon lifted Two Gulps tenderly up to what was left of the roosts between his spinal plates, where he was roped up to a half dozen cleats for his own and their safety. But curiously, the Imperial did not appear concerned for his small companion.

'I don't understand,' Quenelda said tearfully for the dozenth time, head in hands with despair. 'What he is saying is all nonsense...his thoughts are all jumbled up. He's going mad. And Storm says he is not ill at all!'

She pressed her palm with its dragon scale against Two Gulps again, but her fingers failed to tingle. Not a hint of power trickled from her to the dragon. 'I can't heal him; I can't even work out what is wrong. I don't understand, I've never failed before. I don't want to lose him, too!' She started to cry helplessly.

'Hush, Goose,' her father comforted her, wrapping her in his maimed arms. 'You're tired. Sky Above! You have just fought the Maelstrom and lived and stood vigil all night at my side! You have to regain your strength before you can help him. I will pilot Stormcracker, with,' he turned, searching blindly for Quester, 'my Sword.

'You three care for Two Gulps. No one is more learned in dragon-lore than my Dragon Master, or healing than you, Goose; and Drumondir has great wisdom and knowledge that I can only guess at. They will help you.' Turning, his hand lightly resting on Quester's shoulder, the Earl headed towards the pilot's chair.

The sea remained calm as they skulled swiftly over the waves heading westwards towards the Brimstones, with no sign of pursuit or interception. Then barely half a bell into the flight, Quenelda came running.

'Papa! Papa! Tangnost! Come and look! He's alright!'

'Well,' Tangnost shook his head as Two Gulps slobbered all over Quenelda, searching for honey tablets. 'He certainly seems to be himself again. That is welcome news, indeed.'

As dusk fell, they approached the foot of the Brimstones and the Octarine Pass that would take them through the Shard mountains to safety. They decided to press on despite the treacherous winds and crags that killed so many.

'My Lord Earl, you should rest!'

'No, Bearhugger. Pursuit is bound to be close behind. We must make the safety of the Howling Glen. Then I shall rest, I promise.'

'Then let Quen-'

'No. My daughter is many things, but the winds are perilous here, and the mountains have claimed many lives. Stormcracker and I have flown here many times, often in the dark. We will make the fortress of the III Firstborn by dawn.'

'My Lord!' Tangnost acknowledged the order. 'Strap in and flying tethers on,' he ordered the rest of his crew.

'This is going to be a difficult passage.'

Root wilted. He just knew he was going to be sick!

The fearsome spikes of the Shards reared upwards, pitch black against the deep blue night sky speckled with cold stars. Only the snow reflected light faintly in the deep ravines and gorges, the ridges and passes beneath the mountain that led to the other side. It was bitterly cold, even in summer the sun never touched here. The rising moons lit the snow and threw dark shadows, and the wind grabbed greedily at them. They seemed to break free, only to be caught again.

'Not long now,' the Earl told his hapless navigator, who was being too sick to care, unlike Quenelda and Drumondir who were both sleeping deeply and missing all the fun.

'What's happening? What is that?' Quester asked as they swept around a ridgeline and the distant glen came into view for the first time. 'It can't be dawn already!'

'No, boy it can't be. Think! The sun doesn't rise from the north...' the Earl said.

But Quester was right. It was as if snowy ridges of the Howling glen were lit by a rising sun. Then it seemed as if the stars had fallen and twinkled in bright pinpricks of fire.

Then faintly, as they drew closer, they heard them: pops and cracks, bangs and the dull whumph of detonations.

'They're under attack,' Tangnost said grimly as

explosions bracketed the slopes of the glen.

As they broke free of the Octarine Pass, they saw the glen far below engulfed by battlemagic. Imperial Blacks swooped like shadows over the snow, flaming as they went. Hobgoblins poured down the slopes.

'There must be three banners at least!' Tangnost cursed.

'Bearhugger!' The Earl called his Shield forwards. 'They must think we are here already, and are throwing everything against the fortress in the hope of overrunning it. By the time Dragon Isle reaches them, it may be too late. This fight is not for us. We will head south to the Smoking Fort. Fly till daylight, and then put down during daylight hours. It is the winter solstice, the shortest day of the year, which favours our flight if we wish to stay hidden. We should make the fort by tomorrow night if the wind is behind us.'

CHAPTER FIFTY-FIVE

The Winter Solstice

The bell softly struck the witching hour, and outside the watch changed. All was quiet, save for the hoot of a nearby owl. The Earl was asleep, under the watchful eye of Drumondir, in the Tower of the White Star, one of the two massive gatehouse towers that guarded the southern gate, where the defences and wards were strongest. The three esquires were below.

'He's exhausted,' Drumondir assured Tangnost, as she came down into the eating hall to join him. 'I thought we were going to lose him to madness when the Maelstrom struck. But the seadragon city was a place of great power and healing. The Dragon Lords of old lived there...it strengthened both him and his dragon.' *Will he become like a Dragon Lord of old?*

'Seadragon city?' Calder asked eyes wide. He had thought that nothing could surprise him anymore.

Tangnost nodded and turned to Drumondir. 'You have yet to tell us what you found...you and Quenelda.'

'That tale will wait, Bearhugger, for another night. I will join Quenelda and rest now.' She smiled. 'And so should you.'

Calder had met them as they dismounted on the Stangate,

as light left the sky. He looked exhausted. 'We've been hit by attack after attack since you left,' he told Tangnost. 'They've been testing our defences all along the Wall, probing for weaknesses. I only have four battlemages beside myself, and one of them is badly injured. I have posted the others to league turrets along the wall where the building is incomplete.

'Then there was a storm last night, killed two patrols barely a league north of here, and the wards were damaged as if something sucked the power from the very stones. We flew out to take a look this morning. I've never seen anything like it.'

Stormcracker's long tail uncurled, gently setting down a figure from the pilot's seat. Not the Earl's daughter surely, but a man swathed in rough homespun and furs. The air prickled with tension.

Calder's eyes narrowed. This was no dwarf, there was an aura about this figure, strange, dark and fractured, weak, and yet, and yet...

'My Lord Earl,' he husked, going down on one knee, fist against heart in salute. 'My Lord,' he swallowed, blinking back tears, trying to find his voice. 'By all the Gods...' taking his ArchMage staff from his back, he offered it.

'Commander, I will lay down my life for you.'

Amusement tinged the reply. 'Then let us make sure it does not come to that.' The voice was the same, but even in the dark he could see the man was not. The Earl smiled, teeth gleaming in the dark as a crippled hand accepted the battlestaff. 'Get up, man.'

'Papa!'

There was a moment's hush.

'Papa! Your aura!' Quenelda whispered. 'It's not fractured any more!'

'My Lord Commander! It is true!' Calder affirmed. 'Your aspect has changed, it is no longer dark! Faint, my Lord. But true! Your power returns!'

'Take my chambers, Commander, and rest easy. The couriers for Dragon Isle have flown and Imperials out of III Firstborn should arrive two days hence if the winds are favourable. They will see you home safe. If you need anything, my Lord, send your esquire. Sleep well.'

'Major! My thanks.' The Earl nodded, then hand on his esquire's shoulder, he turned away and Quester closed the door.

Calder led Tangnost up to the guest quarters over the Dragon Port. Pulling the poker from the fire he offered him a goblet of mulled wine, then clapped the Dragon Master on the back.

'You've done it, man! By all the Gods! You have him when all had thought him dead. And...,' he said wonderingly. 'He can pilot his dragon, blind?'

'Aye,' Tangnost nodded. 'He can. His daughter did it. They have bonded as the Dragon Lords of old did, and so he gains strength from it. But his body is still frail, still healing. There is a weed; the bone casters call it Dragon's Leaf or Dragon's Bane. We think we have found some, but it made her Sabretooth sick.'

Calder nodded. 'Your Bone Caster has already asked. I have sent our healer to aid her. He is old but very wise and learned. He studied at the Battle Academy and may have heard of it.' He rose and stretched, then buckled on his sword.

'I must go and check the watch. I've doubled the guard. If our Lord Protector is as dangerous as you say, I doubt he has given up. Sweet dreams, Bearhugger.'

CHAPTER FIFTY-SIX

Sweet Dreams!

Tangnost relaxed for the first time in three moons. He pulled his boots off and his pipe out, and sat wreathed in smoke watching the fire burn down, letting the tension ease out of his aching muscles. His boots steamed on the hearth. Tomorrow he was going to the bath house to soak in steaming water heated by the battledragon roosts. *Now we're surely safe?* Stormcracker lay along the length of the Stangate, a formidable presence that bolstered the fort's morale. Two Gulps was in the sabretooth roosts, eating his fill of brimstone, meat and thistles.

Three dozen of the Major's Tower Guard were guarding the Earl, the remainder posted around the Star Tower or on patrol on their black vampires. With the Howling Glen under siege, the entire fort was on battle alert.

Slowly, Tangnost slipped into sleep.

A bell began ringing, its tones urgent, strident.

Clang! Clang! Clang!

Clang! Clang! Clang!

Tangnost's head snapped up. Three bells...attack.

'Hobgoblins!' Even the thick walls could not dull their

ululating cries! With a curse he leapt to his feet, pulling on his boots, reaching for the axe that was never more than a hand span away. As he reached the chamber door, it was flung open.

'The Wall is under attack.' Calder informed him tersely. 'Come!'

He has found us!

'Quester, with me,' Tangnost decided to take the Earl's esquire. The boy needed experience of battle if he were to serve the Earl.

'What is it?' Root knuckled his sleepy eyes, as his friend pulled on his boots, hauberk, and buckled his sword on. 'What's happening?'

'Sit fast. They have been attacking up and down the Wall for the last few moons. There is no cause for concern,' Tangnost reassured them. Root rolled over gratefully and fell asleep almost immediately.

They met Drumondir on the stairs. She had been resting in a small chamber next to the Earl's and looked alert despite the late hour. 'Stay with him,' Tangnost advised. 'This may be nothing. I'll be back as soon as I can.'

Tangnost and Quester raced up the turnpike stair and out over the frost-rimed gantries to the anchored dragon pads on the heels of the Major, his standard bearer and bugler close behind, to where three harriers were being hurriedly prepped for takeoff. The pads rose swiftly skyward.

'Go! Go! Go!'

Far below, troops were pouring out of the barracks and along the Wall, to join the Watch Tower garrison. There was activity in the sabretooth and spitting adder roosts as the battledragons were saddled, rapidly forming up on the parade ground to the east of the fort, ready to charge if the hobgoblins broke through.

'Incoming! Incoming!' Thin cries rose up in the cold air.

'Shields up,' came the order as bolts arced over the wall, falling in a deadly black shower, thudding into wood and leather and flesh, skittering across the ice and stone to rattle off the tiled roofs in the fort below.

'Weapons free!' Already the standby squadron of harriers had been scrambled and were swooping out over the attacking hobgoblins, the downdraft from their wings raising swirls of snow on the lower pads. Beams of colour lanced out, striking again and again against the cliff face, and outer ditches of the Watch Tower. Ice and earth exploded, creating a hail of dirt and stone that clattered off helmet and shield.

'Fire! Fire!' an officer shouted from the battlement embrasures.

Thunk! Thunk! Thunk! Thunk!

As the granite counter-weights swung down, the thick beams of the huge oak catapults slammed against the crossbar, releasing their deadly cargo of dragon fire, their impact shivering through the stone bones of the wall. Out on the moor, fiery colour exploded, so that soon it looked as if the star-filled sky itself had fallen to earth, and blurry waves of heat warped the frigid air.

And still the hobgoblins kept on coming.

'Sir!' A breathless officer reined in his mount on the Major's dragon pad in a flurry of snow. He was young, half trained, and frightened. He pointed to where a watch beacon flared through the dark, and beyond it another and another. 'They are attacking the watch towers in force...the couriers say the beacons are lit for ten leagues before they turned back. They have broken through the Wall between Mountain Hare Tower and the Blue Eagle Tower.'

'So soon?' Calder's eyes narrowed as he donned his helmet. 'We bloodied them barely three days ago. Watch how the battle goes, Bearhugger. I'll leave the Tower Guard under your command, should the need arise. Captain Stramach,' he turned to the young officer astride his armoured frost dragon. 'You and your men are at Bearhugger's disposal. Do whatever it takes to protect the Earl.'

'Sir!'

Tangnost, with Quester at his side, was invited by the Captain to watch the battle unfold from the Smoking Fort's command centre in the Runestone Tower at the centre of the fort. They stepped out onto the balustrade that ran around the Ops Room. Colour now blazed along the length of crenelated Wall as far as the eye could see; save for where the cliffs rose a thousand strides high from the moor in front of the fort itself. The noise carried on the thin cold air was a swelling tide of hobgoblin cries, the wet slap of arrows, swords and spears finding their target, cries and shouts of pain and fear and triumph, and the thump and explosion of battlemagic. Comets of dragon fire blazed through the night from the battlements, but still the hobgoblins kept on coming.

'Look! Look! They're over!' Quester pointed to the nearest watch tower half a league to the east. Tangnost peered through the confusion of colour and movement and shook his head.

'Your eyes are better than mine...' He raised the spyglass and frowned as he saw the snow flowing as if it were alive.

'Thor's Hammer' The dwarf swung the eyeglass; an avalanche of hobgoblins was pouring over the Wall, pushing the defenders back towards the fort!

A heavy brigade of Sabretooths, supported by swifter Spitting Adder lancers on the flanks, pounded eastwards to meet them. Pulses and detonations, grenades and hexes rained down on the thick press of warriors straddling the defences, from the circling Vampires and Frost dragons commanded by the Major. The hobgoblin banners began to slowly fall back, drawing the defenders with them away from the Smoking Fort. Cheers erupted around the battlements, but Tangnost's instinct was aroused.

'Captain, I don't like this,' the Dragon Master admitted. 'It doesn't feel right.'

'No, Sir!' the SDS Officer agreed. 'They have never attacked this close to the fort before. Why tonight? I think they have been waiting for you.'

'But they're getting beaten back!' Quester protested.

'Yes,' the Captain agreed. 'But they are drawing out our reserves.'

'I agree. I think they know the Earl is here. This was a trap. Tell Quenelda to prepare Stormcracker for combat takeoff, dress the Earl, and get him mounted up.

'*Now,* lad!' Tangnost repeated, 'We'll form a corridor with the Tower Guard. Go!'

The Earl's esquire raced away.

Tangnost turned. 'Captain, form an outer perimeter about the Imperial with air cover and an inner shield wall.'

Barely had they left the battlements than a banner of hobgoblins, hidden by the snow and the battle to the east, rose silently up over the cliff edge in their hundreds and crept around the now thinly defended fort.

'We h-have to prepare to leave! Now!' Quester was bent double with exertion; he had already stopped by the Earl's chambers and passed on Tangnost's orders to Drumondir. Root and Quenelda gaped at him through bleary eyes. Root rolled out of bed grabbing at his clothes on the floor.

'Quenelda, Lady,' Quester urged. 'You must get Storm ready for combat take off.'

'Why?' Quenelda asked as she headed for the door. She had fallen asleep in her clothes she was so tired. 'I thought we were safe?'

'Tangnost thinks the attacks are diversions, that their true target is your father. He thinks the attack on the Howling Glen was deliberate, that they knew we would think ourselves safe here and flee south!'

'But I thought the fort ha-' Root began, when the strident alarm of the bell drowned him out. There were shouts, and the sounds of running feet. Below them, the gatehouse guards struck the winch with a mallet and let the portcullis fall with a roar and a rattle as the Tower Guard raced for the dragon pads. The fort itself was under attack!

'I must go and dress the Earl!' Quester departed.

Quenelda paused at the door. 'Can you collect Two Gulps from the roosts?' she asked. 'Storm needs time to warm up. I may have to help him.'

Root nodded.

Quenelda ran through the emptying streets of the fort towards the South Port and Stormcracker. All around her those not fighting were streaming towards the Unshatterable Tower for safety. Her feet felt heavy as lead. They had not even had so much as a single night's sleep, but danger was on them again. She was *so* tired.

Already two troops and a dozen frost lancers in the white and silver of the Tower Guard had fanned out about Stormcracker, forming a defensive perimeter facing the battlefield. Others were forming an interlocked shield wall between the fort and the dragon's tail.

Battle..? Stormcracker said hopefully, as his tail lifted her up to the pilot's seat, accidentally knocking five soldiers to the ground, breaking an arm and knocking one out. His nostrils were full of the hobgoblin's scent, and smoke threatened eager retribution for the Westering Isles.

No, not unless we have to fight to break free... We must take Thunder Rolling over the Mountains home as swiftly as we can...this is a trap....

We fly?

Yes! Home to Dragon Isle as soon as they bring my father here... Stretch your wings, prepare for immediate flight...

Standing on the dragon's shoulders, she searched the South Port for a sign of Root or Tangnost. Where *were* they?

The roosts had emptied, the curses and cries and sound of hobnailed boots now silent. The air was sharp and cold as icicles. Bloodcurdling cries and the clash of arms spilt over the huge outer wall as Root frantically searched for Two Gulps. He had to get him mounted up onto Storm. The juvenile would never survive if the hobgoblins found him. No sign! He must already be with Stormcracker. He could see the Imperial's spinal plates looming above the battlement walls, almost white with hoar frost.

With huge relief he reached the protective corridor formed between the fort and the battledragon, who was rumbling ominously, smoke pouring from his nostrils and pooling on the freezing ground as he flexed his wings.

Where is Tangnost? Quenelda thought she saw Root arriving, and went down to greet him.

'Ro- Where's Two Gulps?'

'What?' Root looked up in alarm. 'He isn't with you? He wasn't in the roosts!'

'What? No!' Quenelda found panic rising. 'No, he's not here!' She looked around wildly. 'Where is he?'

Storm...where is Two Gulps...?

He was hungry...

Quenelda groaned out loud. 'Oh no!!' *Where would he go?* The answer came swiftly. *The brimstone pits. He has to be there!*

Two Gulps? She sent out an urgent appeal. *Two Gulps!*

There was no answer; nothing distracted the young dragon from food! Quenelda suddenly realised the wisdom of Tangnost's warnings. Two Gulps' lack of discipline, her own poor training and neglect, had led to this moment, and now the greedy juvenile sabretooth was in real danger. He couldn't fly. He couldn't fight! What a fool she had been!

'Quenelda! Root cried after her as she scrambled down the icy girth rungs, slipping the last few strides. 'Quenelda, wait! Where are you going?'

'I have to find him!' she called over her shoulder.

'They still haven't got Papa on board. I'll be back in a heartbeat!' And she was racing towards the brimstone pits.

Chapter Fifty-Seven

Save the Earl!

There was a flurry of wings, and Calder's harrier dropped down beside Tangnost as he waited impatiently by the Port. The battlemage's armour was dented and scored, his staff smoking. Blood dripped from his harrier's claws and beak; she had a tattered hobgoblin bone in one claw.

'There are nigh on four banners out there!' Calder shouted above the din, as he swung his shield pricked with arrows around onto his saddle's pommel.

'Four!' Tangnost was stunned. 'A hundred thousand hobgoblins?' This must have been planned from the moment they were discovered, even before they left Dragon Isle!

'The moor and woods beyond are infested,' the Major reported. 'We cannot hold the Wall; they'll overrun the Frost dragon roosts soon, and be upon your Imperial! Get the Earl out of here! Now! It's a trap; they have been waiting for you!'

Calder called his bugler forwards. 'Sound the retreat!' He ordered calmly. 'We'll fire the moat.' He turned to Tangnost one final time as red stars briefly lit the night, leaning down to offer his hand in farewell. 'Never fear.

We will hold them off long enough for you to fly,' he promised them. The pair clasped arms, and then Calder spurred his mount into the air, followed by his bugler and standard bearer, and was gone.

Rounding the corner bastion where the catapults and stingers had stopped firing, for fear of hitting their own troops, Quenelda headed for the deep brimstone pits that lay to the east of the fort. The ground beneath her feet trembled to the concussion of battlemagic ripping into the front ranks of the hobgoblins, but she didn't notice it. Nor did she notice the hobgoblins break through the shield wall on the right flank, or the thunder of the sabretooths as the reserves stormed down the slope to meet the rising tide of hobgoblins. She only had thoughts for Two Gulps, and returning with him before Tangnost found out what had happened.

Galtekerion's warriors, tasked with diverting the Sorcerer Lords, had done their work well. A small war band of hobgoblins in their white armour slipped silently unseen along the west wall of the fort. Only numbering five score, they had lost twice that in the climb up the sheer ice cliffs that protected the north west approach to the fort. But unlike the swarm attacking the Wall, many young untried warriors, these were his Chosen. Their task was to shield him whilst he killed the Dragon Lord and his spawn, as the WarLock had demanded. Swiftly covering the ground with their large webbed feet, they stealthily approached the blind side of the Imperial still on the ground; the hobgoblin WarLord was nearing his quarry.

Two Gulps! Quenelda's terrified cry pulsed across the battlefield. The young dragon raised his head as she ran up to him. *Come now*, she commanded. *Now*! She tried to throw a bridle over his head as he skittered backwards, frightened by her anger. Dipping into a well of strength she never knew she had, she dragged him away. As she was pulling on his bridle, a riderless sabretooth nearly ran them down, before collapsing, pricked with spears. Horrified, Quenelda looked up to find a wedge of hobgoblins racing towards them, and more were now between her and Stormcracker!

They were cut off! She swung round to where the East Port behind still lay open, although the portcullis was dropping slowly. The hobgoblins were so fast, she wouldn't make it!

Two Gulps! She threw herself on his back as adrenaline gave her strength. *Run!* She flung the full weight of her power behind the command, *compelling* him to instant obedience. Never had she thought Two Gulps' greed would jeopardise their safety. Yet Tangnost had. She should have taken his warnings more seriously!

Soldiers and troopers were desperately fighting a rearguard action, all along the nearest section of the Wall, falling back in controlled shield ranks towards the

Frost Tower drawbridge to the fort, as the Earl finally stepped onto the gantry. Body exhausted from flying over a day in the pilot's seat through danger and darkness, it had taken far longer than Quester hoped to get the Earl dressed and up to the steps that wound steeply about the Star Tower, where his escort anxiously awaited on the gantry. They had a Frost Dragon with a double saddle waiting for him.

'My Lord Earl, Lord, mount my Frost,' the Captain of the Tower Guard offered. 'He is swift and strong, his name Frost Bite.'

The Earl was alert but clearly weak, and all too obviously blind. The Captain took the bridle. 'Hold tight, my Lord,' he said softly, not wishing to embarrass the crippled Dragon Lord riding pillion like a novice, who had once commanded all the Queen's armies; and wondering if the rumour that the blind man could see when flying his Imperial, were true. What an age of wonders and woes he was living through!

'Prepare to fire the moat!' Calder commanded.

'Prepare to fire the moat!' The call echoed down the battlements, and archers dipped their tarred arrows into the glowing necklace of braziers that were strung out along the battlements.

Caught up in a stampede for the safety of the closing gates, Two Gulps leapt forwards, carving a path through the soldiers streaming for safety. Taking huge strides, aided by flapping his wings, he ate up the distance in easy bounds. Despite the danger, Quenelda found it was exhilarating!

He's grown! The Earl's daughter realised as she felt the muscles bunching and flexing, and the large feet kicking out. *I can ride him now! And his wings are getting stronger*! Ducking and weaving with the ease of a cave dragon, the juvenile sabretooth thundered over the drawbridge. Fireballs and sizzling lances of light struck again and again about them from above, as armoured harriers swept in low overhead to snatch hobgoblins up and then drop them before swooping in again.

The noise was deafening as they made the safety of the fort, while exhausted soldiers and dragons milled about on icy cobbles in confusion. Officers gathered their men. Orders were given, troops mustered, ranks formed, fresh arrows and spears collected. The wounded were being carried to the hospital. Panic fogged Quenelda's mind as she tried to catch her breath, and now with the chase over, she trembled with fear and shock.

What now? Where now? She stopped, barely able to think, as soldiers knocked and jostled around her heading for the battlements, until Two Gulps protectively spread his wings about her and grumbled warningly. Behind them the portcullis slammed down with a crash, making Two Gulps bugle with fright. Above, along the gate tower embrasures, the catapults thumped with the regularity of a heartbeat.

What would Tangnost do if he found her gone? What

if Storm stayed and her father was killed while they looked for her? *Think!* Combat take off; but could they do that so close to the fort and Wall? Not with all the missiles! She had to see what was happening. Get up as high as she could, that is what Tangnost had drilled into his esquires, should they ever become separated in battle.

Up, Two Gulps! Up to the battlements...

Intent on scrabbling up the icy steps, she barely noticed Two Gulps leaping in three strong bounds behind her.

'Where *is* she? Where *is* she?' Standing next to the empty pilot's chair, Root was beginning to panic. The press of battling sabretooths and soldiers was drawing nearer. Dragonfire blazed out, lighting a nightmarish scene. Men screamed and dragons were overwhelmed, whilst overhead, Harriers and Vampires struck again and again. And where on the One Earth were Tangnost and the Earl?

CRACK!

A wave of sorcery struck the East Port where the tribes were pouring into the ditch and clustering against the portcullis. In heartbeats they were gone. Already weakened, the foundations of one of the towers fractured under the impact, and tons of masonry began to tumble.

Quenelda blinked, temporarily disorientated by the explosions, not fully understanding as the stone beneath her feet wobbled and then shifted. A gathering rumble filled her ears. She staggered; nearly losing her balance, then part of the wall collapsed, taking the steps she had just climbed with it. Screams and shouts of fear and anger carried over the din, and a rising cloud of choking dust blossomed. She couldn't see a thing any more, let alone Stormcracker. Where were they? Her heart choked with sudden fear, leaving her shaking: what if they had already gone? What if she and Two Gulps were on their own?

'Fire the moat!' the Major commanded as a tide of hobgoblins clambered up the rubble of the East Port. The bugle sang out. 'Fire the moat,' the cry was echoed along the battlements. Next second, with a thump that thundered through the ground, dragonfire ignited. A wall of blue flame hid the fort from view, and everyone trapped in it.

The outer shield wall guarding the South Port was collapsing under the weight of hobgoblins, but shields interlocked like a tortoise shell, they still they fell back in ordered ranks towards the battledragon.

'Go! Go! Go!' The Captain urged the guards surrounding the Earl as Stormcracker lay down a withering fire that rolled across the hobgoblins like a flood tide, buying them some time to mount the Imperial.

'Quenelda!' Tangnost slid from the saddle of a dragon, and ran towards the pilot's chair. 'Combat lift off! Lift off!' There was still no answering cry. He ran for the pilot's chair to find Root standing hopelessly at the reins.

'Where is she?'

Root swallowed, and bit his lip. He knew he shouldn't have let her go, but he would have done the same for Chasing the Stars. 'She went to find Two Gulps.' He felt sick. 'She's cut off, she's in the fort.'

Tangnost didn't need to ask why. He looked down to where the hobgoblins had overrun the brimstone pits and leaping flames had cut them off from the fort, and cursed in dwarfish. Wherever Quenelda and Two Gulps were, if they were still alive, they were in trouble.

It was just as well Root's language skills were poor, nonetheless he got the gist. And Quenelda's father certainly had.

'I'll take the pilot's chair, Bearhugger' the Earl moved forwards, groping for his seat with Quester and Drumondir's aid.

'My Lord Earl, I-you-'

'Prepare for immediate takeoff,' the Earl ordered, pitching his voice for Tangnost alone. 'See if you can find my daughter, old friend; I can be of no use to her except here with Stormcracker. Find her, Bearhugger!'

He searched for Tangnost's hand and gripped it with surprising strength. 'Take the Guards if needs be, for a drop, and we'll execute a combat lift. I cannot lose her, too.'

'My Lord!' Immediately understanding, Tangnost

turned into Root who was anxiously hopping from foot to foot right behind him. 'I- I tried!' He blurted miserably. 'I tried to s-'

'Hush, lad, it's not your fault,' the dwarf hugged the shaking boy to him. 'Once she's made up her mind there is no stopping her.' *Nor that juvenile,* he thought grimly, *but now is not the time for that.*

'Root, find the bugle and sound combat take off. Repeat it every sixty heartbeats. It's the only way we can get a message to her; she'll know what to do. Quester, find her! Use those keen eyes of yours!'

'Sir! Yes, Sir!' Root ran down to the tent and dived into the baggage, casting frantically about for the bugle. Where had he put it? He ripped open another bundle of equipment. *Where is it?*

Thunder Rolling over the Mountains, the battledragon turned anxious eyes on the Earl being buckled into his flying harness by Quester, echoing the dwarf's concern. *Have you the strength?*

*Yes...*the Earl lied, trying to still the trembling that shook his body, as he reached out to his battledragon and felt the now familiar punch of adrenalin race through his veins, when he lifted his dragon's eyes to the chaos of the battlefield.

Behind them, Galtekerion's warriors silently rose up from the snow.

CHAPTER FIFTY-EIGHT

Find My Daughter

The clarion cry of the bugle carried over the battle. A little wobbly and hesitant, it ended on a true note, and then repeated. Quenelda's head snapped up. *That's Root!* He never quite got the hang of it before he became her esquire.

Combat take off!

Stormcracker was taking off! Her father must be safe on board. This message was for her! She ran towards an embrasure that jutted twenty strides beyond the battlements, to see if she could see them beyond the wall of flame that thundered like a waterfall, sucking in the air. But the rampart was slick with blood and melting ice that gushed over the stonework, pricked here and there by black darts.

Quenelda slipped with such force it knocked the breath from her, and she screamed as a dart pierced her thigh. She lay there stunned, ears ringing, lips bloodied, wound leaking onto the ice, congealing in the cold. Blood thundered in her ears as hobgoblins already in the fort, who had survived, climbed the rubble between her and the gates and sniffed the air...fresh blood! Suckers gripped the ice, and pale avaricious eyes turned towards the fallen girl. A warrior bared his rows of serrated teeth and screamed his delight. Quenelda opened her mouth to scream back, but nothing came out. She tried to find her feet, but her boots wouldn't grip, and her leg was agony. The hobgoblin was coming towards her in easy strides, suckers popping on the ice.

This time she managed to scream.

'Combat take off, combat take off!' Back on the ground, Tangnost urged the surviving guards to get on board up the dragon's tail as Stormcracker's great wings swept down. Darts and spears were already finding their range, and exhaustion was taking its toll, but the inner shield wall of veterans was still holding. The battledragon would lower his wings one final time for stragglers before a running take off. *But can he manage with an injured leg and a weakened wing, both stiffened? Imperials need dragon pads...*

The Earl watched through Stormcracker's eyes as the Guards fell back towards him, feeling the battledragon's desire to fight. As the shield wall fell back beneath the dragon's wings he unleashed Stormcracker's power, and a wave of purple plasma rolled out, incinerating hundreds, buying precious moments for those cut off from the fort, giving them time to reach safety.

'Quenelda!' Root screamed, as Stormcracker's muscles bunched, poised to begin his take off. 'Quenelda, where are you?' Lifting the bugle, he threw all his might into a trumpet call...

Combat take off! Long... long... short... long... Combat take off....

Quenelda no longer heard Root, saw nothing but the hobgoblin rushing towards her. There was nowhere to run, nowhere to hide. Two Gulps was not going to reach her in time, they both knew that, and despite Drumondir's words, no power came to her in this moment of deadly danger. It was going to end here. *Two Gulps and You're Gone...* She whispered to her dead battledragon. *Two Gulps...*and she widened her arms to accept her death...he would be waiting impatiently for her across the rainbow bridge...

In this last dance of dragons
I will wait for you
For surely as the sun sets
You must dance with dragons too...

She could smell the rank fishy stench that rolled before the hobgoblin, could hear its bone armour jangling with kill fetishes, see its rows of gleaming serrated teeth opening in slavering delight; the Seven Kingdom's ancient foe, her ancient foe. It raised its sword.

Dragon fire wrapped about Quenelda and the attacking warrior in a blistering embrace, leaving the charred warrior to crumble at her feet, and Two Gulps came to a screeching halt behind her, talons scoring deep grooves in the stone. There was a moment while the two of them were frozen, and then the young sabretooth awkwardly hugged her wounded body to him, enveloping her in fiery kisses.

Stiff and cold, Stormcracker stepped forwards, feeling the satisfying crunch of hobgoblins beneath his great claws. Exactly at that moment, when the Imperial was outflanked on his blind side, he was boarded by Galtekerion's warband. Unseen and unchallenged, they were swarming about the battledragon's hind claws, hindering his movement, and swiftly climbing, crawling, spreading rapidly out along the underside of Stormcracker's starboard wing, before the dragon screamed his outrage and turned to snap.

The Guards, facing the wrong way, fell before they even knew the warriors were amongst them swinging battle mallets and swords. Tangnost turned to see dragonbone swords rising and falling, and a standard, barely visible, white against white, of skulls and fetishes of the thirteen tribes topped by a dragon skull, carried by a phalanx of tall heavily armoured hobgoblins, armour heavy with kill bones and tattoos.

Pale, heavy-lidded lambent eyes skewered Tangnost, lips were curled back from rows of teeth, and then the WarLord hissed his challenge, spread his arms and let out the hobgoblins' ululating war cry.

Galtekerion! Tangnost breathed, as a shiver of cold went down his spine. The hobgoblins would never have thought of these tactics on their own! The Lord Protector was closing his trap.

'Repel boarders! To me! To me!' Tangnost shouted, and with a cry he leapt out onto the wing, axe raised high. Behind him he heard Quester shouting 'DeWinter DeWinter!'

'No!' Tangnost caught the Earl's esquire in an iron grip. 'Stay with the Earl. If they break through before we are airborne, you are his only defence! Go!'

Rising twin moons now bathed the battlefield in a cold light. Calder turned his mount, desperately searching through the battle-seared darkness behind the fort for the Imperial, hoping to find it airborne and the Earl safe. The blazing dragon fire encircling the Smoking Fort made him night blind. His spurred his lathered mount forwards towards the South Port, when his heart caught in his throat.

Sluggish from the cold and injury, infested by hobgoblins, the Earl's battledragon was struggling to get airborne. Calder's men lay strewn about the Imperial's wake, or fighting in isolated knots.

'Abyss below!' he cursed. 'Alpha Wing! Alpha Wing! To me! To me! Protect the Earl!'

Behind Calder, the major's standard bearer raised his staff, and the sigil of the Smoking Fort rippled into the air. All over the battlefield, pilots turned their frosts and vampires and sabretooths towards their commander. They had been summoned where the need was greatest. From all over the battlefield, Calder's airborne Wings converged on him.

CHAPTER FIFTY-NINE

A Reckoning and a Frying Pan

They had fought bravely, but the young Tower Guards were no match for the WarLord's battle-hardened veterans, who relentlessly carved a passage through the press towards the Earl. Crying with rage and despair, Tangnost swung his axe again cleaving a skull, feeling his broken ribs grate together in a blaze of agony, aware that they were falling back with every heartbeat and about to be outflanked by warriors on the dragon's wing. Quester stood, drawn sword at the ready, but the Earl was oblivious to everything but the need to take off and find his daughter.

A phalanx of eager hobgoblins was swiftly converging on the pilot's chair when Stormcracker turned. Striking swiftly as a serpent, he plucked them away, and took another huge stride, half bounding above the battlefield.

'Weapons free! Weapons free!' Calder shouted. 'Down, Alpha Wing! Hunt and destroy!'

The hobgoblins on Stormcracker's left wing suddenly found frenzied frost dragons in their midst, as Calder and his battlewing dropped down and set about with staff and sword to drive them back. Highly trained to kill with hind or fore talons, the dragons spun about, biting and kicking, a whirling scythe of death. Galtekerion hissed as one of his Chosen, protecting his back, fell to those snapping jaws. Within moments, black vampires swooped down. Clutching warriors in their claws, they rose into the night before releasing them. With a cry, the soft skinned hobgoblins fell to burst like soft-skinned slugs on the hard ground. Galtekerion's fury rose. He must kill the Dragon Lord soon, or the dread dragon would be airborne, and his warriors could be picked off one by one! 'Clear a path for me to the Dragon Lord,' he hissed to his Chosen.

Eyes blazing gold, the Earl's head was pounding and his veins were on fire as he fought as one with his dragon. Screaming power flowed through him, hot, burning. But broken body forgotten, infused with Stormcracker's mighty power, the Earl lashed his spiked tail out, killing scores, struck out with his stiff and aching wings trying to rid himself of these foes who swarmed over him, trying to bury him. He flamed fiery destruction, and stamped hobgoblins beneath his claws in raw fury, oblivious to the weakness of his own body as he tried to get airborne. He had lost his daughter and his world lay in ruins!

Springing, Stormcracker frantically beat his wings. Pain blazed through the Earl's fragile body. Legs buckling he fell to his knees, as the last of the Tower Guard protecting him fell to the Chosen.

As the battledragon stumbled, Galtekerion lifted his

dripping sword and raised his eyes to the witchwood chairs astride the Imperial's neck; finally, a reckoning with this crippled Dragon Lord who should have died under his blade at the Battle of the Westering Isles. He had waited many moons.

'My Lord!' At the Earl's side Quester leapt forward to protect the fallen Dragon Lord with a cry, the Earl's sword in a two-handed grip. 'Behind you!' Tall as he was, the esquire was dwarfed by the hobgoblin WarLord who stalked towards him.

Sparks flew as their weapons clashed. The weight of Galtekerion's first blow drove the Earl's esquire to his knees. He twisted and rolled as the huge sword cleaved Stormcracker's armoured hide, where the esquire had been but a heartbeat before. As Quester desperately tried to get to his feet and crabbed sideways, the flint sword whickered round in a lazy arc and the boy crumpled without a sound, the sword flying from his grasp. But the Earl didn't see, because Stormcracker was intent on the battle in front!

'Quester! Nooo!' Dropping the bugle, Root ran forward to his friend, small shield raised to protect Quester from further harm, almost tripping the hobgoblin stepping over the body. The WarLord hissed with irritation and struck out with the pommel of his sword. Root's shield shattered under the contemptuous backhanded swing, and the gnome was thrown violently sideways. Pain and numbness shot up Root's arm as Galtekerion pushed past; pale dragonbone armour and lambent green eyes, ghostly as he advanced on the blind Earl. Looking round on hearing Root's cry, the Earl heard his danger but could not see.

'Quester?' he called. 'Bearhugger!' Where was his Shield?

Casting about him in the wreckage of battle for a weapon, grabbing a nearby heavy frying pan, with a cry of rage and pain, Root leapt onto the piled bodies of hobgoblins and guards and thumped the advancing hobgoblin on his head with all his passion and might. Helmet fracturing under the blow, the WarLord collapsed at the Earl's feet.

CHAPTER SIXTY

Fly!

Quenelda lay on her back. She couldn't hear a thing.

The stars above were so bright and cold, and soot floated down soft as snow. Her boots and clothes were smouldering; so was her hair, although she didn't notice, and her eyes were white behind a mask of greasy black.

Comets of dragonfire trailed lazily northwards across the sky. *Like shooting stars...* she thought dreamily. Bright colour lanced out as vampires swooped overhead, blocking out the stars. Then a hot tongue, rough as sandpaper, licked her face; Two Gulps was feeling peckish after all his exertions.

Food?

Dazed, she struggled to her feet, hands and feet sticky with puddling black goo, as Two Gulps nudged her happily. His red gold scales were also oily black; only his long tongue was pink and wet as he looked in vain for caramelised honey tablets.

Quenelda looked around. They were totally alone now. The wall still glowed cherry red about her as the dragonfire slowly died down, and a choking oily smoke clung like morning mist. There was a rumble as the second gate tower collapsed into the moat. Then the battlefield beyond came into focus and her hearts slammed into her chest.

Stormcracker was still on the ground, and circling him a dozen vampires and frost dragons, dark and silver under the moons. Pulses of battlemagic crisscrossed about him as the Mages tried to clear a path for the battledragon to take off.

As she watched, a dart caught the nearest vampire's hind leg, and the battledragon was down into a sea of hobgoblins, flaming as he went, his rider wielding his staff to send an arc of battlemagic about them while waiting for reinforcements. The wings of a second dragon collapsed as a poison dart took her in the flank, and a heartrending scream split the air as the jubilant hobgoblins jumped to catch her and pull her down.

If only Two Gulps could fly...if only I could fly...

Two Gulps responded to her silent panic. *Fly? We must fly?*

Fly... she was frantic. *There is no other way to escape...*

*But you cannot...*it was not a question.

No, and despite their danger, no magic was tingling at her fingertips. *Then I must.* Without hesitation, he nudged her... *mount....*

Mount? Still she didn't understand

Let us fly together...

You can fly!?

Standing on his taloned claw, Quenelda vaulted onto Two Gulps' back again, and tucked her legs beneath his wings...could he truly fly?

This way! She turned Two Gulps northwards towards the cliffs, where the northernmost battlements were still empty of life, to where sticky dragonfire still licked cracking stone.

Fly!! Fly!!

Two Gulps stomped forwards, his juvenile gait rocking her from side to side as she hung on to his neck crest.

Fly! Fly!

Talons gouging the ice, the little dragon barrelled along the smoking battlement, gaining speed. Ululating cries and darts and arrows skittered off the ice behind them as they were spotted.

Fly! Fly! Two Gulps echoed, till his thoughts drummed in Quenelda's head like a heartbeat.

Thump, thump, went his huge feet, and then, wiggling his bottom like a cat about to pounce, with a great bound, he leapt over the crenelated battlement. With a clumsy half flap of his wings and another bound, over the smouldering ditch to the Wall, and with another bound up and up.

With a hope and a prayer, dragon and girl soared out into the greater darkness.

CHAPTER SIXTY-ONE

Cry Havoc

'Bearhugger!?'

He was fighting back-to-back with the remaining Tower Guard when Tangnost heard the Earl cry out.

'My Lord! Rufus!' Tangnost shouted, desperately swinging his axe, trying to cut through Galtekerion's bodyguards. 'I am coming!' He was exhausted, they all were. 'Rufus! I -'

Without warning, purple Imperial dragonfire lit the night. The hobgoblins swung about confused, as Tangnost's eyes widened in surprise. It came from his starboard flank, and could not have been Stormcracker. Fireballs followed. Explosions bracketed either side of the Earl's battledragon. Darts of light crisscrossed the night, wreaking havoc amidst the attacking hobgoblin banners, sweeping them off Stormcracker's wings. A wave of gold rippled out in front of the Earl's battledragon, burning a furrow in the ground and clearing a path. Wings shed of the hated weight of his enemy, the battledragon finally rose up into the night.

There the sound of rushing wind and the snow swirled and gusted, filling the air with ice crystals.

Tangnost looked up. The stars flickered and went out, and the ground trembled as six Imperials rippled into existence about Stormcracker, and dragonfire lit the battlefield about him in a ring of fiery purple.

Barely had the hobgoblins infesting Stormcracker blinked, than a troop of Bonecrackers abseiled into their midst, shields smashing and axes whirling. Within heartbeats, Galtekerion's Chosen were falling back in disarray. A protective shield wall was formed again about the Earl.

Find them, Stormcracker, *find them,* the Earl frantically urged his battledragon, searching the battlefield below with his dragon's eyes, his reptilian senses. Where was his daughter?

As one of the Imperial's wing tips almost brushed Stormcracker's in passing, a Dragon Lord stepped calmly across the fleeting air bridge and removed his helmet. Tangnost found himself looking at the SDS Commander, Jackart deBessart.

'Bearhugger!' the Dragon Lord greeted him with a wolfish grin. 'We've come to give you a hand! We can't let you keep all these hobgoblins to yourself! Where is the Earl? '

'In the pilot's chair.' Tangnost thanked the gods. They had done it! The Earl was finally safe!

DeBessart's grey eyes opened wide. 'In the-? He is well enough?'

'Come, Commander, see for yourself.' Tangnost

limped forwards.

'My Lord Earl,' DeBessert gathered the crippled man into his arms in a heartfelt embrace. 'My Lord Earl,' he repeated, overwhelmed. 'Rufus...by all the Gods! I never thought to see you again!'

He doesn't realise he's blind, Tangnost thought.

Dragon Isle's Commander stepped backwards as the Earl raised eyes that glowed sulphurous in the near dark.

'My daughter, Jackart! Find my daughter! She's out in that hell somewhere!' Then with a groan the Earl collapsed.

CHAPTER SIXTY-TWO

Crash Landing

'Aaaaaaaaaaaaaaaaaaaaaaaaaahhhhhhhhhhhhhhhhhh!'

Down, down, dragon and Dragon Whisperer fell into darkness, barely clearing the cliffs. The air was thick with missiles trailing ribbons of fire. Down and down and down they fell, towards the burning moorland. Sounds of the cliff top battle faded in the rush of the wind. Her leg was aching, the wind freezing, making her eyes water. But they were flying! Quenelda was exultant.

Two Gulps! You can fly! You can fly!

But her joy soon changed to concern, because they were swooping further and further out over the moor and away from safety. And, as she peeked over Two Gulps' withers, she saw that the marshes below were alive with hobgoblins! As the small dragon and girl sank ever lower, they were soon spotted. Darts and arrows were arcing upwards, as warriors raced after them.

Two Gulps' wings were now beating frantically and the juvenile was rapidly tiring. His muscles and tendons were not yet strong enough for his weight.

Two Gulps! Quenelda's heart slammed in her chest. They were going down! And rapidly.

Then the air rippled, and an Imperial materialised

immediately below them, flaming as it went. Its huge length glided below, its vast spinal plates rising protectively up to either side of them. It was heavily armoured, and still carrying a full complement of Bonecrackers, half of whom were deployed on the flanks laying down a withering fire of arrows.

As it swept beneath the sabretooth, Quenelda saw that the back of the dragon had been cleared for them to land, and a dragon-cradle harness was stretched out, held by ranks of Bonecrackers shouting encouragement!

'Quenelda,' Tangnost's voice bellowed. 'Put him down!'

But Quenelda and the overweight juvenile were rapidly losing height, anyway, and needed no encouragement! Two Gulps was exhausted. Wings spread wide, huge feet splayed, frantically scrabbling, the ungainly dragon landed badly with an undignified thump, and bounced. Rolling from side to side in an attempt to stop, he tumbled head over heels, throwing Quenelda, who bounced several times before landing in the pile of fodder and cloaks heaped at the end.

Rough hands and grinning faces surrounded her, helping her up, patting her on the back, warming her with words of welcome.

'Tangnost! Tangnost!'

The dwarf looked up at the blackened, smoking apparition running up to him, leaping over the netting; arms spread wide, a white-toothed grin gleaming in the moonlight.

'He did it, he did it! He did it!' She hugged Tangnost. 'Two Gulps flew! He saved me! Twice!'

'He did that,' the dwarf returned her hug; crushing her close in his arms despite the dreadful stink of smoked hobgoblin...*I thought I had lost her!*

She cried out in pain.

'What is it, lass? You're injured!'

'No! Yes! I'm alright! How is Papa?'

He could not lie; he took her hands in his and held them against his heart. 'He took the pilot's seat; he was desperate to find you. He felt helpless unless he bonded with Storm. He was airlifted out straight away for Dragon Isle in the company of Healer Mages. Drumondir went with him.'

'He's not dying!' Her face crumpled.

'No! No, lass,' Tangnost reassured her gently. 'But he is very ill. He was not strong enough to bond during the heat of battle yet. And in truth, neither was Storm. They were both exhausted from their injuries, but together they managed. He has just been airlifted out for Dragon Isle too, in a cradle.'

'Whose Imperial is this?'

'This is Northern Nemesis; Commander DeBessart is in the pilot's seat. He swore to find you, or die trying. I chose to come with him.'

'And Root?' she looked around for her friend. 'Did he not come with you?'

'Root has a badly broken arm, his shield arm. He was injured protecting Quester, who was struck down by

Galtekerion. Drumondir put on splints but he was in great pain and may lose his arm. He flew with the Earl, as did Quester. They defended your father with great honour, we can be proud of our Dragonsdome esquires.'

'Galtekerion?' It had taken her a few moments to take it all in. 'He boarded Storm? The Lord Protector, he betrayed us again!'

'Oh, yes!' Tangnost nodded. 'Yes, they were waiting for us; he must have planned it even as we left Dragon Isle. There were four banners thrown against the Wall. It is carnage down there!'

A thought struck her befuddled mind. 'But where is Galtekerion?'

Tangnost smiled, grateful for some good news to tell. 'Root captured him.'

'Ro-? Root captured him?' Quenelda was awestruck.

'Knocked him out cold...' Tangnost nodded. 'With a frying pan...'

'With a...? A frying pan?!'

Tangnost nodded, grinning. 'That will be one for the story tellers! He has fulfilled your Lord father's trust and more. He has brought great honour to his people!'

'Where is –?' she looked around, half expecting to see the hobgoblin WarLord.

'In chains. They have flown for Dragon Isle, where no doubt he will be put in the dungeons from the Mage Wars, they are warded. It is,' he chose his words carefully, 'good fortune in one way, because we can use him to prove that the Lord Protector is a WarLock and not the hero all think him to be.'

'The Queen!' Quenelda suddenly remembered. 'We have to stop the wedding. We-'

'One thing at a time, lass,' Tangnost planted a kiss on her forehead. 'Dragon Isle first. And then...'

'And then?'

'And then, lass... Why, we have a Queen to save, and a Kingdom to retake.'

ooOoo

THE STEALTH DRAGON SERVICES

Volume 4 of the Dragonsdome Chronicles will be published in Autumn 2013.

Watch out for Quenelda's and Root's latest adventures!!